B.P. DONIGAN

FATE BROKEN

BOUND MAGIC SERIES: BOOK 2

Fate Broken
Bound Magic™: Book 2
Red Adept Publishing, LLC
104 Bugenfield Court
Garner, NC 27529
http://RedAdeptPublishing.com/

---

1.   http://StreetlightGraphics.com

Chapter One

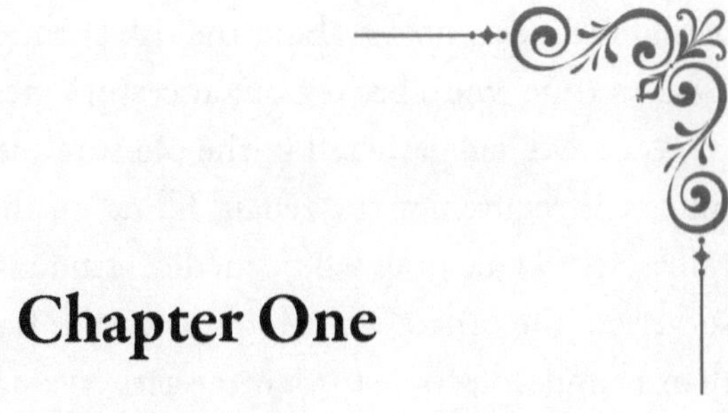

The threads of magic wavered around us, dangerously unstable. More than one of the faces around us tightened with concern as I pushed my thick auburn braid off my shoulder and wiped the sweat building on my brow.

I squeezed the small metal charm hanging from the chain around my neck as I ran my thumb over the engraved sigil of our people. *Marcel's charm.* It was the only thing I had left of the brother who had died trying to bring me home. The magic I was anchoring swelled up in response to my surge of emotion. I gritted my teeth. *Steady.*

Like many historical sites on Earth, the abandoned hospital campus we'd purchased and transformed into residential space just outside of Boston was built over a pocket of deep magic. But even with the extra boost and a twelve-person conjuring circle, channeling this much magic was taking its toll on all of us. We just had to hold it together for a few more minutes.

"Last one!" Tamara said, her face scrunched in concentration. Perspiration shone on her dark skin and slid down her face as she wove the final binding layer into the conjuring.

Tamara was convinced her latest magical configuration would patch up the crack in Earth's magic source, and we'd all agreed to give it one more shot, but if we couldn't figure it out—well, messing around with this much magic was just plain dangerous. But I wouldn't dare complain about the risk or the effort, especially since I was the one who'd broken our ancestor's greatest creation.

A crowd had gathered in the old surgical theater to watch the Inner Circle attempt the repair, filling up the four levels of vertically stacked balconies where medical students used to observe live surgeries. The ornate waist-high balconies framed spaces for more than a hundred people to view the activity on the circular first-floor stage. We'd named it the circle room for its shape but also because it was the location of the Inner Circle's meetings.

Instead of leeches and bone saws, the stage held a round stone table with carved sigils representing each of the twelve layers of the Source's magical binding. My ancestors had built the altar when they bound all of Earth's magic, and we'd salvaged it from our old Amish town and brought it to the campus. It was the only thing that hadn't burned in the fire.

The six members of the Inner Circle and an additional six people carefully chosen to balance the magical construct stood in front of each section of the table with their right hands on the carved surface as we worked together to fix what I'd broken. I tried not to let the guilt consume me. I'd had good intentions—namely, stopping Titus and the Brotherhood from stealing our powers and gaining control of Earth's magic. I'd reversed Titus's super conjuring, but in the process, the backlash of magic created a crack in the binding layer around Earth's source.

I inhaled deeply, allowing as much magic energy as possible to flow through me. As long as I anchored the circle, every person channeling magic within our group was safe from burnout. With the power Marcel stole from the Brotherhood and transferred to me, not to mention the cataclysmic events involving Titus's super conjuring, I could absorb a hell of a lot of magic. But that didn't make it easy. I had to concentrate. Plus, the backlash would be a bitch if I lost my focus.

If we failed—yet again—to fix the crack in the binding, we'd continue to be vulnerable to our many enemies. And that list hadn't gotten any shorter. Lord Elias, the traitor on the Aeternal Council aiding the Brotherhood, was hiding somewhere with the remnants of his rebels. Lord Nuada and Lady Treva, the Council's Fae representatives, revealed themselves to be Elias's coconspirators when they led the Fae right off the edge with Elias and disappeared overnight.

I couldn't forget the Aeternal Council, which was still on the long list of problems. Despite the alliance we'd struck, we couldn't trust them unless they also happened to be acting in their own best interests. As the only ones who could access the vast untapped magic of Earth's source, my Sect couldn't afford to fully trust our supposed allies, who desperately wanted that power for themselves. Everyone wanted to get their hands on the power we controlled, and thanks to the crack I'd unintentionally made in the binding around Earth's magic, we were more vulnerable than ever before.

A hundred people held their breath as we worked to repair that mistake. No one would risk a distraction that might unbalance the complex and sensitive conjuring we hoped would seal the leaking magic, but I was dangerously close to distraction all on my own. I focused on the energy flowing through me. The magic was like air, filling me with an increased awareness of all the life around me and an incredible, deep sense of joy. But that feeling could quickly turn to pain if I pushed past the limits of my capacity and took in too much.

All I had to do was anchor our circle and provide a direct connection to Earth's magic. What I didn't need to be doing was thinking about how much I'd already screwed everything up.

White waves of magic flowed from Tamara as she directed the threads of energy into an elaborate conjuring growing in the middle of the Inner Circle. The threads twisted and connected together, weaving into a perfectly symmetrical shape. It was beautiful to watch, and as she neared the end of the binding layer, a little spark of hope flitted through our circle. We'd already gotten farther than the previous times. Tamara was right—the modification she'd designed for the final binding was going to seal together the entire conjuring, and we could put this all behind us.

"Maeve O'Neill!"

I jerked my head up and locked gazes with a man in a suit standing at the top level of the viewing balconies. I'd never seen him before. He leaned over the chest-height balcony wall, peering down at the tiers of gaping people. My stomach lurched as he held up a gun, pointed it in my direction, and cocked the hammer.

I stared stupidly, lost in my own complete shock. In the space of time it took for his finger to squeeze the trigger, I pulled on my magic and threw out my hands. The bullets slammed into a wall of magic a foot in front of my face. Twelve inches between me and death—the space of a heartbeat. Pulling on my magic that suddenly had caused the energy within our circle to flex dangerously, and I gritted my teeth with the effort of stabilizing the conjuring wobbling between us.

Like a robot programmed with new coordinates, the man shifted his aim, and bullets ripped into the balconies. Shocked cries and screams echoed across the circle room. Three, four, five rounds tore through the densely packed space as everyone ran for the exits on each balcony, panicking and pushing. Dozens of people drew on their magic, attempting to conjure their own shields and skim out of danger.

The intruder reached into the inner pocket of his suit jacket and pulled out a small round object.

"Grenade!" Casius yelled as he pulled out of the circle, drew enough magic to skim, and landed next to the man. He grabbed the shooter's hand, preventing the man from pulling the pin.

They struggled on the top balcony as everyone ran for their lives and magic flashed wildly. The weight of the magic Casius had been channeling within the circle fell on me, and the ripple of power knocked me back a step while I struggled to rebalance the conjuring. The entire circle was off-balance, and energy sloshed violently like a bowl of water being tipped side to side. My insides clenched as if I were poised at the top of the roller coaster, momentarily weightless as the magic spun out of control.

Casius ripped the grenade from the man's hands and pinned him against the railing, but the intruder struggled until he managed to turn the gun under his own chin. We made eye contact just as he pulled the trigger. I lost my grip on the magic.

Energy whipped backward through our circle in a cascade of magic power. Tamara got hit first. Her knees buckled, and she fell on the hard wood stage with a loud thud. Seth dropped to his knees next, clutching his head. The power rushed through our circle like a tsunami, gathering strength as each member collapsed, until finally, Rhonda went down directly to my left and Jason on my right. I braced myself.

The wave of backlashing magic slammed into me. My vision went black around the edges, and I staggered to my knees. A dozen images flitted through my brain way too fast to absorb.

Crimson high-heeled shoe prints on a white marble floor.

Blood-soaked hay scattered across a dirt floor, and a glimpse of dark skin.

A white Councilor's robe billowing across someone's shoulder.

I shook my head as I recovered from the shock of the magic and the vision sequence it had triggered. Unlike the suppressed memories I'd recovered when the binding spell on my powers had disintegrated, I felt distanced from the experience, as if I were seeing images on TV. The scenes had been fragmented. Nothing made sense, and there was no context to any of it.

Absorbing the backlash felt like getting kicked in the stomach, and I squeezed my eyes shut as I struggled to breathe. I couldn't process the images I'd seen. Maybe that much magic had just over-loaded my brain for a hot second, letting random images from my life rise to the surface.

By the time I recovered, almost everyone had fled, and the shooter's body was crumpled on the ground floor. Blood formed a wide arc across the hard floor in front of me, and the entire left side of the shooter's face was missing. My stomach turned, and heat stung my eyes as I fought back my gag reflex.

"Dammit!" Casius skimmed to the ground, swearing. "Fates curses in all five hells!"

"What happened?" Tamara asked, clutching her head. "Who is he?"

"He's a Mundane." I felt flat, emotionless. I was so damn tired of the death surrounding me.

"How do you know that?" Casius asked.

"He used a gun. Anyone with magic would know that a gun is useless against a basic shield."

That was why I'd spent most of my life training with blades, which could slip through a protective conjuring with a negligible amount of magic. Some swords were crafted with magic embedded in the steel, but I preferred Mundane weapons, which could be coated with magic for the same purpose. A bullet couldn't be mod-ified in the same way—something about the ratio of material to magic and the physical distance from the conjurer. All I knew was that guns were exclusively Mundane weapons, and swords were more reliable, anyway.

"Plus, our perimeter shield is designed to keep everything and everyone with magic out. If the man had even a drop of magic in his blood, he wouldn't have been able to get in."

Jason stumbled over to us, gripping his shoulder with his opposite hand. "That grenade could have killed half our Sect."

"He didn't demand anything," Tamara said. "He wasn't angry or upset or... anything. He just started shooting, and then he calmly shot himself in the head." Tears welled in her eyes. "I don't think he was acting for himself. I think he was under a compulsion."

Everyone took in the Mundane man with new horror. He was a complete innocent, and someone had sent him to kill us. Casius swore again.

"He called your name," Jason said to me. "Someone sent him here for you."

The shock was beginning to wear off, and anger started to surface beneath my skin, hot and prickly. That man didn't deserve to die, and the people gathered on our campus certainly didn't either.

"Could it be Elias?" Jason shifted his sore shoulder, wincing. At least he hadn't been shot.

"There's nothing left of the Brotherhood but a few stray Rakken licking their wounds," Casius said.

"I thought he was with the Fae in some other realm," Tamara said.

The previous fall, when I accidentally led Titus to our Sect's hidden town, we'd trapped the entirety of the Brotherhood's forces between us and Silas's Guardians. Casius was right. Most of the Rakken had been killed, and any who weren't had been taken prisoner in Aeterna. Silas believed a handful had escaped, but the Brotherhood was broken. Elias was still out there with the Fae defectors, but they couldn't survive outside of magic-rich environments. And with all of our realm's magic stored safely inside the Earthen Source, only my Sect could access it.

"Whoever put the compulsion on that Mundane knew he could get through our shield," I said. "It could be Elias. He lost everything when Silas and I exposed him for the traitor he is. He may not have enough people left to mount an assault in our realm, but he definitely wants me dead. He could be acting alone, and if he knows where we are, he would be capable of something like this."

"Subtle," Tamara griped.

I agreed. Sending an innocent Mundane with a grenade was extreme even for Elias. Apparently, he'd given up his long-term power plays and manipulations in favor of more direct action after we destroyed his power base.

"But how did he find us?" Casius asked. "We did everything the Mundane way. We purchased the campus through a shell corporation, coordinated our move from the old town in small groups, and didn't even use our magic until the shield went up. We were untraceable. No one in Boston has any reason to suspect we're anything other than an antisocial religious community."

"I have no idea," I said. "But who else would compel a Mundane to suicide bomb our campus? Very few people even know that's possible." My anger flared, transforming quickly into resolve. I hated being responsible for more deaths. "We have to stop him. This is only going to get worse."

"We should modify the shield to keep out anyone who isn't part of our Sect," Jason said.

I frowned but didn't disagree. We'd all hoped to stay hidden, maybe not forever but at least until we'd set up better defenses. If Elias knew where we were, then we needed a major shift in our plans to keep our people safe.

"We can't just keep out everything," Tamara said. "We're in the middle of Boston. People are going to notice if they suddenly bounce off an invisible wall."

Jason grimaced. "Jamaica Plain isn't what I'd call the *middle* of Boston. There's not *that* much foot traffic."

Tamara shook her head. "We have Mundanes on our campus for garbage pickup, electric-meter checking—hell, with almost five hundred people housed here, we've got pizza deliveries every night, not to mention stray cats and birds in the air. Nothing would get through a shield modified like that. Trust me, people will notice, even in JP."

"We don't have a choice," Casius said quietly. "Modify the perimeter shield so no one gets in or out—even with our Sect's sigil. Everyone can go through a single access point for now. We can't risk Elias or the Council leveraging this particular weakness. And tell people to knock it off with the deliveries. We have to keep a low profile."

I didn't try to argue with him. Casius was a paranoid bastard who was never going to accept our new allies with open arms, but he wasn't wrong. The Council had a long track record of shifting allegiances. Even with Silas on the Council, there was only so much he could do to help us out.

Thoughts of Silas brought a familiar pang of loneliness and the instant wish to finally getting him alone and naked. I forced myself to focus. Not only did I miss him, but I also could really have used his advice about Elias. It felt like forever since I'd last seen Silas.

"We should keep trying to repair the binding around the Source." I patted Tamara's shoulder. "I'm sorry. I thought that one was going to work."

"It was already starting to unravel." She sighed deeply. "I don't know if I can do this again." Her generally upbeat attitude had taken a beating over the past few weeks of failures.

"We'll keep trying," Jason said gently.

We all stared at the dead Mundane on the ground between us, lost in our own frustration and fear. Twisting Marcel's charm between my fingers, I considered the exhausted members of the Inner Circle and the few people who had returned to the auditorium to gape at the intruder and the carnage he'd left behind. Since we'd retrofitted the old hospital campus into residential housing for our

Sect, we'd managed to erect a protective shield, but as the intruder so graphically demonstrated, it wasn't enough. I didn't know when we'd feel safe again.

"We should post additional guards until we get the shield modified," I said.

We all knew there was no way to patrol the entire perimeter of the huge campus every minute of the day and night. The truth was, we simply didn't have the resources or the knowledge to protect ourselves. Our ancestors had bound all of Earth's magic into a single source of energy, and we couldn't even put up proper shields. It was depressing to say the least.

Casius's head bobbed in agreement. "We'll also move everyone back into the central buildings. There's plenty of room, and it will make it easier to secure the campus."

"We'll try again tomorrow," I told Tamara.

She managed a weak smile. "At least we're on the right track."

I was grateful for the quick return of her optimism, mostly because I couldn't muster any of my own. I looked down at the dead man, and the sick, angry feeling in my stomach transformed into fury. A lot more people could have been hurt, and I didn't need that added to my conscience. Elias needed to die. The world would be a better place for it.

"Check his pockets, and see if he has any ID. We need to find his family." I tugged on my braid. "Maybe I should—"

"No," Casius said.

I scowled in his direction. "You don't even know what I was going to say."

"You want to find that lunatic," Jason said. "Lord Elias."

"We have to stop him before more people get hurt."

"It's not a good idea, Maeve," Casius said in a tone of finality. He waved his hand toward the dead Mundane now covered by a sheet someone had the presence of mind to fetch. "Look what Elias is capable of."

I sighed, giving up the idea for the moment. I didn't really have a way to find Elias anyway, and without either Jason or Casius on my side, the Inner Circle would never agree to let me go looking for him.

"It's all right. We'll figure this out as a team," Jason said.

Jason was our resident diplomat and Casius's right-hand guy. Although he wasn't a full Empath like Stephan Valeron, everyone liked Jason and immediately trusted him. He was one of the most influential members of the Inner Circle, despite not having as much raw magical ability as Casius and I did. In fact, his magic was weakest within the Inner Circle, but it didn't seem to matter. When he spoke, people respected his opinion, and over the past few months, I'd grown to like him a lot. With his longish light-brown hair and baby face, he seemed barely old enough to drink, but he was thirty, only a few years older than me.

A young woman with shoulder-length chestnut hair ran through the ground-level door onto the stage, panting. I couldn't remember her name. *Sheila? Sharon?*

"Mel?" Jason asked. "What's wrong?"

Damn. I suck at names.

Mel bent over her knees and gasped for air between words. "The Idaho delegates are here."

"What?" Casius's spine went instantly rigid. "The summit doesn't start for another two days!"

"*They* demanded to see the Inner Circle right away," Mel said. "I tried to stall... left them with Jonathan. They're right behind me."

In unison, we all turned toward the dead body on the ground. There wasn't time to hide him.

Our Sect had split apart when the Brotherhood found us and murdered my mother. She'd bought us enough time to escape, but our people had scattered across the globe, and most were still too scared to come back. Almost ten years later, we'd invited delegates from the last of the splintered tribes to attend a three-day summit so we could convince them it was time to come home. We had to show them how safe we were with our new campus and help them see the benefits of our alliance with the Aeternal Council. If the splinter groups returned, we'd finally be strong enough to rebuild everything we'd lost. But if they realized Elias could send someone waltzing into our campus at any time, the summit would fall apart before it ever got started.

Casius rushed outside, and the rest of us followed him to intercept the delegate. Just a hundred paces outside, Alannah Rourke, the leader of the Mountain West tribe, marched her way up the linoleum hallway. Her eyes widened at the sudden appearance of all six leaders of our Sect blocking her path. I schooled my expression into something less desperate as I looked her over. It had been almost ten years since I'd seen her, but she was the same as I remembered and still larger than life.

Alannah was a soccer-mom type with bottle-blond hair and fake nails, but her physical appearance was deceiving. As the leader of the largest group to split from our Sect and the only one to hide in plain sight, Alannah was tough as leather and wicked smart. Her people didn't follow her because of her meticulous grooming. She had a cunning mind underneath all that blond. Underestimating her based on her physical appearance would be a big mistake.

By our estimate, there were almost seven hundred people in their Mountain West compound, many of whom were Mundanes, and winning her over was critical to the success of the summit. Her splinter group was the largest, and if they rejoined the Sect, the other tribes would follow.

I did a double take when I spotted her son, Ethan. He was twenty-nine with sandy-brown hair and had his mother's all-American good looks, without the salon polish. In high school, he'd been cute, but the intervening years had transformed him into a handsome man. I hadn't seen him since his people split from the Sect, and my stomach flipped with unexpected nerves. Ethan wasn't supposed to be here.

Ethan scanned the crowd, and a smile flashed over his face when he spotted me. It was the same lopsided grin that had made my teenage heart swoon. I waved limply, plastered on a diplomatic smile, and pushed down the confused emotions coursing through me.

With Alannah's unexpected arrival, I had to deal with my past in addition to the suicide attack. No one had told me Ethan was coming to the summit, and because I was an oblivious idiot, it hadn't even occurred to me that it was a possibility. I wasn't Alannah's favorite person, so I'd planned to give her a wide berth and let others handle her, but Ethan being here changed things.

A nasty suspicion popped into my mind, and I glared over at Casius. He'd been after me for months about my relationship with Silas. To say he didn't approve would be a wild understatement. With Silas on the Aeternal Council and me in the Inner Circle, there were plenty of people on both sides who weren't happy to see us together, potentially muddying our allegiances.

But Casius had gone so far as to ban the entire Aeternal Council from setting foot in our realm, despite the alliance between our people. And the portal to Aeterna was locked down tighter than a nun's panties, preventing me from visiting Silas. Because of that, I hadn't seen him since the day I left Aeterna almost six months earlier.

And then my high school boyfriend shows up. This little reunion with Ethan had to be more than coincidence, and I was pretty sure my devious mentor was behind it.

Casius stepped forward. "Welcome, Alannah! We weren't expecting you until Friday."

Alannah smiled at him with bright-red lips. "Casius! It's good to see you again. We decided to pop in a little early." She took his offered hand and looked through her eyelashes at him.

"I didn't realize you were bringing Ethan," he said, grasping her hand between both of his.

"I was eager to reintroduce my son to all of you." They held each other's eyes a little too long, and something unspoken passed between them, further fueling my suspicions. "I was sure you wouldn't mind him joining us. We're both eager to rekindle old friendships."

Casius and Alannah glanced at me. If Casius hadn't put her up to bringing Ethan, then Alannah was pulling a classic power play. She was pushing the boundaries by showing up early and bringing an uninvited guest. Either way, Alannah was seeing how far we'd be willing to go to accommodate her demands, and every time we gave her a concession, she gained the upper hand.

As Ethan and I locked gazes, heat crept up my cheeks.

"Welcome back, Ethan." Casius moved to give him an enthusiastic firm handshake. "You're all grown up since I last saw you."

Ethan's grin spread wide, lighting up his handsome face. "Time changes all things, Master Casius. I'm so pleased to be here."

"You both remember Maeve O'Neill, of course," Casius said.

I swiped away my worried frown and replaced it with a friendly grin that felt constipated. Casius had made me practice being friendly, but I wasn't prepared for this.

"And you look just like your mother, don't you?" Alannah took my hand and held it between both of hers. "She was a wonderful woman and a great leader. Her death was a loss for all of us."

I swallowed back an unexpected lump in my throat and managed to get out one of my canned lines. "Thank you for coming to the summit, Alannah. Since you were last with us, we've made a number of changes. We're pleased to show you around for the next few days." Casius had made me work on that one too. I was stuffed full of appropriate things to say.

"Yes, yes. Wonderful. I believe it will be a productive use of our time. Do you remember my son, Ethan? You two used to be friendly."

Friendly was one way of putting it. I bit the inside of my cheek and held out my hand to Ethan. His face twisted in an ironic smirk that meant he was about to be a smart-ass.

"Balls of Steel O'Neill!" He used my offered hand to pull me into a crushing hug.

Alannah's mouth popped open in horror.

I laughed despite myself, enjoying her expression, as I pulled free of Ethan's bear hug. "Ethan, you may be a grown-ass adult, but you're obviously still a delinquent."

He shrugged, and a roguish glint lit his gaze. "Some things never change."

I took a deliberate step back, putting some distance between us. The way he said that definitely had weight behind it, and he was looking into my eyes like someone very interested in rekindling our *friendship*.

Everyone was looking at us. Suddenly, I was sixteen again, and a blush spread over my cheeks. This obvious romantic setup needed to be squashed—quickly.

Alannah's attention was drawn to something behind me, and I turned. A group of our people stood shoulder to shoulder, blocking the entrance to the circle room. The dead man lay just a few feet inside. It was too obvious, and we all froze, terrified that Alannah would start asking questions.

"So, uh, you all are early," I said, "but I think your rooms are ready, right, Jason?"

Jason took the cue and led them away from the auditorium. "Yes, absolutely. Follow me, and we'll make sure you're settled in before dinner."

I sighed with relief as Alannah followed Jason away from the circle room. One crisis averted—probably a hundred more to go before the summit was over. At some point in the next five days, Ethan was going to want to talk to me... alone. I didn't feel like dredging up the past, and I didn't look forward to fending off his attempts to rekindle our relationship. *This week is going to suck.*

I headed back inside the circle room and was immediately confronted with the remains of the intruder. Blood had soaked through the thin sheet covering the body, and his polished black loafers pointed at unnatural angles. He'd probably gone to work that morning with no idea that he'd never return to his family.

No matter how irritated I was at the little manipulations of Casius and Alannah, seeing this reminded me of the bigger picture. There was no excuse for this innocent man's death. We had to stop Elias, and we were only going to do that if we reunited the splintered groups of our Sect.

Chapter Two

Jason rushed into the old operating room with a flushed face and an air of panic. "Thank the gods... I lost her." He dropped into the chair to my right and opened one of the water bottles waiting on the large oak conference table.

I didn't even have to ask who he was talking about. Alannah had been a terror for the past forty-eight hours, and Jason had to bear the brunt of it. I let a wry grin slip onto my face and whispered, "What would Casius think?"

"I think I have a solid two minutes before they show up. Let me have this."

While Jason had played host, I'd focused on coordinating our security improvements around the campus... and avoiding Ethan. We quietly moved everyone into the central admin building and the two nearest it. The other three buildings would remain empty, which allowed us to set up a reasonable perimeter patrol. I also anchored the conjuring that modified the perimeter shield so no one could pass through except at the main gate to the campus. Even Casius couldn't complain about the progress we'd made.

The other two representatives of the splinter tribes had arrived the previous night, and Jason spent the evening entertaining them even though official introductions wouldn't start until morning. I felt bad for him. Jason had a long couple of days ahead of him. As I watched him hunker down in his seat and hide from Alannah, I was immensely glad I wasn't host material.

The other members of the Inner Circle settled around the table, preparing for the day's official kickoff. Tamara and Rhonda chatted quietly across from Jason and me, and Casius took his spot on my other side, wearing slacks and a button-down shirt.

"Alannah will be so impressed," I joked. "I can't remember the last time I saw you so dressed up."

He frowned, clearly too stressed for humor, before he leaned in to whisper to Jason and me, "Do you have any questions about your assigned delegates?"

I widened my eyes in fake surprise. "There were assignments?"

Casius's face jerked. "You didn't read the briefing?"

Flustering Casius was a favorite hobby of mine, but he was usually a harder target. The summit had really stressed him out. The "briefing" was a stack of papers the size of a dictionary with background about the delegates and their tribes. It included a detailed history of the years since they'd broken from our Sect, information about their financial situations and political alignments, and Casius's best estimate of their current head count. As much as I liked to tease him, I had actually read it. Well, most of it. I'd flipped through it twice and fallen asleep both times, but I had managed to finish the stuff about my delegate.

I'd been crossing my fingers that Ethan's unexpected arrival wouldn't get me assigned to him and Alannah. Whether or not Casius planned it, he would have loved an opportunity to steer me away from Silas, but angsty teenage feelings aside, we all knew I wouldn't be a good host to Alannah or her son.

I plastered an innocent expression on my face. "They all hate each other, and someone is allergic to peanuts?"

Jason snickered.

Casius sighed. "That's two months' worth of research you're mocking."

"I read all about the Alaska group," I said, feeling bad for adding to his stress. "I'm ready to be a good host—don't worry."

"We got some new information," Casius said quietly. "Gerald Thompson retired just last week, and his oldest daughter, Gia, was voted in as his replacement."

I suppressed a groan. *All that reading for nothing.* "What's her deal?"

Every one of the splinter tribes had a special reason they hadn't returned home. Alannah's group had financial assets they likely didn't want to share, as well as the complication of their religious-based community, which included Mundanes who believed in miracles and faith healings and didn't realize their entire religion had been fueled by magic.

A second group had relocated to Europe and had been living nomadically to keep themselves hidden from the Brotherhood. Their leader, Levi Fenwick, had adamantly refused to come until only a few days before. We didn't know exactly what had changed his mind, but we intended to find out and leverage it. And lastly, the Alaskan group, led north by Gerald, had sought safety by creating distance between them and the location where Titus had found our Sect and murdered my mother. Most of the briefing about the Alaska tribe had been about Gerald's concerns. I had no idea what Gia would add to the negotiations.

Casius cleared his throat. "They don't like your personal ties with the Aeternal Council."

Awesome. That was his super-subtle way of telling me, for the hundredth time, that I shouldn't be involved with Silas. I crossed my arms and leaned back in my chair. "You know damn well that I haven't seen him in months, Casius."

"Yes, well..." Casius's sour expression said more than his words. "There are still concerns."

I hadn't seen Silas in person for twenty-four weeks and four days, to be exact. Not since I'd put my people before my heart and left Silas behind in Aeterna. We'd exchanged notes via delegates traveling between our realms on official business, but it was hard to build any kind of relationship—especially one so new—on sporadic letters. We'd promised to be together soon, but I was beginning to doubt if there was a way forward for us when there were more barriers than ever.

The Council, the Circle, and all our responsibilities—none of that had changed. Silas was still fulfilling the deal he'd made with the Aeternal Council to take up the Guardian's seat when he bargained for my life, and he'd made a vow to help the people of Lower Aeterna after Atticus's death. The Lower City citizens needed him to help right the injustices piled on by the Council under Lord Elias's rule and to rebuild their government. Not to mention the situation with Aria and Silas's half brother Stephan and the unborn child Silas had claimed as his heir. Ultimately, Silas couldn't walk away from the bond-mating with Aria until he'd found some way to make things right for all of them.

For my side, I was the only person in the Inner Circle who could effectively anchor the magic that allowed us to connect directly to the Source. Despite our previous failed efforts, my participation was required if we were ever going to fix the cracked binding around the Earthen Source and put our Sect back together. Piled on top of the reasons we stayed in our respective realms was the fact that treaty or not, my people didn't trust his people. Admittedly, the lack of trust came from a long history. The Aeternal Council had spent a thousand years ruling Aeterna by force. The last hundred years had been particularly brutal, leading my people to defect over a disagreement about draining the Mundane realm of its magic power.

In short, my ancestors believed that we didn't have the right to steal all magic from Earth while the Council counted Mundane lives as acceptable collateral damage to keep the Aeternal society running. So my ancestors protected all of Earth's magic by binding it behind a barrier that only we could access, and they vanished overnight. We'd been hiding ever since, but now that we were finally on equal footing with the Council, we were just starting to put our Sect back together. Gathering the splinter groups was the final piece.

Which brought me back to all the reasons a relationship with Silas was a bad idea—reasons I knew better than even Casius did. Silas had been the Council's enforcer and had a reputation both from his family's power and Silas's own history with the Guardians, which had earned him a terrifying nickname: Death's Fury.

Neither of us could walk away from our responsibilities, and a relationship between Silas and me would jeopardize everything we were trying to build for our respective people. But I couldn't help the way I felt. I loved him, and he felt the same for me. Plus, it really pissed me off that Casius thought he could tell me who I could and couldn't have feelings for. I was really sick of Casius disparaging our relationship yet again.

The door to the conference room swung open, admitting our guests. Alannah was the first to stride confidently into the room, followed by Ethan. Half a step behind them and looking like he badly needed a good night's rest was Levi, the delegate from the Eastern Europe tribe. Levi's long blond hair was pulled back at the nape of his neck and tied with a leather cord. His narrow face was stern, and a thin, hawkish nose gave him an eighteenth-century schoolteacher vibe. He wore traveling clothes, wrinkled and layered, with a leather vest and a matching leather satchel draped over one shoulder. The bag hadn't left his side since he'd arrived, giving off the impression that he was prepared to hit the ground running.

Rhonda, the final member of our Inner Circle, walked in with the last delegate, Gia Thompson, an average-height woman with a curvy build and lovely dark-brown skin. She wore her curly hair long, and as she walked into the room with one arm cradling her stomach, I realized she was pregnant.

My heart skipped a beat as I was pulled into a vision.

I'm standing in the middle of a barn. It smells faintly of animals, but the mildewed hay and the doors hanging off their hinges scream abandonment. The horizontal slats are old—gaps of sunlight show through—and I know instantly where I am. Sheer agony burns through me. This is the barn where I hid and watched my mother die all those years ago.

Dread makes my feet heavy as I move forward, drawn like a magnet to a woman lying facedown on the ground. Her dark curly hair is splayed over the straw-strewn floor. My heart pounds in remembered fear as the smell of death and blood assaults my senses. I move around her, afraid of what—and who—I will see.

Her face has been eaten off. Her body is a bloody mess. Everything is gnawed down to her bones, except a swollen stomach that protrudes grotesquely under a fitted royal-blue shirt. Blood soaks the hay beneath her, and I suddenly realize her stomach isn't swollen—she's pregnant.

The vision spat me out, and my heart pounded violently against my ribs as the delegates took their seats around the conference table, totally oblivious to my episode. As I recovered from my shock, I remembered the vision I'd experienced when the magic backlashed through me two days before. I'd discounted it as fragments of memories and completely forgotten the episode.

I twisted the charm hanging around my neck and worked to slow my racing heart. I mulled over the possibility that I'd just seen Gia's gruesome end on the remote Idaho farm where my mother was murdered by the Brotherhood. It couldn't be a coincidence. If that was some kind of premonition brought on by the aftereffects of the magic I'd mishandled, then Gia was going to die horribly sometime in the next month, judging by the size of her belly.

I stared at Gia, completely absorbed in my own thoughts until I realized she was scowling fiercely at me. I forced myself to focus on the introductions happening among the other tribe leaders. We were a large group—three delegates plus Ethan and all six members of the Inner Circle, including me.

Since all Circle meetings were open to the entire Sect, spectators filled the remaining seats placed around the walls of the room, and the first hour was spent on introductions and posturing. Lots and lots of posturing. I tried to listen to everyone's special concerns, but my mind kept returning to the possible premonition.

Did I really see Gia's death? Should I tell someone? For all I knew, the backlash of magic was causing my brain to short-circuit. *But if it was a true vision, would telling someone cause it to happen—self-fulfilling prophecies and all that?* I let my mind run in circles until after a while, even my speculations weren't much of a distraction from the tedium of the meeting. Stifling a yawn, I discreetly checked the clock again. We'd been at this for three hours.

"Thank you for explaining your unique situation, Alannah," Jason said with more patience than I could have worked up. "We recognize that there are complications to your people returning home."

Ethan spoke up for the first time. "Our *home* is in Idaho. A third of our people weren't even born before the death of your previous leader." His eyes flicked toward me, and he grimaced apologetically. He must have realized that he'd just invoked my dead mother.

My mother's death was the thing no one wanted to talk about—the thing that had broken our Sect apart. It was the catalyst for my disappearing act with my father, when I chose to block my own memories and my magic, and for the scattering of people desperate to save themselves and their families from the Brotherhood. When she died, the hope of our Sect had gone with her.

"Half our people have no capability for magic," Ethan continued. "And the rest of us don't consider this Sect to be their home any longer."

Alannah put her hand on his arm. "Which is why we require special consideration if our people are going to make a successful transition."

Jason cleared his throat. "Do the Mundane members of your community know the details of your abilities?"

Jason's tactful wording was what made him a great moderator. We all wanted to know how much the Mundanes in Alannah's group knew about magic. We had no idea if they planned to bring them all back with them, and it was an issue we needed to discuss. Transitioning Mundanes into our community would be a big change.

Alannah shifted in her seat and studied her manicured nails. "No one without magic abilities is aware of the full extent of our powers. We haven't decided who will be made aware yet. We're considering splitting from the church."

Across from me, Levi snorted. "You took over a backwater religion based on your 'miracles' and convinced them to shelter you. Now look how quickly you cut ties when a better offer comes along."

Levi, the leader of the smallest tribe, had said very little even though he'd traveled the farthest for the summit. But he'd already taken a few potshots at Alannah, which made me think they had a history. I would have to make a point to check Casius's briefing and see if he mentioned what that was about.

Alannah's face darkened, and her eyes narrowed. "Your dirty homelessness is not a badge of honor, Levi. You travel around like beggars, using your powers to steal things and cheat people out of their money. You're a plague!"

Levi jumped to his feet. His fists banged down hard on the tabletop. "I'd rather be a beggar than an overgroomed prostitute willing to sell my body and my magic to the highest bidder."

Alannah and Ethan shot upward, and then the entire room was suddenly on its feet. I expected Levi to grab for his magic, but he showed restraint even as his face distorted with rage.

Casius nodded in my direction. I curled my lip. I was hoping it wasn't going to come to this. He raised his eyebrows, and I sighed. The theatrics went against my nature, but he'd insisted, and I'd agreed to put on a show if needed. As Casius was fond of saying, sometimes being a good leader meant doing things you didn't like to do.

I opened my mind to the Earthen Source and let the magic flow. The energy filled me, and despite my annoyance, I shivered with the joy of it. Joining with magic was like taking a huge gulp of fresh air and realizing you'd been suffocating without knowing it. The sweet power filled every cell in my body as everyone stared in awe at my aura. The pure white magic flooded the room with a strength and clarity that normally only the entire Inner Circle could achieve while linked to the Source. It was the magical equivalent of ripping my shirt down the middle and flexing my huge muscles.

The ridiculous amount of energy at my disposal was somewhat of a fluke. Between the powers I'd absorbed fighting the Brotherhood and my access to the Valeron Source through the bond I shared with Silas, I had a lot of juice. Being directly joined to Earth's source balanced the magic and turned it white.

They could all feel the power radiating from me, no doubt spilling over them with the same sweet euphoria that tingled across my own flesh. Everyday colors were sharper, more brilliant, and every detail was brighter. It was just as potent as the first time I'd experienced it, when my aunt Deanna anchored me to their circle and burned away the block on my powers. She'd done it to return my true memories and my magic. I felt a pang of guilt. She'd died because of her faith in me.

Even while I let the power pour through me, I was careful. It was dangerous to access the Source directly without an Anchor. If I drew too much, I could burn out my abilities or even lose myself to the magic. Casius wanted me to find a permanent partner, bonded by blood and magic, and had even presented a few options, all of them young single men—more of his not-so-subtle attempts to get me to move on from Silas.

But I wasn't confident in making that kind of bond yet. I wouldn't want to share a permanent connection with someone I didn't really know, especially when I was still figuring out my role in the Sect. I'd learned from my bond with Silas that those kinds of connections could be very personal, so even though it was yet an-other thing Casius disapproved of, I'd delayed choosing an Anchor.

When everyone was quiet, I released the magic, and the power faded away. It was hard to let all that joyous magic go, but I cen-tered myself and spoke quietly into the bubble of silence. "Please sit down."

I studied each of their faces and saw fear. Fear had caused us to hide from the Aeternal Council for generations and then from the Brotherhood. Fear had split us apart after my mother died. This summit was about putting our fears behind us. I met the eyes of every delegate and paused on Gia. Like me, she was young for someone with so much responsibility. Her group in Alaska was smaller than the others, with only fifty people total, but she was new to her role, having taken her father's place just weeks before. She had to be feeling the same kind of pressure as I did, stepping into a leadership role for the first time.

But Gia didn't seem to feel any kinship with me. Her face was scrunched in anger, and she'd spent every moment since she arrived throwing me icy glares. I'd never met her before the summit, so I was confident it wasn't anything I'd done. As a young leader, I empathized with her situation, but it was getting hard not to take her sour mood personally.

The vision of her death surfaced again, but I pushed it back as I dragged my gaze away from her and spoke to the group. "We're not in the business of forcing people to leave their homes. If you don't want to come, don't. You're free to go home and stay there. You'll be alone without allies, but it's your choice." I paused to let that sink in.

Jason and Casius had matching expressions of surprise, although Casius's leaned hard toward irritation. I waited, half expecting either of them to jump in to correct me. When they didn't, I decided to return to the script, because we all knew I was not a diplomat, and there was too much at stake for me to screw this up. "We're building something here that matters, and none of us have to run or hide anymore. Our alliance with the Aeternal Council has rebalanced the scales."

Gia snorted, ruining my moment. "You really think screwing the Council's enforcer will guarantee our safety? What do you think is going to happen when Lord Valeron gets sick of you in his bed?"

I ground my teeth—*that* was definitely personal. "Who I sleep with is none of your business."

"Of course it's our business!" Gia rose to her feet, her stomach protruding over the table. She cradled it with one hand and pointed at my face with the other. "Everything you do affects us—including running away after your mother died!"

I stood up, curling my hands in anger. Things had escalated quickly, but I wasn't above slapping a pregnant woman. *That wouldn't hurt the baby, right?*

Casius rose and cleared his throat. "Maeve's involvement with the Lord Commander is not intimate."

My face flamed red. It was technically true—Silas and I hadn't slept together. Not for lack of desire, though. There hadn't exactly been time while we were being chased all over multiple realms, running for our lives. But Casius had no right to bring that up in front of everyone, especially since I'd shared that intimate detail with him in confidence. He just wouldn't quit guilting me about our relationship, and I'd blurted it out in the middle of one of our arguments. I instantly regretted it, but my mouth had a way of moving faster than my brain.

Gia transferred her glare to Casius. "But she's bonded to him. Valeron is her *Aegis*." She nearly spat the last word.

Casius walked behind me and put his hand on my shoulder. I let him push me back into my chair, feeling like a chastised teenager who had thrown a fit. I sat, but my anger burned hotter as I glared back at Gia.

"The bond was a matter of protection," Casius continued calmly. "Their alliance benefited our treaty negotiations with the Council, and as you know, we are completely independent of them. You don't see any Council members here today, do you? That's because we've banned them from this realm." Gia sat as Casius walked slowly around the table to his seat. They all turned their heads toward him, except Ethan, who gave me a secret sympathetic grimace. "We hold the key to the Earthen Source. The Council can't harvest any magic in our realm unless we allow them to. We are not their puppets or their bedmates."

I didn't appreciate his choice of words, but they seemed to pacify the tribe leaders. Gia was still scowling, but at least she'd stopped glaring in my direction.

"We have several days for further discussion," Jason added after a measured pause. "Let's end our day on a positive note, remembering all we have in common. Please join us for dinner. We've prepared an excellent feast with the harvest from our own gardens."

Everyone rose, eager to stretch their legs and eat, while Jason talked some more about our self-sustainability as he led them out of the room. Casius put a heavy hand on my shoulder, urging me to wait until everyone left.

"My sex life is none of their business!" I blurted as soon as only he and I remained in the room. With Casius, it was better to go on the offensive before he could start in on the chastising. "I'm a gods' damned adult."

He pursed his lips. "Then maybe you should act like it. I need you to rein in your infamous temper, Maeve."

A wave of shame rolled over me. I'd let Gia bait me so easily, and I'd lost my temper in front of the delegates.

His expression softened, and he let out a deep sigh as he sat in the chair next to me, slightly favoring his injured leg. The old training wound made his leg stiff, but he must have been really tired to let it show. "They're concerned about your alliances. Who you're sleeping with is an easy way to judge that."

"I'm not going to hash this out again, Casius," I said carefully with as much control as I could muster. But the anger and guilt coursing through me made it hard to look him in the eye, and I rose from my seat and paced across the floor.

"Maybe you should sit this one out," Casius suggested not unkindly. "Let Jason and I kiss their asses tonight at dinner. I'll ask him to step in with Gia tomorrow, and you can take over with Levi.

We just need you to keep it together until the summit's over in a few days. We have to show a united front."

"Whatever you think is best," I replied woodenly.

I did not slam the door on my way out, nor did I stomp back to my room. I stalked. Like an adult—one who'd been sent to her room without dinner because she'd thrown a tantrum.

I marched toward my dormitory, trying to outpace my anger and annoyance. I never spent any time in my room unless I didn't have anywhere else to go. It wasn't home. Truthfully, nowhere on this campus felt like home. Home was a place with family and friends, and I didn't have either.

It was true that I was part of the Inner Circle, included in their ranks because of my abilities and my parentage. But it had been a decade since any of them truly knew me, and I'd been a teenager then. Even after months with my people, I was still struggling to carve out my identity within the Sect, trying to figure out when to lead and when to follow. Leadership seemed to come so naturally to people like Jason, who could remember everyone's names and talk anyone into just about anything. Or Casius, who radiated natural authority like my aunt had. But this was all so hard for me, and Casius was constantly reminding me of my responsibilities as I stumbled through one disappointing mistake after another.

And unfortunately, my spat with one of the tribe delegates hadn't helped me impress anyone. I had no idea what I was doing most of the time, and clearly, I wasn't good at making friends. Mostly, I was angry—angry that the Brotherhood had stolen my family from me, angry that so many had died because I'd convinced them to fight instead of run, angry that all my happy memories in Boston with Father Mike had been a lie, and angry that I was being forced apart from Silas because our people would never get along. I decided the best use of my time would be to hole up in my room and learn more about my new responsibility, Levi. Since he hadn't planned on coming until just a few days ago, there wasn't much to review in Casius's briefing, but I'd give it another read and try to redeem myself the next day.

I paused when I found Levi standing in my path, as if I'd just summoned him with my thoughts. I took a moment to really look at him. He came across as rugged, with that ever-present satchel slung over his shoulder, but his clothes were clean and not at all worn. His face was clean-shaven, and his brown eyes were clear and kind. I knew from his dossier that he was forty-three, but like most people who used magic, he could pass for much younger.

I pulled on a friendly expression. *Time to start redeeming myself.* "Hey, Levi, are you lost? You're supposed to be at the dinner."

"I needed a bit of fresh air. All this talking is..." His face scrunched.

"Exhausting," I finished for him.

He chuckled. "I'm not really cut out for all the political maneuvering. I'm more of a fresh-air-and-outdoors kind of guy. So I asked after the restroom and went for a walk. I hope that's okay."

"I can't begrudge you some fresh air. I probably should have done the same thing before I blew up back there."

He grinned. "If you recall, you weren't the first to lose their temper today."

A real smile spread across my face. "Thanks for that—makes me feel a little better."

He flinched as if I'd alarmed him, but before I could figure out what I'd said wrong, his expression cleared, and his smile returned. "Would you like to finish my walk with me? I'd love to get the poor man's tour of your campus. I understand it used to be a medical facility? And you have the only remaining access point to Aeterna somewhere around here, right?"

He held out his arm the old-fashioned way, and I looped my arm through it. "Sure. I'll show you the portal room first—it's not far from here."

As we walked, we chatted casually about the new campus and all the renovations we'd done to make it livable after being abandoned for almost a decade. I was surprised to find that despite his gruff exterior, Levi was easy to talk with. When we arrived at the portal room, I paused at the edge of the expansive lobby and waved casually at the two folks on guard duty.

"There's a shield surrounding the portal," Levi noted.

"Casius is a paranoid old—" I cleared my throat and considered more politically correct phrasing. "He cares a lot about security. Since this is the only portal between Earth and Aeterna, we have extra shielding in place to secure all entries. No one can travel through the shield on their own."

"Even members of your own Sect?" Levi asked.

"Not currently," I said carefully. "There are actually two shields here. The Guards have to let down the outer shield to let anyone through, and only members of our Sect can pass through the inner shield." I held up my arm to show him my Sect sigil—two overlapping triangles that flared out to the sides as they connected in an endless loop. "Casius wasn't kidding when he said that no one from Aeterna is allowed to be in our realm. Not only has he banned all the Councilors, but no one else from Aeterna can set foot outside this building without an escort either. We have an agreed-upon schedule for official visits and guards posted twenty-four seven. There's a handful of meeting rooms along the edges there that also fall under the shield, and we use them to—"

The portal came to life, flexing like a wave of liquid-silver magic into the atrium space. We froze as a woman walked through, and the containment shield around the portal activated in a rush of magic. I was shocked to see a familiar face.

"Tessa!" I called.

Tessa was in her Guardian uniform, the standard-issue black fatigues they favored while on duty. Her light-brown hair was boy short again, showing off slightly pointed ears that revealed her Fae heritage. Her lavender eyes brightened when she spotted me. "Maeve!"

I motioned to the guards, who let the outer shielding down, and then I passed through the inner one on my own so I could greet Tessa. Unlike Silas, Tessa hadn't been banned from Earth, but I still hadn't seen her in months, and the pang of happiness surprised me.

Tessa pulled me into a huge hug. "Maeve O'Neill of Earth, well met. What's up?"

Her mishmash of greetings made me chuckle. "Well met, Tessa. It's been forever since I saw you."

She frowned. "It's been eight cycles since last we met. Doesn't Earth's time run at the same rate as Aeterna's?"

"It's just an expression." I chuckled, knowing that both realms always had and always would run on the same time schedule, unlike some of the other realms. "And eight weeks is a long time. What brings you to Earth again? Not that I'm not happy to see you."

She grinned and held out a beautifully carved wooden box about the size of a box of tissues. "I came to deliver a gift from Silas."

My heart turned over, and a flutter of bittersweet emotion bubbled in my stomach. *Gods, I miss Silas.* "Oh! Levi. This is Tessa D'Nali of Aeterna."

I turned back to Levi on the other side of the shielding and was startled to see his shocked, angry expression as he gaped at Tessa. I put myself in Levi's shoes. I'd just told him everything was safe and secure, and then a Guardian for the Aeternal Council showed up bringing gifts.

"Hey, uh, I know this is a bit strange to take in, but Tessa is my friend. It's not official Council business or anything."

"She's a Guardian," he said. "And a Fae halfling."

Tessa narrowed her eyes, and I quickly stepped closer to Levi, who still stood just outside the shield. "I'm sorry. I didn't mean to alarm you," I told him.

He pulled his gaze off Tessa and seemed to shake himself out of his surprise as he ran a hand over his face and half turned away. "No, no. My apologies. I'd just heard all the Fae defected from Aeterna." He glanced back at Tessa again. "I should go. You catch up with your friend, and I'll just head back to my room."

"Sure. Good idea. It's been a long day." I waved over one of the guards. "I'll have someone show you the way."

I watched Levi leave, hoping I hadn't just ruined my relationship with a second delegate. *That* would not make Casius happy at all. I'd have to apologize to Levi again tomorrow and make sure he understood that Tessa was here as a friend, not a representative of the Aeternal Council.

I returned to Tessa with a sigh and escorted her into one of the visitor rooms housed under the shield. The waiting space had been set up with a square table and four chairs for quick meetings. A small sofa sat in the corner, and a television was mounted on the wall. The TV was currently off, but I was pretty sure it only played the nature channel for our Aeternal guests.

"How long can you stay?" I asked.

"Not long. I just came to deliver the gift." Tessa handed me the box with a twinkle in her lavender eyes. "Go ahead. I promised Silas a detailed recounting of your reaction."

Inside the velvet-lined box from Silas was a pure-white crystal. I ran my fingers over the sharp edges, remembering a similar one from Lord Councilor Alaric's office in Aeterna. *A memory catcher.* It was cool against the tips of my fingers, and my heart stuttered as I channeled a tiny scrap of energy into the crystal.

Silas's memory hit me, as crisp and real as if I were living through it for the first time from his perspective. I watched from Silas's eyes while Father Mike and I said goodbye outside the shelter in Boston. My father hugged me, and the unmistakable love on his face made my heart squeeze painfully.

As I sat next to Tessa in the visitor room, a lump formed in my throat, and my stomach churned with guilt. It was the last time I'd see my father before Titus killed him—the last time he would hug me. At that time, I had no idea who he really was. I'd never even gotten a chance to tell him goodbye or to thank him for saving my life and sheltering me after my mother died.

A strong sense of Silas's irritation accompanied the memory of the first time we met. I smiled. The gift of the memory catcher was twofold. Not only did it capture the final moments with my father, but it was also a glimpse into Silas's feelings, implanted into the crystal. I didn't know it at the time, but Silas admitted later that he wanted to gain my trust so I would reveal more about who I was and possibly lead him to my people. But it was irritating for him to pause the search for Titus and coax the information out of me while chaperoning me to the Fate's temple.

Despite our rough start, we'd managed to find something more, and the annoyance coating his first memories of me made me smile wryly. Unfortunately, the gift hadn't been delivered in person, and I had no idea when I'd be able to see Silas again or kiss him and melt into his strong arms. The uncertainty of our future together made my heart hurt.

The memory catcher shifted into a new scene, and I choked back a sudden burst of rage embedded into the scene. Two women appeared in the middle of the Council's chambers, causing a flurry of alarm through the Councilors and the Guardians stationed around the grand hall. A scream of panic and pain ripped from Aria's lips as we landed in the middle of the hall.

I winced, seeing myself as Silas had seen me. The woman in the memory was on her hands and knees, beaten to a bloody mess. What was left of my clothing was torn and bloodstained, and my puffy, unrecognizable face was covered in bruises and cuts. Other than the long auburn braid over my shoulder, I wouldn't even have recognized myself.

Having the living hell beaten out of me hadn't been any more fun than it looked, but I was surprised at the intensity of Silas's feelings for me at that point in our relationship, when he was actively trying to distance himself from me. Fortunately, the memory shifted quickly to that night in his bedroom, when I asked him to stay and he turned me down. With the aid of the memory catcher, I could tell how much it tore him apart to walk away. His feelings for me were on the surface of the memory, fear and love and confusion all rolled into a tense ball, with a healthy dose of desire too. Walking away that night had been hard for him, and through his memories, I learned that he'd slept against the outside of my bedroom door.

For someone as private as Silas, sharing his most intimate feelings through this memory catcher was a sign of trust and love. It was bittersweet for me to understand exactly what he was going through during that rough period of our relationship, and it made me feel more connected to him. Even though we were being kept apart by our responsibilities to our people, I knew that he had deep feelings for me and that what we shared was worth fighting for.

I noticed a note he'd included with the memory crystal, tucked into the box. I opened it to find one word scrawled across the paper: *Soon.*

Guilt washed through me. I hadn't been able to keep that promise either. We hadn't figured out a way to make our relationship work for the past six months, and I didn't know if it ever would when the Council and the Inner Circle stood between us. I was letting *everyone* down—Silas, Casius, and my entire Sect.

"His gift has made you upset," Tessa noted with a small frown.

"No, I just... I don't know how to make things work the way I want them to, Tessa."

"You'll find a solution. It just needs time."

"Silas is literally banned from Earth with the rest of the Councilors. The Circle would never agree to me spending any time in Aeterna. How do we get around that? And even if we could visit each other..." I sighed. "The list of problems goes on and on. I'm trying to fix it, but I keep screwing everything up."

"Why do you feel these things are your fault?"

I leaned back in my chair. "The Circle will never accept Silas and me until they believe in me as a leader. I've been trying so hard to earn their trust, but I'm not making any progress. I'm trying to be the kind of leader my mother was, but I just keep disappointing everyone."

Tessa frowned. "You cannot be someone else—only yourself. They will accept you or they will not, but your path is your own to forge. You have to do what you believe is right, and the rest will follow."

I let her words roll around in my head. Tessa was right. I had to figure out what kind of leader I was, not who everyone believed I should be. Casius was constantly telling me to stay focused, to just try a little harder. This summit was my chance to show our Sect that I could be a good leader in my own way. And maybe, with more trust in my leadership, the Sect would understand the benefits to our alliance with the Council and come to accept my decision to be with Silas.

I'd nail it with Levi, try harder with Gia, and do whatever it took to get Alannah on board too. Our people were stronger together, and I had to show them the way home by building their trust in me. With their trust, Silas and I just might have a chance. And somehow—*Fates curse us*—I would have to figure out a way to do all that without hitting anyone.

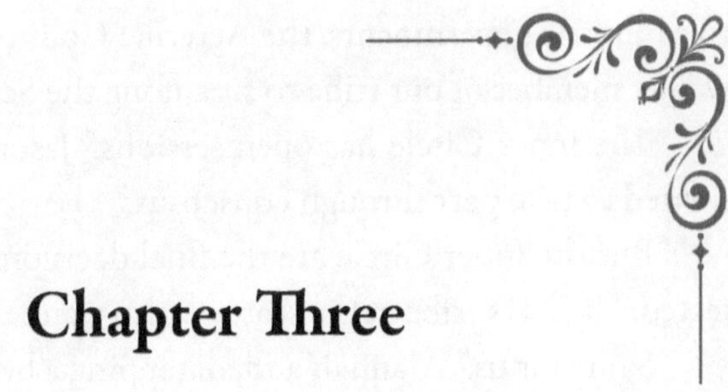

Chapter Three

"Let's discuss what we each need to reunite the Sect," Jason said to the delegates.

We'd already suffered through another full day of endless talking, subtle digs, and posturing. All they'd done since that morning was argue with each other. I'd played nice through all of it like a good leader, even though I hated every damn second of it.

I'd managed to read up on Levi and his group, but there wasn't much in Casius's files. I'd learned on my own that Levi mildly disliked eating fish and really disliked the government—no surprise there—but there wasn't anything about whatever was fueling the hate fest between him and Alannah. I was mildly surprised that he hadn't brought up Tessa's visit to the broader group and had easily accepted my explanation about our friendship. He seemed just as anxious to let it blow over as I was.

Of course, Alannah despised Levi and disparaged his lifestyle every chance she got. And Gia—well, she hated everyone, apparently. But she seemed to hate me most of all, if her continued death glares were any indication of her feelings. I'd managed to avoid the social gatherings or any more direct conflicts with her, but she hadn't stopped throwing a side-eye my way since our argument. It was getting old, but I was determined to make it work with these people.

"We want a guaranteed place at the table," Levi said, his voice rising. "We are a *free people*. We won't be subjugated to anyone. Not to Mundane governments, the Aeternal Council, or the Circle. We want a member of our tribe to sit among the Sect's leadership."

"The Inner Circle has open sessions," Jason said. "Everyone is invited to take part through consensus."

"But the Inner Circle are the final decision makers," Gia interjected. "If Levi's tribe gets a seat, we also want a representative."

"Same for us," Alannah added, tapping a bright-red nail on the conference table for emphasis.

I glanced at Ethan, who had remained mostly silent. He didn't speak up much in the official meetings, but I'd seen him chatting up the other delegates at breaks and meals. He was a good balance to his mother's direct, almost bullying approach. Ethan must have sensed me watching, because he looked up, and his face softened into a smile. I looked away quickly.

"We're prepared to offer each of your groups one seat in the Inner Circle," Jason replied. "Does that meet your needs?"

Everyone waited for someone else to speak, clearly unwilling to give in first and accidentally lose any unknown perks. I refrained from rolling my eyes. I was not looking forward to dealing with these three all the time. Maybe we could talk them all into appointing someone else as their representative within the Inner Circle.

"Yes," Gia finally said. "That works for me."

Levi bobbed his head curtly. "Agreed."

Alannah paused dramatically while everyone waited for her to speak. "We will have a representative in the Inner Circle. But we still have further concerns. The most important is that we maintain financial control of our assets."

Alannah's tribe had acquired a financial fortune in their Mountain West stronghold. We didn't know how much of it came from their church tithes or their subsequent investments, but Casius estimated that they had as much as thirty billion squirreled away.

The Inner Circle had already discussed how to handle this, and Jason was ready with financial estimates and contracts. He pushed a small binder across the table. "That is acceptable, so long as you assume responsibility for your share of community expenses."

Alannah waved her fingers casually over the binder. "Our lawyers will review this. I'm sure it's reasonable."

Jason's eyebrows rose in surprise. "So we're settled?"

We expected a lot more discussion and a prolonged argument over what the shared expenses would be. We'd prepared a list of items to haggle over and already planned out a separate session for Alannah just to go over her financial concerns.

I narrowed my eyes. *That was too easy.*

"I have one more requirement." Alannah inspected her nails again, almost bored. "I propose a bond-mating between my eldest son, Ethan Rourke, and Maeve O'Neill, to be executed within the next three years and formally fulfilled with the birth of an heir."

I froze, in shock. All eyes shifted to me, but no one said a single word. A glance at Ethan convinced me he was either a lot better at covering his surprise, or he'd known this was coming.

Gia's face lit with vindictive delight as heat built under my skin. I opened my mouth to tell Alannah where to stick her proposal. Then I closed it again. Another outburst from me would probably blow up the summit.

Casius cleared his throat, gathering everyone's attention.

Thank all the gods above and below. Casius could tell her where to shove it—in the most diplomatic way possible, of course. He would reject the crazy lady and her ridiculous proposal without destroying everything we were trying to build.

"A bond-mating with the Anchor of our Circle would be a very advantageous connection for your House," Casius said. "What are you proposing in exchange?"

Excuse me? My mouth literally dropped open.

Levi swore under his breath, probably upset at missing the opportunity to suggest himself as my baby daddy.

"We are prepared to contribute one-third ownership in all of our assets upon agreement and another third upon the birth of a child."

Casius's eyes went wide. "And what of the offspring from the mating?"

"As the more established House, we offer the child the position of Prime and heir of House Rourke once he or she comes of age. We're offering a huge portion of our financial assets and showing that we are committed to the success of our reunited Sect. We want an equal commitment."

My head felt like a ping-pong ball as I watched them barter over my uterus. My heart was pounding so hard in my ears that I felt light-headed. This couldn't really be happening. Casius and Alannah couldn't really be discussing the purchase price for my unborn child in front of the entire Sect.

I couldn't take it any longer—someone had to stop this. I rose to my feet. "Are you out of your fucking mind?"

Alannah's face was impassive, cold. "Wouldn't this arrangement be better than other... *outside* connections?"

She was talking about Silas. Rage boiled through my veins, and I let my magic burn through me until it burned through the room. "You can fly on your broomstick back to the backwater town you crawled out of and take your trained monkey with you!" I waved angrily at Ethan. "I will not be sold to the highest bidder! I don't care how many millions you're offering. The answer is no. Never!"

Alannah sat back in her seat. After a deliberate pause, she looked around the room, and I followed her gaze. Everyone was gaping. Levi, Gia, and Ethan were aghast at my outburst—even my own people were shocked. Jason, Tamara, Seth, and Rhonda—all of them clearly thought I was doing something wrong.

Alannah sneered condescendingly. "No one is forcing you to do anything against your will, child."

"Listen, you heartless bitch—"

"Mae!" Casius shouted. "That's enough!"

I slammed my palm on the table. "No! I mean it, Casius. I will not consent to this."

He gave me a look I knew well, although I hadn't seen it directed at me in years. Casius had been a part of my life since I could hold a knife, training and mentoring me. That look was reserved for the times when he thought I was acting like a spoiled, impetuous child who should know better.

I walked out of the room before I really lost my temper. Ranting under my breath, I stalked down the halls, away from the crazy people. I marched through the dark, abandoned hallways of the outer buildings until I reached my favorite spot on campus, the rec room. It had been a high-risk maternity wing during its hospital years, but we'd since torn down the walls and added a spring-padded sparring mat, customizing the large open space for weapons training.

The sparring platform filled most of the room, but there were two soft-surface practice pads on either side of the ring, complete with top-of-the-line practice equipment for blade and archery practice. I spent all of my free time here, and I was starting to rebuild the skill and strength I'd lost during my years in hiding. It also provided much-needed stress relief.

I stomped over to the section dedicated to all things sharp and pointy. I still favored a knife, but I was working on expanding my hand-to-hand skills, so I grabbed my new favorite, a blade inspired by the fifteenth-century German Messer. Almost as long as my arm, it was light enough to be a single-handed short sword or a double-handed combat weapon in a pinch. I named her Missy the Messer, in honor of a pig-faced boss who insisted on calling me "missy."

Muttering in anger, I rotated Missy in a small figure eight, warming up my wrist and shoulder. The curved blade had an angled handle similar to a knife with a straight cross guard and a short nagel—a small piece of metal jutting from the hilt to protect my hand. It was a workhorse blade, just like I preferred.

With a burst of my magic, I called Ripper to my left hand, gripped the bigger sword in my right, and set my sights on the practice dummy. I was working on becoming more proficient with both hands, and I needed to blow off some steam before I lost my temper and hunted down several people on my shit list. I toed off my shoes and bowed before stepping onto the mat. I ran through my forms slowly at first, jabbing the dummy with angry thrusts.

Casius had designed the spring-loaded machine so it spun and flexed with each impact. It moved in every direction and whacked you with hard wooden arms if you weren't fast enough on the rebound. I suspected Casius had infused just a tiny bit of magic into it, because the thing moved against the laws of physics. If I didn't keep on my toes, I ended up with wicked bruises the next day.

I replayed Alannah's demands in my head. She wanted me to mate with her son, have a baby, and then hand it over to her family. All for the price of fifteen to twenty billion dollars. I kicked the dummy, and it flexed backward. When it rebounded, I hacked at the wooden arms and sent it spinning clockwise with a kick. Twisting, I moved in to punch it in the face with Missy's metal hilt. The solid thump was very satisfying. I ducked under the swinging arms and fantasized about melting Alannah into a puddle of overpriced makeup.

My skin itched with anger as I worked up a sweat. I couldn't believe Casius was discussing how much they could sell me off for. He might be my mentor, but I was ready to skin him alive. There was no way they were going to sell my future child to the highest bidder. Just the thought made me murderous. And Ethan—*ugh*. The bastard hadn't fallen far from the tree after all. He just sat there, letting his mother plot out his life.

Footsteps squeaked across the gymnasium floor. My magic blazed as I whirled to face my unexpected visitor, peering into the dark edges of the gymnasium until a figure materialized.

"Ethan?" I relaxed my ready stance and wiped sweat from my forehead with the back of my hand. "Do you have a death wish?"

He stepped toward me. "Sorry to startle you."

I gestured around the deserted space. "You must be lost. The bride store is on the other side of campus."

His eyes were on my aura, which still blazed with magic. To his credit, he didn't act scared, and he didn't take the verbal bait either. "I came to apologize."

I set my anger aside. It was one thing to fantasize about melting the Wicked Witch of the Wasatch Mountains, but it was another to hurt her son, who might or might not have known what she was planning. With an effort, I let the magic go, but my anger was still simmering.

He took a tiny step closer and planted his expensive loafers on the practice pad. "I was hoping we could talk."

I glanced pointedly at his feet, but he didn't get the hint. "I think your mother has done enough talking for the both of you."

"If it makes you feel better, I tried to talk her out of it."

So he did know. "You're both crazy if you think you can buy me, breed me, and steal my future child. I don't care how much money you have."

He ducked his head. "I totally get it—you're not a prize to be won."

The angry retort died on the tip of my tongue. "Did you just quote Princess Jasmine?"

He flushed, and my anger cooled a tiny bit. I probably couldn't kill someone who just quoted a Disney character.

"Can we just... start over?" he asked. "There's a lot of history here that I'm not proud of. I'm sorry my mother is crazy, and I promise not to impregnate you against your will." The corners of his mouth twitched.

An almost amused huff escaped me. With a quick weaving of magic, I sent Ripper back to its spot in my room and then placed Missy back on the weapons rack. We were long overdue for a conversation. "Honestly, Ethan, I'm probably the one who should be apologizing."

His head tilted, and a sly grin tugged across his face. "For calling my mother a bitch?"

I rolled my eyes. "No. I have no regrets about that."

He chuckled, and I remembered why I'd liked him in high school. He was nothing like his mother—or he hadn't been, anyway. It had been quite a few years since I'd dated the slightly awkward kid who'd gone behind his mother's back to sneak out at night to meet me. He'd bring me presents, little Mundane things he'd messed around with, adding magic to make them work better or do something unexpected.

"Are you still tinkering with magic?" I asked, stalling the awkward feelings this was dredging up.

"We're not really supposed to expose our magic to the others," he said cautiously. "It's all carefully orchestrated by the church leadership."

I arched a brow. "Come on... I know you have something you're working on."

"I may have a little project." He grinned. "It's a short-wave field that disrupts the pockets of magic, rendering the entire space magic free for a limited period of time. I've been tinkering with the impact radius. I think I can modify it to generate a stabilized field with a few tweaks to the underlying conjuring."

Ethan kept talking, and I grinned fondly. Hearing him describe his latest pet project made me strangely nostalgic. I was a decade late, but I really did owe him an explanation for leaving without a word after my mother died. "I should have talked to you before I left. I..." I swallowed back a flash of residual pain. "When my mom died, I just wanted to forget what I saw. Everything fell apart so fast. But I shouldn't have left like that, with no explanation. No good-bye."

His eyes softened. "Oh, Mae. I won't say it didn't hurt, but I understand." His voice was gentle, and he took a step toward me, taking my hand in his. "I can't imagine what you were going through. I'm so sorry for everything that happened to your family."

My heart squeezed with remembered pain. Locking away those memories had only delayed the inevitable need to deal with the emotions and memories of my mother's murder, and I'd been sorting through a lot in the past few months.

"I'm glad we're back together again," he murmured softly.

I took a deliberate step back, breaking his touch. My teenage feelings for Ethan had been resolved a long time ago, and we were different people now. "Look, I hope your people choose to come back to the Sect. I really do. But you need to know I will never, ever be part of the deal. I'm not interested in rekindling our relationship, Ethan. Join the Sect or don't, but I'm not part of the package."

He spread his hands wide. "I completely respect that. My mom botched the proposal, but there's a lot of sense to a mating bond between us—"

"Oh, and how much would you have offered for me, then?" I crossed my arms.

"I'm not like that, Mae. You know me." His voice was calm, reasonable. "All I'm trying to say is, bonded-matings are part of our culture. Nobody is forced to do anything they don't want to. Take me. My mom has set me up with countless potential matches, but nothing's stuck, and that's totally fine."

I gritted my teeth. "Maybe you just really suck at dating."

"Or that," he said with a self-deprecating chuckle. "You tell me. I recall some good times from high school." His chocolate-brown eyes were full of memories.

My face flushed, but I gave him a flat look. I was so not falling for that trip down memory lane. "A lot has changed since then, Ethan, and I'm with someone else who I love very much."

He held up his palms in surrender. "I get it. I'm not pressuring you—I promise. All I'm saying is an alliance between us would be beneficial for everyone. It's not like we have to get married. We were good friends once, and I'd like the chance to get to know you again and see where things go. It doesn't need to be anything more than that."

I frowned but didn't say anything.

"We both had some growing up to do, but we were really good together, Mae." He took another step onto the pad and grabbed my hand again. "Maybe we could find that spark again. And if it benefits everyone in the Sect, is that such a bad thing?"

So much for not pressuring me. If I used magic to blow his head off his shoulders, I'd probably regret it later. At the very least, it would make Casius angry.

"Time to leave, Ethan," I said.

"Okay. Okay. I'm not trying to push anything." He flashed the lopsided grin that used to make my stomach flip and now made him roguishly handsome. "But I'm not giving up, either."

I let my anger fizzle out as he left. A lot had changed since high school, and I didn't have—or want—romantic feelings for him. But he wasn't a bad guy, despite the misguided attempt to get the two of us back together.

After the door closed behind Ethan, I counted to ten in my head and then called, "You can stop lurking, Casius."

Casius stepped into the rec room from the hallway, and I didn't even try to contain the snarl on my face. "Plotting more ways to sell me off? Maybe you could harvest my organs for the black market next."

He glanced pointedly at my aura, and I realized I'd accessed my magic again. My control was slipping, which was the opposite of helpful when dealing with Casius. I exhaled and let the magic fade away.

Casius stopped a few yards in front of me and crossed his arms. "He seems like a quality young man. I forgot you two had a history to build on."

"Nice try."

"What's wrong with considering someone *without* ties to our enemies?"

"Nope."

Casius's hands moved to his hips. "A bond with his family would bring in much-needed allies."

"And finances," I added.

"We can't afford to be splintered if we're going to stand against our enemies."

"I said no."

"You're acting like a child, Maeve."

I planted my fists on my hips. "A child you want to sell off to the highest bidder!"

He sighed with exaggerated patience. "These arrangements are a completely acceptable part of our culture."

"Gods' dammit, Casius! I am not a bargaining chip."

"I'm not saying you have to marry the boy, but it's your responsibility to our Sect to at least consider—"

"You don't get to sell me and my future child to the highest bidder! How could you even think I'd go along with this?" I snatched up my shoes. I'd officially had enough of being manipulated, and it was time to go. If I truly lost my temper, we'd both regret it.

"Maeve, just listen to me. The *possibility* has to be a part of our bargaining process with Alannah. No one is forcing you to go through with it against your will, but not considering the proposal is making people question your loyalties."

"You've got to be kidding me!" I snapped. "I've given everything to these people! I have nothing left to give, but somehow it still isn't enough. What else do you want from me?"

"*Our* people need an opportunity to see your leadership firsthand. You were gone most of your adult years, and you're bonded to an Aeternal. Gods, not just any Aeternal—Silas bloody Valeron, the Council's enforcer! How do you think that looks?" He took a deep breath and visibly settled himself. His voice was quieter when he spoke again. "A lot has changed in our Sect since you left, and they need to build their trust in you."

I slipped my shoes on, feeling guilty for continually letting Casius down. "I'm working on that. I know I need to earn their trust. But I'm still not going to make babies you can sell to Alannah."

Casius grimaced. Like all magic users, Casius hadn't physically aged much in the past twenty years. But there was a haggardness to his expression that made me feel guilty every time I disappointed him. He was the closest thing to family I had left, and he was a good man who worked hard to mentor me into becoming a leader. I had to remember that we were on the same side. He didn't like Silas, but that didn't make him a bad person.

"I promise I will try to be more diplomatic," I said with a resigned sigh. "But I love Silas, and our people are going to have to accept that at some point." He opened his mouth, and I held up my hand. "Let me finish. They're not ready yet, but I'll help them get there. We don't need to sell off our future in order for this summit to succeed. We have the alliance with the Aeternal Council, and we'll get the splintered tribes back home where they belong. We'll be stronger than ever."

Some of the energy seemed to return to his face. "You sound like your mother."

"I miss her." Memories of my family were bittersweet. "I feel bad about how things were left between Marcel and my father after she died. Marcel was right—I shouldn't have gone into hiding. They never had a chance to make peace, and now they're both gone."

"They loved you, and they loved each other. One fight doesn't change that. What happened to your family is a tragedy. But this is your opportunity to make them proud. You just need to try a little harder, Maeve—I know you have it in you to be the kind of great leader your mother was."

There was plenty of tragedy to go around in our Sect, and I was well aware that I wasn't measuring up to my family's legacy. I tried to see it from Casius's perspective. "So, should I pretend to want to mate with Ethan? What then? Have a pretend bonding and birth a pretend child? When does the charade end, Casius?"

"Just be nice to the boy while we smooth things over. We need you to put on a good face until the negotiations are over."

Casius hadn't outright accused me of being selfish, but I had to admit that I wasn't being particularly helpful either. I wasn't doing what the Sect needed me to do, and honestly, the suggestion wasn't so crazy. My parents' own marriage had been arranged—although no one forced them into it—but they'd fallen in love after Marcel was born, and then they'd had me. If I looked at it rationally, I should do what my mother did and put our people first.

"I know we need to put it on the table, but it just rubs me the wrong way. I feel like a piece of meat."

Casius's mouth twitched. "Think about it this way—once Ethan spends time with you again, he'll probably decide you're not worth the trouble."

"Very funny."

"Just don't let your emotions cloud your judgment. You know what's best for our people, and this is part of being a leader. In the end, no one can push you into a bonding you don't want, but you can at least allow us to keep the option on the table while we negotiate."

"So, if he decides he doesn't like me...?"

A devious spark lit Casius's eyes. "All's fair in love and business, Maeve."

"Don't you mean war? Love and war?"

"Business is war." He started tapping his fist against his thigh. "Alannah knows that. She could have introduced the proposal to you directly or alone to me. She could have let you and Ethan spend some time together first and rekindle the romance. She chose to bring up her proposal in a way that was guaranteed to tick you off in a very public setting. And no offense, but your temper is not a secret, and you're easy to provoke. Why do you think she would do that?"

I clenched my jaw. "She wanted me to freak out in front of the entire summit." Alannah had played me like a child, and I'd let her do it. The realization redirected some of my anger back to Alannah, where it belonged.

Casius pursed his lips. "I don't know what her endgame is yet, but the best way to handle this is to agree to the charade for now. Let us bargain. I promise no one is going to force you to make babies with Ethan, but I just need you to keep the proposal on the table while we work out the rest."

"Fine. But I'm not going to go around batting my eyelashes at Ethan and fake laughing at his jokes."

Casius squeezed my shoulder and flashed a grin. "No one would believe you if you did. You're a terrible liar."

The door to the rec room slammed open, and Tamara rushed in. "There's a Mundane government agent here, and he's asking for Maeve!"

Chapter Four

"Where is he?" Casius asked.

"I left him in the old chief of staff's office in the administration building," Tamara replied as we double-timed it back toward the administration wing. "The delegates and the rest of the Inner Circle are still at dinner on the other side of the campus."

"What does the government want with us?" I asked.

"I have no idea," Casius said. "We've filed the right permits, paid our taxes, and kept our heads down around town. Whatever he wants, a personal visit right now is not ideal. The last thing we need is the delegates thinking we have more problems we can't handle. Let's see what he wants and try to keep this quiet."

We fell into silence as our quick steps echoed down the empty hallways. The campus was huge, made up of multiple buildings connected by long, tiled halls. With so many buildings, we hadn't had time or funds to remodel everything, and this area hadn't been touched yet. It was a nice quiet place to meet with the agent without anyone seeing him.

The man waiting inside the office was in his midforties and tall with cropped blond hair, broad shoulders, and a little extra padding that hinted at glory days spent playing high school football. Everything about him screamed government lackey.

"Maeve O'Neill? I'm Special Agent Lennart."

I shook his hand and bit my tongue so I didn't blurt out anything incriminating. "That's me," I managed. "And this is Casius Palmer."

"Sorry for showing up without an appointment," Lennart said. "I didn't have a good way to get ahold of you, and I need to ask you some questions."

His words were completely polite, but something about him set me on edge. Although he'd barely said anything, I got the sense he was gauging my reactions and judging my character. The deep lines around his mouth and eyes spoke of a perma-scowl, and I suspected his nice-guy routine was a thin veneer that he would shed as soon as he got any resistance.

I motioned him to two leather chairs positioned in front of the massive mahogany desk left behind by the hospital. "What did you want to talk to me about?"

Lennart sat down, and I leaned on the edge of the desk. Tamara and Casius hovered near the door, trying to act casual, but all three of us had accessed our magic, and white energy glowed around everyone but the agent. Not surprisingly, Agent Lennart didn't react to the sudden flash of magic in the room.

Definitely Mundane.

Lennart's tight smile didn't reach his dark-brown eyes. "You remember an incident last September in Pennsylvania?"

Something definitely wasn't right with this agent showing up here in Boston, asking questions about that night. I frowned at him and let an edge of annoyance creep into my voice. "When our entire town burned down? Yeah, I remember that."

"You received a very large insurance settlement for the damages to your town buildings and surrounding farmlands, which triggered a mandatory investigation into the claim."

"Okay?" We'd done a significant amount of cleanup to make the destruction from the battle appear like an accidental fire. But that was all insurance business, and I didn't know how the government would be involved. Still, a bubble of worry started to build in my stomach, twisting around uncomfortably.

Casius cleared his throat. "That was all settled. We already got the check from the insurance company."

"I'm part of the official police investigation, and I believe Miss O'Neill will be able to shed some light on some recent incidents."

"What incidents?" I asked.

"Two people have gone missing, and we have reason to believe they have a connection to you."

Casius moved closer as Lennart reached into his bag, retrieved a small tablet, and handed it to me. The display showed two headshots. The first I didn't recognize, but the second—shock struck me as I recognized the second man. He'd just tried to kill me and blow up our Sect with a hand grenade.

I forced my voice to stay neutral as I said, "I don't know either of these men. You say they're missing—what does this have to do with me or the insurance claim?" I handed the tablet back. "I'm not, like, a beneficiary on the policy or anything."

"I'd like you to look at something before we continue," Lennart said. "Just so we're all on the same page."

My mind was spinning as he flicked his fingers over the screen and turned it back toward me. It was a blurry image of our previous town and the surrounding fields. I felt cold in the pit of my stomach. *Aerial satellite images.*

Lennart swiped a finger across the screen, and the next image zoomed closer to the fields just outside the town. The picture was so distorted that it took me a minute to recognize what I was seeing. The image was filled with people—the Guardians, the Brotherhood, and my Sect.

Once I knew what I was looking at, it wasn't hard to pick out the animal shapes of Shifters and the fallen bodies of the dead. The results of a massive battle lay scattered across several crushed fields of grain. Taken from above, the entire picture was obscured by the wind and debris Titus's super transference had kicked up, but it was clear enough.

My palms started to sweat, and I struggled to keep my face neutral. "What is this? It's blurry."

"I was hoping you could clear that up," Lennart said in a tone that dared me to answer.

I swallowed. "No, sorry. I have no idea." I tried to think of something more to say, but I was a terrible liar and decided to keep my mouth shut.

Lennart's lips pressed flat together. I glanced at Casius for help. *Sweaty palms, shifty eyes. Could I be any guiltier looking?*

Casius squinted at the image. "Is that a field?"

"We believe those people are engaged in a conflict," Lennart said.

I made a point of examining it again. "I don't know. It's very blurry."

"It looks more like animals to me," Casius offered smoothly, pointing at one of the dead Rakken. "I'm confused. What does this have to do with Maeve?"

Agent Lennart dropped the tablet back into his lap, and his lip curled on one side. "Her aunt was the primary policy holder for your insurance. You inherited a lot of money, Miss O'Neill."

"She died in the fire," I whispered, letting true grief color my tone.

Casius folded his arms. "Maeve is not the beneficiary on the policy. The Community Trust is."

Lennart leaned in. "About that. You all sure have a lot of business savvy for an Amish community."

"We're progressive," Casius said, sounding offended.

"Clearly." Lennart dragged his eyes over our clothing. Casius was in slacks and a button-down shirt for the summit, and I was in jeans. Tamara, at least, was in a dress, but none of us appeared properly Amish.

"The Lord provides in mysterious ways," Tamara said from her spot across the room.

A sudden coughing fit overtook me, and I held back a totally inappropriate burst of nervous laughter. With a scowl, Lennart handed me a printed photo that was clearer than the others.

I gaped in shock as a dozen emotions slapped me in the face—surprise, anger, and finally terrible, crushing guilt. In the photo, I knelt in the bloody trampled field. A dark-haired man with broad shoulders stood on my left side in bloodstained leather armor—Silas. On either side of me lay dead bodies. Titus, Atticus, and my aunt Deanna were clearly visible. The fourth person, mostly obscured by the angle of Silas's back, was my dad. Dead.

My throat closed, and tears started to burn behind my eyes.

"What is this?" Casius grabbed the photo out of my trembling hands.

"We've only been able to identify one of the people in this photo—your aunt," Lennart said. "And she didn't die in a fire."

I swallowed hard and worked on composing myself.

"That person there"—Lennart pointed at the top of my auburn head in the photo—"looks an awful lot like you, Miss O'Neill."

"This is a religious rite for the dead." Casius tossed the photo into Agent Lennart's lap. "How dare you photograph our private rituals."

"You didn't report these other deaths. Who are they?"

"This is religious persecution!" Casius declared. "You'll be hearing from our lawyers."

"A lot of people seem to die or go missing around you, Miss O'Neill. Why don't you tell me what happened to them and ease your conscience?"

"I have nothing to do with those missing people," I said.

He held the photo out to me again, and my gaze locked on Atticus's scarred, lifeless face. He was so young. His short life had been full of inequality and betrayal, and he'd gone on the undercover mission to infiltrate the Brotherhood because I'd asked him to. It was my fault he was dead.

"Then why did both of the missing men receive a text message from your mobile phone directing them to meet you here?" Lennart asked.

I twitched in surprise. "What?"

"They were meeting you here at your compound, and now they're missing. You were the last person to see them alive." He pointed at the photo again. "And what we have here are a whole lot of extra bodies that haven't been accounted for. Just what kind of weird ritual shit are you into here?"

"This is conjecture and defamation," Casius said. "People go missing all the time—maybe those people decided to leave town for the weekend. Can you even prove Maeve sent those texts in the first place? Truthfully, I don't even know what you're accusing Maeve of, so unless you have a warrant for her arrest, you need to leave. Now."

Lennart unfolded his large frame from the chair and stood to leave. He handed me a business card with the photo and leaned down until I met his eyes. "When more bodies start to show up, I'll be back with that warrant, and it will be too late for you. Or you could do yourself a favor and tell me what you know about the missing people. Do the right thing, Miss O'Neill. Their families deserve closure."

I held it together as Tamara escorted Agent Lennart out of the office, but as soon as their footsteps retreated down the hall, I slumped into one of the vacated chairs. My hands shook as I gripped the photo. "I think someone is setting me up."

"I agree," Casius said. "I don't know if we can believe everything Agent Lennart said, but have Rhonda wipe your mobile, and let's get you a new number."

"What about the photos of the battle?" I couldn't look away from Atticus's face. My heart was beating too fast, and pressure squeezed my chest.

Casius took the photo from me and set it facedown on the desk. "He can't prove anything."

"Lennart didn't believe a word we said." I swallowed thickly. "What if he has some other proof from the old town?"

"They don't have anything else, or he wouldn't be here asking questions." Casius sounded calm, but his fist started tapping against his thigh.

My brain raced with all the ways the government could expose us—the battle and all those unexplained dead bodies. The true cause of the fire. The existence of magic. There were so many secrets, and Agent Lennart was digging in all the right places. I *did* have a connection to the missing man—because someone had sent him to kill me. And whoever did that was making it look like I was responsible for his disappearance.

The irony was that Lennart was right, not about the missing people but about my guilt. I *had* caused a lot of other deaths. All the deaths from the battle with Titus were my fault. I'd led the Brotherhood there, and I'd convinced the Sect to fight. Lennart was right, just not in the way he suspected.

We sat in tense silence until Tamara returned. "He's gone. I think the religious-rite argument will hold him off for a little while.

That was quick thinking." She patted my shoulder sympathetically and seated herself in the chair adjacent to mine.

"What if it's not enough?" I asked, examining the business card Lennart had given me. The bottom line read Department of Defense, Special Interests. *Special Interests indeed.* "They're not going to just stop digging. They've got those images, and the government has all kinds of technology. They're going to find something else."

Casius positioned himself in front of the window, gazing out over the main quad. "I'm more concerned about the missing people and whoever is setting you up with the Mundane government. We need to inform the rest of the Circle, but it will have to wait until after the summit ends tomorrow. We have enough problems to focus on without creating more."

Tamara's face pinched. "Maybe this goes without saying, but we can't afford to attract the attention of the government."

"Too late," I muttered, chewing on the inside of my cheek.

"The cell phone trail is concerning," Casius said, "but they can't prove anything other than what we said happened."

"Agent Lennart doesn't seem like the kind of guy who's going to back down," I replied. "He's going to keep digging until he finds proof. Thanks to those satellite images, he's going to scour our old compound. We could have missed anything in those fields—a single broken blade, a lost piece of armor, a patch of blood-soaked ground, for crying out loud!"

Casius frowned, but Tamara said, "Maeve's right. We need to deal with this before it gets worse. It doesn't matter what we say. Did you see all that blood soaking the Lord Commander's armor? No one explained the blood."

"Or the armor," I said.

"At least he didn't still have his sword," Casius offered quietly.

"We need to take this to the Circle now," I said with a sigh. "We can't afford to wait."

Tamara chewed on her lip. "If we call an Inner Circle meeting, the entire Sect will hear about it. The summit would fall apart. Even after the summit, the second the delegates get wind that the government is about to descend on us... everything we've been working for is over."

"The delegates can't find out," Casius agreed. "We don't say anything until we know more or Special Agent Lennart comes back with a warrant. They don't have any evidence on us, and we don't need to blow it out of proportion. Reuniting the Sect is too important."

A throat cleared from the doorway behind us, and all three of us jumped.

"And wouldn't that be a disaster," Alannah said dryly.

Casius jumped to his feet. "Alannah—"

She held up a perfectly manicured finger. "Don't, Casius. This is exactly why we don't trust you. You're exactly the same—keeping secrets and afraid to take action. Nothing has changed."

I shot to my feet. "Were you eavesdropping on us? Did you *follow* us?"

She scowled. "Haven't you caused enough problems today? Maybe you should take a time-out." With that, she turned away from me and said to Casius, "This threat needs to be dealt with, and I demand that this matter is brought before the full Inner Circle, including the delegates."

"Alannah, there's no reason to panic everyone," Casius said. "We need to gather more information before we tell everyone about a potential issue."

Alannah's heels clicked on the floor as she moved into the office and planted herself face-to-face with Casius. "The *potential* issue was when you did a piss-poor job of cleaning up your own mess in Pennsylvania. Now you have the government showing you evidence of your problem, and your plan is to close your eyes and *hope* it goes away?"

Casius gestured at Tamara, who glanced up and down the hallway before she closed the office door. "We can't risk everyone finding out about this," he said to Alannah. "Surely, you realize how important it is that we not panic the entire Sect. Look what happened last time."

Alannah leveled a look at him that didn't require any words to decipher. She wasn't going to keep silent.

"It would be irresponsible to bring this to everyone's attention," Tamara pleaded. "The Circle is not a closed forum. You'll panic everyone for nothing."

Alannah's face was shrewd. "Your current leadership is failing because you let the uninformed lead by consensus, and it's time to make an Inner Circle that is truly empowered and able to govern our people."

I huffed, unable to contain my disgust. "No time like a crisis for a power grab."

She ignored me. "I'm talking about government by representation. You need to appoint leaders who represent the people and close your meetings to the rest of the Sect. You can't even confer on important issues without everyone knowing every detail. It's a security risk. You have weak leadership, without a true leader at the head."

"Let me guess who you think that leader should be," I said.

"I'll tell you who it shouldn't be," Alannah said. "Just because you're the offspring of the previous leader does not mean *you're* a good leader. You are childish, unpolished, impulsive, and inexperienced. You've proven that with your unwillingness to even consider an offer that would fortify and build your people!"

"You sure make a lot of demands, but I don't see you making any personal sacrifices!"

Alannah's voice was a low snarl. "You have no idea the sacrifices I've made to secure the future of my people."

"Enough!" Casius's eyes swept over me and Alannah. "Please. Just stop." He turned away and gazed through the darkened windows overlooking the campus.

Shame flooded me. *Dammit, I did it again.* I couldn't muster self-control when I needed it most. Fighting with Alannah was stupid. We needed her to work with us, not against us, and I wasn't winning any leadership points by goading her.

Outside, lights glowed through hundreds of windows across the campus, shining from dorm rooms filled with families. I felt responsible for each and every one of those people. I would give my own life to keep them safe, and I'd worked my ass off for months trying to do all the right things for them. Even though Alannah had no right to waltz in with her own agenda, making demands and derailing my credibility, I was too quick to lose my temper and make things worse.

Casius massaged the furrow between his brows before he finally spoke. "We will call a closed meeting with the Inner Circle and decide what needs to be done. Alannah, I'm asking you for twenty-four hours."

"I will agree," she said, "if Maeve will publicly agree to the bond-mating with Ethan."

"You made me look like a hot-tempered child in front of everyone. You don't need to humiliate me any further."

"Oh, I was serious about the bond-mating, my dear. I want our people to be united fully, and mating you and Ethan is the perfect way to do so. So you can step up and make the decision a true leader would, or I can reveal your dirty scheming to your people."

Tamara gave me a sympathetic grimace. I didn't know what to say. I looked to Casius, whose eyes were rimmed with exhaustion.

"News of a government investigation will panic every member of our Sect," he said. "The summit will be called off, and you know how important it is to reunite our people." His brow rose, silently asking me to agree to do the right thing. "Remember what we talked about earlier, Mae. It's time for you to think ahead about what's best for our people."

I had to remember that I trusted Casius with my life. He knew I would never agree to a bond-mating with Ethan. He'd told me he would never force me into it. We just needed Alannah to believe the offer was on the table while we worked through the current crisis.

I inhaled deeply through my nose before I forced the words out of my mouth. "I agree to *consider* the proposal, and I will do it publicly. But nothing will be finalized until your people have formally returned to the Sect."

Alannah's smile was wide and pleased. "Agreed. But you must arrange a public date with Ethan."

"What? Why?"

"Because the two of you have things to discuss. Romance to rekindle. You shot down my proposal publicly, and I want it clear to everyone that you're considering Ethan as a potential mate. Unless you're not serious about the bond-mating?"

I gritted my teeth. "Fine."

Everyone was going to think I was a child who'd thrown a fit and had gotten schooled by Alannah. I was losing credibility left and right. To top it off, everyone in our Sect would prefer to see me bond-mated with Ethan because they'd never accept Silas. His reputation, his family name—everything about Silas was a problem. Ethan was the easy choice. Everyone would think he was the *right* choice. Except he wasn't right for my heart. But I would do it. Even though my heart clenched in my chest, I would play pretend with Ethan, because a good leader made sacrifices for her people.

I flashed my teeth in a terrible approximation of a smile. "I'm looking forward to it."

Chapter Five

The sun rose bright and early, shining over the main quad as Ethan grinned knowingly. "So, what threat did my mother use to get you to agree to this?"

I adjusted my backpack and smirked despite myself. Ethan knew his mother well. I almost felt bad for pretending to go on a real date with him, except for the fact that Ethan had gone along with this bond-mating plan from the beginning. He'd come out to Boston and ambushed me with that plan. It was his own fault Alannah had twisted my arm to take him out.

So I threw him a smile. If he wanted a fake date, he'd get a fake date. "I wanted to show you the town where we used to live."

The silver lining to this forced outing was that we'd have an unsupervised opportunity to talk. The night before, I'd gone to bed dreading the next day, but I woke up with a brilliant idea. It started with the realization Ethan's mother and Casius could push us all they wanted, but if one of us said no, there wasn't any way they could force us to make babies together. The key was Ethan. While we were alone on this date, I could talk to him and explain why a bond-mating would never happen and why his people should still return to the Sect. I could get Ethan on my side against Alannah, and our old town in Pennsylvania would be the perfect setting for that. I would get a chance to make sure we'd cleaned up all the evidence, and the destruction would serve as a physical reminder of what happened when we stood alone. If I could get Ethan to see

67

reason, maybe we could convince Alannah to rejoin the Sect without a bond-mating as part of the deal.

After I showed him the town, we would get lunch together on the campus—publicly, like Alannah wanted. It was a solid plan, but the idea of returning to the old town gave me chills. I remembered exactly what the destruction had been like after the battle—the dead bodies of friends and family and the ground soaked in their blood and magic. A shiver ran down my spine, and I forced myself to take a pause. I was getting worked up for nothing. We'd poke around, make sure there was nothing to worry about, and then get out.

I handed Ethan a hat and fitted one over my own distinctive hair. It wasn't a perfect solution to potential satellite surveillance, but it should keep us from being identified.

Ethan's expression morphed into a confused frown. "Didn't the town burn down?"

"Well, the buildings and the fields are mostly burned, but the surrounding area is really lovely. And it's private. Your mom wants us to discuss... things."

He held out his hand. "All right. Sounds like a plan."

I frowned at his outstretched fingers. "Look, I agreed to the mating bond. Don't forget, I haven't agreed to hold your hand and be your baby mama."

"I've never been to your old town," he said patiently. "I'll have to follow your flare when you skim, and the physical contact will make that a lot easier."

He was right, of course. Without a line of sight or familiarity with the location, it would be a lot harder for him to skim there. I grimaced out of embarrassment, took his hand, and opened myself to the magic, leading us both to Pennsylvania.

The sun's cheery glow turned harsh, revealing the mess we'd left behind in our old compound. The town was in complete ruin.

The fire had burned everything, and the fields were a sea of black stubble. The buildings were reduced to charred wood and ash except the town hall, our largest building, which boasted the remains of two blackened walls. It looked as if a giant fireball had landed directly on top of our little Amish-style town as an act of God. *Or demons in human skins.* Not quite the picturesque stroll I'd described to Ethan.

It had been six months, but the air still smelled like smoke. I half expected the insurance company to have bulldozed the whole place, but apparently, the demand for remote Amish farmland wasn't that high. Nothing had been touched.

Ethan let out a low whistle. "Damn."

"Yeah," I whispered. "It was..." The memories tore through my heart. There were no words to describe what had happened here. So many people lost their lives when Titus unleashed the super transference and tried to steal our magic. Hundreds of our people died to stop him, including Atticus and the last of my family. I spun in a slow circle, remembering. "Bad," I finished. "It was bad."

I turned my back and paced deeper into the dead field so he wouldn't see my tears welling up. I hadn't expected this to hit me so hard. Everything around me was my fault. The Sect had hid for years, safe and undiscovered, before I brought the Brotherhood crashing down on them with my carelessness.

Our battle with the Brotherhood had brought about the treaty with the Council and, hopefully, a full reunion of all the scattered people of our Sect, but the price had been too high. We'd lost so many. I stopped in the exact spot where Deanna and my father had died. A dozen yards to my left, I'd let Atticus die.

Squatting, I touched three smooth oval rocks I'd stacked on top of each other as their only memorial. A small, pathetic token for each life. The stones were cold and hard under my palm. Lifeless. I squeezed my eyes shut.

Ethan crouched at my side, the smell of his cologne drifting around us as he placed his palm on top of my hand. "I know you miss your mom," he said. I opened my mouth to tell him this memorial wasn't for her, but he seemed genuinely sad. "I miss her too."

"Really?" It was so rare to talk about her. Most of the people in our Sect had already mourned her and moved on years before. Or they didn't know her. Just a decade after her sacrifice to save our people from the Brotherhood, she was more legendary than real to most. But for me, the pain of losing her was fresh with the recent return of my memories.

"Remember that time she busted us for breaking into your parents' liquor cabinet? She could have really nailed my ass, but she was cool about it. Never did tell my mom."

I chuckled softly. "She thought you were a good influence on me. She used to say you softened my hard edges."

He snorted. "I liked your hard edges. If anything, you influenced me to be more assertive. Stand up to my mother occasionally."

Because of that, Alannah's opinion of me as a teenager had been about what it was at the moment. *Not very high.*

He held my gaze. "I'm really sorry about what happened to your family."

A lump formed in my throat. "Me too."

Ethan squeezed my hand. "I know you don't want to talk about this, but you're not alone, Mae. There's no reason we can't pick up where we left off. A bond-mating between us doesn't have to be about obligation."

I pulled my hand out from under his. My heart was beating too fast. It had been a lifetime since I'd felt anything for Ethan. Even after my memories returned, I hadn't thought about him until he walked onto our campus a few days before. All these feelings and memories and being where so many had died—it was too much. I swallowed a thick lump in my throat and leaned away from him. "That was a long time ago, Ethan. I spent most of the time since then not remembering who I was, and I'm a different person now. I've moved on. I already told you that."

His blue eyes searched mine. "I didn't mean to push. I just wanted to say I'm sorry. For all of it. I'm here if you need me, okay?" He stood, giving me the space I needed to pull myself together.

I appreciated that about Ethan—he knew when to just let me be. After a few more minutes, I rose and adjusted the backpack hanging from my shoulder. It was time to stop dwelling in the past and move forward, and at the moment, I needed to finish a different conversation with Ethan. Together, we had to convince Alannah to return her people to the Sect without an archaic bond-mating alliance to seal the deal.

"Actually, I wanted to talk with you—"

A flash of brilliant-blue magic filled the space in front of me, and I jerked back, my own magic forming around me reflexively. Lord Nuada, the exiled Fae Council leader, stood in front of us, glowing with deep-blue magic. His long near-black hair was shaved on the right side of his head, exposing one pointed ear. His unexpected appearance in the field was even more jarring because of the jeans and T-shirt he wore, and I froze in midsentence with my mouth hanging open.

"Who the hell are you?" Ethan demanded, stepping in front of me.

Nuada made a flicking motion with his hand, and Ethan flew into the air. He landed hard on his back with a pained grunt, plowing soil and ash underneath him for several feet.

I threw unformed magic at Nuada, hoping to knock him backward and give us time to escape, but he countered it with ease. He deflected wave after wave of power with skill that it would take me lifetimes to acquire. It probably *had* been acquired over many lifetimes. I had more raw power at my disposal but not nearly the knowledge and technique required to fight a master conjurer like the former Lord Councilor.

I changed tactics and launched myself at Nuada. The physical attack surprised him, just as I'd hoped. A solid kick to his thigh sent him staggering backward, and before he recovered, I dropped low and swept my leg at his ankles. He fell.

I conjured Ripper into my hand.

"Maeve!" Ethan called.

I glanced at Ethan. In that split second of delay, Nuada's arm shot out, and he grabbed my leg. His magic rose around us.

My stomach lurched as his magic caught me, and I blacked out.

Chapter Six

I woke with a pounding headache and a sandpaper tongue. A small cloud of dust exploded into my eyes as I coughed and lifted my face out of the dirt to find that I was alone and surrounded by trees in some kind of densely wooded area. Birds chirped from the ancient oaks that stretched high above my line of sight. Vines as thick as my wrist wrapped around their trunks, flowering with exotic-looking blooms, and from somewhere not too distant, I could hear running water. Above the canopy of leaves, the sun shone brightly, casting dappled shadows on the ground. Beautiful, but not super helpful for pinpointing my location.

I pushed to my feet, but I froze when I saw what surrounded me. At my feet, a perfect circle of complex magic sigils was etched into the dirt. Carefully, without moving, I examined the corresponding dome of magic over my head. It had four layers, and the runes tied to each element were drawn in four concentric circles around me. Judging from the symbols, the first layer was conjured with air, the second with earth, the third was tied to the element of water, and the fourth, farthest from me, was pulled from fire.

Holding back my rising panic, I tried to access my magic. *Nothing.* Where my powers should have been, it felt like I was hitting my head against a brick wall. I couldn't access or absorb any outside magic.

I was trapped inside an Elementari.

I let out a string of expletives that would have made Silas proud. The Elementari was similar to the conjuring Titus had used to block my powers when he kidnapped me. But that spell had been conjured with a small portable sigil disguised as a necklace. This spell was a level-four conjuring, and a different master-level practitioner had formed each layer from four unique elements. There was no way to break out of it without magic, and by design, the Elementari blocked my access to magic. Depending on the way it was built, an elemental trap could even suck the energy out of anything that touched it, and I had zero desire to experience that particular kind of death.

Outside of the unbreakable magic prison, I could see the energy winding around every branch and radiating from every leaf in the forest. I blinked, surprised at the amount of power threading through the trees. Considering who'd brought me here, I realized I was in a Fae haven, a place that didn't exist in our Mundane, non-magic realm.

Nuada had trapped me in an Elementari in another realm, with no way out and no way to let anyone know where I was. My heart felt like it was about to race out of my chest as I stood stock-still in the center of the circle, taking in my dire circumstances. I was careful not to touch any of the runes on the ground while my brain shuffled through my options and focused on the facts.

First, Nuada didn't want me dead. If he did, he could have killed me while I was unconscious. Second, this took a lot of planning, and he wasn't acting alone. Conjuring a complex Elementari would require more than one person and a hell of a lot of magic power. And it would have taken some time. He wanted something from me, and he'd gone to a lot of effort to keep me prisoner. Third, it had to be something he wanted from me specifically, because he hadn't taken Ethan.

Ethan had been conscious when Nuada grabbed me and pulled me to the haven. If Ethan made it back and told the Sect I'd been taken... they'd still have no way to know where I was. Nuada had taken me to another realm, and I had to assume there was no rescue coming.

I sank to my knees, careful to avoid disturbing the sigils in the dirt, and pushed down my rising panic by searching for anything that could help me escape. First, I needed to find a weak spot in the conjuring and get out of this magic trap. Then I could freak out.

I turned slowly, examining the runes on the ground intently, but I froze in my tracks as I completed the circle. A man had appeared outside the Elementari, sitting cross-legged on the ground. His thoughtful brown eyes matched his short chestnut hair, and he wore a plain tunic with loose-fitting pants. He appeared to be in his early thirties and generally had an average-Joe look about him—neither remarkable nor unattractive. Normal. I wouldn't have noticed him in a crowd. I didn't think I'd ever seen him before, but still, there was something compelling about him and almost familiar.

His expression was amused, and when his lips curved upward, a shiver twisted down my back. "Gods' day. Or rather, evening." He raised his chin at the sky, which had transformed into a dark night with a full bloodred moon shining overhead.

What the hell?

The giant blood moon glowed above us exactly as it had the night Titus attacked. It had to be some kind of trick. My heart started racing even though I knew it had to be an illusion. But if the man was doing it, I couldn't see an aura of magic around him. The space around him was almost a blank, without any magic at all.

The back of my neck tingled. "Who are you?"

He winked at me. "You can call me Four."

This guy was setting off all my internal alarm bells. I had no idea who he was, but something about him was tugging at my subconscious. "What do you want, Four? Why did you bring me here?"

"I didn't bring you here. The Fae male did. As to what I want, now, that's an interesting question. I don't believe I've been asked that before. So many questions, but never that one." He tapped his chin with his index finger.

His actions were stiff, and I felt as if I were watching an actor on a stage. I narrowed my eyes, and his narrowed too. I shifted, and his head tilted with mine, mimicking. There was something really, really off with Four.

"What *do* I want?" he continued. "I suppose the answer is change. I want change." He chuckled to himself. "But of course, that depends on you. What do *you* want?"

Irritation sparked in my chest. He wasn't Fae—that much was obvious from his appearance—but I didn't know what he was, and no magic flared around him, giving away his species.

"Are you going to help me, or are you just here to gawk at the idiot trapped inside the magic bubble?"

His face morphed into a wide smile that seemed out of place. "Truthfully, I haven't decided yet. Your death brings change, but so does your life. I can't see which way it will go."

Another shiver ran down my spine. "Tell me what you want, or go away. I don't have time for this."

He winked again, and suddenly, he was sitting inside the Elementari. I scrambled backward on my hands and heels, wiping away a swath of the runes on the ground. I froze, waiting for the Elementari to respond. Three heartbeats pounded as I held my breath, but nothing happened. The trap didn't collapse or burn me to a crisp, but relief didn't come, because I realized who—or what—was sitting inside the Elementari with me. There was only one being who possessed the astronomical magic power it would take to pop in-side an Elementari like Four just had.

I was trapped in the Elementari with a Fate. All the curse words I knew ran through my mind, but for once, my mouth wisely stayed shut. I swallowed around a dry throat. Slowly, I righted myself and faced the Fate who called himself Four. My pulse pounded in my ears, and I rocked with adrenaline as I stared at the all-powerful be-ing who could wipe me from existence with nothing more than a thought.

When I'd tracked one down in Alaska to help me get rid of my magic, I'd had no idea what I was getting into. I didn't have the luxury of ignorance anymore. Fates didn't just pop in for tea. They didn't bother with mortal lives and events. A Fate taking notice of me meant I was in some deep shit, and nothing good was going to come from this visit.

"What do you want with me?" I asked.

"A lesson." His eyes glowed completely white, and foreign mag-ic rolled over me as he raised a single forefinger and drew a straight line in the dirt between us. "Mortal life is a linear progression of events. Each event affects the outcome, but mortals have choices, Maeve O'Neill. Choices that drive change." He placed the tip of his finger on the line, and it bent a few degrees. "A doctor misses the di-agnosis of a patient's disease." His finger moved a few inches farther down, and the line bent again. "The dead woman's husband drives drunk and kills the future father of your children." The line shifted a third time, and he ran his finger down the length of it. "You do not meet him, and you bear no children. Each event changes the total trajectory of the thread."

Despite my fear, I listened in fascination. He was talking about predetermined destiny. I'd experienced a moment like that when I stopped Titus's super transference, and for a split second, I understood the many events that had brought Silas and me to that exact moment. It was... fate.

"We don't care about those. Too small. Too... mortal." He waved his hand above the dirt, and a hundred lines appeared, intersecting each other in an intricate web. "What you and I care about are Moments." He emphasized the last word, capitalizing it. "Large-scale change, Maeve O'Neill, is the potential you have now."

He placed the tip of his finger in the center of the web of lines, and they all shifted around that intersection point. They moved and flexed until a pattern emerged. "Every life is part of the bigger pattern. A tapestry of potential and free will."

I was struck completely speechless. Even inside the Elementari, where magic was supposed to be nonexistent, I felt the power emanating off the Fate. The pattern he showed me was three-dimensional, imitating the structure of magic but so much more complex and vast. He was showing me only a glimpse of his powers, and it was absolutely intoxicating. My mind felt as if it had just expanded as his magic surged across my awareness. I let it wash over me as I tried to absorb the meaning of his lesson.

"Would you like to see your own personal Moment?" His expression was filled with curiosity. "Most mortals don't get one, but you will."

"No," I answered immediately. I didn't want to know the things that would change the course of my life or the lives of everyone around me. It was too much responsibility. If I knew something like that, I'd second-guess every action, every choice.

"Very wise of you. Instead, a gift."

A tingling sensation spread from the base of my spine. My brain told me to run, but I couldn't. He reached for me, and I wanted to move away, but my body wouldn't respond. I was frozen until the tip of his finger touched my forehead, and my vision shifted.

Bloody tracks on a white floor. A woman's high-heeled shoeprints.

A pregnant woman with curly black hair lying in the middle of an empty barn, her face brutally chewed away.

I'd seen those things before, but I still didn't know what they meant. White magic flared in front of me, and I moved into a new vision.

I shade my eyes and squint into a cell carved from stone. A blond woman lies on the bare floor in a heap. A man strides purposefully into the cage and drags her out to a dark stone hallway. Her limp form is too weak to stand or fight back. He lets her go, and she looks up with defiance burning in her amethyst eyes.

The vision shifted again, leaving me with nothing more than vague images and a sense of dread.

I am inside a building, surrounded by a thousand people. They press around me, screaming. No... cheering. My eyes snag on a billowing white robe flowing over several shoulders. It's concealing something—a body. The man bobs lifelessly on the shoulders of the crowd. Dark hair. Strong wide shoulders. A sword hangs from a scabbard on his hip.

"No!" My entire body shook as I gasped for air. I tried to pull out of the vision, but I couldn't.

They lower the body to the ground and lay him at my feet.

Stephan Valeron's eyes are rimmed in red. "He's dead. We couldn't stop him."

"Silas!" I screamed and jerked myself free of the vision for only a moment before I was dragged back into the next one.

I am outside the compound in Boston. The entire campus is flooded with people running in a blind panic across the grassy quad. They're dying, and the sounds are terrible. Shrieks of rage and death, the clash of swords from Guardians fighting to the death in the central quad. Flashes of blue magic—Fae.

I watch from above as a new group advances. Men clothed in black tactical gear surge forward from two sides of the quad, trapping the bulk of the people in the middle. Families and children run for their lives, but they're indiscriminately mowed down by the soldiers with guns.

My eyes jerked open, filled with tears, as I processed what I'd just seen—Silas's death and the slaughter of my people. My heart hammered in my chest as I looked at the Fate in terror. "Is this real?"

Four's eyes were filled with power and completely void of emotion. "It is the future that might be."

"Can I stop it?" I demanded. "I can't let them all die."

"Your Moments are filled with death. It's time to embrace who you are, Maeve O'Neill." He placed his finger in the dirt again, and the web of intersecting lines melted back into a single row. He drew five tick marks along the straight line. "The next point draws near."

"Are those the visions you showed me? Will stopping these Moments prevent the next one?"

"They are tied in the linear way of mortals. You may choose to stop the Moments, but you cannot alter the path of others. Free will is the great equalizer to all of us, mortal and immortal. But heed my warning. Tell no one, or you will not be able to change the outcome."

"Where do I start? How will I know it's working?"

"What will happen is already happening. The visions will guide you to shift the trajectory."

The weighty feel of his magic disappeared as if he'd yanked it all inward, and I inhaled sharply. One moment, I was bathing in the surreal feel of almost unlimited power, and then—it was gone.

"I suggest you get started. He'll be arriving soon, and you'll need to be most of the way done before then." He winked and disappeared.

"Wait!" I yelled, but he was already gone. "Don't leave me in here!"

I quieted as I realized what he'd said. I could stop the visions. Silas didn't have to die. My people wouldn't be overrun by the Fae and the Mundane government. Somehow, the visions would guide me, and I could stop those horrible things from happening.

With determined fingers, I wiped the moisture from my eyes and examined the path he'd drawn in the dirt. I had to remember the Moments—each of the visions he'd shown me was a turning point. The first time I'd seen the visions, there had been bloody footsteps, and Gia's death had been next. But this time, the blond woman in the stone cell had come after the footsteps, followed by Silas's death. The final vision had been the all-out attack from all our enemies—the Fae and the government converging on our home, killing families and children. My heart clenched in my chest as my brain tried to sort through everything. I'd do anything to stop those terrible events from happening.

Four had said each one led to the next and I could stop them. But I had no idea how. According to Four's parting comment, I couldn't risk telling anyone else what I knew, or I would lose the chance to stop this all from happening.

I swore. I was trapped inside the Elementari in a foreign realm with no idea how to stop the events in the visions from happening. I sat for a long time, contemplating the words of the Fate and committing everything I could to my memory, until a group of Fae in long green robes emerged from the forest.

I immediately recognized Lord Nuada and Lady Treva, the former Council Members who'd defected from Aeterna. Nuada had ditched his Mundane clothing for the more traditional garb the Fae favored, but it was the woman at the front of the group who drew my attention. Her long silver-white hair flowed loose almost to her hips, and she was flanked on either side by two creatures the size of large cats. They had pointed ears, bobbed tails, and coloring like a Doberman. Black collars studded with black gems twinkled in the evening sunlight as they glided on either side of the woman, moving in perfect sync with each other like puppets.

She paused just inside the clearing, and the other Fae gathered around her. I'd heard stories about a Mother Nithia, the Fae queen, but no one had seen her for at least a decade—or at least, no one had lived to talk about it. She looked at me from the edge of the trees, and I held my breath as the power of her stare washed over me, ancient and heavy.

This was the moment when she would decide if I lived or died.

She tilted her head, and Nuada bowed in her direction before the entire group advanced on me with supernatural grace that, along with their Fae features, exposed them as something other than Human.

As the Fae queen turned away with her animals, I glimpsed her hands—or where her hands should have been. Her forearms ended in stumps, and each wrist was adorned with a wide metal cuff that matched the collars on the animals—black with black gems.

Surprise made me gawk at her retreating back long after she'd faded into the trees. It was rare to see a missing limb in the magic community, and especially among the Fae. Their Healers could do nearly miraculous things with magic. Birth defects were almost nonexistent, and most accidents, if caught soon enough, could be repaired, assuming they had the original body part to reattach. I wondered if someone had intentionally maimed her.

My attention was drawn to Nuada as he stood in front of the Elementari and spoke in a grand, loud voice for everyone to hear. "Welcome to Haven, the Earthen seat of the Fae High Council."

A flash of shock rolled over me. *I'm on Earth?* The Fae shouldn't have been able to create a haven in our Mundane realm. There wasn't enough magic.

But I realized the answer before I'd even posed the question—the magic leaking from the Earthen Source had to be giving the Fae enough power to sustain themselves in our realm.

I'd only heard of three Fae havens over the course of our entire magical history. It took a long time to grow a self-sustaining power source like this—at least a decade, maybe two—and it required a specific magic-rich environment to draw from. I might have thrown fuel onto the fire, but they had to have started their haven long before Nuada disappeared from Aeterna.

"I have to admit," I said to Nuada and Treva, "I never guessed you'd become Elias's henchmen, going around doing his dirty work. Whatever he's promised you in exchange for me, I wouldn't count on getting it."

Lady Treva's lip curled in disgust. "We do not do the bidding of that selfish, greedy worm."

I felt my brow scrunch in confusion. Silas had told me that Nuada, Treva, and Elias had been working together to undermine the Council for years. They defected from Aeterna after Elias was revealed as the Brotherhood's secret leader, taking all the Fae with them. They'd been working together all along. Or so everyone had assumed.

"Are you saying the Fae just... defected? The timing was a coincidence? You're not in league with Elias?"

"We grasped our moment and fled when the Council fell apart," Nuada replied. "We do not intend to be ruled by them, or anyone, ever again. We are a free people."

"But you were on the Council—you were the leaders for the Fae. You defected... from yourselves?"

"The Council forced us to live in the way of Humans," Nuada answered. "They banned our natural magics and cut off access to our true powers, but as a free people, we intend to return to the natural order of the Fae."

"But the Council will not leave us be," Treva added.

"If you just want to be left alone, then why did you kidnap me?" I demanded. "My people will come looking for me."

"Our daughter, Lady Kianna, has been taken by the Council," Lady Treva said.

Without warning, everything went dark, and I slipped into another vision.

The floor is stone and cold. A Fae woman with filthy blond hair reaches out to me on the other side of iron bars, her amethyst eyes pleading. I want to reach out to help her, but a flash of magic fills the entire cell as soon as she touches the bars. It's like lightning. The magic is so bright and sudden that I throw my arm over my eyes and cry out in surprise.

The whole vision cut off just as suddenly as it had started, and I blinked at my captors, my sense of reality spinning out of control around me. "The Council kidnapped your daughter?"

"We received their proclamation," Nuada said. "The Fae must surrender to the subjugation of the Aeternal Council in exchange for Lady Kianna's life."

I snorted. "You think the Council will trade for me instead? I'm flattered, really. But if they want you back in Aeterna, they aren't going to trade Lady Kianna for me."

Treva leaned forward, her amethyst eyes sparking with fierce promise. "I promise you this: if Lady Kianna is not returned safely to us, we'll return you in pieces." She pushed her long, intricately braided hair over her shoulder and said to Nuada, "The time draws near. We must prepare."

My stomach dropped as they walked away. I yelled after them, but no one so much as glanced back as the entire entourage slipped silently back into the forest. I didn't have time to sit around. Not only did I have to stop the visions from happening, but it was also only a matter of time before Nuada and Treva realized what a colossal mistake they'd made. The Council wouldn't trade their leverage over the Fae for me, and when they realized that, I was as good as dead.

Chapter Seven

Sitting on the hard-packed dirt got uncomfortable fast. I ground my teeth and resisted the urge to yell at the Elementari trapping me in the Fae's haven. Every minute I wasted in here was one minute closer to Silas dying in some vision from a stupid Fate, and I wasn't going to let that happen. I closed my eyes and reached for my magic. Stretching my senses as far as I could, I pushed against the multilayered prison. *Nothing.* I couldn't feel a single drop of energy beyond the trap.

I'd spent hours testing the boundaries of the Elementari, trying to figure out some way to unravel or absorb the conjuring, but I still had no idea how I was going to get out of it. For the hundredth time, I tried to pick out the patterns of magic in the spell, but my knowledge of Elementari was less than basic, and I'd done very little with elemental magic in general. It was an advanced magic that most Humans didn't have the aptitude for. Fae were almost exclusively the ones who wove elements through their magic. Under Thomas's tutelage, we'd been required to study each of the elements, but I'd never attempted to conjure anything with a specific element. And even though I'd learned about these kinds of traps, I'd never seen more than one element in an actual conjuring.

Most of my formative years had been focused on self-defense, hiding, and escape, and at some point, I'd learned about Elementari. Theoretically, I should be able to unravel some of this conjuring and work my way toward escape. *Maybe. Possibly.* I rubbed

Marcel's charm between my fingers as I thought. If I could absorb some of the conjuring, I could potentially leverage that boost of power to get free. Our ability to absorb magic was the reason all the members of my Sect had learned about these kinds of traps, but it was all just theoretical.

I tried to identify threads of magic that might belong to certain elements, hoping to decipher where I could start, but after another twenty minutes or so, I exhaled through clenched teeth. There was no hope. Each layer was intertwined within the others, building a tapestry of multilayered magic that changed from every angle. I didn't recognize any specific element, and I'd smudged most of the sigils on the ground, making them useless to me. With a sigh, I decided to just start somewhere.

I pushed on a random thread with my mind, separating it from the intricate pattern of elemental magic in the hopes that I could create a gap in the conjuring. I needed something I could untangle and absorb. I followed the thread of magic deeper for at least ten minutes, tugging it loose from the other layers of the conjuring. Like untangling yarn, I worked along the threads, pulling and twisting the energy until finally—*finally*—a single thread broke free from the conjuring.

The thread of magic I'd extracted was a delicate, almost lacelike pattern made of light, interwoven energy. I'd found the air layer of the Elementari.

"Yes!" I slapped my hand over my mouth and looked around to make sure I hadn't accidentally alerted anyone with my outburst.

The entire layer of elemental air was looser than it had been, and I wondered if a good tug would pull it all apart. I closed my eyes and visualized the power around me. I lifted my hands from the dirt—gripping the threads of woven air in my mind—and pulled with everything I had.

A rush of air hit me like a slap in the face, and I fell onto my back, knocking the breath out of my lungs. Loose magic danced around me, trapped within the Elementari, and as I opened myself to the power, it sank into my bones like a gust of fresh air.

Triumphant, I sat up on my elbows and beamed. The first circle was mine. Conscious that I was running out of time, I sucked up every bit of power and braced myself. I still had three layers left to unravel, but the magical void around me was beginning to lessen. Already, I could feel a small trickle of magic through the weakened Elementari.

With one layer removed from the conjuring, it was easier to tell the remaining three apart. I focused on finding the next elemental layer and identified the interwoven elements of Earth. The pattern was incredibly dense, with threads that wove through each other. The individual layers were each wafer-thin, but they joined together in a thick, strong weave, almost like two woven tapestries stacked on top of each other.

I pushed against the conjuring, hoping I could spread the layers apart and pick out a thread to pull free, just like I had with the conjured air element.

Lady Treva stepped out of the trees. "You've dismantled the air conjuring."

I froze and squeezed my lips together. Treva had felt my attempt to escape, which probably meant she'd been the one to build the first layer. It shouldn't have surprised me. Conjuring an element as part of an Elementari was master-level work, and she was on the Aeternal Council because she was strong and skilled in magic. But she'd come alone, and she hadn't sounded the alarm.

"Are you going to stop me?" I asked.

She cocked her head. "I am told that you regained memories previously buried, and you now lead the Lost Sect."

I blinked at the change in topic but went with it, responding carefully. "Yes, that's true." *Sort of.* I wasn't *the* leader, but I wasn't going to correct her under the circumstances. I would let her think I was more powerful and important than I actually was.

Her head tilted from side to side, and she licked her lips. "Then you understand the weight of responsibility. Even before you learned of your true identity, I could sense your determination when you stood in front of the Council, a child with no memory or allies and still possessing the will to defy a superior power."

"In my defense, you all have a lot of rules, and I didn't know I was breaking them."

She ignored my snarky comment. "Many of your people died in the fight against the Brotherhood."

The familiar guilt tightened in my gut. "Yes."

"You led them to their deaths," she said matter-of-factly.

It was a relief to finally have someone say it out loud. All those deaths were my fault. I knew it, everyone knew it, but no one was willing to hold me responsible.

I swallowed the lump in my throat. "Yes," I whispered.

She moved closer to me, watching me intently. "Would you do it again, knowing what the outcome would be?"

I exhaled through my nose. The Brotherhood had been broken, and my people were now free. But almost half of our number had died, including my aunt, my father, and my friend Atticus. Even though I knew objectively that hundreds and maybe thousands of lives had been saved—possibly even all of Earth—the price of our freedom had been steep. *Would I do it again?*

I answered truthfully, "I don't know."

"The Aeternal Council will kill my daughter if we do not give in to their demands and return to Aeterna." Treva's face pinched in pain. Her long blond hair fell forward, hiding her expression, as she lowered her head. "Mother Nithia asks that we sacrifice our child for the freedom of our people, and Lord Nuada will obey our queen without question. He believes in the old ways and values our freedom above any individual life."

"But you don't want Kianna to die."

"We have rejected alliances within the Council and the Brotherhood, even though we are not yet strong enough to stand on our own. My daughter's life should not have to be the price of our freedom."

Even though they were willing to kidnap me and bargain with my life, I felt compassion for Lady Treva. If the Fae truly weren't allied with Elias, then her daughter was also an innocent, and the Council was using her as a way to control the Fae.

"Why are you telling me this?" I asked slowly.

When her eyes met mine, they were tight with pain. "If my daughter still lives, I cannot sacrifice her. I cannot pay that price—even to free all our people."

"Let me out, Lady Treva. I can talk to the Council—to Silas. I'll do everything in my power to return her to you. You know they won't trade Lady Kianna for me. It doesn't have to go down like this."

She wet her lips as she held my gaze, and my heart rose to my throat. This could be my only chance to convince her to let me go, but it all depended on Treva believing I could save her daughter.

"I cannot," Treva said.

My whole body slumped.

"I don't have the ability to release you from the other elements," she clarified. She took a step back from the Elementari. "When you dissolve the next elemental layer, the conjurer will feel it as I did. You don't have enough time."

My brain went into overdrive as I scrambled to find some way to get her to help me. Surely, the two of us could work together to find a solution to our mutual problem, and I couldn't let her walk away when she was my best shot at getting out of there.

Treva started to back away. "I suggest you save your energy until we hear from the Council. If they refuse the trade... I will do what I can to spare your life."

"Wait! I've seen a vision of Kianna! I can figure out where she's being held. Help me out of here, and I'll tell you about the vision I had. She's blond, right? Kianna? With amethyst eyes, like yours? The woman in my vision was blond, and she was being held in a cell carved from stone."

Lady Treva's eyes narrowed in suspicion. She wasn't stupid. The blond hair and purple eyes would be an obvious guess, given they matched Treva's own coloring. But she was also a desperate parent searching for any scrap of hope.

"She had a ring! On her right hand, carved like a flower. A white flower."

"Tell me where she is." Treva's voice was full of desperate hope.

"Help me get out of here first."

A loud boom echoed from deep within the forest. Lady Treva whirled toward the sound as shouts followed.

"What is that?" I demanded. "What's going on?"

Another explosion rocked me back on my heels. Magic blazed somewhere in the distance. There was enough of it that I felt the energy through the remaining three layers of the Elementari, which meant something powerful was headed our way. Maybe the Council had decided to answer Nuada's demands by killing us all.

The deafening crack of massive trees breaking and toppling sent Lady Treva fleeing toward the opposite side of the clearing, where she disappeared into the forest without a word. My heart thundered in my chest as I craned my neck toward the ominous noise, trying to see through the dense forest. The sounds grew louder.

Something destructive was coming my way, and I was out of time to escape.

More shouts. A fight was drawing closer, and I gritted my teeth. Whoever was headed my way was moving fast, and I didn't want to be stuck in this trap, defenseless, when they arrived. With the magic I'd collected from the first layer of the Elementari, I threw myself into disassembling the next. Loosening the thick layers of the Earth conjuring felt like digging a tunnel through rock with nothing but my bare fingernails. The layers were heavy and tangled, but I kept pushing and was soon drenched in sweat and tired to my bones.

Shouts rose out of the forest, and another explosion shook the ground. *Closer.*

My heart burst into a sprint as I frantically pulled and twisted, breaking through threads of magic as fast as I could. Finally, the tapestry of magic separated, and I grasped a single thread from the Earth conjuring. I paused, scanned the forest around me, and then pulled with all my strength. With that last yank, the earth circle collapsed in a cloud of dust. The released power flooded me as I coughed through the dirt and debris.

The noises crashing through the forest were so close. I heard yelling. Someone screamed in mortal terror, and the sound cut off.

Faster. I have to be faster.

Exhausted but out of time, I grabbed the threads of the water circle and ripped it apart without finesse, sinking all of my stored magic into the effort. The circle popped, and I was instantly soaked in actual water. I gasped. The freezing-cold liquid soaked me as if I'd jumped into a lake, but the magic it released renewed my depleted powers. There was only one more layer left—fire.

A blast of magic tore from the tree line, and Nuada flew out of the forest. His arms and legs flailed as he spun through the air and landed hard on his backside. I froze, my eyes glued to the trees, as

I waited for my certain death. A dark-haired figure emerged from the woods, glowing with golden magic.

My heart skipped a beat. *Silas*!

Chapter Eight

"Stop!" Nuada yelled, scrambling to his feet. He raised one arm toward me, his fingers curled in the air like a claw.

Silas slid to a stop a dozen feet from the Elementari with a fierce snarl on his face. Golden-yellow power radiated around him, bright like a starburst that blurred into white at the edges. He looked like an avenging angel. I had never been happier to see someone in my entire life.

"You can save her!" Nuada yelled at Silas. "Or you can chase me." Nuada closed his hand into a fist, and the final layer of the Elementari—fire—destabilized around me as he disappeared in a burst of magic.

I used my last scraps of power to form a shield around me, and it slid into place a fraction of a second before the destabilized magic would have burned me to a crisp. The weight of the broken fire element pressed down on me, and I cried out as I dropped to my knees. The magic was completely unstable, and actual flames burned through the air. It was too heavy. I wasn't going to be able to hold the shield for long.

"Maeve!" Silas rushed to me. "Shite! It's collapsing!"

My wet clothes started steaming from the heat. I couldn't breathe. "It's crushing me!"

"I'll hold the shield. You break through the conjuring." Magic rose around Silas. He thrust his palms against the outside of the El-ementari and tried to push his magic through the barrier.

I could see the power he was channeling, but I could barely sense a trickle inside the trap. "It's not getting through!" I yelled.

Heat licked my back, and my panic flared with it. Sweat started to drip off my forehead from the rapidly rising temperature and the effort of holding the shield. Silas's magic needed an opening to reach me, but I found nothing as I searched the threads of the fire circle. The previously ordered conjuring was a tangled mess of unstable magic energy.

As quickly as I could, I ripped apart individual threads of magic, but the heat kept growing, and my skin felt like it was blistering. I willed myself to move faster, pulling the threads apart, twisting and breaking them without pausing. The pressure increased every second. I felt like I was breathing fire.

Faster, faster. Don't panic. Faster!

A tiny crack appeared in the threads of the tangled conjuring. Silas's magic flowed through in a rush of power and formed into a protective dome around me. I sagged to my knees and dragged in a deep, full breath. The mad dash to rip apart four master-level conjurings and then hold that shield had completely exhausted me.

"Ung," Silas grunted outside the conjuring. "The destabilized element is heavy." His brow was tight with strain against the magical weight of the broken fire element.

Only a tiny fraction of his power had made it through the Elementari, and it was taking all of Silas's effort to maintain the shield around me. I couldn't pause for a rest—I wasn't free yet, and I didn't know how long Silas could bear the weight of the destabilized magic. If his shield collapsed, I'd be crushed. I had to get the threads of magic separated so I could absorb the power of the spell and break free. Great plan—except the magic was a tangled mess.

I willed myself to think despite my exhaustion. The broken threads of the trap were all fused together. Dismantling it thread by thread wouldn't work, even if I had days to pick apart the collapsed conjuring. I could absorb it all, but without a circle to take the excess power, that much power would fry my magic abilities and most likely be fatal. There was only one option left... and it was very stupid.

"I'm going to absorb the power from the fire element and then let the excess energy loose when the Elementari falls," I informed Silas.

Silas gritted his teeth. "The kickback will kill you."

"I can hold it. It's just a few seconds." The timing would have to be perfect. I'd have to absorb all of the magic at once to dissolve the entire layer and then release it before the sheer amount of magic crushed me to death. It was risky. Even if the timing worked, I didn't know if I could absorb that much power without someone acting as an Anchor to keep me grounded. I could be overwhelmed by the sheer amount of magic, but we were out of options.

"Maeve," Silas growled, and his arms shook as if he were physically holding the weight of the magic. "Don't do it."

"We don't have time to argue about it. You can be mad at me later."

I raised my arms and reached for the magic embedded in the conjuring, searching for the best place to start. I'd only get one shot at this, and it had to be perfect. Once I absorbed the power, I had to hold it until the Elementari was completely dissolved. If I only got partway before the magical pressure overwhelmed me, or if I released the raw power while I was still trapped inside, it would rebound inside my little bubble and literally crush me.

I picked a spot within the conjuring and reached for it. "Here goes nothing—"

"Where is my daughter?" Lady Treva demanded as she pressed the point of a bone-handled dagger under Silas's chin, right against his artery.

Treva's teeth were bared, and the muscles in her arm tensed tight. Silas strained away from the edge of the blade, but he couldn't go far. If he let go of the shield protecting me, he would be able to defend himself against Lady Treva. But I'd be crushed.

"Treva! Stop!" I yelled.

She bared her teeth. "Where is my daughter?"

"I don't know!" I yelled. "I told you everything I know!"

"The Council took her," she accused Silas. "You know where she is."

"The Council did not take your daughter." Silas's face was tight with strain, but his response was confident.

"The Council has her!" Treva insisted. The tip of the knife dug into his flesh, and blood trickled down Silas's neck.

He hissed, and the shield around me pulsed. A wave of heat hit me, and I threw my arms over my face as the air within the Elementari blazed. I couldn't breathe.

"Silas isn't responsible for the Council's actions. He's innocent!" I yelled.

She let out an angry, mocking laugh. "'Death's Fury' is far from innocent. There is more blood staining his hands than runs through the veins of everyone you love combined."

Silas opened his mouth, but Treva dug the edge of the blade deeper into his flesh. Silas gritted his teeth as fresh blood wet Treva's knife.

"Your lies will fall on deaf ears," Treva warned.

"Killing him won't free Kianna!" I yelled. "Let us go, and I'll swear to do everything I can to bring her back to you."

Treva's hand was steady as her gaze flicked to me.

"If you kill Silas, you get nothing," I continued. "Think about it! We can help you!"

"I gain vengeance for my daughter's death."

"She's not dead yet! We can help bring her home."

"Swear it first!" she demanded. "Make an oath sealed with magic."

I waved my hands frantically around me. "I'm trapped inside your freaking Elementari! But I swear it. You have my word. I'll do everything I can to find Lady Kianna and bring her to you."

I held my breath as Treva's knife dug into Silas's flesh. If she didn't see reason, Silas was as good as dead, and I would get crushed to death. Finally, she stepped back and lowered the dagger to her side.

Silas pivoted away from her and in a surprisingly calm tone said, "Get the Elementari down, Maeve."

My shirt was soaked in sweat, and I was dead tired, but I focused on the energy surrounding me and picked up the thread of the fire element again. "When I tell you, drop the shield. It should collapse before the magic overwhelms me."

Lady Treva took a small step toward us. Silas tensed as she put herself within striking distance.

"You must anchor to your Aegis," Treva said. "Then channel the excess through your bond. I will expand your circle." She reached her hand out toward Silas, who didn't move a muscle. "I believe the Earthen saying is, 'No harm, no foul.'"

He bared his teeth. "And only fools give second chances."

We didn't have time to second-guess her. A small circle with a murderous Fae was better than no circle.

"Silas, she could have killed you already, and she needs us to get her daughter back. We're on the same side... for now."

Silas didn't move for a heartbeat, and I opened my mouth to urge them to trust each other, but then he grabbed her extended hand with an unfriendly yank and a scowl. Both their auras burned with magic.

Through the tiny crack I'd made earlier, I quickly reached for Silas's magic. The bonded sigil I shared with him made it easy to connect, and the feel of his distinct cool power vibrated pleasant-ly through my body. My training kicked in, and I anchored my magic to him, preserving our core energy and preventing a possible burnout for both of us. Through him, I could sense Lady Treva's magic like a light, airy breeze. I focused my attention on the fire element, and with a deep breath, I called all the power out of the conjuring at once.

The rush of magic slammed into me first, burning every cell in my body with incredible power. I pushed the magic outward to my little circle as the explosive energy of the fire layer tore through the three of us. Silas and Treva rocked backward as the magic hit them.

Without even a heartbeat to spare, the threads of the destabilized magic withered and disappeared, and the excess energy exploded out and upward from all three of us. Fresh, cool air lapped against my skin, and I dropped to my knees, exhausted. I gulped the air in greedily. The Elementari was gone, and I was alive. With a small shudder, I realized that if I'd attempted to absorb all that unstable elemental magic without my emergency circle, I probably would have died a horrible, painful death. Treva had just saved my life.

Silas helped me stand, carefully keeping Treva in sight, as he held me at arm's distance and looked me over. "Are you injured?"

My skin felt like crisped bacon, but I didn't see any burns. I was drenched in sweat, but my clothes weren't on fire, so that was a win. I seemed to have use of all my limbs too. "I'll live."

Being this near to Silas did funny things to my brain. For the first time in months, I felt him through our shared Aegis bond, and it was better than magic. I suddenly didn't care that I was sweaty, dirty, and exhausted or that our reluctant ally was watching—I was alive, and all I wanted was Silas's arms around me. I leaned into him, and he pulled me closer, wrapping me in his arms.

It felt so damn good as I inhaled the crisp, fresh scent of him, and I let myself relax against his strong chest. Even in the middle of enemy territory, I knew I was safe. Silas was my home, and I was his. I tilted my head back, and our lips connected, sending a spark of heat through me as I draped my arms over his shoulders. I needed to get closer. It had been way too long since I'd had the opportunity to kiss Silas, and my entire body tingled with excitement as our kiss deepened and a flood of desire spread through our shared Aegis bond.

Lady Treva cleared her throat, and I reluctantly pulled apart from Silas to peer at her.

"Do you swear upon your father's memory that you do not know where my daughter is?" she asked Silas.

"I swear it," Silas said. "To my knowledge, the Council didn't have anything to do with her kidnapping."

"But the Council said they'd release her if the Fae returned to Aeterna," I said.

Silas's eyebrows rose. "We did not issue such a proclamation."

Treva pursed her lips, and I could see the calculations behind her eyes. "It's possible that someone in the Council acted on their own. If you find out the truth of that matter, I will be in your debt, Lord Valeron."

Silas nodded gravely.

"Lord Nuada took your Aegis to lure you here," she continued. "We knew you would tear down the Inner Circle's shielding to get to her if you had to. He hopes your actions will drive a wedge between your two peoples."

Surprise slapped me in the face. *I was bait?* Nuada had never intended to trade me to the Council—he wanted to lure Silas to Earth. And by coming to Earth, Silas had just violated the treaty between my people and the Council. *Oh, shit.*

"My mate wants retaliation against the Council members more than our child's safe return. He is focused on our people's freedom at the expense of Kianna's life."

"What do you mean by retaliation?" Silas's expression changed to anger as he glowered at Lady Treva.

"I cannot say, other than he intends something... widespread."

"Like starting a war between the Council and my Sect?" I snarled.

Her head tilted. "Perhaps."

"Why are you helping us stop him?" I asked. "I already promised to do everything I can for Kianna. You didn't have to tell us any of that."

"The altar of history has too much blood upon it, and I am tired of contributing."

"On that, we can agree," Silas replied.

"I should not be surprised that Death's Fury would feel that way." Treva fished a long chain out from under her tunic and unfastened a white ring carved in the shape of a flower. "My daughter has the matching bone ring, as you know. Perhaps you can use it to find her, but my tracing spells have been unsuccessful thus far." She moved backward toward the forest. "Do not forget our bargain, Lady Maeve. Your freedom in return for my daughter's safe return."

"I'll do everything I can," I promised.

She inclined her head in my direction before she disappeared into the forest.

"Tell me you didn't tear down the protective shielding around the portal to get to me," I said to Silas.

"I could tell you that," he replied carefully, "but it wouldn't be true."

I let the air puff out of my cheeks. "We have to get back to the Inner Circle and explain what happened before this goes too far. We need to make sure no one freaks out and tries to break the treaty."

"Are you recovered enough to skim?" Silas asked, running an assessing eye over me.

"I think so, but I have no idea where we are."

"We're in a forest just north of Boston called the Fells. I followed our bond to find you."

I felt like an idiot. The Fae had been building their haven in our backyard. It shouldn't have surprised me. Boston—like all big cities—was built on a magic pocket where the energy was strongest. The magical hot spots not only provided a boost in power—they would also help to hide flares of magical energy. The Fae had hidden here for the same reasons we'd bought the abandoned hospital campus in the city—Boston was one of the oldest cities in the United States, and it was built on a particularly strong pocket of magic.

"I'm ready. Grab my hand, and I can take us back to the campus," I said.

"No need," Silas said. "I can skim on my own."

I was too exhausted to think clearly. "But the Valeron Source is too far from Earth."

He held up his arm—the one I'd branded with my sigil—with a wry grin. The symbol of my Sect gave him access to Earth's source. "I believe the Fate called it a 'balance of power.'"

"Dang, and all I got was this lousy tattoo." I held up my opposite arm, the one with his brand.

Silas's full-throated chuckle warmed my heart. His arms wrapped around me as he pulled me close, and I sank into his embrace. He lowered his mouth to mine, and every part of me tingled from my head to my toes as the kiss deepened and our mouths moved together. I wanted more, and he responded just as eagerly until we were both breathing heavily.

Silas pulled back much too soon. "As much as I want to continue this delightful reunion..."

I sighed and let him release me before we decided to tear each other's clothes off in the middle of the Fae's haven. "When we're done saving the world—again—I want to spend at least a month alone with you on a beach somewhere. Naked."

"I couldn't agree more." The look Silas gave me was all heat as one of his hands slipped into my hair and the other cupped my face.

Shivers rushed across my skin. Our Aegis bond was wide-open, and I felt his love and desire through it, just as he could sense mine. My breath hitched in my chest.

"But first..." I sighed as I resigned myself to waiting a little longer. "Let's go see just how much damage you did. Casius is probably about to have kittens."

Chapter Nine

We skimmed to the perimeter of the campus, and I froze when I realized the protective dome of magic was missing. "Did you also take out the shield on your way out?"

Silas's face was equally alarmed. "No." He held up his arm with my sigil, indicating the magical symbol that would have allowed him to travel through the shield. "I had no need to—I walked out."

We'd destroyed all the other known portals between our realms in the past two months. I took particular relish burning down the small warehouse where Titus had tortured and killed my brother, and I'd destroyed the portal in the attic along with it. But that meant Nuada only had one portal he could use to get back to Aeterna—a portal that was normally protected by multiple shields.

"I think Nuada's plan was about more than just threatening our treaty. Do you think he—"

"Yes." Silas pulled me into a run, and we headed toward the portal in the center of campus.

When we entered the large atrium where the portal was located, it took me a moment to confirm that I was in the right place. It looked like a bomb had exploded. Loose magic floated everywhere, and large chunks of the marble floor were torn out, leaving scattered piles of debris all over the place. And most notably, a wide scorch mark marred the white floor, from the stone pillars of the portal to the first-level doors of the administration building where we'd entered.

The entire Circle was gathered around the gateway to Aeterna, examining the damage. I noted with dismay that the double shields we'd constructed around the portal were missing. It had taken weeks of planning and hours of conjuring with the full Inner Circle to get that in place.

"Maeve!" Ethan spotted me almost instantly. He was covered in dirt, but he pulled me into a hug, and I felt a rush of relief that he was all right. "Thank all the gods you're okay. I thought the worst had happened when that Fae took you. I came back here, but everything has been in total chaos."

"Did Nuada attack?" I asked. "Is anyone hurt?"

Casius marched over to us, glowing with white magic. His mouth tightened into an angry slash, and a magic-coated broadsword landed in his hand, which he pointed at Silas. "You! You son of a bitch! You tore down our shields!"

I held up both palms, taking in the serious death glares coming Silas's way from every member of my Sect. "Wait a minute. Wait. It's not Silas's fault. Nuada set us—"

"Like hell it's not! Look at the damage he did!" Casius flung his hand around the atrium.

Silas's magic rose around him, adding even more pressure to the already tense situation. The amount of power Silas radiated wasn't a joke, and he knew how to use it. His offensive magic abilities were legendary, which had even more people grabbing their magic as they stepped back, clearly aware of how bad this could go.

I stepped between them. "Casius, wait—"

Silas stabbed a finger in the air at Casius. "I told you Maeve was in danger, but you wouldn't heed my warning!"

"She looks just fine to me!" Casius countered.

"She was almost crushed to death in a destabilized Elementari, you shite licker!"

Casius's face drained of color. "Mae? Is that true?"

Everyone was staring. "Yeah," I admitted, embarrassed. I really wasn't the damsel-in-distress type. "I'm fine. Really. I'd already unraveled three of the elements. If Nuada hadn't decided to collapse the fire conjuring, I would have been able to get out." I remembered how exhausted I'd been after I dismantled the earth layer. "Probably."

Silas's voice rose to carry across the atrium. "The Fae have created a haven in your territory. They kidnapped Maeve in a misguided attempt to free themselves of the Aeternal Council."

"Dear gods," Casius said. "What did the Council do now?"

Silas's hand slashed angrily through the air. "Nothing. Which you would know if you hadn't banned us all from Earth!"

Casius ignored that. "You should have sent a messenger!"

"*I* was the messenger," Silas growled.

"Stop!" I yelled at both men. "This is why communication needs to stay open between Earth and Aeterna, and you're not helping the situation by yelling at each other. The Fae took advantage of our division, and look what happened!"

"Silas is the cause of all of this! He completely ignored our orders to return to Aeterna, and then he ripped down the portal's shielding! He basically held open the door for Nuada, and as far as I'm concerned, all of this is his fault. They're probably working together!"

Silas stiffened at my side, and his anger boiled through our shared bond as he shifted onto the balls of his feet. *Shit. I have to de-escalate this situation.*

I raised my hands again, stalling another fight. "Silas isn't working with the Fae. That's ridiculous. Nuada wants us to be at each other's throats, and it's working!" When both men settled a bit, I added, "We can repair all the damage, but we should start with the perimeter shield. We're vulnerable without—"

"He broke our treaty! There should be consequences for his actions!" Levi pushed through the crowd, sporting a puffy left eye.

"Maeve's life was in danger," Silas snapped, picking up the fight again. "Every second you kept me behind your outrageous barrier was a threat to her life. As her Aegis, I had every right to act, or she would have died."

"You should have explained the situation!" Casius crossed his arms and glowered again. "You didn't need to tear apart the portal shield."

"I told you she was in danger!" Silas barked back.

"You left our entire Sect vulnerable!" Alannah said, shoving her way into our angry knot and practically steaming.

I rubbed my temples. This was not going to get better quickly. Even Ethan scowled at Silas, and Silas... well, he was almost snarling at all of them. I had to stop this before someone got murdered.

"Silas wouldn't have come here if my life weren't in danger. He saved my life," I said in my most reasonable voice. "He maybe should have *used his words* before tearing apart the shield around the portal"—I threw a frown at Silas—"but this was all planned by Nuada to break apart our alliance. We can fix this." I waved my hand around the room, indicating the destruction and the missing shield. "Don't let Nuada win by tearing our alliance apart. We're stronger together."

People were throwing major side-eye at Silas and me, but at least everyone stopped yelling. "I think we should focus on the perimeter shield first," I said. "What do you think, Casius?"

"I have to return to Aeterna," Silas said suddenly. "Nuada has already had too long to enact whatever he's planning, and I must warn the Council."

Levi threw his hands in the air. "The Circle can't just let a member of the Aeternal Council saunter into Earth any time he wants, destroy our shield, and then return to the Council without consequences. He was specifically banned from this realm. If you allow this gross infraction, your authority is useless. He should be detained while we discuss the appropriate reaction."

"We've been over this already," I said.

"I think you misunderstand your authority," Silas interrupted, his voice dangerously flat. "I obliged your request to stay out of Earth. I came to tell you that the life of one of your own was in danger, but you chose to ignore me. You forced me to act." His voice sank menacingly, and Levi stepped back. "If you attempt to stop me from warning my people about an imminent threat, there will indeed be consequences."

I put my hand on Silas's arm and spoke to Casius, who was gripping his sword too tightly for my comfort. "Nuada used me to lure Silas here. He's trying to start a war between the Council and us. Don't fall into his trap."

The almost-physical tension in the room was built on decades of distrust. Even Ethan was glowing with magic as if ready to attack. I had to get them to calm down and see reason.

"The power-sharing alliance with the Aeternal Council has allowed us to become allies for the first time since our ancestors left Aeterna. We're no longer hiding, and we're actually working together for our mutual benefit. Do you really want to throw that away over Silas saving my life?"

I'd just pulled the ultimate trump card. If the alliance fell apart, the splinter tribes would never agree to rejoin the Sect. They'd be too scared that the Aeternal Council would hunt us again for the magic contained in the Earthen Source. The Inner Circle might be pissed at Silas, but they wouldn't risk further breaking apart our Sect.

Casius loosened his grip on his sword. "The Lord Commander is free to go. His actions were a result of his oath to protect Maeve as her Aegis."

Silas snorted softly beside me, but fortunately, he didn't say anything snarky about being *allowed* to leave.

Without warning, the portal flared behind us, and everyone dove for cover. Silas pulled me with him, his magic forming a protective barrier around us before I had even managed to step out of the way. Four figures ran through before the magic stabilized and disappeared.

Magic burst all around as people prepared to defend themselves against the unexpected intruder.

"Tessa!" I yelled, recognizing the tall Fae Guardian with her short boy-cut hairstyle. "Wait! Everyone, stand down!"

Tessa and three other Guardians stood tensed, with weapons and magic ready, as they glowered at the group of people surrounding them.

I hurried to Tessa's side. "What are you doing here? What's wrong?"

"Maeve, I wish our greeting were under better circumstances." Her eyes locked on Silas. "You must return quickly. The Citizen Source has been poisoned!"

"Poisoned? How?" Silas demanded.

"We don't know, but it's spreading. The Council has quarantined the entire Lower City. People are killing each other in the streets, trying to get out."

I was still trying to process Tessa's words as Silas strode to the posts of the portal and placed his palm over the closest one. His magic blazed in a brilliant golden-white aura before the doorway activated, and magic flexed away from us.

He turned back to me. "What's your decision?"

Silas and I had talked about the best plan to find Kianna, and it started with the Council. I'd already attempted a quick tracer spell on the ring Treva had given me and had come up with nothing. If the Council had taken her, she was most likely in Aeterna, and

I needed to get there to question the Council and to try another tracer spell. We hadn't yet known what Nuada was up to, but I was hoping to quietly convince Casius to let me talk to the Council while Silas hunted Nuada down.

But Nuada poisoning the Citizen Source changed everything. I couldn't wrap my brain around the enormity of what had happened. Aeterna was built on magic, and everyone in the Lower City relied on the Citizen Source for everything from getting around Aeterna to heating their homes. During my time there, I couldn't even get through doorways without accessing magic.

All those people had been poisoned. Good people, like Atticus.

"I'm going to Aeterna," I declared.

Casius started shaking his head.

"Thousands of people could die, Casius. I might be able to help. And it would be a sign of goodwill between our people if I—"

"No, Maeve," Casius interrupted. "You can't involve yourself in the affairs of the Aeternal Council. Your concerns are with our people, not theirs. Plus, there's no way to know if you'll be safe over there. You need to stay in our realm."

I was so surprised that I just gaped at him. I couldn't believe he was banning me from helping. It was one thing to try to keep Silas and me apart, but a lot of people were going to die in Aeterna, and I could help.

"The people in our Sect aren't our only responsibility," I said. "I won't leave innocents to die if I can do something about it. If you think that makes me disloyal, then that's on you. Helping is the right thing to do."

From the looks on their faces, the Circle agreed with Casius. Even Ethan shook his head, silently pleading with me not to go.

Alannah put her hand on Casius's shoulder. "Let her go. She's made her priorities clear. In the meantime, we need to take care of the mess they've made. Without the perimeter shield, anyone and anything can get onto the campus. And the portal shield needs to be repaired right away, before the Lord Commander informs his colleagues about the damage."

Alannah's words sent equal parts anger and guilt flaming, hot and prickly, along my spine, but I knew I needed to help, and that conviction steeled me. Over the past months, I'd gotten used to letting Casius guide me as I figured out my place in the Sect. But if I was being honest, I had a lot of regrets about the consequences of my past behavior, and letting Casius make the decisions for me had been easy. I'd lost sight of the fact that a good leader had to make hard choices, even if they were unpopular. With Nuada poisoning innocents to strike back at the Council, the greater need was in Aeterna, and I had to help.

"I'm going to do the right thing, Casius. I hope you'll understand later." I didn't wait for Casius's approval or more snide remarks from Alannah. I walked through the portal to Aeterna without looking back.

Tessa and the Guardians followed, and I emerged side by side with Silas into a gray stone room deep within the main portal facility in the center of Aeterna. The room was bare, without any visible exits or windows, and the only item in the room was the portal frame made of three rectangular stone blocks.

I paused to reorient myself. Traveling through a portal between realms was a lot like being on one of those spinning rides at a carnival, and I felt dizzy as my body materialized in a new location. Plus, I was so far away from my normal source of magic that I felt disoriented until Silas's familiar cool rush of magic flooded through our shared bond, settling me.

"It's a battle zone in the Lower City," Tessa said. "Dozens have died, and all the Guardians have been dispatched to stop the rioting. I haven't seen anything this bad since our hostile training unit in Krittesh."

Silas squeezed my hand. To Tessa, he said, "Place all the portals on lockdown. No one gets in or out of Aeterna without my personal approval."

"Already done," Tessa said. "No one has left Aeterna since we discovered the poison."

"Good. Then Nuada is still here."

"Lord Nuada?" Tessa asked.

Silas's face was set in hard lines. "Go to the Council, and tell them Lord Nuada is responsible for the poison. He's here in Aeterna."

Tessa's face went blank with shock. To her credit, her surprise transformed quickly into resolve, and she thudded her fist over her heart in a quick salute. Blue-green magic flashed around her, and she disappeared.

"We need to get to the Council chambers." Silas held out his hand to me. "Can you follow me if I skim?"

I took it. "Lead the way."

Last time, before I knew how to use magic, Silas had used a transport pod to take us through the Lower City to the skimming ports located at the base of the mountain, and we'd climbed a gazillion stairs to the guarded entrance at the top. This time, Silas and I each wove the magic into a skimming spell, and we stepped through it like a doorway, exiting at our destination. It was easy with access to Silas's family source, even so far away from my original source on Earth. I blinked, and we were standing just outside the upper levels of the Council Chambers.

Carved straight out of the stone cliff, the building was an impressive sight, towering above the Lower City, with open-air walkways and stone arches carved into the face of the building. Twisting spires capped in gold stretched straight up and created the impression of a castle floating in the sky.

It shouldn't have surprised me that the elite Houses in Upper Aeterna had their own private entrance located at the top of the mountain, with not a stair in sight. Skimming into the building was blocked for security reasons, but this Upper City entrance was clearly the most direct route—if you had enough magic to get there.

We took the elite entrance into the Council's chambers through a huge arched doorway carved directly into the mountain. As we wound our way through the interior of the stone building and down endless connecting hallways, I was thankful to have Silas as a guide. This building was like a maze built into the side of the mountain, with a series of paths that I couldn't have navigated without a map.

The noise of several heated voices talking over each other reached us as we approached a room at the end of one of the hallways. Silas waved his hand in front of the extra-wide door, which melted away to reveal a meeting room in a flurry of activity. All of the Aeternal Council members sat at a large horseshoe-shaped table whose open end faced the doors. Each of them was elbow deep in consoles and surrounded by aides. Several disorganized debates appeared to be happening at the same time while brown-robed servants rushed around the room.

Lord Nero, the Shifter representative who oversaw the citizens' labor assignments and justice system, was engaged in two loud arguments simultaneously, one on his left and another on his right. In the middle of that, he pulled aside an aide, growled instructions at him, and sent him running off. Nero was broad with wide dark eyes and brown hair, and even in his human form, he resembled the enormous bear-buffalo hybrid he changed into. He was intimidating on an average day. Right then, he looked ready to bite someone.

I stood there gawking. The last time I'd been to the Council chambers, the Councilors had presented themselves on a raised dais, glowing majestically with their combined powers and sitting on individual thrones. The intended effect was of a stately, united front of power. This was... chaos.

I recognized Lady Octavia, the Shifter representative overseeing Aeterna's economic resources, who was tapping furiously on a console pad. Lord Alaric, Aria's father and the other Human representative along with Silas, sat next to her. Normally immaculate in his dress, Alaric's long true-blond hair was tied back in a severe knot that had come halfway undone, falling across his strong brow. He pushed the loose strands away from his face as he called over an aide with an impatient wave of his hand.

Two aides bowed to Silas as they squeezed through the doorway where we stood before they hurried past us to do their business. One aide carried a stack of consoles, and the other balanced several trays of food and drinks precariously in her arms.

I took a moment to center myself in the midst of the frenzy. Two faces were new. Presumably, they were the replacements for Treva and Nuada. From the shades of the new Councilors' magic, I could tell that one was mostly Human and the other was mostly Shifter. I noticed immediately that neither had the full-blooded and pure glow of Human or Shifter, like the other Councilors. It was noticeable because every other member of the Aeternal Council was like a supercharged power pack of magic thanks to their private House sources, and they were all pure-blooded Human, Fae, or Shifter.

The Council's standard setup of two Humans, two Shifters, and two Fae—all pure blooded—seemed to be changing. I wondered if that would affect the balance of their magic, perhaps altering the pure-white hue of the Council's combined conjuring circle.

With Silas as the representative on the Council overseeing the Guardians, that left only the Lord Councilor seat open. I had no idea if they'd elected a new one since Lord Councilor Elias had fled, but I felt bad for whatever poor soul they found to fill his shoes. *They're inheriting a total mess.*

"Good of you to show up, Lord Councilor," Alaric said.

I actually looked behind us to see who he was talking to. Silas squeezed my hand, and a sinking feeling filled my stomach.

"*Acting* Lord Councilor," Silas corrected blandly.

Everyone in the room stopped what they were doing to watch us.

"Are you kidding me right now?" I whisper hissed in Silas's direction.

How could he not tell me? Silas accepting the Lord Councilor's seat was not going to help my people accept him as a part of my life. There was no way in hell my Sect would be okay with the two of us being together now.

As Silas led me to the spectator seating in front of the conference table, the Councilors' expressions weren't any friendlier than they'd been the last time I'd appeared before them. *And last time, they wanted to kill me.* In particular, I noticed the less-than-friendly welcome from Lady Octavia, who was her counterpart's opposite in both looks and animal form. Petite and narrow with refined features, she was able to shift into a massive falcon. Her lips curled in a sneer as she saw me standing with Silas. Apparently, my absence hadn't made her heart grow fonder.

Silas took his seat in the center of the table, and I glared at my boyfriend, the new leader of the Aeternal Council.

Chapter Ten

"Your warning came too late," Lord Nero said to Silas. "The Citizen Source has been poisoned, and the Lower City has been quarantined."

Silas ignored the dig, picked up several consoles, and started scanning them. "I heard. What's the latest?"

"We've received a message from Lord Nuada," Alaric said.

"We won't give in to his demands!" Lady Octavia declared immediately. "Especially without any evidence of his supposed antidote."

"What demands?" I asked.

All six Councilors frowned at me.

"What *is* she doing here?" Lady Octavia snarled. "This Earthen is not welcome in our business."

"I'm here to help stop Lord Nuada. And I'm offering the Council my assistance during this crisis as a leader of the Earthen Sect of Harvesters, under our alliance agreement."

Silas's eyebrows rose in surprise.

I smiled sweetly. *See, I can be diplomatic when I need to.*

"Your Circle sent aid very quickly," Octavia sneered, making it clear how she felt about my Sect's governing body.

"I'm here to help," I said, skirting the details about how exactly I'd gotten here. The Inner Circle hadn't exactly sent me, but I would make the most of my presence in order to benefit our alliance.

"Your offer is gracious, Lady Maeve," Alaric said diplomatically, but his narrow-eyed gaze contradicted his words. "We welcome you as an ally."

I shifted my best smile toward him, and his face flickered with enough confused emotions to make me nearly laugh. After a few tense moments when none of the Councilors could figure out a way to argue with my presence, everyone finally decided the show was over.

Alaric handed Silas a console. "Lord Nuada's demands."

Silas scanned it. "Declare the independence of the Fae. Dissolve the Aeternal Council. Revoke our alliance with the Earthen Sect of Harvesters... and return Lady Kianna, unharmed."

Silas tossed the console on the table in disgust. There was no way the Council would do all of those things. Nuada might as well have asked for cotton candy from the moon.

"Typical Fae bargain," Nero said. "They demand the impossible and, in return, promise nothing more than to solve the problem they created in the first place."

"What about just releasing Lady Kianna?" I asked, rising from my seat. "If you release her, they might be willing to negotiate the other demands."

Even though Silas didn't think the Council was responsible for Lady Kianna's disappearance, one of the Councilors could have acted independently. I intended to fulfill my vow to Lady Treva, and I would do everything I could to return her daughter to her. Silas had agreed that bringing up the kidnapping in front of the entire Council would be the perfect way to gauge their reactions. I moved to the center space of their horseshoe-shaped table, scrutinizing their faces for any sign of guilt.

"Are you implying we have kidnapped Lady Kianna?" Lord Nero asked, his voice rising.

I folded my arms. "Definitely. Kidnapping Nuada's beloved daughter and threatening to kill her unless the Fae return to Aeterna and under your control sounds exactly like something the Council would do."

The room went silent, and the glares spread. I didn't care. I was right, and we all knew it.

"We have done no such thing." Alaric's expression was a study in cultivated outrage.

"Unless someone on the Council acted on their own, I am confident we didn't order the kidnapping of Lord Nuada's daughter." Silas took in the reactions around the table. "In point of fact, the Council didn't know the Fae had built a haven on Earth. We believed the Fae to have escaped to another realm with more readily available magic resources. We may need to revisit some of our assumptions."

Their collective expressions went even sourer.

"Well, Lord Nuada sure as hell thinks you did." I waited for someone to twitch with guilt, but everyone seemed equally outraged by my accusation.

"If we knew her whereabouts, we'd gladly trade her for the antidote," Alaric said. "Citizens are rioting in the streets! We've lost all control of the Lower City."

He had a point there. The Council would always act in its own best interest, and returning Kianna had just become the key to solving all their problems.

Despite Octavia's glare, I picked up the console and read the message from Nuada. "But there *is* an antidote?"

"He implies there is," Silas said. "But we have no guarantee."

"Nuada may be an opportunistic, self-centered Fae-hole," Lord Nero said, "but the Fae cannot lie. It would break the truth oath that binds them to their magic."

"No," Silas agreed, "but they can stretch the truth until it chokes you."

"It doesn't matter!" Octavia said. "Even if we were so inclined, we can't meet any of Lord Nuada's other preposterous demands!"

"What about the people in the Lower City? What can we do to help them?" I asked.

Lord Nero pounded both fists on the table, and his eyes shifted to yellow for a second. "If you wanted to help, your people should have stopped Lord Nuada from getting to Aeterna in the first place! What good is a treaty that blocks us from Earth but allows our enemies into our realm?"

"The Sect of Earthen Harvesters isn't to blame," Silas responded calmly. "Lord Nuada lured me to Earth, knowing I would break through their defenses to rescue Lady Maeve as my Aegis oath requires. He used the opportunity to slip through the portal."

"Fate's bollocks," said Lord Nero with an inhuman growl.

"Indeed," Silas agreed.

One of the new Councilors cleared her throat conspicuously. She was dark-skinned with serious brown eyes and wore a sleeveless tunic that revealed well-toned muscles. Her weak red aura pegged her as a Shifter but not someone who was magically strong.

"We know that the poison has only infected those who accessed the Citizen Source directly," she said. "Many trapped in the Lower City are not infected. We must release those who are not yet sick from the compulsory quarantine."

Lord Nero waved his hand dismissively. "Lady Cecilia, with all due respect, we don't know if the poison can spread even without direct contact with the Citizen Source." His tone carried a heavy dose of condescension. "Releasing anyone who has been exposed could risk all of Upper Aeterna."

Lady Cecilia's hands clenched on top of the tabletop. "Guardians within the quarantine zone report that those who followed the mandate to stop accessing the Citizen Source appear un-affected. We must separate the sick from the well and bring them to the Upper City before it's too late. More lives will be lost if we do not act."

"We're not going to risk the safety of our entire realm for a few lower-house citizens," Lady Octavia objected.

"You have more than three thousand people down there," I said, shocked by her callousness.

Lady Octavia's jaw clenched, but Lady Cecilia jumped in. "Yes, and our most aggressive estimates put the infected at less than thirty percent of the population. Are you willing to throw away the lives of over two thousand citizens?"

"You overstep your position," Octavia said coolly.

Silas held up a hand, cutting off whatever retort the other woman might have made. "Lady Cecilia has been tasked to represent the voice of the citizens, and we will let her speak. We cannot leave behind the mistakes of our past if we refuse to hear the voices of those we govern."

A little thrill went through me even as Octavia's nose wrinkled in distaste. Silas had promised to help the citizens of Lower Aeterna, and this was tangible evidence of the changes he'd made so far. I bit back my smirk as Octavia sat back silently in her seat, and I let my pride for Silas radiate through the Aegis bond. If they would listen to Lady Cecilia's concerns, the Council could make some real progress.

Silas leaned to his left, giving Cecilia his full attention. "What do you suggest?"

"Acting Lord Councilor, if I may be frank, the citizens don't trust the Council. They're scared and trapped in the Lower City. The public announcements not to access the Citizen Source aren't enough, and if they become desperate enough, they'll do so despite the warnings. You must understand that the citizens need access to magic in order to live their lives. They haven't been released from their daily assignments, and without their daily labor token, they can't purchase the food they need for their families. But how do you expect them to travel to the fields and markets without magic? We've asked them to do the impossible. We must explain how they will be provided for during the quarantine, and we must release those who are not sick."

"Until we know definitively if the poison can spread person to person, we cannot risk infecting thousands more in the Upper City," Silas said. "But we can separate those who are symptom-free within the Lower City."

Cecilia frowned, but her hands unclenched. "It's a start. If you want to quell the panic, you need to send in food and resources for all of the citizens. Explain why they must stay home and why they must not access the Citizen Source."

"Good." Silas motioned for an aide near the wall. "Inform Acting Commander Corin to mobilize the Guardians. Create separate quarantine zones, and update the public announcements with this information as well. We need to move quickly. I expect a report on progress within four hours' time."

The aide bowed. "Yes, my lord."

"Lord Nero, how long can we feed the inhabitants of the Lower City from Aeterna's supplies?" Silas asked.

Nero tapped on one of his screens. "If we ration everyone to two meals per day, we can feed approximately three thousand citizens in the Lower City for six days."

Lady Cecilia's brow furrowed. "That's only accounting for registered citizens. There's perhaps another two thousand in Lower Aeterna who are unregistered."

"That high?" Alaric asked.

"We search every cycle," Octavia said. "But some of the registered citizens help them hide so they can shirk their daily assignments and operate in the illegal markets."

"Unbelievable." Alaric tsk-tsked.

Lord Nero grumbled in agreement. "They've made their choice, so let them reap the consequences of their actions. We will feed only the loyal citizens."

"The Council won't provide for those who don't contribute to the greater good of our society," Alaric agreed.

Lady Cecilia growled so loudly everyone stopped talking and looked at her. "Those unregistered citizens don't have enough magic to qualify for any of the Sects. They could register and become your unpaid servants in exchange for meeting only their most basic needs, or they could operate in the illegal markets, with their dignity and freedom intact. You've left them no other choice. They have to provide for themselves and their families however they can."

"But Silas opened the Sect registration to any level of magic ability," I said. "They can be merchants or Healers or artisans. They have options."

"Which will help future generations tremendously," Cecilia said. "But these things don't change overnight. The citizens relying on the illegal markets can't just start over at the lowest levels of a Sect. And many are afraid to register. They're scared of retribution for their past choices."

Color crept up Alaric's neck. "The Council provides for anyone willing to share in the burden of running our civilization. Those who reject responsibility must live with the consequences."

"The Upper City would live in abundance while people starve!" Cecilia argued. "Empty your private stores, and feed *all* our people! You want to know why the Brotherhood exists? Take a listen to yourselves. It's time to build your legacy on something besides tyranny and fear."

The expressions on the Councilors' faces ranged from outright anger to annoyed disgust. They clearly didn't appreciate what Lady Cecilia had to say. Silas's brow was scrunched in concern, and I knew the continued inequality of the situation bothered him as much as it bothered me. Changes had been made, but it wasn't enough to help everyone.

Lord Nero's rumbling bass broke the silence. "Your plan is shortsighted, Lady Cecilia. We won't beggar ourselves to save disloyal citizens."

Cecilia's hand slashed angrily through the air. "You asked me to tell you the needs of the citizens, but I can't make you listen."

From what I'd seen so far, I had to agree with her. She wasn't making much progress with Aeterna's elite rulers. Of course, the Council didn't want to hear what she had to say. They were used to being on top and were perfectly happy to climb over the backs of others to stay there. Lady Cecilia had openly challenged the most powerful people in the entire world, calling out their prejudices, and the hostility between the Councilors and their newest member was almost physical.

She had balls—I'd give her that. I'd only defied the Aeternal Council when I had no memories and nothing to lose but my life. Lady Cecilia knew full well what these people were capable of—had probably spent her whole life bowing down before their will—and she was still standing up for what she believed was right.

Just like that, I decided I liked her. If she believed the right thing to do was to empty the supplies, I'd back her. "If the Council wants to regain the trust of your people," I said, "you should make the disaffected citizens your top priority. Provide for them in their time of need, and they might return to the fold. Your goodwill is critical to building trust with your citizens."

Lady Cecilia nodded in solidarity.

"You suggest we continue to support the cause of our problems?" Alaric challenged.

"I'm suggesting you take a long-term view. Earth has a saying: 'Actions speak louder than words.'"

"How long can we feed the full five thousand from our stores?" Silas asked Lord Nero.

"With some additional rationing, I believe we could manage for about two days. However, I would advise against completely depleting our resources."

"People will panic when they realize there's only two days of food available," Lady Cecilia said.

"We wouldn't tell them that, obviously," Alaric said.

Cecilia tapped her pointer finger on the table. "Emptying the reserves of the Upper Houses would give you the resources to feed everyone for another day, possibly two. Four days total. It's the best option."

I decided to put my resources where my convictions were. "If you agree to feed all the people in the Lower City, my Sect will bring in the needed goods from Earth."

We'd planned on using the remaining money from the insurance payout to renovate the rest of the hospital campus, but we could work on it over time. Those funds could buy supplies from our realm and save lives in Aeterna. We didn't need all the extra room anyway—our people fit comfortably into the two buildings we'd already fixed up. Casius would be mad that I'd offered assistance without consulting with the Circle first, but it was the right thing to do.

Nero's face twisted into an angry snarl. "Are you implying we don't have enough funds to feed our citizens?"

The other Councilors looked equally irate, and even Silas had a small frown. I must have insulted them. "Umm..." I said carefully.

"You pay for it. We'll just transport it from Earth so you don't have to deplete your stores in Aeterna."

That would make Casius much happier, anyway.

Lady Octavia cleared her throat. "At the rate this poison is spreading, there's a good chance we'll all be dead by then, unless we find an antidote. We mustn't waste resources and time in Lower Aeterna when we should be focused on finding Nuada and protecting those who are not yet infected."

Cecilia and Nero started arguing. Then Alaric joined them. Silas tried to get them back on track, but soon, everyone was arguing with each other.

After a few minutes during which no one so much as glanced my way, I realized the Council wasn't going to be doing much more than fighting with each other, so I slipped out one of the side archways onto an outside balcony. I needed some fresh air. Two of the Guardians peeled off from the room and followed me. No doubt, Silas had sent them to keep me safe. They stayed at a polite distance behind me as I paced along the length of the balcony and turned a corner. It ended up being a full breezeway lined with arched openings that overlooked the Lower City. The walkway wrapped around three sides of the Council's meeting room before a small alcove connected two additional breezeways from other directions. When I reached the intersection, I leaned on the railing and gazed out over the city.

Despite its ugly politics, I couldn't deny that Aeterna was beautiful. The sun had set, and the glow of magic from the city lit up the entire valley. Spanning the distance above the valley floor, the Upper City floated on a network of graceful stone bridges, which spiderwebbed from each of the Upper Houses carved directly into the mountainside. At the center of it all, the graceful column of the City Centre rose from the Lower City to the Upper, connecting them to the portal to Earth.

The obvious splendor of the Upper City cast a long shadow over the streets of Lower Aeterna. The working people lived down there, those born without the right family name or resources, and they had to rely on the Citizen Source to supplement their magic. They were the servants and merchants and the fodder for all the politics of Upper Aeterna. Atticus had lived in Lower Aeterna, and hundreds of young people just like him still lived and worked and dreamed down there. And they were dying while the Councilors debated about doing anything to help them.

I remembered the bone ring Lady Treva had given me and pulled it out of my pocket. With a few moments of concentration, I wove a tracer spell over the ring. The magic settled on the surface of the delicately carved flower but stayed dormant. I swore softly. Wherever Kianna was, she wasn't anywhere near me—and possibly not anywhere in all of Aeterna.

I wasn't really surprised. I didn't think the Council had kidnapped her anymore, but that left me without any real leads. Unfortunately, if the Council wasn't responsible, then Kianna was probably still on Earth. I slipped the ring onto the chain I always wore around my neck, next to Marcel's charm.

Footsteps sounded up the path as I tucked the necklace away. When I saw Tessa, an automatic grin spread across my face.

"Gods' evening," she said, pulling me into a friendly hug.

"Hey. I was hoping I'd get to see you again."

Tessa was one of the few Aeternals I genuinely liked. Although she was a Guardian, and therefore under the command of the Council, I never felt like I had to watch my back around her. She was also Silas's close friend and had gone through training with him and Atticus. Mourning his death had brought us closer together.

"Are you off duty?" I asked.

She shrugged. "Silas asked me to keep an eye on you."

I sighed. "I'm more than capable of taking care of myself." Even in their most protected stronghold, with two Guardians trailing me, Silas felt the need to pull Tessa from her assignment to babysit me.

"Silas is overprotective," Tessa offered. "But he has enemies, as do you."

I lifted my chin toward the Lower City. "What's going on down there?"

"The citizens are scared. Everyone knows about the poison, but no one knows what it means. Who will get infected next? How can they survive without access to the Citizen Source? Why can't they leave the Lower City?" She sighed and leaned back against the railing. "There are no answers. It's a disaster, and it's going to get worse if the Council doesn't do something soon."

A thin translucent barrier of magic supported the railing, keeping Tessa from falling to her death. Even though she couldn't see the threads of magic inside the conjuring like I could, she propped herself against it blindly, trusting that the magic would keep her safe. Everything in Aeterna functioned by magic. It was intertwined into people's daily lives and the fabric of their society. The people in the Lower City couldn't function without it.

They had to figure out how to remove the poison from the Citizen Source. That thought brought me right back to Nuada's impossible demands and the reason for his actions—his missing daughter. I had to figure out what had really happened to Lady Kianna. I hoped that with Treva backing us, returning Kianna might be just enough leverage for us to negotiate for an antidote.

"We were just starting to recover from Lord Elias's duplicity," Tessa continued. "Silas was making real progress. He even forced the Council to take in a representative of the citizens. I'm guessing you met Lady Cecilia."

"She was trying to talk sense into the rest of them, but they weren't listening to her."

I had to give Lady Cecilia credit—she'd tried. Her suggestions made sense, but the Council would never put any other interests above their own.

"The Upper Houses fight change any way they can. They're still trying to restore the balance of power in their favor. They can't see... what's the Earthen expression? The writing is on the wall."

"The old way isn't working anymore," I agreed.

She gazed out over the city. "It never worked."

"Is the Council doing *anything* to help? I'd hoped without Elias sabotaging every positive move, things would have improved."

"Silas is trying. But as *Acting* Lord Councilor, he doesn't have enough political power to sway the other members. He's essentially a tie-breaking vote."

My annoyance from earlier surged. I couldn't believe Silas hadn't told me about his new role. Despite that, I felt bad for him. He'd been pulled into the middle of it all because he cared. He was trying to do the right thing for the citizens, but the Council was full of a bunch of useless bureaucrats fighting for their own selfish interests.

"Why Silas, though? He's the newest Councilor. Why not Alaric?"

"Lord Sergius, Silas's father, was the Lord Councilor before Lord Elias. Silas was literally raised to follow in his father's footsteps, and even though he shunned that path, his family name and pedigree carry a lot of weight. But more importantly, Silas is probably the only person who isn't interested in a power grab to take the position in a long-term capacity, which makes him uniquely qualified in the eyes of the other Councilors who want to hold the seat permanently."

I frowned but didn't push further. That argument was one I needed to have with the new *Lord Councilor.* "I guess it was naïve to think things would get better with Elias gone and the Brotherhood broken."

"Flushing out the traitors did help," Tessa continued. "Opening up the enrollments into the Sects helped even more. But changing the Council from within will take time."

A messenger in a light-blue tunic jogged up the breezeway. "The Council has come to a decision. Lord Silas bids you return."

I chewed on my lip as we followed the messenger back to the chamber. The Council coming to an agreement about anything was a surprise. And I'd only been gone less than twenty minutes. Something told me I wouldn't like what I was about to hear.

When we entered, Silas waved away the gaggle of aides surrounding him, and they scattered to the walls with their consoles. It might have been my imagination, but the other Councilors watched me with expectant expressions, and Alaric was downright smug. Silas looked determined, and our Aegis bond was locked down, giving nothing away.

Whatever this is, I'm definitely not going to like it.

"Nuada must be forced to give up the antidote," Silas said to me, "and the Council is willing to commit a legion of Guardians to the task."

"Uh-huh..." I almost looked around for that other shoe. It was about to drop at any second.

"The Council believes the best way to draw Nuada from hiding is to capture his people. We know where their haven is within Earth. With Nuada's followers as collateral, he'll be forced to give over the antidote."

"We... you..." I'd lost my words. All I could do was bark out a harsh laugh. *I expected something bad, but wow.* They wanted to send a hundred Guardians to Earth to kidnap and torture a bunch of innocent Fae in order to force Nuada into giving up the antidote. This plan was disastrous on so many levels that I didn't even know where to start.

"The Council is in agreement," Silas said. "We will leave this evening for Earth."

"No," I finally managed to say.

"No?" Silas's eyebrows rose.

Every single person on the Council went still, watching us. If it hadn't been so tense, it would have been comical—they expected him to get me to bend over. His reputation as the new Council leader was probably on the line.

Bring it on, buddy. I raised both my eyebrows. "You heard me correctly. The answer is no."

Chapter Eleven

"I can't allow you to send a hundred magically trained fighters storming into my realm," I said.

Silas leaned back in his chair. "It's the fastest way to gain the leverage we need to force Nuada to give us the antidote."

"You're willing to use innocent people as leverage? Lady Treva accused the Council of this exact thing. I thought you agreed with her about sacrificing innocents for your own purposes."

"Nuada is already killing innocent people. You're tying our hands with morals that don't apply," Silas retorted.

"Then capture Nuada and get the antidote from him. His people shouldn't pay for his crimes. And morals always apply!" I snapped.

Someone scoffed. I took a step closer to their table. "Did you even stop to consider what would happen if you took a hundred Guardians into Earth? The Mundane government is watching us. If they realize magic is real and see what your Guardians can do with it, they will shit their pants and then try to kill us with whatever weapons of mass destruction they can pull the trigger on."

Silas folded his hands calmly in his lap. "We know how to be discreet. We've been making excursions into other realms for centuries, including Earth."

"And what will happen when you storm the Fae haven?" I argued. "You think they're just going to surrender? No! We're talking about an all-out magic-fueled battle. Last time that happened, the government caught us on satellite! They have pictures of your Guardians on the battlefield. Mundane technology isn't a joke. The magical community can't risk the kind of exposure you're talking about."

Silas ran a hand through his hair, and the other Councilors shifted in their seats. I'd hit a nerve with that one. Aeterna existed in the first place because the earliest magic users had been feared and hunted by Mundanes. The discovery of this realm rich in magic and resources allowed them to escape persecution and certain death. Keeping our abilities secret had kept *all* of us alive for centuries. We were stronger now, but the need for secrecy was deeply ingrained in everyone in the magical community.

"We have to do something to stop the spread of the poison," Silas said.

"Then use your resources to help the innocent people in Lower Aeterna. The portal has been on lockdown, and Nuada can't get back to my realm. Do everything you can to find him—but Earth is off limits."

"Your alliance with the Aeternal Council has an aid stipulation," Lady Octavia noted.

I snorted. "Your plan isn't about aid—it's kidnapping and torture. You want help? Here I am. All my considerable powers are at your disposal to help those suffering in your Lower City. In addition to personally being here, I've offered to bring in food to feed your citizens. We have more than fulfilled the aid stipulation."

Alaric leaned forward, placing his elbows on the table. "What kind of ally would thwart our attempt to save the lives of thousands of citizens of Aeterna?"

"Oh, please," I scoffed. "You couldn't even agree to feed these people half an hour ago." I glowered at the group of powerful magic leaders. "I won't allow your Guardians access to Earth."

Silas's brow furrowed, and I braced myself for round two. This could get ugly.

"You're right," he said.

"I—what?"

"It was a bad idea. Capturing innocents as leverage is not acceptable, no matter how effective it would be. Lord Alaric, Lord Nero, Lady Octavia, we tried your approach, and it failed."

The Councilors seemed thoughtful but not particularly upset that I'd refused their demands. My brain spun. They'd been testing me, and if I'd rolled over, they would have sent a legion of Guardians to Earth to kidnap and torture people. I glowered at the scheming bastards of the Aeternal Council, Silas included, unsure if I was more pissed off at their manipulations or relieved that they'd relented so quickly. It was an even break, and the mix of emotions left me reeling.

"We need to focus on finding Nuada and helping those who are sick," Silas said.

Lady Octavia bared her teeth. "Nuada is trapped in our realm. We'll turn over every rock and tear through every hiding place until he has to crawl out of his hidey-hole. Starting with the Lower City."

"I agree," Lord Alaric said. "We need to search every home in Lower Aeterna and make sure we question anyone who is associated with him or who had ties to the Fae Sects."

Other voices rose as they discussed how to hunt down Nuada in the Lower City. I bit my lip. If they tore through the Lower City, accusing people of harboring a criminal, they'd be fueling the panic down there.

Lady Cecilia spoke up, her voice pitched loud enough to cut through the noise. "We must shut down the Citizen Source. It's the only way to stop the spread of the poison."

The Councilors stopped talking—possibly out of shock.

"Can you do that?" I blurted.

She'd basically just suggested the equivalent of shutting down the sun. A magical power source wasn't something you turned on and off. It was a force of nature, and it was permanent.

No one spoke, which meant none of them knew if it was possible. The silence was thick until finally, Alaric cleared his throat. "We would need to research this idea. It hasn't been attempted before."

"Have your Magisters research it," Silas said. "If it were possible, it would help tremendously."

"We must close the Lower City," Lady Octavia added. "If we order a mandatory home quarantine, it will make it easier to find Nuada and force him to give us the antidote."

"Barricading them in without access to healing is not an option." Cecilia's jaw was set. "Especially not when we can only feed them for a few days. You're asking for a riot. At least consider other possibilities before you act rashly."

"Agreed," Silas said quickly. "We will research our options, break for the evening, and convene before dawn tomorrow to discuss this further. Lord Alaric, I trust that will be sufficient time to consult your Magisters?" Alaric nodded, but he didn't look hopeful. "I'll dispatch Guardians to begin the search for Nuada. We'll start in the Upper City until we have a more detailed plan. We're convened for now."

The Councilors left one by one, taking the flurry of aides and servants with them until the last one bowed and scurried away, and Silas and I were alone. I waited for him to finish tapping along his console pad. Finally, he set the console aside and looked at me. His face was hard, but I couldn't tell if he was angry with me. *Hell*, I was angry with him. I'd shut down his attempt to invade Earth with Guardians, but he'd set me up to either roll over or fight with him in front of the Council. And he'd surprised me with the *Lord Councilor* thing—which was really irritating.

Silas shrugged out of his Council robe and tossed it carelessly over the back of his chair. The long strand of rough-cut gems that had kept the fabric around his shoulders thunked loudly on the wood. The Councilor's pendant was meant to impress, but it was the white fabric of the robe that caught my attention. It reminded me of the vision from Four.

Every good defense starts with a strong offense. "Why didn't you tell me you're the new Lord Councilor?"

One eyebrow rose sardonically as if he knew I was going on the offensive before he could, but he answered the question. "I'm the *Acting* Lord Councilor until we vote in a permanent leader."

"Did you even think about what this means for us? My Sect is not going to look the other way on this. I've been busting my ass to build their trust so we can figure out a path forward for us. And then you go and do this! There's no way in hell they're going to be okay with your new title."

He stalked around the table, and I resisted the urge to take a step backward as he approached. He was damn imposing when he wanted to be. I supposed that came with the territory of leading a lethal force of magically trained warriors, but it didn't do anything to settle my rising temper.

So I did what I did best and lashed out first. "And I'm sorry, but you don't get to be mad because I didn't allow Guardians into Earth."

"You took a strong position," he said, his expression not relaxing even a fraction.

"Did you seriously think I would just fall on my back and let you—"

He pulled me into a kiss, pouring all the frustration I'd sensed rolling off him into the act. I kissed him back just as urgently, eager for more, until we were both breathless.

He pulled away long enough to ask, "What is this expression, falling on your back? Sounds promising." His eyes sparked with humor and desire.

"I—stop that," I said firmly. But his eyes stayed locked on my mouth, and I ran my tongue over my lips, tasting his kiss. "I'm still annoyed with you. Why did you push me to let the Guardians into Earth when you didn't even agree with the plan?"

"As the Acting Lord Councilor, I was tasked with negotiating the plan the majority agreed to." He shrugged.

"Did you expect me to go down without a fight?"

He chuckled. "Earthens have the best expressions. Are you propositioning me?"

I swatted him on the chest and then ruined all my righteous anger when my fingers lingered there to trail over his sculpted muscles. Then the vision of his death flashed in my memory, and my throat tightened. I couldn't lose him. *I wouldn't.*

I forced my face into an annoyed smirk, hiding the sudden pain in my heart. "You know what I mean."

One side of his mouth quirked up. "Why would I want you to submit when fighting with you is so much more fun?"

I stretched and kissed him on the lips. He kissed me back, pulling me tighter into his arms, and as his hands slid lower, I pressed myself flush against his hard body. Tingles spread across my skin, and I moaned into his mouth. I'd been dreaming about being alone together practically since I'd met him, and it looked like we were headed down the right path, finally.

"Thanks for admitting I was right," I said, coming up for air. "You should do that more often."

He kissed my palm and placed our twined hands over my heart. "You keep my heart with you always."

A warm shiver spread through me at his unusual display of emotion. "I love you, Silas."

And gods, did I love him. When I first met him, I would never have guessed he could be this emotionally open and tender. I'd thought he was an arrogant, self-centered asshole who always got his way. Sometimes he still pushed all my buttons, and he definitely got his way too often, but he'd let me past that hard exterior, and I'd fallen in love with the person on the inside.

Plus, I was just as stubborn and strong-willed as he was. And despite his rough edges, the man beneath all of that was worth fighting for. I didn't have to be alone in this world, because Silas would be there at my side when I needed him. And I was going to keep it that way, fate be damned. If only the whole world didn't seem to want to get in our way.

"Do you ever just want to hide out and let everyone solve their own problems?" I asked.

"I have an idea." Silas grabbed my hand and pulled me out of the room.

"Where are we going?" I'd been sizing up the sturdiness of the conference tables and checking to see whether there were locks on the doors, but Silas seemed intent on thwarting my plans as he dragged me toward the short-distance skimmers located on the upper side of the mountain.

A boyish grin spread over his face. "I want to show you something."

He whisked us through the Council building, outside to the skimmers, and finally, into the reception room at House Valeron, which was about the size of a small apartment. On the far wall was a carving of his family's sigil, which matched the one I had branded on my arm—two vertically overlapping circles running together as if they had no beginning or end. Under the sigil, in a language I couldn't read, was the family motto Silas had once translated for me as, "The House of Eternal Might."

Silas placed his hand on the far wall, and a doorway appeared, leading into the grand ballroom. The first time I'd seen it, I was overwhelmed by the sheer size and splendor of the space. It was as wide as three football fields stacked side by side, with a half dozen different hallways connecting to the rest of the cliff-face mansion.

The ceiling soaring twenty feet above us was a stained-glass masterpiece that floated under a dark evening sky. In daylight, it cast brilliant, multicolored light over the center of the obscenely ornate space. Gemstones embedded in the floor formed an image of Silas's family crest. He'd called it ostentatious the first time I was there, and it was. But it was also beautiful.

He led me quickly down one of the side hallways, heading away from the main areas of the house. I'd never been in this part of his gigantic mansion, but Silas wouldn't tell me the secret of where he was taking me. Our footsteps echoed off the stone as I kept up with his long strides, heading deeper and deeper into the mountain. Several turns and doorways later, we descended a staircase carved straight from the rock, and when the path got dark, Silas's magic rose around us, lighting the way. The air cooled as we traveled farther and the smooth walls blended to rough-hewn stone. Despite a few more attempts to figure out where we were heading, Silas wouldn't relent.

I began to hear a buzzing, and as we descended another long staircase, the sound increased, matched by the pulsing of energy in my chest. We were surrounded by strong magic, and like a dense fog, the power tingled on my skin and through my blood. I inhaled and let the cool, fluid energy soak into my skin, but I couldn't see anything through the thick darkness.

Silas wound his fingers through mine, pulling me to a stop. He stood behind me and wrapped his arms around my waist. His strong hold was perfect in this strangely energizing space, making me feel entirely safe even though I was blind to my surroundings.

I had to raise my voice over the noise. "Where are we?"

His magic pulsed, setting off a cascade of embedded spells that illuminated the space with soft ethereal light, revealing that we were standing inside a large stone cavern. "Look down."

My toes were inches away from the edge of a cliff. With another step, I would have fallen more than twenty-five feet. My stomach squirmed, and I scooted back into his arms. A huge deluge of water rushed from an opening in the rock face opposite us, falling straight down into a pool of aqua-blue water. The source of the buzzing was a waterfall.

As the initial shock passed, I noted that the cascading water was infused with magic. Threads of energy danced and tumbled down into the pool below us, shimmering with energy. The power of it thrummed inside my chest, pulsing with magic that seemed to soak inside the fibers of my soul. It was the most beautiful thing I had ever experienced.

"I used to come here as a child," Silas said quietly. "I spent endless hours swimming in these waters. As heirs of different Houses, Stephan and I weren't raised together, but we were allowed to spend time here to boost our powers. Our mother didn't like my father much—Sergius Valeron was a difficult man—but she negotiated access for her future offspring as part of the bond-mating that produced me as my father's heir. It was very smart on her part, and it allowed Stephan and me to have at least a bit of shared childhood. We are half brothers, after all, and I'm grateful Sariah placed more value in that connection than Sergius ever did."

I gazed into the swirling fog of misty magic until I suddenly realized what I was looking at. This was the Valeron Source. Silas's familial source was legendary because it was so strong and one of the few pure sources of magic energy remaining in any realm. A source like this wasn't a result of bound magic like the Earthen Source. It generated magic, like the Fae's haven, and had been protected with a conjuring that allowed only people with their House sigil to access it. An elemental source was so rare, and so well guarded, that probably only a handful of people had ever even seen the source of the Valeron magic. This raw power was the reason his family negotiated mating bonds and brokered political deals and the reason the Council wanted him as part of their ranks.

Silas's magic had always felt like a cool rush of power to me, and now I realized that was a literal interpretation of it. Through our shared bond, I had access to this magic, and being this near his source sparked something deep and joyous in my soul. But Silas seemed wistful, almost sad.

"Your childhood sounds kind of lonely. You only got to see your mom once a week?"

Silas shrugged. "Upper Houses enter into mating agreements in order to produce an heir for a specific House, and the offspring doesn't usually have much contact with the other House. I suppose I missed out on a relationship with my mother, but I was lucky to get a brother out of the arrangement. Stephan and I joined our Houses after they both died, and I made him Prime of House Valeron when Alaric forced me into the bond-mating with Aria. It worked out in the end."

"Stephan told me about that. Bold move, going against the Fate's prophecy and the Lord Magister. I bet Alaric was apoplectic with shock."

"He wasn't pleased with me." Silas smirked. "But I was stubborn and very angry. I found a way to strike back at Lord Alaric and walk away from all the House politics at the same time."

"Do you regret it?"

"Some days," he admitted. "Life was simpler before that damn prophecy. But I feel responsible for the opportunity my name brings with it. I can use that power for something bigger. There are a lot of things that need to change in Aeterna, and I have a part to play in that now."

"I completely understand what you mean. I can't walk away either—even when I feel like I'm getting crushed under the weight of it all." I leaned against his chest, intertwining my fingers with his as I ran my eyes over the cascading water spilling into the shimmering pool. We were silent for a while, just holding each other and basking in the magic surrounding us. "I didn't know your source was elemental. Harnessing this much magic is impressive."

"The falls spread through a system of caverns reaching miles back. It's the reason my ancestors found this realm and built the Valeron House on this cliff face." He shrugged. "I'm not sure there's anyone left alive who could contain an elemental source of this magnitude. It took a great deal of power to harness it."

I could relate. Over the generations since my Sect had left Aeterna, we'd lost so much of our knowledge. The hiding and infighting and divisions had cost us all.

He released me, and a boyish grin spread suddenly across his face. "Up for a swim?"

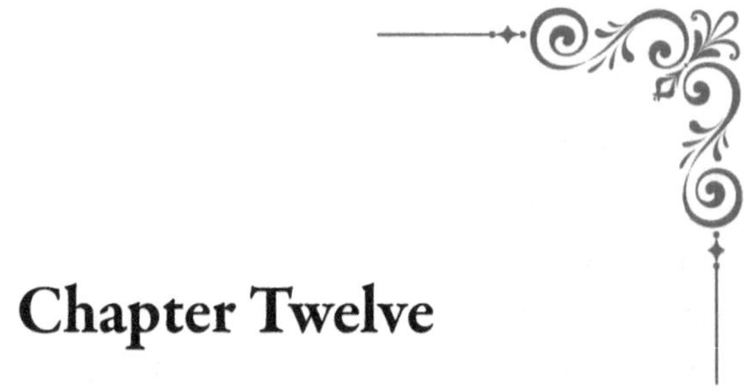

Chapter Twelve

I laughed, and then I realized he was serious. "Um, I didn't bring a swimsuit."

He smirked, reached down, and pulled off his shirt. Heat burned through me as I ogled his carved torso. Years working with a sword had transformed his body into a finely tuned weapon, and it wasn't hard to appreciate the view. He tossed the shirt onto the rocks behind us, and I admired the beautiful magic tattoos worked along his bare skin. They filled every available inch of space from his collarbone and across his shoulders and upper back before continuing down his left side.

He toed off his shoes and reached for the waistband of his pants, clearly aware of my lingering gaze. "Would you prefer to go first?"

Uncharacteristically shy, I flushed and averted my eyes, focusing on the sheer cliff face. "How are you going to get down there?"

I heard his pants hit the ground and then turned in time to see him launch himself off the cliff in a streak of bare flesh. A distant splash sounded before he surfaced with a whoop.

"Jump in!" he called up to me.

"How are you gonna get back out?" I yelled, my stomach twisting as I leaned over the drop.

It was a perfectly reasonable question. The cliff face was almost thirty feet above the surface of the water, and I didn't see a ladder. Skimming relied on familiarity with where you wanted to land and a solid understanding of where you started. A flexible element like water screwed up any sense of a starting point and would throw off a person's ability to get back out.

"You're afraid?" he taunted, treading water.

I grumbled, and he laughed. A little thrill of excitement went through me as I contemplated jumping in after him. *Naked.* I suddenly wanted to go for a swim. "Turn around so I can get undressed."

"I've seen you unclothed before."

"You're making this weird." I certainly didn't mind getting naked with Silas, but I wasn't quite planning on a cliff-top striptease.

Laughing, he turned his back and continued to tread water. I stripped and jumped feetfirst into the pool before I could talk myself out of it. A little scream escaped me before I hit the water. It was warmer than I expected, and I came up laughing. Magic and water surrounded me, filling me with pure happiness.

"So, a pack of Rakken is nothing to fret over, but you're scared of heights?" he taunted.

I splashed him in the face.

He wiped the water off and narrowed his eyes in mock outrage. "Did you just attack me?"

I splashed him again. "Someone once told me to be prepared for attack at all times. Maybe you should take your own advice."

He dove under the water and grabbed at my ankles. I kicked to get away, but his grip was strong, and he pulled me under the surface. When I emerged, a fresh wave of water hit me in the face. Gasping and splashing, I retaliated blindly, splashing water in his general direction while trying to block the steady stream pounding me in the face.

"You have terrible aim," he said, laughing, somewhere to my left.

I launched myself in his direction. My quick action landed me on top of him, and he went down like a rock. Kicking, I attempted an escape, but his hands wrapped around me. Suddenly, I was pressed against a hard body, and I quit fighting his grip.

We bobbed on the surface, chest to chest, treading water. His eyes dropped to my lips, and a delicious tingle spread through my body. I leaned forward and kissed him. He tasted of spice and warmth and Silas. Then he threw me one of his feral grins before he took a deep breath and dove under the water.

Where is he going? This was just getting good. The crystal-clear water allowed a nice view of his backside as he swam toward the waterfall... and disappeared.

I dove toward the base of the waterfall and fought against the current as I swam after him until I saw a light flickering ahead. I kicked hard for the surface. Breathing heavily, I surfaced inside a cave the size of a backyard pool and lit with softly glowing magic spells that twinkled across the gently bubbling water. My toes touched the smooth stone bottom, and the deliciously warm water lapped against my collarbones.

At the far end of the pool, Silas lounged on a natural ledge, submerged up to his chest and waiting for me. A set of stone stairs behind him answered my earlier question about his exit plan.

Tiny bubbles of energy burst against my skin, releasing power that left me shivering with pleasure. Like a champagne hot tub, the bubbles prickled across my flesh. "It's so warm," I said. "And the magic..."

"There's a natural hot spring running through the mountain," he said, his voice low. He shifted, stretching his arms along the stone ledge to either side of him, drawing my attention to his muscular shoulders and biceps. "Come over here."

In true Silas fashion, he was commanding. But far from angering me, his words sent shivers of anticipation through my body. I moved slowly through the warm water, enjoying the sensation of magic and his gaze on me, until I stopped a foot in front of him. Only the gentle movement of the water lay between us.

His eyes dropped to my mouth and then kept going south through the crystal-clear water. Butterflies fluttered in my stomach. I wondered if he was as nervous as I was. Technically, I'd seen him naked, but it had been in close quarters when we'd just about had sex in a sleeping bag in the Alaskan mountains. A pack of Rakken had interrupted us, and we hadn't had a chance to start again. I'd been waiting for this moment for almost as long as I'd known Silas. I already knew I loved him, but we'd never been together fully.

He didn't seem nervous, and the emotions emanating through the Aegis bond were eager but restrained. He was holding back. Aeternals were very forward about sex, and Silas was no exception. On top of that, he was confident, aggressive, and used to being in charge. He was letting me lead—giving me a chance to back out if I wanted to.

I let my eyes drift over his body, biting my lip as I took in the sight of Silas naked and aroused. He leaned toward me slowly and placed his mouth over mine. Carefully, intently, he sucked my lower lip between his. My heart thudded in my chest as our mouths moved together, and our tongues danced. My entire body ached to be closer to him.

He leaned back, and a small disappointed noise escaped the back of my throat. He gazed at me, waiting.

He is so damn sexy. Deliberately, I moved closer until only inches of space lay between us. I could see his heartbeat pulsing in his neck. I let the tips of my fingers drift across the skin there and traced the top of his shoulders and down the sigils covering his arms until our fingers wound together.

He lifted our entwined fingers and kissed the back of my hand, his steel-gray eyes locked on mine. I wrapped my arms around his shoulders and slowly slid my body flush against his. His hard muscle against my skin felt like molten silk as our bodies molded together perfectly. He groaned with restraint, and pleasure flooded through our bond.

This was the best kind of torture. His eyes were dilated with desire, and I bit my lip in anticipation. Gods, I loved him, inside and out, all the good with any bad. I appreciated that he was holding back and letting me lead, but he was an idiot if he thought I was going to back out. I'd never wanted him more. I let all of those feelings flood through the Aegis connection.

Something shifted in the bond, and I gasped at the sudden rising of his magic. Here inside his source, the connection between us was an almost solid, tangible force that overwhelmed me with its intensity. Silas's desire hit me, wrapped in pure magic, and the longing building low in my belly caught fire.

Unable to resist any longer, I straddled him, kissing him deeply as I unleashed my own magic. The feel of him right where I ached most fed my hunger as we kissed, hungry and aggressive, running our hands over each other's bodies. I moaned as his mouth and tongue traveled over sensitive flesh. Everything about this moment felt right.

In a sure, swift movement, Silas lifted us out of the water and tipped me back onto the smooth stone floor. He settled on top of me, his hard, warm body fitting perfectly over my own. The heat between us kept me warm as our mouths and hands explored each other, the bond between us intertwining our magic and amplifying every sensation.

"Silas, I want…" The waves of pleasure and magic were melting my brain. "I need…" I needed to get closer to him. I needed him inside of me. A steady ache grew. I needed *more*.

"Fate's bollocks, Maeve." His voice was gravelly and rough. "If you're going to tell me to stop and find a Mundane contraceptive or invoke Earth's religious deities—do it now."

I nearly laughed at the reminder of the first time we'd almost had sex, before I'd recovered my true memories. The realization that we had no Mundane birth control had kept me from going any further with him, even though I'd burned with equal parts irritation and desire. With my memories and magic restored, I knew a simple spell would prevent unwanted side effects.

"I need you to say yes," he said.

I'd wanted him all those months ago, but the desire building inside of me now, coupled with the feelings and magic pounding through our bond—the love we shared—was like a bonfire raging inside me. I *needed* him. Every part of him. And I was so sick of waiting, sick of being apart, and sick of being told how to feel about him. I'd given this man my heart long before, and I wasn't willing to wait any longer either.

"Say yes," he repeated against my skin as his mouth kept moving south.

"Yes. Sweet baby Jesus, yes. Don't you dare stop." The magic around us rose up, matching the wild beating of my heart. "I don't care if the whole world blows up. Don't. Stop."

My entire body caught fire as I moaned and writhed while he brought me to the verge of screaming. When I couldn't wait any longer, Silas positioned himself above me, his mouth trailing kisses and nips along my overheated, sensitive flesh. My hunger had built into painful urgency. I wrapped my legs around his hips, arching into him. Silas rocked against me, building the aching sensation in my body as he slowly pushed inside. We both moaned at the sweet agony of the pleasure building between us.

"Are you...?" He gritted his teeth, his entire body strained and tight as he paused above me. "Do you need a moment?"

I rocked my hips against him. "Don't stop," I repeated, breathless.

The Valeron Source responded to us, vibrating with power as our bodies moved together. Around us, the magic flowed and swirled in a frenzy of energy. This moment was everything—the magic between us, the feel of Silas inside me, the love we shared. Nothing else mattered. I pulled the magic toward us and pushed it through the Aegis bond.

Magic flooded through the bond, and we both gasped in shared pleasure as magic shattered through us, binding our lives together. Always.

Chapter Thirteen

Light glowed cheerily through the single window as I woke early the next morning in Silas's bed. The handsome green-velvet drapes had been pulled back, drenching the small but cozy room in morning sun.

"Gods' morning, my Maeve," Silas said.

"Ung," I groaned as I kicked free of the tangled silken sheets.

"You're adorably rumpled in the morning," he said, standing over my side of the bed.

Forcing my eyes open a crack, I found Silas's steel-gray eyes focused on me. They crinkled handsomely as he laughed silently. Being so damn chipper on so little sleep was a crime against humanity.

"I didn't get much sleep last night." I stretched my entire body, feeling a perfect mixture of contentment and muscle ache from a long night of bliss. Being with Silas was even better than all the fantasies I'd harbored.

He hummed in self-satisfied pleasure as his hand traveled across my bare back. I shivered, remembering the things he could do with his hands. And his mouth. And the rest of his incredible body.

"I regret nothing," he said smugly.

"Me either," I admitted, earning myself a very nice good-morning kiss. I managed to open both eyes before I got fully distracted. "How did the meeting go this morning? Did the Council agree on anything?"

Silas stripped out of his white robe and tunic and slipped back into bed with me. He wrapped his arms around me from behind, and I snuggled against his broad chest, completely happy.

"The only thing we agree on is the need to find Nuada. We're searching the Lower City today, and I managed to convince them to deliver food to each of the residences during the search."

"Smart. Did Alaric's Magisters find a way to shut down the Citizen Source?"

"Nothing viable. They're working on a theory to restrict access—not unlike Earth's bound magic—but it would require an incredible amount of energy. I'm not hopeful. We need to find Nuada and get the antidote."

We fell into contemplative silence as I nestled into his chest and our legs tangled together. He ran his fingers slowly through my loose hair, and I started to drift back into blissful unconsciousness. If I ignored all the problems outside of this room, this was an absolutely perfect moment in time. I wanted to freeze it and live there forever.

"Do you truly regret nothing?" he asked. "When first we met, your only desire was to get back to your Mundane life." He propped his head on his elbow to peer into my eyes. One hand trailed lazily over my bare shoulder to the necklace I always wore with Marcel's charm, which was heavy against my chest with the addition of Lady Treva's ring.

"My Mundane memories weren't real." Running away from the memories of my mother's murder and hiding in Boston had only delayed the inevitable. The weight of all my responsibilities had settled back on my shoulders. "I shouldn't have run away from my responsibilities in the first place."

"After all this is fixed, we'll find that beach. Just you, me, and the sun... somewhere without clothing." His fingers ran down the side of my neck. "Maybe we won't even come back."

His tone was light, but there was a serious intent behind his words. I let myself consider it for a minute. He'd first made the offer to leave our responsibilities behind after we killed Titus, but at the time, his government was in shambles and my people had been scattered across the globe.

Six months later, things weren't much better. We still didn't have a solution for Aria—Silas's legally bonded mate—or Stephan, his half brother. Although he'd claimed their unborn child as his own, Silas was bound by an unbreakable bond-mating with Aria until the child was born. And those personal reasons were only the start of our relationship problems.

After the session with the Aeternal Council, it was painfully obvious that the situation with Lower Aeterna wasn't going to get better without Silas's intervention. Not to mention my people still needed the magic I could channel to protect us from the Fae, whatever Elias was up to, and even the Mundane government. The Fate's visions had confirmed that all those threats were real.

The visions. I tensed when I remembered the visit from Four. *Silas dying. My people slaughtered by our enemies. Kianna.* I still had no idea where to start, but I knew that finding Kianna in her stone prison was the best lead I had. No matter how badly I wanted to escape to a beach with Silas and never come back, there were bigger things at risk.

"I can't ask you to give everything up," I finally said. "Your family, your people. I just... we can't. They all need us."

"No good act goes without punishing someone, as they say."

Silas lay back, and I rested my head on his chest. I kissed the sculpted dip between his pectorals. His incorrect use of Earth's sayings was freaking adorable.

"Fratch, Maeve, I don't care about any of it. I dedicated my entire life to the Council, to my House obligations, my people... I didn't know I wanted more before you came and flipped my world upside down, but I finally have something worth living for. And even though you're right here in my arms, you're still out of reach. It's killing me."

I knew exactly what he meant. But I didn't have an answer for our problems either. "I know. I love you so much, Silas, and I promise we're going to find a way through this together. It's just going to take a little time."

"Consider that beach as a standing offer."

Three loud bangs sounded on Silas's door before it flew open. Silas was out of bed, his magic blazing around his stark-naked body and a sword in hand, before Tessa made it two steps into the room. Neither of them seemed embarrassed as I pulled the sheets up to my neck and gaped at her.

"Lady Aria's been poisoned. Come quickly!" Tessa ran out of the room, leaving me and Silas staring at each other in confusion.

We threw on pieces of clothing and chased after Tessa. Since we couldn't skim inside the house, we ran to the other side of House Valeron and through living spaces I'd never seen before, which wasn't surprising, since the building was as big as a palace.

"What happened?" Silas demanded as we ran.

"Lady Aria became ill sometime during the night. Stephan brought Healers to the Prime suite this morning, but they can't help her. She has the same symptoms we've seen spreading through Lower Aeterna. Fever, vomiting—she's been in and out of consciousness."

"Did she access the Citizen Source?" I asked as we tackled a staircase two steps at a time. "Or come into contact with someone who did?" If the poison was spreading person to person, we were in a lot more trouble than we'd imagined.

Silas grunted in understanding as we sprinted up a hallway and into a somewhat familiar area of the house but said, "Aria doesn't need to access the Citizen Source."

"We don't know how she became infected," Tessa replied.

We ran through the halls at a dead run and didn't stop to admire what I was sure amounted to a fortune in art hung in tastefully gilded frames throughout the long hallways we traversed.

Why is his house so damn big?

"What are you doing here, Tessa?" I panted. "At House Valeron, I mean."

Instead of answering me, Tessa's gaze slid to Silas.

"Tessa's been assigned to you indefinitely," Silas said. "Where you go, she goes."

"Silas! That's ridiculous. I don't need Tessa to babysit me."

"You can be mad at me later," Silas replied, using my own words against me.

We neared a large double doorway with real wooden doors, not the magical barriers that I'd gotten used to in Aeterna. They hung open, and worried voices floated out as I slid to a stop outside, but Silas barged through without knocking, so Tessa and I followed.

From the front entry, I could see that the suite was larger than my apartment back in Boston, and multiple rooms branched off of it. An entire family could live there. We walked through three richly furnished rooms until we arrived at the last room, dominated by a large four-poster bed. Each post was hung with gold fabric that matched the heavy draperies framing a large picture window with a stunning view of the Upper City.

A knot of tense people stood around the bed. Kneeling at the bedside with a grim expression was Stephan Valeron, Silas's half brother and mirror opposite. They shared the same mother, but Stephan's father had been Fae. Where Silas had dark hair and exuded seriousness and intimidation, Stephan was blond and lighthearted. Silas was irritated by the social fame that came with his family name. Stephan found it amusing, and he often pulled pranks to see how far he could push the lemmings hanging on to his every word.

They both had good hearts and strong ties to each other—their only remaining family.

But Stephan wasn't smiling now. He didn't even glance up when we entered. His attention was completely focused on Aria, who lay in the giant bed.

The last time I'd seen her, a pregnancy glow had enhanced her natural beauty. Now dark circles shadowed her closed eyes, and her skin was pale and waxy, giving her delicate feminine features a frail look. Her long blond hair was limp and damp with sweat. A male and female pair of Healers, each glowing with magic and clad in green robes, concentrated intently on helping Aria. The expressions on their faces made my chest tighten with fear.

"What's her condition?" Silas asked the Healers.

The slight shake of the man's head was enough to confirm what the tension in the room already told me. Aria wasn't doing well.

The female Healer swiped at her forehead. "We're doing our best, my lord, but the poison is attacking her magic. We've never seen anything like this before. I think we've slowed it, but it's still spreading. We only have a small amount of time before her body can't take the stress any longer."

Silas laid his hand on Stephan's shoulder. "Did she access the Citizen Source or come into contact with someone who did? Think carefully, brother."

"No." Stephan's voice was emphatic. "She wouldn't have had a reason to, and we've been together since yester eve. I don't understand how this happened."

"Tessa," Silas said, "find Lord Alaric."

Tessa took off at a run.

A flash of visceral anguish slapped across my awareness, and I inhaled at the sudden wave of pain, but the feeling dissipated just as quickly as it had come. Some of Stephan's Empathic magic had just washed over me. I grimaced at the small window into his suffering, unable to imagine bearing what he was going through.

"Is she going to be okay?" I asked quietly.

"Will she live?" Silas added.

Two sets of uncertain eyes gazed back at us. The woman spoke hesitantly. "We cannot guarantee an outcome, my lords."

"Most of the master Healers defected with the Fae Houses," the male Healer said softly. "If I may speak candidly, we're novices, and we're out of our depth."

I took in their yellow-green auras and realized that they were both part Fae and part Human. When all the full-blooded Fae defected with Nuada, they'd left Aeterna with the least skilled Healers.

Silas's mouth turned downward. "You must do everything in your powers to help Lady Aria. What of the baby?"

"The child is not in any duress currently," the woman confirmed. "But we don't know how long we can... we're doing all that we can."

Aria's eyelids fluttered, and her face scrunched in pain. Her breathing was fast and shallow.

"We sedated her," the male Healer said quietly. "She was in pain."

Stephan looked at us without hope, and I felt the weight of his sadness as though I'd never have a reason to be happy again.

"We can't stop the poison," Stephan said in a rough voice. "We don't know what caused it."

Silas squeezed his brother's shoulder.

"Our House was attacked," a new voice said from behind me. Alaric stood in the doorway, his skin pale and clammy. He shuffled into the room, clearly in pain, his white Councilor's robe dragging as he made his way to Aria's bedside.

Silas swore. "Lord Alaric, what happened?"

The male Healer brought Alaric a chair and started scanning him with magic.

"Help my daughter." Alaric waved the man off. "I was attacked by Lord Nuada and four Fae. I tried to defend myself, but I was outnumbered. They injected me with… something. A poison, I suspect. I fell ill, but I didn't realize it had spread through me to Aria until Tessa brought word. It must have infected her through our family bond." Alaric leaned over the bed and stroked Aria's fevered brow. "My personal guards saved my life… chased the Fae through the Lower City and to the City Centre, but they escaped through the portal. Two other Primes of Upper City Houses were also attacked."

"Nuada's back on Earth?" I exclaimed. "How did that happen? I thought it was secure!"

"Three Guardians died trying to stop him," Alaric said.

Silas swore and said to me, "Let me send a legion after him. We'll find him before he causes any more damage."

The Inner Circle would never let Silas bring a hundred Guardians through the portal. And if I just showed up with them, they'd never forgive me. I'd lose every ounce of trust I'd built with the Circle. "I can't, Silas. I—we'll have to find another way." I rubbed Marcel's charm between my fingers and resisted the urge to apologize. I didn't have a choice.

Silas frowned but didn't push.

"Where's Tessa?" I asked Alaric.

"I sent her to update the Council. They need to know that Lord Nuada has escaped."

"You need a Healer," I said. "We can call someone here for you."

"The poison does not spread as long as I do not access my magic. I feel ill but no worse."

Aria moaned, and we all turned toward the bed. The Healers went into overdrive, and magic flexed around them as they wove more of their energy into complex healing spells.

"What's happening?" Stephan demanded.

The female Healer spoke quietly, her efforts focused on the conjurings building around Aria. "The poison is still spreading. It's feeding on the magic within her."

"But she's not accessing our Source," Alaric said, his hand on Aria's forehead. "My own exposure was limited when I ceased access. How is the poison still spreading?"

"The baby draws energy through the mother. It will spread as long as either accesses the tainted source," the male Healer said.

"Oh my gods," I whispered. The baby was killing Aria.

"Then terminate the pregnancy," Alaric said decisively. "You can sire another heir, Lord Silas. The bond-mating allows for two miscarriages. It will still be valid."

I stared at Alaric in shock. *Who the hell cares about the bond-mating agreement right now?*

"Do you think we haven't thought of that?" Stephan replied in a choked voice. His head dropped onto the bed, Aria's hands grasped between his own.

"She forbids it," the female Healer clarified.

Alaric furrowed his brow at Stephan before he looked to Silas for confirmation. Aria was willing to die before she killed the baby. But as long as the baby lived inside her, it would draw from the tainted magic source and kill them both.

This couldn't be the way Aria died. She was a light in a dark world, a woman of grace and kindness. And Stephan... *Dear gods, Stephan can't lose her like this.* I couldn't imagine what it would be like for him to lose the love of his life and his baby at the same time as poison spread through them like a disease.

"She needs a transfusion," I said suddenly.

"A what?" Silas asked.

The idea was still forming in my head, but I explained what I was thinking. "Mundanes are susceptible to diseases that attack their blood. I'm not a doctor, but the cure involves replacing the bad blood from your body with new blood that isn't infected. Aria needs a transfusion of magic."

Silas frowned, but Stephan perked up. "Can you do that—replace the tainted magic within her?"

"I can try."

"But the fetus will continue to draw on its native source after this transfusion," Alaric said.

"Not if you strip her of her old source and give Aria access to another one." I looked up at Silas and raised my eyebrows. "How do you feel about sharing your House sigil?"

Silas said, "It's long overdue."

"And you can cut her off from House Certus's source?" I asked Alaric.

"It is... possible," he said. "Usually in cases of disowning, but yes, I know how to do it."

"Accessing your own magic will mean additional exposure to the poison within your family source, my lord," the male Healer pointed out.

Alaric lifted his chin. "I will do it."

"Okay, then, we have a plan," I said, infusing my voice with confidence.

My plan was full of theories about things we'd never tried before. If even one part of this failed, Aria and her baby were going to die. I wiped my sweaty palms on my jeans. We didn't have time to come up with a different plan. Aria's breathing was labored and shallow, and in just the last few minutes, her color had gotten worse.

Silas held up his hands. "Wait. If you drain out the poisoned magic, there's a possibility you'll get infected yourself."

"It's a risk we'll have to take. I'm the only one here who can absorb the tainted magic." I twisted my loose hair into a braid over my shoulder, trying to sort out all the steps as Silas scowled in disapproval. "Get ready to infuse her with fresh energy."

"This isn't a solid plan," Silas argued. "There's no plan if you're infected also."

I laid my hand on Silas's arm. "I've done this before, Silas. It's exactly like when I absorbed the power from those Rakken on Earth. I know what I'm doing. I know how to hold magic without absorbing it. I just need a safe way to release the tainted power."

Alaric saved us from further argument as he grabbed a wooden hairbrush from a nearby table and thrust it into my hand. "You can channel the tainted magic into an object. The natural wood element will be a fine conductor."

I frowned dubiously at the brush and then back up at Alaric. "Are you sure?" Other than summoning sigils, I'd never tried to channel magic into an object before. It felt ridiculous.

"Yes," he said with confidence.

I'd have to trust him. He was Aeterna's leading expert on all things magical, and he wanted Aria to live. Plus, his office was full of knickknacks someone had channeled magic into, so he was clearly familiar with the concept. It made sense in a strange way.

"Okay." I steeled myself. "Okay. We're gonna do this."

"What happens to Aria when you drain all of her magic?" Stephan asked.

I'd drained those Rakken of all their magic, and it had killed them. But I knew what I was doing now. *Sort of.* "I'll cycle in clean power as I drain out the bad. It may take a few rounds, but hopefully, that will be enough to overpower the poison in her system. Then you can give her access to the Valeron Source."

Silas narrowed his eyes. "Exactly how dangerous is this for you? I want the truth, Maeve."

Aria was my friend, and I couldn't just let her die without trying to help. But I couldn't lie to Silas and tell him it wouldn't be dangerous for me. "I don't know. There's a chance I'll get infected, but Aria needs help now, and we're all she's got."

Silas frowned. "Your death won't help anyone, including Aria."

"I won't put myself in any more danger than I absolutely have to."

"Promise me you'll be careful. Please, Maeve."

My heart thudded in my chest as I nodded. "I will do everything I can to get us both through this."

I moved closer to Aria's bedside. Stephan released her hand reluctantly, and I took his place while Alaric and Silas waited on the other side of her bed.

Aria's eyelids fluttered open. "Maeve?" Her voice was weak, and her eyes were dilated. "What... you doing here?"

"I'm going to try to help you, okay? We're going to pull out the tainted magic."

Her eyes were wide in her face. "No," she protested weakly. "The baby."

"It's okay. Your baby will be fine. We're going to give you access to the Valeron Source and cut you off from House Certus. But we have to drain the tainted magic first. You just need to hang in there a little longer. You can do it."

I turned to the Healers. "Can you help her numb the pain? This is going to hurt."

The woman nodded, and the pair began building another conjuring between them.

"Stephan, come hold Aria's other hand. Help her stay calm."

"Not like this. The baby... I have to..." Aria searched around the room, panicked, until she spotted Alaric. "Father!"

"Dear heart, we have to act quickly," Alaric said gently, stroking her brow. "The baby will be fine."

Aria shook her head weakly. "I won't accept... the Valeron sigil."

Alaric flinched in surprise. "Why ever not? Of course you'll accept the Valeron sigil. It's part of your treatment."

Aria tried to push up onto her elbows, but she was too weak. Stephan caught her when she collapsed and lowered her gently back down to the pillow. She was too sick to resist, and her breathing was ragged.

"I want... the mating bond... annulled."

Alaric's eyes went wide. "You're pregnant with Lord Silas's child, Aria. It's too late to go back on the bond-mating."

"It's Stephan's. The baby is his."

Chapter Fourteen

Alaric's face flushed an unhealthy shade of red. He didn't move for several long seconds while everyone in the room froze, waiting for him to react to the revelation that his daughter was pregnant with the wrong Valeron's baby. Alaric had intentionally misinterpreted a Fate's prophecy to manipulate his daughter and Silas into a bond-mating because Silas, not Stephan, was the prime and heir of House Valeron.

Alaric glared at Stephan. "Is this true?"

"Yes," Stephan replied without flinching. He gathered Aria's limp hand in his own. "I love your daughter, Lord Alaric, and her child—our child—grows in her belly."

Alaric's fists were clenched at his sides, his anger visible in the unhealthy red-purple shade of his skin. For a moment, I was afraid he might strike Stephan. The younger man squared his shoulders and faced Aria's father.

"Father," Aria whispered, "I want the bond annulled... and..." She dragged in raspy, shallow breaths. "Your blessing... Stephan as... my life mate."

Alaric's wrath refocused on Silas. "Did you know about this?"

"I won't object to the annulment," Silas replied carefully.

The color continued to rise on Alaric's cheeks. "Gods dammit, Aria! No! This is foolishness. Your child is already accepted as the future heir to House Valeron. You can't renege on this bond! I won't allow it."

"Then I refuse the treatment." She looked at the Healers, her gaze steely and determined. "Witness... my final desires."

"So witnessed," the female Healer replied formally, her eyes as big as saucers as she watched the drama unfold.

"Aria!" Alaric snapped.

"Father. Do you want..." She paused as she struggled for breath. "Me to die without... heir to our House?"

Alaric's face went from red to purple. He glowered at his daughter. She stared back, unwilling to submit even though death was knocking on her door. The family resemblance was obvious in the stubborn set of their jaws. Neither was going to budge.

"I love Stephan," she said.

"We're running out of time," I whispered.

Silas spoke urgently to Alaric. "Do it, and I'll cede my rights as Prime. If you allow their formal mating, Stephan's child will inherit the Prime rights to House Valeron."

Alaric snorted. "There is no precedent for permanently ceding your birthright while you're alive, you obstinate arse. No one would recognize Stephan as Prime of this House. How can they when you could reclaim your right at any time?"

"I will not reclaim the Prime title," Silas said. "You have my word as my bond."

The two men stared at each other. I clenched Marcel's charm in my fist. Every moment wasted was a step closer to Aria's death. We didn't have time for Alaric to negotiate a deal over his daughter's deathbed, and this offer would solve all of our problems.

"I accept your word as your bond," Alaric finally said. "But this is a slight to my House, and I demand recompense."

"Oh, for crying out loud!" I exclaimed. "You're willing to let your own daughter die over your wounded pride? Aria would still be bonded to the Prime of one of the most powerful Houses in Aeterna, and their child will inherit all of this."

I waved my hand around the room angrily. Obviously, the power and wealth were what he wanted, even if no one else was blunt enough to say it. If I hadn't known firsthand how much Aria loved Stephan, and the fact that Silas wanted nothing to do with the politics and fame that came with his family name, I would be kicking Alaric's ass instead of helping him get his greedy hands on exactly what he wanted.

"If you don't agree to Silas's deal," I continued, "I'll make it my personal mission to make sure everyone knows how you abused your position as Lord Magister. *You* misinterpreted the prophecy to force Aria and Silas into a bond-mating neither of them wanted—all for your own benefit." I hit him with my hard stare. "Take the damn deal."

"You can't do any such thing," Alaric said with a huff of indignation.

"Technically," Silas said, "as a rightful party to the original prophecy, she can bring her grievance before the Council. The Fates only know if they will vote in her favor, but I will do everything within my power as Acting Lord Councilor to make sure the investigation is as public and scandalous as possible."

"You wouldn't dare!" Alaric said with a hiss.

Silas's eyebrows rose. "Wouldn't I?"

They stared at each other in a battle of wills that had the color rising on Alaric's cheeks again. Alaric grunted and muttered words that sounded a lot like "ungrateful" and "blackmail," but his magic rose around him. "As Lord Magister of the Aeternal Council, I declare the bond-mating between Lady Aria of House Certus and Lord Silas of House Valeron to be annulled."

Threads of magic uncoiled between Aria and Silas, sparking a small flare in the room.

"Thank you." Aria exhaled weakly before her eyelids fluttered, and she crumpled into unconsciousness.

"Hurry!" Stephan said.

The Healers' magic flooded the room as they laid their hands on her body, chanting to keep their magic in tandem, and the conjuring settled over Aria.

I held the brush in my left hand and placed the other over Aria's heart. "I'll draw the tainted power first. Silas, I'll let you know when to form your House bond."

"Stephan will do it," Alaric said. "As the Prime of House Valeron."

Both Silas and Stephan jerked in surprise.

"The Prime ritual takes days," Silas objected.

"Forget all the pomp and circumstance," Alaric replied. "We just need to transfer the Prime rights."

Stephan blinked. "It's a blood ritual. We don't have time for that."

"You'll do it, or I'll consider this an attempt to renege on your word," Alaric said.

Silas's jaw clenched, but his magic blazed around him, and a large dramatically serrated knife landed in his hand. The carved hilt bore the Valeron House sigil.

Alaric held out his hands in a cupped position, and Silas ripped the knife across his own forearm in a long gash. "I, Silas Valeron, hereby release the Prime rights of House Valeron, and name Stephan Valeron in my stead."

Silas's blood pooled into Alaric's hands as he turned to Stephan and said, "Anoint yourself in the blood of your kin, and claim your Prime rights, heir of House Valeron."

Alaric smeared the blood on Stephan's forearm as the Lord Magister's magic wove into a relatively simple two-layered conjuring. Alaric placed one palm over Silas's cut arm and the other on Stephan's, and his magic sank into both men, as the Prime rights transferred between them.

"It's done," Alaric declared.

"You're such an asshole," I told Alaric as Silas's flesh knit back together.

Alaric's mouth thinned. "But not a fool."

"We need to get started," Stephan said. "Aria doesn't have time for any more delays."

If it weren't a life-and-death situation, we'd all be celebrating the release of the bond-mating, but we would have to save that for after this magic transfusion was finished.

This has to work. Aria and the baby can't die on us after all of this.

I let my magic fill me. It was a little strange to access Silas's source instead of my own, more familiar source, but the sweet power still filled me with familiar ecstasy. I sank my magic into Aria and instantly realized she was going to need a hell of a magic transfusion. Her energy was barely a blip in my awareness. The amount of magic I would be able to transfer to her without a direct bond wasn't going to be enough, and I needed a stronger connection to her. I made a split-second decision and built the layers of the bonding spell so I could connect with her directly.

I pushed the magic over Aria's forearm, and my sigil appeared on her flesh—two overlapping triangles looping together in the center. But the sigil had another layer I wasn't expecting. The connected circles of House Valeron crossed, perpendicular, over the triangles, linking themselves into the pattern.

"Whoa! Did you see that?" I asked Silas. He would have been able to see the brand for a moment just before it faded into her flesh. "Did I just give her the Valeron brand with my own?"

Silas's face was pinched in confusion. "What did you do?"

"I was trying to create a direct bond, but it's... that's your House sigil combined with mine."

"It's not possible for anyone but the Prime to pass on a House sigil," Alaric mused.

"It shouldn't be," Silas agreed. "She's right. I can feel Aria's presence through the bond, but it's filtered through Maeve."

I glanced at Stephan. "Can you sense her too? Is it connected to both of you?"

"Figure it out later!" Stephan snapped. "We must hurry."

Right. We had more urgent things to worry about, like doing the first-ever magic transfusion. Now that we were connected through a bond, I could feel the poison within Aria's magic, spreading through her like ink soaking into the fibers of paper. I could also sense the smaller life energy of the baby inside her. I didn't allow myself time to dwell on the too-weak connection to the tiny, fragile life inside my friend.

I reached for Silas's hand. "I'm ready to channel your source."

He placed his hand in mine, and I focused on the bad energy in Aria. I reminded myself not to absorb it. I didn't want to get myself poisoned.

"Stephan and Silas, get ready to channel as much clean energy through your source as you can. I'll transfer it to Aria. But not until I tell you, okay? We have to time this really carefully."

The energy was like a dark mass inside of Aria. I reached for it and drew it slowly away from her. Even with the obvious tainted feeling, it was hard not to absorb the power. All magic was slightly addictive, and the urge to control it was instinctive, but I gritted my teeth and focused on pushing the power into the wooden brush gripped in my hand. A sour taste filled my mouth. I exhaled through my nose and focused on not allowing a single drop to enter me.

Through the haze of my concentration, I heard the soft, distant voice of the male Healer. "She's fading."

"I'm holding her heart steady," the female Healer said.

Closing my eyes, I pulled as much as I dared, channeled it into the wood element, and then paused so I could reach for Silas's magic. He was strong and steady through the bond, and beyond him, I felt Stephan, also connected to their family source. Once I was certain I had a good grasp on that power, I felt back through the bond to Aria and directed power into her. I did it twice more, but she was still weak. The transfusion was helping, but not fast enough.

"She's not breathing," the female Healer said, her voice rising in pitch. The energy in the room pulled tight as another healing spell settled over Aria.

I couldn't risk delaying any longer. "Silas, Stephan," I whispered, "channel as much as you can to me now."

A huge infusion of magic swelled from them, and I braced myself against it, funneling the energy to Aria in a controlled stream through our new shared bond.

"Come on, Aria." I pulled more of the tainted magic away in smaller bursts, storing it inside the brush and alternating with influxes of good energy. The wood warmed under my hand as each new wave flooded Aria and filled her body with fresh energy. Each round cleared out more and more of the tainted magic, but she still felt distant, and the baby was a barely flickering presence.

"She's not improving," the female Healer said.

"The infant is in distress," the male said.

I gritted my teeth. Between the three of us, we'd pushed enough clean magic into her to fuel two people, but she wasn't responding. "Stephan, try to draw her back. She's got to help us fight this. Throw everything you've got at her."

A sense of love and belonging filled the room. I felt it through the bond and through Stephan's empathic projection. I squeezed Silas's hand tighter as the feelings washed over us all, and I hoped Aria could feel it too. She had to fight her way back to us.

"Aria?" Stephan stroked back the hair from her face. "Come back to me. Please don't leave me. Come on, love. Fight."

My whole body started shaking as I pulled magic from Silas, Stephan, and myself, straining to give Aria more fresh energy. Everything inside of me focused on pressing every last drop of magic back into Aria. She wasn't going to leave us like this. I wouldn't let her. I thrust wave after wave of magic into her as fast as I could until I started to feel faint, but I didn't dare let up.

"The infant's heart is in arrest," the male Healer said. "It's too much stress."

I couldn't let them die. I wouldn't be responsible for that level of tragedy. "Alaric, cut her off from your source now," I said.

I felt a wave of new magic wash over us—Alaric's. The taint within it was like a film of grease on my subconscious, and then it was gone.

Alaric's voice was rough and gravelly. "It is done."

Aria's entire body convulsed, shaking the bed as her head rocked back and jerked wildly. Her arms and legs started twitching violently.

"She's in seizure." The Healers worked frantically, weaving healing spells for her failing vitals.

I pushed more magic into her, drawing from deep inside my own well of magic. *Please, please, please.* Magic streamed through me and into her, more than replacing the bad we'd drawn out, but she wasn't recovering. I kept pushing.

"Cardiac arrest. Respiratory failure."

"She's not breathing!" Stephan cried out.

No! I wouldn't allow even one more death. I gathered everything inside of me and slammed it into Aria. I didn't hold anything back. Something inside of my magic expanded so wide it made me gasp, and my eyes flew open at the almost audible popping sensation from deep inside of me.

I cried out as a burst of magic left me and flooded through our bond. A brilliant flare of pure magic filled the room with power so strong it was translucent. Like the dead rising, Aria jerked upright in the bed. Her blue eyes were wide as she drew a sharp breath, and her face flushed a healthy pink color.

"Aria!" Stephan pulled her into his arms.

They embraced in a fit of tears and relief as the Healers confirmed what we could already see with our eyes and feel through the bond—Aria and the baby were cured. Alaric and Silas converged over Aria, and the Healers congratulated each other. I sagged onto my knees at her bedside, so overcome with relief that I almost fainted. My vision went a little blurry around the edges as I wiped away tears.

Silas flashed another one of his rare smiles, and my heart flooded with happiness. We'd done it. Aria and the baby would both be okay.

When I stood, my vision warped into black smudges. I rocked back on my heels and reached for Silas to steady myself.

"Maeve?" Silas's concerned face slid sideways.

The room kept moving as my vision narrowed to a tiny tunnel of light. My body felt hot, like a fever had broken over me.

"Shite!" Silas grabbed me and lowered me to the floor as everything went dark. "She's infected!"

Chapter Fifteen

The Healers hovered over me, their warm magic spreading through my body.

"If she took too much..."

Blood pounded in my ears. The magic was burning me, and I was so hot. *Fire. I'm on fire from the inside out.*

"Without an Anchor."

"Are you sure?"

My head was spinning. I couldn't follow the conversation. *Oh dear gods, I'm going to die. Why did I have to be so stupid?* Silas had warned me that my plan was risky, but I'd been so sure I could do it. If I died, there'd be no one to stop the prophecy about Silas's death. My Sect would fall under attack from all our enemies at once. My panic reached up and gripped me around the throat.

"She's not..."

"But we don't..."

The cool rush of Silas's magic flowed over me, and I gulped greedily at the wave of fresh energy spreading through me. Another wave of power sent tingles shooting from my head to my toes, like a numb limb coming back awake. Slowly, the world stopped spinning, and the fire burning me from the inside out started to retreat.

I opened my eyes and found myself in one of the sitting rooms in the Prime suite with Silas glaring down at me. Giving him a wary glance, I pushed up to a sitting position and waved off the Healers hovering around us. "Is Aria okay? The baby?"

Silas's voice was a near snarl as he said, "They are fine. Unlike you."

Might as well get this fight over with. The risk of absorbing the poison had been worth saving Aria's—and the baby's—lives. My hand went to my forehead. "How did you get the poisoned magic out of me?"

"Gods dammit, Maeve! You weren't poisoned. You overextended yourself and drained too much of your own magic."

I blinked at him as that settled in. "It wasn't the poison?"

"Maeve!" Silas threw his hands in the air and started pacing. "You burned through your magic, and you could have died! You put yourself in serious danger. I had to pour energy into you through our bond."

Relief flooded me. "Thanks for giving me a boost. I'm fine now, and you're overreacting."

Silas growled. It was kind of sexy. The tingling started to spread to other parts of my body. A posttransfer sexual buzz was definitely building. I was growing more familiar with this side effect. I eyed him speculatively. Maybe I could take advantage of some alone time with Silas.

He huffed, exasperated. "Can you access your magic?"

"Buzzkill." I reached for my magic, because he wasn't going to let it go until I showed him that I was fine.

Nothing.

I tried several times, but I couldn't get a handle on my magic. Even though I could sense it, I couldn't do anything with it. It slipped through my fingers like sand. A shiver of fear welled up inside me.

"As I suspected," Silas said, his eyes narrowed with anger. "You burned out your magic."

"I don't have *any* magic?" True panic bubbled up my throat. Without my magic, I was defenseless against the Fae, the Brotherhood, and the Council. And I was trapped in Aeterna. *Fates curse me—I'm useless without magic.*

"It's temporary—it's only until your power regenerates." Silas raised an irate eyebrow. "It could be a few days or a week. It depends on how close to *dying* you actually were."

I swallowed back the panic. I'd been without magic before, and this would pass eventually, but the spike in my adrenaline made me shaky. Silas helped me stand, his arms around my waist. Everything felt wobbly, and I couldn't seem to coordinate my feet with my legs.

Without warning, Silas swung me up into his arms and walked out of the suite.

Oh no, he didn't. Not again. I waved my hands at the ridiculous position he cradled me in. "This is really not necessary, Silas. I can walk... I just need a minute."

His footsteps pounded down the long marble hallway as he focused straight ahead. "Don't argue with me. I'm quite livid right now. You're not taking any consideration for your own life."

I smacked his chest. "You don't get to go self-righteous on me, buddy. I just miscalculated how much magic it would take to heal Aria."

His scowl deepened.

"I will even admit that I panicked when she didn't respond, and I went too far. But you..." I poked him in the chest. "You don't get to point fingers, Mr. 'Death's Fury.' How many times have you risked your life on the battlefield?"

"That is different." His steps pounded down the hallway.

I snorted. "When you went into a fight against Titus without your full magic capacity, did I call you out for being reckless? No. Because I knew you could handle it. It's what you do. High-powered magic mojo is what I do. You owe me the same respect."

"Almost dying isn't 'handling it,' Maeve."

His mouth was set in a stubborn line, and I had the sudden urge to run my lips along the stubble edging the strong planes of his jaw. I inhaled the crisp, clean smell of him. The posttransfer tingles were getting stronger.

"I took a calculated risk," I said.

He opened his mouth to argue, and I did the only thing I could think of to end this fight—I wrapped my arms around his neck, and I kissed him. Silas stopped walking and kissed me back, his arms pulling me tighter in his embrace until my whole body lit with anticipation.

He pulled back suddenly. "What are you doing?"

I kissed up the side of his neck. "What does it look like I'm doing?"

"You're experiencing a side effect of the power sharing."

"Don't tell me you're not feeling it too." I rubbed my fingers across the hard muscles of his chest. "I'm sorry I scared you. Let me make it up to you..."

He snorted and started walking again. I positioned myself in his arms so I could slide my hand downward. A throaty moan slipped out when I found the bulge there.

He came to a full stop in the middle of the hallway. His eyes drifted to my mouth. Butterflies went wild in my stomach.

"You're magic drunk, and I am very angry with you right now." He shifted, removed my hand, and dropped it back into my lap before he started walking again, his eyes fixed down the hall.

"Everything turned out fine. Aria's healed, and I'll be recovered in no time. You can't seriously be mad at me."

He set me down on my feet so suddenly that I had to lean against the wall to keep from falling over. "Fine?" His face was twisted with serious anger. "You almost died, Maeve! Do you even know how close that was? You released your core energy into Aria!

Did you even think about what you were doing before you let your never-ending guilt push you into recklessness yet again?"

"Excuse me?" My voice rose as my temper steadied my legs.

"Your guilt is going to get you killed! It radiates off you every moment of every minute, and I'm tired of you making stupid, reckless decisions."

I wanted to object but could only manage an indignant huff before he was in my face again.

"It wasn't your fault," he said.

"What the hell are you talking about?"

"Titus killed half your Sect in that battle. Not you. He's responsible for the murder of your entire family. Not you."

My chest thumped painfully. "Shut up."

He pushed closer to me as I took a shaky step backward. "Atticus's death wasn't your fault. He knew the risks when he agreed to infiltrate the Brotherhood."

"I said shut up, Silas." My heart pounded furiously in my chest, and tears stung behind my eyes.

"No." He got right in my face. "I want you to say it. It wasn't your fault."

"Screw you." I pulled away from him. "I don't have to stay here and listen to this."

He grabbed me by the arm. "I'm too selfish to watch you continue down this path until you end up dead. So we're going to deal with this right here and now." His magic rose around him, and the ceremonial dagger appeared in his hand again.

"What are you doing?" I asked.

He jerked me closer to him. In a quick, angry movement, he bared the flesh of my forearm. He slapped the knife into my free hand and shoved up the sleeve of his own shirt. I examined the four parallel scars across his forearm. The last mark was from Atticus's father—penance for Atticus's death.

"Commanders bear a mark for every failure. Make your mark, and move on," he demanded.

"I don't—"

He pushed the blade's edge against my forearm, while his other hand gripped mine. His steel-gray eyes bored into me. "If you were responsible for their deaths, then admit it, and take responsibility so you can move on. Do it."

With the knife poised over my flesh, a well of emotion sprang up inside of me. I wanted the pain. I wanted to suffer for the mistakes I'd made and bear the scars for everyone to see. Fresh hurt flared inside my chest. The guilt of all the deaths had been eating me from the inside out, and Silas was right—I hadn't dealt with it.

"It *was* my fault," I whispered.

"You're wallowing in guilt that isn't yours."

I fought back the tears stinging my eyes. "I told them to fight. I convinced them we could win."

"You enabled your Sect to fight their enemy, and you won. You stopped the Brotherhood from controlling Earth's magic."

"I got hundreds of people killed."

Silas's face was hard. Unyielding. "You saved millions."

"We could have run. They didn't have to die."

"Titus would have followed you to the very ends of your realm and any you fled to."

"I should have..." My voice quivered as I gripped the knife. "I could have... my family..."

"What?" Silas demanded. "What exactly did *you* do to cause their deaths?"

I wanted so badly to tell him how I'd caused all the deaths of everyone who died fighting the Brotherhood—and how I could have stopped my mother's death all those years ago. I opened my mouth several times to do just that, but nothing came out. If we'd run, Titus would have chased us. If we'd hidden, he would have found us. We fought, and so many had died, but I hadn't killed our people—Titus had. I couldn't have saved my mother. The Brotherhood had hunted my people for almost a decade, picking us off one by one, and she'd been a victim of their actions, not mine.

I felt responsible for the deaths of Marcel, my father, and my aunt. I even blamed myself for my mother's murder, but I was just a child. Titus was the one who'd killed my family because he wanted our ability to absorb magic, not because of anything I'd done. With the knife poised over my flesh, ready to brand me for each death I'd caused, I couldn't take responsibility for all of that.

But I had directly caused at least one death. My throat tightened painfully. "What about Atticus? I... I held his life in my hands, and I let him go, Silas. I let Titus take Atticus's life as a distraction. I could have saved him."

"Atticus sacrificed himself to save all of us. I was there, and I saw it all. You didn't ask Atticus to do what he did. That *distraction* bought you the time you needed to kill Titus and save everyone on that battlefield. You're diminishing Atticus's sacrifice by claiming his actions as your failure. Honor his decision, and lay the blame where it belongs."

My guilt had made me second-guess every part of my life since that day. I had no confidence with the Inner Circle, letting them dictate how I could be a good leader instead of trusting my instincts. I'd nearly given up my commitment to find a way for Silas and me to be together, and I'd been downright miserable for months.

"Every single person went into that battle willingly," Silas said gently. "Even Atticus. It wasn't your fault, Maeve. Let your guilt go."

Tears leaked from my eyes, and the knife clattered to the floor as I folded myself into Silas's arms. He held me as I cried. I cried for my family and for all the families who had lost loved ones. I cried for my lost childhood and the bad choices I'd made in the wake of grief. And I cried for Atticus—my friend, who had chosen to sacrifice his life to save mine.

"It wasn't my fault," I whispered into his tear-soaked shirt.

Silas held me, quietly stroking my hair until I'd cried myself out.

Eventually, I untangled myself from Silas's arms. "Thank you. How did you know what I needed to hear?"

He wiped the tears from my face with a tenderness that I never would have suspected him capable of when we first met. "Tessa paid me the same favor once."

"Did you cry like a baby?" I asked, wiping under my puffy eyes.

One side of his mouth lifted. "Only after she kicked my arse three ways to the post and back."

I let out a small chuckle. "Thanks for skipping that step."

Silas led me down the hallway and into the dining room. He set me down at the table, and I had a flash of memory back to when Atticus had sat there and tried to steal my bacon. It seemed like a lifetime ago. Fresh guilt welled up as I remembered him eating through three people's worth of food.

I didn't let myself wallow this time. Atticus deserved better. My people deserved a leader who didn't second-guess her every decision. They deserved better, and I would do better, starting with finding Nuada. He was back in my realm, and I knew what I had to do to stop him, even if the Inner Circle would disagree. It was time to step up and lead.

A servant appeared with a tray of crunchy root vegetables, and Silas handed me something that resembled a purple carrot. "It's no cow burger, but you should eat and keep up your strength."

I bit into it with a wry laugh and grimaced at the bitter taste. It wasn't quite so nasty a few bites in—I was hungrier than I'd realized. When I finished, he handed me another one and pushed a glass of water toward me.

It was time to make the leap. Casius was always saying a leader had to make the hard decisions. "We need Nuada to give us the antidote," I said. "But it's going to be impossible to pry him out of the Fae haven."

Silas stopped chewing. "Are you reconsidering the legion?"

"No." I leveled my purple root at him. "You can't take a hundred super-conspicuous, magically powerful warriors into Earth to start a battle with the Fae." I paused, trying to sort through the plan forming in my mind. "How many Guardians would you need to search for Kianna?"

"Lady Kianna?" His brow scrunched. "Her safe return was only one of Nuada's demands. What about the rest?"

"If we find Kianna and prove that the Council had nothing to do with her kidnapping, *all* Nuada's demands will be unjustified. The Fae are all about truth and bargains, right? We'll safely return Kianna, prove that the Council wasn't responsible, and demand the antidote. But you'll have to promise that the Council won't retaliate against the Fae for what Nuada did."

"You can't be serious," Silas said. "Nuada must face punishment for his actions. People are dying. He attacked Lord Alaric!"

"Nuada isn't going to agree to any deal that doesn't give him immunity. As much as I'd love to see him pay for what he did, we have to work with him to get the antidote."

After a moment, Silas said, "The Council is not going to like it."

"I don't like it either, but helping the people in Lower Aeterna is more important. Do you think the Council will agree to the terms if we can negotiate a deal with Nuada?"

Silas grinned sharply. "Well, there's at least one good thing my new position can offer. I get to make that decision. The rest of the Councilors may not be happy with me after the fact, but it's better to ask forgiveness before permission, as your people say."

"That's not exactly what they say, but that makes this easier for sure." I toyed with Treva's bone ring hanging on my necklace. "I don't think Kianna is in Aeterna. After Nuada poisoned the Citizen Source, the Councilors would have released her for the antidote. Whoever took her was from Earth."

"I agree. And access between our realms has been restricted. If she went missing in your realm, she's still there."

"Even a legion of Guardians wouldn't be able to find her without some idea of where to start. Lady Treva gave me this ring, but I haven't been able to get a tracing spell to work on it."

Silas hummed thoughtfully. "We can't trace her location, but maybe we can use it to scry on her."

"Isn't that like hokey witchcraft stuff? Hit or miss?"

Scrying was simple in concept—you could infuse an object with a small amount of magic and use it to view or listen in on the owner. The practice had fallen out of favor, except in Mundane folklore, because scrying an object left an energy trail that made it obvious the object had been tampered with. It was also notoriously unreliable.

"I happen to know someone who spent her entire first year in Guardian training hiding scrying objects in a certain lieutenant's quarters. She said it was for blackmail, but I think Tessa had a crush on her."

"Tessa?" I suppressed a smirk.

"Oh yes," Silas said. "Tessa got more punishments than any other first-year trainee. She's quite proud of that, and her arcane scrying skills are legendary."

I laughed and then sobered quickly. "Then the three of us need to get back to my realm as soon as possible. We might be able to return through the portal without drawing too much attention if we arrive during one of the already scheduled windows." I swallowed the last of my purple carrot. "We could hit the evening one today if we hurry."

"You're worried the Circle won't approve of bringing me and Tessa back to Earth."

"It's the right thing to do." I shrugged. "And I hear it's easier to ask for forgiveness than permission."

He looped his foot around my chair leg and pulled me closer to him, kissing me until I forgot my insecurities about disappointing my people. I decided to let my worries go for a minute and enjoy finally being with the man who had my heart. Kissing Silas was like magic—all tingles and happiness—and I needed as much of that in my life as I could get.

"I'm going to have a big mess to sort out when we get back. Casius wasn't happy when I left."

A sly grin spread across Silas's face. "He'll be even less pleased that I'm returning with you."

"He'll deal," I promised. Silas was a part of my life, and a good leader knew when to listen to what others wanted and when to follow her heart. My mother had taught me that much. I bit my lip. "Speaking of getting my powers back... we've got a couple of hours. Do you want to go for another swim?"

Chapter Sixteen

A couple of hours later, I was feeling much more emotionally centered. Even though sharing power through our Aegis bond didn't fully replace my depleted magic, sex with Silas was still mind-blowingly good. My powers were just strong enough that I could generate a small flare, but nothing else. I didn't have enough magic to even conjure a simple first-level spell.

When we arrived through the portal to Earth that evening, we found that the atrium had been cleaned up but not yet fully repaired. The scorched marble floor was a vivid reminder of how much repair work lay ahead of us—especially between Silas and my mentor.

I'd hoped to casually slip into our realm, but the guards stationed there had specific instructions for my return, and they marched us to Casius. I tried not to question my own conviction as my own people escorted us like enemies to the circle room to appear before the Inner Circle.

Casius's expression immediately darkened when he saw me return with Silas and Tessa by my side. The same reaction spread across the faces of everyone seated around the circular stone table, including Alannah, Gia, and Levi. Even Ethan, leaning against the wall behind Alannah's chair, withheld his ever-present grin as he took in my entourage.

What the hell is Ethan doing there? Technically, he wasn't sitting at the table, but he wasn't sitting in the spectators' seats either.

That was when I noticed that those seats were empty for the first time that I could remember. The Circle was in a closed session, just like Alannah wanted. A closed session with her—and her son—in the center of it all.

I wondered what other changes she'd manipulated in the short time I'd been gone. Gods, she wasn't even officially part of the Sect. She'd probably hold out until I produced an actual baby she could rip out of my arms.

As I explained the full details of the situation with Nuada and the poisoned Citizen Source, Gia huffed and shook her head in a way that set my teeth on edge. I didn't know if it was her pregnancy hormones or her natural disposition, but Gia seemed to hate me on principle. Just as well. The entire Circle was about to drag me over the coals—maybe she would be able to work out some of her irrational hatred of me in the process.

As soon as I finished, Alannah jumped in and got the party started. "You have no authority to promise our help to the Aeternal Council. Tracking down Lord Nuada's daughter is not our concern, nor will we allow *him* loose in our realm."

The "him" in question stayed blessedly quiet at my side, but I could feel his annoyance through our bond. My own anger was about to boil over from the incredible amount of misplaced authority coming off Alannah, but I managed to keep my mouth shut as I waited for Casius to weigh in. It didn't matter what Alannah thought or said. Casius was the person who could block us from finding Kianna and send Silas back to Aeterna permanently.

When he finally spoke, his brows furrowed, and his voice was accusing. "How can you justify involving our Sect in a conflict between the Aeternal Council and the Fae? Finding Nuada isn't our problem to solve."

That comment was aimed at my guilt and insecurities. And I would have let it score a direct hit, too, if I hadn't realized how all those misplaced fears had made me a worse leader.

I squared my shoulders, meeting each person's eyes. "It's the right thing to do. Thousands of people will die in Aeterna if we don't do something. But if that isn't enough of a reason, try this: our Sect can't fight Elias *and* the Fae. If we allow the Fae to weaken the Council, which I feel I should remind you is our only ally at the moment, we're setting ourselves up for a battle we can't win. Because sure as shit, Elias or the Fae will take the opportunity to attack us at our weakest. Ignoring our allies when they need us is shortsighted, even if you don't like them."

Casius frowned. Even though it was hard not to continue to argue my case, I let my words settle. If I pushed him, he'd revert to his natural dislike of the Council, Aeternals in general, and my boyfriend specifically. My logic was sound, and rational argument was the best way to convince my mentor.

"I'd like to point out," Alannah said, "that bringing a member of the Aeternal Council to Earth violates our treaty and undermines our authority."

I glared at her. "Until you sign on the dotted line and rejoin the Sect, I don't remember you being part of 'our treaty,' Alannah. I'm happy to get you a pen right now so you can actually put some skin in the game."

Alannah's nostrils flared. "Gladly. After you finalize your bond-mating with my son."

From his spot against the wall, Ethan's handsome face twitched into a frown. I felt Silas's surprise through our bond, but I kept my eyes locked on Alannah. I didn't need to see her gaze flick to Silas, or the satisfied twitch of her lips, to know she was aware of exactly what she was doing.

"I told you I would *consider* the proposal, and I have. If you want my answer right now, I'd be happy to give it to you."

"Maeve…" Casius warned.

Alannah and I glowered as the entire room went quiet.

Silas broke the tense silence as he stepped forward and said, "I'm ready to renegotiate the treaty between the Council and the Inner Circle."

"Under whose authority?" Alannah snapped.

"Mine. I am the Acting Lord Councilor for the Aeternal Council." The snarl in his voice appeared briefly on his face, but I couldn't sense his emotions through our Aegis bond. He'd apparently locked it down tighter than Fort Knox.

Casius's fist started tapping against his thigh. Feathers were just about literally ruffled all around the table as everyone in the Circle digested Silas's statement. Not only did they have a member of the Aeternal Council on their turf—they had the leader. No one looked happy about Silas's promotion.

Temporary promotion, I reminded myself.

"These are our terms," Silas continued. "In addition to access to Earth to solve the *joint problem* Nuada has created, I also require that the ban on Council members be lifted and never reinstated. I personally plan on spending quite a bit of time here."

Heat crept up my neck, but no one looked at me—not even Ethan, whose unhappy gaze was locked on Silas.

"Why on Earth would we do that?" Alannah sputtered.

"In exchange," Silas continued as if she hadn't interrupted, "I'm going to stop Nuada—the greatest threat to your new autonomy—and I'll teach you how to conjure a new shield around your portal."

Casius planted his feet wide. "The shielding *you* tore down."

Silas didn't flinch. "Yes. I see it's not yet repaired. I'm offering to build you a better one."

"It collapses at the third-layer binding," Tamara offered immediately.

"How long would it take you to research and stabilize your level-three shield?" Silas asked.

"A few weeks probably," Tamara said.

"I can build you a level-five shield," Silas said to the group.

Casius pursed his lips, but Tamara's chocolate-brown eyes danced with excitement. She'd been winging everything since Thomas died. His notes, although meticulous, weren't enough to make up for everything we didn't know, and we'd been struggling. The hope glinting in her eyes made me bite back a smile.

One vote in favor, three more to go.

"In fact, if you'll let me lead your conjuring circle, I'll fortify your perimeter shield as well." Silas sounded only mildly smug until he added, "It might be harder for the Fae to break through it next time."

Casius's face puckered like he'd just sucked on a lemon. Silas threw a challenging smirk at him, and I repressed a groan. Backing my mentor into a corner wasn't going to be good for Silas's long-term relationship with my Sect, which wasn't good for *our* long-term relationship prospects.

"The Aeternals are our allies," I interjected. "Not only do we have a mutual enemy, but we also have an aid stipulation in our agreement." *Thank you, Octavia, for that reminder.* "We all benefit from working together."

Levi leaned forward, his palms flat on the table. "We cannot trust a member of the Council to build the shield for us. He could compromise it without our knowing. He could conjure it in a way that causes it to fail when we need it most. The Council will never give away more than they get in return, which means this deal is skewed in his favor, even if we don't know how yet."

Silas's brow quirked upward. "Your people can see the patterns of magic, can you not? How can I possibly do such a thing under your supervision? Bring your entire Sect to witness it, if you like." His head tilted thoughtfully. "In fact, I insist that the Sect gather to watch."

"Why?" Gia asked, speaking for the first time.

Silas smiled, and it was not friendly. "I want your people to see our alliance in action. The Council and the Circle working in concert to protect them will help pave the path forward."

Gia frowned, but neither she nor Levi voiced any additional objections. Even Alannah was uncharacteristically silent. Silas's argument was sound. It would be hard for him to sneak some kind of back door into the spell, and his offer to repair both shields would put us leaps ahead of anything we could manage on our own.

"Isn't fortifying our defenses worth the small price of allowing our *allies* access to this realm?" I asked. "And think of the positive impact to our magical knowledge. Just by seeing Silas build this shield, we'll save months of experimenting."

"Years," Tamara agreed enthusiastically. "Even Thomas didn't know how to conjure a level-five shield that big."

Slowly, heads started to bob around the table, but our new recruits seemed the least convinced. Levi was positively skittish, his eyes darting around the room like we might come under attack any second. Gia rocked back on her heels, and Alannah glowered. I made a point of not making eye contact with Ethan.

"Pick your battles carefully, *Lord Councilor*. You can't win them all." Casius glanced at me, making his meaning crystal clear. He would never support our relationship, and after this, he'd probably do everything in his power to get in the way.

"I pick my battles to win my wars, Lord Casius." Silas's tone was full of steely promise. "And I'm the *Acting* Lord Councilor. It's not a permanent seating."

"You won't get your way next time, Fates willing." Casius huffed in angry defeat. "Who votes in favor of having him repair the shield in exchange for access to Earth?"

Tamara, Seth, and I were the only ones in favor. I looked around, waiting for anyone else to join us, but no other hands were raised.

"Against?" Casius asked.

Jason and Rhonda lifted their hands to object... along with Alannah, Gia, and Levi.

I cleared my throat. "Since the delegates aren't officially members of this Sect until the binding ceremony, they don't get a vote."

Alannah's face puckered.

Suck that, you harpy.

Without the three votes from the delegates, it was a tie. Almost as one, we all turned to Casius, waiting for his vote. If he sided with Jason and Rhonda, our tied vote wouldn't carry.

Surely, Casius wouldn't let his dislike of Silas keep him from making the smart decision for our Sect—not after all his talk about sacrificing for our people despite our personal feelings.

After what seemed like an eternity, Casius said, "We need to repair the shielding. Although I don't like making bargains with... our allies, our defenses are the top priority." He looked at Silas, and his face was hard. "We accept your terms on behalf of the Aeternal Council."

"I suggest we get started immediately," Silas said. "Time is short."

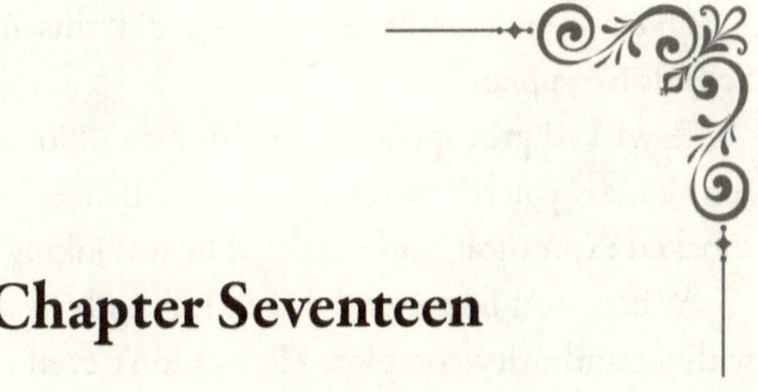

Chapter Seventeen

It took less than an hour for the entire Sect to gather in the grand atrium of the administration building. Everyone wanted to witness Silas build the shields, and the entire space was packed.

Several decades of running had left us with far fewer abilities than our Sect's founders. They'd created the entire Earthen Source, binding all of Earth's magic behind an impenetrable magic barrier that only our people could access, but just a few generations later, we couldn't even put up a level-three shield. So it wasn't a surprise that despite the general mistrust of the Council and Silas's personal reputation as the Council's enforcer, everyone gathered in the central administration building, eager to see him build the level-five shields.

Silas quickly solved the issue of my weak magic flare by asking me to be his Anchor. Combining our power, while separating me from the actual conjuring circle, would make it impossible to tell our magic apart since we'd both share a white aura.

While Tessa waited anxiously, eager to begin the search for Kianna, the Circle connected their magic, pooling the power that would fuel the conjuring. Silas pulled me a little off to the side and spoke in a low voice too quiet for anyone else to overhear. "This far from Aeterna, it would be best if I drew the power from your source. I'll do it through our bond to further aid the regeneration of your magic."

"Not as much fun as what we did this morning, but sure. Sounds like a plan."

A wicked grin spread across his face. "No, not nearly as much fun. Unless you're interested in an audience?" He laughed at my shocked expression, and I realized he was joking.

When we'd first met, I'd seen him only as an arrogant jackass with an authority complex. He wouldn't even crack a smile as we traded information question by question and carefully guarded our own secrets. Trying to decipher his motivations had been a full-time job, and he'd kept the bond between us completely locked down, not allowing me to sense any of his emotions. He'd been ruthless, arrogant, and commanding. But now I knew the depth of his loyalty, compassion, and love. His teasing sent a warm tingle down my spine as our shared love spread through our Aegis bond.

I held out my arm, and Silas slid his hand over the brand on my forearm. The familiar sensation of connecting through our bond flooded over me. Connected like this, I also had a direct link to his feelings. The primary one coming from him was a strong sense of determination and focus, but the little tug of self-satisfied smugness reminded me that he was all too aware of everyone, including Ethan, watching us share power.

The bright-white power of Earthen Source rose around us, and I let the sensation slide over my skin. It felt good to have the familiar magic flowing through me, even if it was Silas who was channeling it. The energy moved through every cell in my body, and I shivered with pleasure. A flash of possessiveness flowed through the bond just before Silas leaned in and kissed me hard on the mouth.

"What are you doing?" I hissed in surprise.

Shocked whispers ricocheted from every pair of lips. Sure enough, Alannah was practically spitting, and Ethan stood right beside her, his face scrunched into an unhappy glower. I didn't dare look to see Casius's reaction.

"Adding my application to your long list of suitors," he said, unrepentant.

"Silas, that was *not* helpful."

He put his lips next to my ear, no doubt further scandalizing everyone. "I'm not giving up that easily. My heart is yours, Maeve O'Neill. I want everyone to know it. Especially you."

My heart skipped. I could literally feel how much he loved me. The tingles that spread through me were more powerful and all encompassing than the strongest magic, and my body surged with remembered passion. I plastered a glare on my face, but Silas wasn't fooled. One of his eyebrows rose, clearly picking up on my frisky feelings through our bond.

"Will you get to work already?" I said. "You've got two shields to fix, Lord Councilor."

"That's *Acting* Lord Councilor, Lady Maeve." He stepped back from me with a formal bow, hiding his roguish grin. "At your command."

More people tittered, watching the display, until Silas pulled magic through our bond. The magic hit me all at once, and it freaking hurt. Every nerve ending stung as if my limbs had all fallen asleep at the same time, and my whole body ached. To the observers around us, I was bathed in Silas's white aura. No one would be able to tell that I was tapped out and magic was being forced through me. I gritted my teeth so I wouldn't give away the truth.

Silas connected to the conjuring circle and manipulated the energy they generated as he wove raw power into threads and the threads into layers. His hands rose from his sides as he built the conjuring like a tapestry. The first layer solidified in a matter of minutes, and he started on the second layer. Through the bond, I felt his concentration as he conjured a complex variation of the personal shield he used to protect himself, except a hundred times bigger, covering the entire campus.

He had a technique I'd never seen. He tied off the first complete layer and then threaded the bonding layer of the second one through the first. I wondered if this was the trick that Thomas had discovered to build out the multilayered shield. I wished I'd had the chance to ask him before he died.

I wish I'd done a lot of things before a lot of people died.

Silas paused his conjuring, and his brows pinched in concern as he looked over his shoulder at me. I remembered that every emotion was amplified when we were connected through our bond like this. I'd been about to continue down the well-worn road of guilt I'd recently decided to stop traveling.

"Sorry." I forced myself out of my old cycle of shame and focused on what we were doing.

The third layer went up and then the fourth. I held my breath as he built the fifth and final layer of magic. From the outside, Silas seemed completely relaxed and confident, but I could feel the strain he was under through our bond. This was hard work that required a great deal of concentration and stamina. Finally, he added an additional bonding layer and threaded it back through all five, finishing the conjuring more securely than any approach we'd tried previously. He tied it and anchored it deep into the Earth around our campus before the circle released the temporary shield they'd constructed after Nuada tore down the original one.

The end result was a dome of complex magic, carefully balanced and harmoniously built. Like a wind spinner, the magic twisted together and around within the conjuring, forming almost geometric shapes moving fluidly within the shield.

"It worked!" Tamara said. "I can't believe it! I mean, I can—no offense, Lord Councilor. It worked!"

I laughed as her joyous enthusiasm spread through the Sect. People cheered, and even Casius cracked a smile.

Silas repeated the process and quickly built a level-five shield around the portal, which was just as complex but took significantly less work because of the smaller size. "The shields around Aeterna require three people to disable, as a security measure. I took the liberty of adding that feature into yours as well, so you won't need a double shield any longer."

Casius was starting to speak when a commotion caught the corner of my vision, and I turned. A man's voice rang out. "Maeve O'Neill!"

Not again!

A man in jeans and a long-sleeved shirt held Gia in a chokehold across her neck, a knife gripped tight in his fist. She struggled, but her protruding stomach made her bulky and unable to put up much of a fight. With his free hand, he held up a pendant the size of a golf ball on a long silver chain.

Terrified cries swept through the crowd as they pushed and shoved to get away from the stranger holding the unknown magical object. I braced myself against the tide of panic as the bystanders fled, leaving only the Inner Circle, Silas, and Tessa, all bristling with weapons and magic. I focused my attention on the pendant in the man's hands, and a cold chill sank into my bones. The Brotherhood had used a pendant just like that to kidnap Aria and me.

I recognized the man's face, although I'd never met him before—he was the other man who had gone missing, the one Agent Lennart believed I'd kidnapped. I had to keep him alive so I could clear my name with DODSI. I stepped forward, holding my hands up. Silas growled for me to stay put, but the vision of Gia's death flashed in my mind.

"I'm Maeve."

The intruder's face was completely empty of emotion. "Surrender yourself, and the mother of your niece will live."

I had no idea what the hell he was talking about. But before I could reply, he dropped the pendant around Gia's neck and plunged the knife into his own chest. Dark, tainted magic rose around Gia, and she screamed before she disappeared.

The man fell dead to the ground with the knife stabbed grotesquely into his chest. I stared in mute shock as his blood spread in a crimson circle, staining the pristine white marble floor. The intruder's wide-open unfocused gaze held no life. My brain numbly registered that he'd killed himself to fuel a skimming spell, but I couldn't believe it. *It all happened so fast.*

Silas and Tessa were the first to reach the intruder. Silas checked his pulse and then shook his head. They searched his pockets and came up with a single folded piece of paper with my name on the outside. Silas unfolded it, revealing a handwritten message.

"It's an address in Idaho." Silas handed it to me with a raised brow.

I knew exactly where that address would be—an abandoned barn on the outskirts of the farm where the Brotherhood had murdered my mother, just like the vision that ended in Gia dying.

Rage flared inside me, breaking through my stupor. Elias had made a man kill himself so he could kidnap a vulnerable pregnant woman, and he had chosen the location of my mother's murder for the exchange. *I am going to kill him.*

My rage solidified into resolve as I realized I'd been so focused on stopping the vision of Kianna and getting the antidote from Nuada that I'd let Gia slip right through my fingers. Each of those visions was important, and I had to stop Gia from dying or Silas was next.

Casius squeezed my shoulder gently. Horrified, I moved away from the body as the pool of blood expanded on the floor.

"He's compelling and killing innocents to send me a message. They have nothing to do with our world." I swallowed back bile.

Elias's level of callous disregard for Mundane life made me sick. He needed to be stopped.

"This has happened before?" Silas's head jerked back.

I was so tired of the death that surrounded me. *What did the Fate say? My Moments are filled with death.*

"He's the second one." I stuffed the paper into my pocket.

"This is the *second* one?" Alannah demanded. "How did the first one get past your perimeter shield? And how did you never think to mention that the Brotherhood knows where you are?"

Casius dragged his hand through his hair as exhaustion wrinkled the edges of his eyes. "Elias is putting compulsion spells on Mundanes. They have no native magic of their own, so yes, they can breach the shield. We were working on a modification of the shield to prevent this, and until then, we have patrols to cover the perimeter."

"The patrols aren't enough," Tessa said.

"No shit," Ethan said.

Alannah's eyes bugged out as she realized the extent of our vulnerability to this kind of attack. But it was Ethan who said, "That man had a magic-infused artifact with him. How did *that* get through your shield?"

Casius opened his mouth and closed it again. He looked at Tamara.

"It couldn't have," Tamara said. "No outside magic can get through the shield."

"Someone on the inside gave the artifact to that man," Tessa concluded, her face grave.

Jason crossed his arms. "No, there's no way—"

"This was not only a kidnapping—it was an attempt to sabotage rebuilding a stronger shield," Silas said. "Did the last attack occur during a critical event?"

Slowly, the pieces started to click in my brain. Elias had known exactly when to send the man with the grenade, sabotaging our attempt to fortify the shield around the Aeternal portal. Then he'd compelled this attack during Silas's efforts to repair the shield. The timing was too perfect—too disastrous to be anything but planned. And someone had helped get that pendant through our shield.

A tense silence fell over us. If there was a spy in our midst, we couldn't trust anyone. The suspect list was too long. Everyone in our Sect knew everything about... well, everything. The Inner Circle meetings were open to the public, and all of our decisions were open votes. It could literally be anyone.

"Why would *anyone* in our Sect betray us to the Brotherhood?" I asked quietly. "It just doesn't make sense. They want us all dead."

"We may not know why until we find out who," Silas said.

"No." Casius shook his head, and his fingers started tapping. "No. Elias sent him. The artifact could have been dormant when he walked through the shield and activated as his life-essence fueled the skim. Or he could have walked through while the shield was down and hidden here until the right time."

Silence sat heavy in the room for a minute, then two. All the theories were possible, and there was no way to know which one was correct.

"If we have a traitor, we can't wait for them to strike again," I finally said. But I had no idea where to start. *How do you find a traitor when it could be literally anyone?*

"Well, shit!" Levi said. "That's our cue to get the hell outta here."

He whirled past Alannah, causing her to take a step backward and place one high-heeled foot in the slowly expanding puddle of blood on the floor. She peered down at it in horrified disgust.

"Levi! You can't leave now," I said. We couldn't afford for the summit to fall apart. "We're stronger together."

"We're a bigger target together," Levi retorted. "And *you* have a lot of enemies taking shots at you."

Alannah tore her eyes away from the blood on her shoe, her face pale. "The Brotherhood can walk through the shield at any moment. And you didn't tell us."

"They knew it this whole time!" Levi accused. "This is the second time."

"Elias is targeting you, not us." Alannah's voice was a hateful snarl as she whirled on me. "You've put us all at risk by not revealing his personal vendetta against you."

"This isn't *my* fault! Elias would be after our Sect either way," I replied.

"I won't put a target on my people's backs. You can't protect them any better than I can. We have nothing to gain from an alliance here." She turned to leave. "Come on, Ethan. We're going home."

Magic washed over me, and I had just enough time to inhale before I was sucked into another vision.

Alannah walks away from me, her back ramrod straight and her heels clicking on the hard stone floor. Each step tracks a single bloody shoe print along the white marble. Ethan glances at me with a sad half shake of his head before he follows her.

Levi pivots between their retreating backs and our Sect. "Guess I'm done here." He turns away with them.

My awareness skips, and I'm in the barn. The smell of old hay and animals assaults my senses, filling me immediately with remembered panic. I search for the woman I know I'll see lying on the ground near the center—and there she is. Gia. She's alive, and I almost sigh in relief at her stubborn, angry expression as she glares up at Elias.

The son of a bitch has her on her knees, flanked by two Rakken.

Elias checks his watch. "Guess she's not coming. Help yourselves, brothers."

Gia's screaming echoed in my head as the vision ended abruptly and I returned to the present. Alannah was still moving toward the exit, her head held high, tracking blood with each step. All our efforts to reunite my people were crumbling to pieces.

Screw me sideways. Somehow, Alannah walking away was part of the chain of visions that would lead to Gia dying and then Silas. Everything hinged on this Moment and convincing Alannah to stay.

I couldn't let her walk out that door, or Silas would end up dead. I didn't fully understand it, but I had to stop that from happening.

"Alannah!" I yelled after her.

She paused and looked back over her shoulder.

I shifted from one foot to the other. This was going to hurt. "I accept the bond-mating."

Chapter Eighteen

Alannah's gaze shifted deliberately over my shoulder to Silas. I could feel him behind me, unyielding as a rock wall, but I couldn't bear to turn and see whatever expression was on his face. Knowing him, it would be stony and impassive, all his emotions locked away.

Seeing it would kill me. For the first time, I intentionally locked down the emotional connection between us. It was like tearing out my own heart, but if I had to walk away from Silas to save his life, I would do it. I'd do anything.

Alannah closed the distance and searched my face. "You're willing to accept the bond-mating before the entire Sect?"

"Yes."

Heavy emotions burned in my chest. Casius and Ethan had nearly identical expressions of shock on their faces. Alannah looked suspicious. I couldn't explain the true reasons behind my sudden change of heart, but somehow, I had to convince them all that I was serious.

I straightened my shoulders. The vision showed Alannah leaving first and then Gia dying. I saw Kianna in a cell next and then Silas dead. And finally, our compound would be under attack. Every step led to the next, and I had to figure out a way to stop them all. I bit the inside of my cheek to keep from howling in frustration. It was truly twisted that I had to give up the man I loved in order to keep him alive. And I couldn't even tell him why. There was no choice but to sacrifice my own happiness in order to protect all the people I loved.

Alannah raised her eyebrows in disbelief.

"I'm sorry," I said to Silas without meeting his eyes. "I've made my choice for the good of my people." I swallowed and forced my voice not to quiver.

I hated doing this to him—hated everything about this crossroad I'd been forced onto. But the vision was clear. If Alannah walked away, Silas would die.

"You held up your end of the bargain, Silas. You and Tessa have access to Earth like we agreed, so... you're free to go. I hope you find Kianna in time."

I still couldn't bring myself to look at Silas, but Tessa's betrayed and shocked expression hit me like a slap to the face. I lowered my eyes. When I stopped the last of these visions, maybe I could explain. I didn't know if I'd be able to get out of the oath I was about to make with Ethan, but I'd have to deal with that later, because I sure as shit wasn't going to produce a baby for Alannah to mold in her own image.

I lifted my chin, determined to see the visions through until the bitter end.

"I was wrong to leave our people in this time of need," Alannah said. "We will stay."

Levi swore and threw his hands in the air. "If she's staying, then we are too. Fates help us all."

"Good," I replied. "That's... good. Good." *What did I just do?*

Finally, I forced myself to look at Silas. His face was absolute stone, not an ounce of expression to let me guess at what he was thinking, and with the bond closed between us, I couldn't sense what he was feeling either. Silas was an incredibly private person who had trusted me with his heart. What I was doing to him was a betrayal on so many levels. Hurting him like this—and shutting down the bond between us—felt so wrong, and I immediately wanted to take it all back. But I couldn't. I had to make Alannah stay, and my only leverage was to go through with the bond-mating to Ethan. Which meant I had to convince Silas that I was serious about the agreement. If he thought I was being coerced, he'd fight it. And if Alannah suspected I was faking my commitment, she'd walk.

I studied each of our guests—the leaders of the splinter tribes and the people our future hinged on. "We're going to get through this together." My voice wavered with emotion. "I'll do whatever it takes to make this work." I desperately hoped Silas would forgive me when I figured out how to undo the mess I'd just made.

Casius's magic rose around him, and a mobile phone appeared in his hand. He punched in a series of numbers and shoved it at Silas. "This is a burner phone. It has my number preprogrammed. Let us know when you've found Kianna, and we'll send backup if you need it, as per our agreement. You have forty-eight hours to conduct your search."

After a long minute of silence, during which I couldn't bear to make eye contact with him again, Silas walked out without a word. Tessa turned away and followed behind him. I hated hurting Silas, and I'd never felt worse about myself.

Everyone was staring. I swallowed down my guilt and heartache and straightened my shoulders. A leader had to make hard choices, personal consequences be damned.

"We need to get Gia back. I have no idea what Elias's message means because I don't even have a niece. But he's going to kill Gia if we don't figure out what the hell is going on."

Casius's head snapped up. "Son of a—why didn't I think of that before?"

"What?" I demanded.

"Gia is pregnant with your niece."

Shock made my brain stutter. "Excuse me?"

"Gia and Marcel dated briefly after you and your father left. They must have rekindled their relationship." He tapped his fingers against his thigh while my brain spun. "Yes. The math adds up. Barely. Gia is eight months pregnant. Marcel probably didn't even know she was pregnant when he left to find you."

"For the love of all that is holy! No wonder she hates me," I said. Marcel had left to find me and died trying to bring me home, leaving her pregnant with his child.

Casius grimaced in agreement.

"We have to save her." A wild, desperate fury was growing inside of me. "Elias won't take my last remaining family. I refuse to let that happen."

"Which is exactly what he's counting on," Alannah pointed out. "He wants you, not Gia."

"I don't care. I'll do it. We have to trade me for Gia."

"We're not trading you for her," Casius said firmly.

"I agree," Alannah said.

Great. Now she cares about me. "I'm not planning on a permanent trade. We'll figure out a rescue plan."

"Elias will be prepared for a rescue attempt," Ethan said gently.

"It's the only option we have," I argued. "Otherwise, he'll kill Gia, and the others will follow."

Casius's brow furrowed. "What do you mean? Does he have more prisoners?"

I realized my slip too late. I didn't know for sure that trading me for Gia wouldn't result in a bigger problem, but what choice did I have? The events I saw clearly led from one to the next. The realization that I had more family to lose to the Brotherhood gripped my heart, along with my terror of Silas's death.

"I meant Gia and the baby."

Casius narrowed his eyes. I was a terrible liar, and I was doing an awful lot of it lately.

"Let's say we trade Maeve for Gia," Ethan said. Alannah and Casius opened their mouths to object, but Ethan held up his hands. "I'm not saying we should, but let me finish. Before Elias releases Gia, he'll most likely transport Maeve to a secondary location. And he'd surely have a plan in place to keep her from skimming out. So he'll likely block her magic. There is no way to follow you to the second location, and—we can assume—no way for you to get out on your own."

Not to mention that I didn't actually have much magic at the moment—which Ethan didn't know, of course. I was nearly as helpless as a Mundane.

"Exactly. Thank you for having common sense," Casius groused.

"Okay," I said, thinking furiously, "but I *want* him to take me in exchange for Gia. Even at a new location, Silas can track me through our Aegis bond and find Elias. Step one, kill the bastard. Step two, easy-peasy rescue."

Assuming Silas is willing to pause his hunt for Kianna and help me out after what I just put him through.

"Unless Elias kills you first," Casius retorted.

"And the Lord Councilor is no longer here," Alannah said.

I barely avoided rolling my eyes at her gloating tone.

"I doubt Elias went through all this effort just to kill her," Levi said. "He could have compelled that man to strap a bomb to himself, and we'd all be blown to bits right now."

"That's not at all reassuring," Tamara noted.

"Exactly," I said. "Elias wants something from me. Which means there's time to follow me and mount a rescue. He's not going to kill me."

"I'm sorry, Mae, but we can't trade you for Gia," Casius said. "If Elias steals your abilities through a blood-transference ritual, the results will be disastrous for everyone."

If Elias absorbed my powers, he would be able to access the Earthen Source, and the whole world would be in danger. Which meant Gia was as good as dead. My heart wrenched at the thought of never meeting my unborn niece. And after Gia's death would be Silas's, and then the rest of my people would die. Which absolutely couldn't happen.

The ironic thing was that I didn't have any magic to steal, and trading me for Gia wouldn't put anyone else in danger. But even if I told the Circle that, they'd never agree to trade me for Gia. A light bulb went off in my head, and an idea started to form.

"I just don't want to be responsible for any more deaths." I let the truth of that statement ring in my voice. I knew what I had to do, but I had to act quickly without anyone stopping me. "Anyone else have any ideas?"

Heads shook all around the room.

"You may not like it, but it's the best choice for our people," Alannah said. "We can't prioritize one life over the lives of the rest of our people."

Exactly. I forced my jaw to unclench. "I know. I just hope we can all live with the decision in the morning."

I stepped around the puddle of blood and forced myself to move slowly until I made it across the marble foyer and into the long hallway leading toward the converted living quarters. I walked calmly down the hall until I was confident no one had followed me. With my heart pounding, I glanced over my shoulder then pushed the door open into the emergency stairwell and ran up two flights of stairs. On the third floor, I sprinted east toward the storage room that held Thomas's belongings.

When I reached it, I punched in the code on the door. Over the years of his experiments, Thomas accumulated hundreds of magic objects. The room dedicated to storing his belongings was stacked with boxes along each wall, each full of knickknacks and research papers.

My ability to retain magic had been short-circuited temporarily, but I could channel the power of a strong magical object. I closed my eyes and let my senses fill with the innate power of the objects around me, searching. Hundreds of tiny sparks of magic registered in my brain, but nothing was powerful enough for what I had planned. Then an idea hit me. I didn't need to limit myself to just one artifact.

I picked up a thin letter opener that used to sit on Thomas's desk and called all the magic from every artifact in the room. The shelves full of trinkets and crystals vibrated with energy as I drew it all out and transferred it into the flat metal blade. It wasn't a lot of magic, but it was enough for what I needed. I twisted my braid into a bun at the nape of my neck and carefully stuck the letter opener through it, securing it in place. The ornate wooden end stuck out of my hair exactly like a hairpin would.

With that settled, I used a tiny amount of magic to summon my mobile and fished Agent Lennart's business card out of my pocket. The Department of Defense, Special Interests was about to learn the truth about magic.

Chapter Nineteen

I sat in a large waiting room, staring at Special Agent Lennart. When he'd asked me to come into their office in Downtown Boston, I'd expected a drab office and a long wait in a sterile gray interrogation room, like on cop shows. But this agency broke the stereotype. The room was paneled with a reddish wood that seemed expensive—perhaps cherry. A round marble-topped table and three wood-and-leather chairs took up most of the space. One entire side of the room had a matching stone counter that ran wall to wall, with a small sink and bar shelves. The counter was stocked with a fancy-looking coffee machine, a collection of mismatched mugs, and a pink doughnut box.

"Can I have a doughnut?" I asked.

"No." Lennart hadn't offered me so much as a cup of coffee, and he glowered from across the table as he hoarded his precious baked goods too.

"Fine. We don't have time to take this slowly anyway. I'm about to shatter your worldview." My talk with Father Mike seemed like a lifetime ago, but the way he'd explained the world of magic made sense. I decided to take the same approach with Lennart.

His expression never changed as I told him the truth about magic. I talked and talked, and he listened without interrupting. Finally, I said, "So everything you suspected about me is true and a whole lot more. But it was Lord Elias who sent those missing people to kill me and then forced them to commit suicide when they

206

weren't successful. You were right about what happened at the old town in Pennsylvania too. What you saw in those photos was the result of a massive battle. Lord Elias was behind that, because he wants to use our magic to rule Earth. I'm trying to stop them, and I need your help."

Agent Lennart was taking this too calmly. When I'd learned about magic, I couldn't believe it. Even after being struck in the chest by pure energy, it was still hard for me to come to terms with the truth, but Lennart barely batted an eye.

Lennart leaned back in his chair. "So you come in here, confess to mass murder, and claim that magic is real. Now you want me to... do what exactly? Besides arrest you and throw away the key."

"As I just said, I didn't murder those people—Lord Elias did. If you help me now, I will give you any information you want. I'll tell you everything about magic and our abilities. You need to know what's coming." I smiled, hoping it looked mysterious, not wildly desperate like I felt.

"What exactly do you want in exchange?"

"I need your technology."

"What kind of tech?"

"I have a prisoner-exchange situation. I need a tracking device to put on the person we're giving to the bad guys."

"Sounds simple enough. Who are you handing over to these 'bad guys'?"

"Me."

He blinked. "That's... interesting. And your exit plan is a tracking device? Why not just do something with your magic?"

Good question. Maybe Lennart wasn't as dumb as I thought. I shared part of the answer, leaving out the fact that, other than the energy I'd just stored, I was pretty much a magical dud at the moment.

"He'll be expecting that and blocking my powers, but what he won't be expecting is Mundane technology. After I exchange myself for the prisoner, I need you to tell my people what happened so they can come rescue me."

I pulled out the paper with the exchange address on it and reached for a pen on the table between us. Lennart twitched, his fingers reflexively reaching for the gun at his hip.

I paused. "For the record, I wouldn't hurt you even if I didn't need your help. I'm one of the good guys, Agent Lennart." I met his gaze and sincerely hoped he believed me. By trusting him, I was putting my life in his hands. I grabbed the pen and wrote Casius's cell phone number on the back of the paper. "After the exchange happens, call this number, and tell Casius that I came to you and asked for help."

"Okay, so your prisoner is released, and you go with the baddies." He held up the paper. "We give your location to your people. That's it?"

"Yup."

"And who's going to fulfill your end of the bargain after you get yourself killed?"

"Your concern for my safety is touching."

"Don't get me wrong. I think you're a psychopathic mass murderer, and maybe your death wouldn't be such a bad thing. But you asked for my help in exchange for information, and since your ridiculous plan is going to get you killed, I need some guarantee we're going to get answers after you die." He leaned forward and tapped two fingers on the table. "And I want to know where the bodies of those missing people are."

"These people are planning to take over Earth and enforce their own rules. Trust me when I say that you won't like that. I'm coming back to give you the answers I promised, and if I don't, you'll have bigger things to worry about."

Lennart thought about it for longer than it should really take. But finally, he said, "How long do we have until the exchange?"

I checked the clock on the coffee maker. Elias had given us four hours, and I'd wasted most of it trying to come up with some alternative to what I was about to do now. "Less than forty-five minutes."

"That's not enough time," Agent Lennart said. "Your plan sucks, and so do your time-management skills, by the way."

"Miss O'Neill," a deep male voice said.

I turned to see a man with dark skin and short-cropped black hair standing a few feet behind me. He wore a baby-blue button-down shirt over pressed slacks, and he radiated authority.

"Who are you?"

"I'm Director Pascal. Head of the Department of Defense, Special Interests. And you are Maeve O'Neill of Boston. Leader of the Earthen Sect of Harvesters and Aegis of House Valeron."

I was dumbstruck. *How does he know about all that?*

"You don't know who I am?" Director Pascal asked.

His question was odd, considering I was currently meeting him for the first time. As usual, my confusion and alarm triggered my snarky side. "Sorry, I'm sure you're a big deal and all, but I don't follow secret-agent-celebrity gossip. How do you know all that about *me*?"

"We've known about your people for quite some time. It's why DODSI was formed in the first place. But thank you for confirming a few details for us."

Lennart's lack of reaction to my big reveal suddenly made sense. I ground my teeth as I realized that I'd been played. Agent Lennart and this Director Pascal clearly knew a lot more than I'd ever imagined—more than they could have known from just watching us since the loss of our faux Amish compound. My stomach churned as I considered how deep this could go.

"Why the charade, Director Pascal? If you knew about us from the beginning, why pretend to be in the dark?"

"Information is our business," Pascal said. "We don't dole it out for free."

Now that more cards were on the table, my brain flew through options and motives as I stared at Director Pascal. He looked roughly middle-aged, but appearances could be deceiving. I wondered if he could be a magic user like me, but I quickly discarded the idea. There hadn't been any gloating at getting the upper hand, and so far, he'd been straightforward with his answers. I decided to take the gamble and put everything out on the table—not that I had any other options.

"You obviously heard everything I just said. And all that wasn't news to you—including the existence of magic."

He tilted his head, not denying my statement but also not admitting anything just yet.

"So you know about us. And now you know about the Brotherhood and what they are capable of. Does that mean that you're willing to help me?"

"Trust is a two-way street, Miss O'Neill, and I'm not going to be the first one to start walking on it. We need a guarantee of your loyalty."

I almost laughed. This was officially the third time my loyalty had been questioned—the Aeternal Council, my own people, and now the Mundanes. *Of course* the super-secret government agency wanted me to prove my loyalty to them when I knew absolutely nothing about them or their agenda.

"I'll do whatever it takes to stop Elias from killing the mother of my unborn niece. If you help me do that, then we're on the same side."

"For now," he said. "Sounds like you're walking in blind with a weak exit strategy."

Ugh, he'd get along great with Silas. "That's my risk, not yours."

"Except you can't fulfill your end of our bargain if you die."

Lennart's smirk was smug as hell. "Told you."

"I have a backup plan," I said, hoping I sounded confident. That backup plan was a voice message on Silas's burner phone that he might or might not know how to check, but it was better than nothing. "And when I get back, you'll get all the answers you want."

"I want information now."

I shook my head. "In about thirty minutes, my time runs out, and the prisoner dies. I need to be in Idaho before then."

"We can't get you to Idaho in half an hour," Pascal said. "That's halfway across the country."

"Terrible time management," Lennart said under his breath.

"I'll get myself there—I just need your tracking technology."

Pascal cocked his head to the side.

"I promised to explain when I get back. Take it or leave it, Director Pascal. I'm running out of time."

Pascal's lips pressed together in a slight grimace. "Lennart, get her gear, and light it up."

"Yes, sir."

Pascal shook my hand. "Good luck, Miss O'Neill."

I followed Agent Lennart out of the break room and down a long hall. The facility stretched deeper than I'd previously guessed. As we wound through the mazelike hallways, we passed several large open spaces filled with desks and people. Between Director Pascal's knowledge of magic and the sheer size of this building, I felt like an idiot. The government was totally onto us, and Lennart had duped me from the beginning.

They even knew I was Silas's Aegis, which meant they had to be informed about other realms. And if this facility was any indication, they were well funded. I had no idea how much they knew, but I'd just promised to give them even more information. I was probably going to regret this later.

I sighed. I already had Elias, the Fae, and the gods-damned Fate to deal with. Now I had this secret government agency to worry about too. Casius was going to have kittens when he found out how much DODSI knew about us.

Finally, Lennart stopped in front of a door marked Locker 9-07. He swiped a card and held his finger against a scanner, and the door clicked open, revealing a closet stuffed full of gadgets. The space was about the size of a large bathroom, its walls lined floor to ceiling with metal shelves. I noticed a large stash of guns locked behind a metal grate.

Lennart plucked a square black box off a shelf and handed me a small piece of clear plastic about the size of a dime. "This is an LWT. It's a low-signal wearable tracking device." He fished out a glass vial of clear liquid and shook it like nail polish. "Where do you want it?"

I pulled down my shirt collar to expose my shoulder blade. Elias wouldn't be checking me for any type of Mundane technology, but somewhere out of sight would be an ideal place for it. Lennart brushed the liquid on my skin and placed the tiny patch of plastic on top of it. It dried in a few seconds, pulling slightly on my skin.

Lennart picked up a handheld device and pointed it at my back. It beeped. "Gotcha. You're geo-tagged like a good doggie."

I ignored his jab. "You'll transfer my location to my people after the exchange? They can trace it from there?"

"The signal is traceable from anywhere in the world, via any mobile phone with a cell signal. Once we give them the transmitter's unique ID, they shouldn't have any issues." He checked his watch. "If your crazy plan has any chance of working, you'd better get a move on. You're T minus twenty."

I swallowed down a lump of doubt. I was about to hand myself over to Elias and the Brotherhood, and my plan relied on a thin strip of plastic glued to my back to bring me home alive. I had no magic and no real backup plan. No one knew where I was going except Agent Lennart and his secret agency. Not to mention, if I lived through all of this, I'd just agreed to give away all of our secrets to the government and then make babies with Ethan. *Not my best work.*

Standing in the locker with Agent Lennart, I weighed all the risk I was walking into against the freedom of everyone in my Sect and Silas's life. I had no choice. I would do anything to stop the visions. Alannah was right. Leaders had to sacrifice for the greater good.

Lennart narrowed his eyes. "You're obviously going rogue on this. And I want you to know that death does not give you the option to renege on our bargain."

"Don't get too excited. I'm planning on living through this." I bit my lip. "But if I don't come back, you're going to have a really pissed-off Guardian who is going to lose his shit. Tell him…" I paused and thought about it. Saying goodbye felt wrong. And doing it secondhand after smashing our relationship to pieces in front of my entire Sect felt even worse. It was time to believe in myself. "Never mind. I'll apologize to him myself."

"Good idea." He tapped the handheld tracking device. "You're ready. Don't die."

Right. Well, at least we're on the same page about that. I pulled all of the stored magic out of the letter opener in my bun and skimmed to the exchange location, enjoying the shocked expression that flashed on Lennart's face as I disappeared in front of him.

One shot. This was my one shot to fix everything or die trying.

I landed on a gravel road outside the barn where my mother was murdered and where Gia was fated to die. There were no signs of other people anywhere. The smell of farm and pasture brought a flood of memories, which I fought down with rising panic. I couldn't afford the distraction of reliving that terrible day. Peeling red paint and a missing door confirmed that the ramshackle outbuilding hadn't been used in years. It was surrounded by a neglected pasture with an old wood fence meant to keep in animals. Dead fields ringed the building, putting the barn right in the middle of nowhere.

The urge to wrap my magic around me was strong, but I had nothing to draw from. The magic I'd absorbed from Thomas's artifacts was gone. I had no more tricks up my sleeve, and my exit plan was shit. With a tug on Marcel's charm, I willed myself to stay calm as I walked through the barn door.

It took a few seconds for my eyes to adjust to the dark interior. *Damn it all to hell. It looks exactly the same.* The musty smell of the hay assaulted my memories, bringing back the terror of the day I'd hid while my mother died stopping the Brotherhood from taking us. The memories hit me hard enough to make me nauseous.

Dread pooled in my stomach as I found Gia sitting in the middle of the barn, gagged. She started squawking and squirming when she saw me, and I realized her hands were tied to a ring in the floor.

Elias and two Rakken emerged from the shadowed edges. It was strange to think I'd once found him attractive. With his dark hair and striking blue eyes, he was objectively handsome, but the ugliness beneath his polished exterior removed any positive attributes I'd once thought he had. His tainted soul shone out of his eyes.

"My lady, such a pleasure to see you again," Elias said with a wide, friendly smile. He held up his hand. "That's close enough."

I hated that grin. Elias was a conniving, scheming bastard. Bringing me here, of all places, wasn't a coincidence. He knew about my mother, and he wanted me to know that the last of my family could die here too.

Anger seethed and itched under my skin. I despised him with everything I had, but I forced myself to stay calm. Gia was yelling again but couldn't say anything around the gag in her mouth. Other than her irate, panicked expression, she seemed unharmed. This was the moment of truth. If Elias decided to take us both, there was absolutely nothing I could do about it. I just hoped he didn't realize that.

"I'm so pleased you came," Elias said as if I were there for a social visit. "I must say, I had my doubts when I realized the truth of our situation, but I think this can work itself through." He rubbed his index finger over his bottom lip as he looked me over.

Elias was acting strangely, but I was way past the point of no return. I stepped farther inside the barn. "Let her go, Elias."

"My pleasure." His magic rose around him.

I flinched and reached for my magic out of reflex, but there was nothing. I couldn't even grasp the little bit I'd started to regain. My powers were blocked—but somehow, Elias still had access to his.

With grudging acknowledgment of his clever plan, I realized that he'd blocked magic in only my half of the barn. It would take an impressive amount of skill to create a conjuring thin enough that I hadn't sensed it yet strong enough to inhibit my powers. Then he'd taken that and expanded it over the large structure with enough precision to cover only the side I was standing on. There was a reason Elias had been the Council's leader. His abilities were impressive.

A small dagger appeared in Elias's hands, and I gritted my teeth as he held the fate of my last remaining relative in his hands—a pregnant woman who hadn't done anything to him. As my vision had suggested, Elias was the type of man who would let the Rakken eat her alive just to send me a message.

I exhaled in relief as Elias cut the zip ties around Gia's wrists. She pulled out the gag and threw it on the ground at his feet. She stalked to my side. "What are you doing?"

I kept my eyes locked on Elias as I spoke to her. "Get out of here. Skim back to our people once you're outside of the barn."

"Are you insane? You can't hand yourself over to him!"

"Do not get yourself killed after I just rescued your ungrateful ass. Go, Gia!"

"You're an even bigger idiot than I thought." She ran out of the barn.

Elias frowned after her. "I can't say I'll miss her company. Hopefully, the baby will take after the father in personality."

"Any chance I'm getting out of this alive?"

He chuckled. "You, on the other hand, are a breath of fresh air." He took a few steps toward me but stopped several yards away—just short of where that magical block likely began. An amused grin lit up his face. "There's no need for you to die this day."

"And if I run?"

The Rakken slid forward on silent stalking paws. Their hard muscle shifted on lean predators' bodies the size of small horses. Each one bared a mouth full of sharp teeth as they flanked me, making any attempt at escape pointless.

"Then my brothers will be forced to take action." Elias waved his hand toward the exit. "By all means, if you believe you are faster than them, you're welcome to try."

"Let's just get this over with. What do you want from me?"

He held out his hand. "I believe we have a date to finish."

I glanced anxiously around the barn. I could run, but he'd already outlined the consequences for that, and I didn't particularly want my face eaten off by Rakken. I could fight, but without access to my magic, it would take a snap of his fingers to subdue me and drag me wherever he wanted. That left me with a long-shot plan that relied on Mundane tech, of all things, and now I had to see it through. *Gia is right—I really am an idiot.*

I shrugged. The little plastic tracker tugged reassuringly on my skin as I placed my hand in Elias's. He grabbed both of my wrists, and his magic flowed around me instantly, wrapping up my arms and spreading over the rest of my body in a tightly woven spell. The layers of the conjuring settled over my skin, like a heavy, wet blanket stitched onto my body.

"You will not access your magic," Elias commanded.

I gulped down the fear tightening in my throat as Traiten bands appeared around my wrists—the marks of a slave under Elias's complete control.

Chapter Twenty

Elias skimmed us inside a small banquet hall. It took less than a heartbeat for my subconscious brain to recognize the room full of predators staring ravenously at us. All kinds of warning bells went off as I took in the five giant men hulking around the dining table that ran the length of the room. Each one glowed with red magic tainted in black at the edges, surrounded by a barely restrained aura of violence.

I tried to swallow my fear and failed miserably. With the Traiten bands, I had no access to my own magic—empty or not—and no free will. The Rakken were hungry and clearly uncomfortable in their human skins. Silas had said that part of the process of making Rakken was to force them into their animal form until they forgot their humanity. I could see the animal in the way they shifted on their feet, their eyes darting at the slightest noise. Nostrils flared and eyes dilated, they watched me with near-palpable hunger.

Elias waved his hand at two empty places set for dinner. "Please, be seated."

The bands around my wrists flared with magic, and I sat. I hadn't decided to move, but the Traiten bands compelled me to act. It was the most terrifying thing I had ever experienced. I had no free will and no way to remove the Traiten bands myself.

I hid my shaking hands in my lap. The transition from the filthy barn to this formal dinner was shocking and almost comical. Across from us, the Rakken had clearly been instructed to dress up, and they tugged uncomfortably at the edges of their button-down shirts and ties.

Elias clapped his hands, and a man and a woman rushed into the room. They were Mundanes, and they were terrified. The woman had straw matted in her long brown hair and looked like she'd been sleeping on the floor of a barn for more than a few days. The man was equally disheveled, and his hands shook as he handed a steaming towelette to Elias.

Elias wiped his fingers and then unfurled his cloth napkin across his lap with a crisp snap of fabric. The Mundanes placed two silver-domed plates in front of us, filled two glasses with red wine, and retreated quickly to the side of the room. None of the Rakken were eating, although they seemed ravenous enough to attempt to take a bite out of *me*. One of them snapped his teeth at the Mundane woman as she hurried past him. She jumped, and the asshole laughed.

"Can you stop with all the mind games? Just tell me what you want from me," I demanded.

Elias scooted his chair closer to the table. "First, we should clear the air. I am appalled about the kidnapping of your kin. I never would have resorted to such an act against a woman in her condition, but I am grateful we have a chance to talk regardless."

"Wait. Are you saying you didn't kidnap Gia?" I suddenly remembered the strange way Elias had behaved at the barn. He'd said something about showing up and realizing the truth.

"No, no. Of course not. Such crude manipulations are hardly necessary. I didn't arrange our meeting." Elias waved his fingers, and the terrified woman approached to lift the covers off our plates. The delicious smell of steak wafted toward me, but I had no appetite for Elias's hospitality or his lies.

I eyed the steak knives. "Then who did?"

He picked up his knife and fork but paused before cutting into his filet. "I can see that you're not going to be companionable until I've put your mind to rest. I don't know who kidnapped your... what was her name again?"

"Gia."

He cut a piece off the steak and put it in his mouth. His eyes closed, and he hummed in appreciation. "I thought *you* had invited me to meet. It wasn't until I arrived early and found Gia tied to the floor like an animal that I realized the truth of our situation. I do believe we were meant to surprise and then kill each other."

"You expect me to believe that?"

"I know, I know. I'd hardly believe it myself, but it's the truth." He chuckled. "I was so eager to meet with you that I walked right into a trap. You ought to be grateful for my quick thinking, or this evening would have taken quite a different turn."

"What about that magic blocking spell you put over the barn? You had that planned out."

"Oh, that? I conjured that quickly. Admittedly crude, but once I realized what was about to happen, I couldn't risk you attacking without hearing my proposition. I know how rash you can be."

My mind was spinning. *Was Elias telling the truth? If he didn't send those Mundanes to attack us—which I have to admit doesn't seem like his style—then who did?* My mind returned to the potential traitor in our Sect, and I frowned.

"And if I hadn't showed up?" I asked, racking my brain for anything in the vision that contradicted his claims.

"I probably would have killed her." He shrugged. "No offense, but I could hardly take her with me. If she were traced, it could risk giving away my location. Plus, she's not very good company. I had to gag her to stop her obscenities. Hardly worth the hassle."

Well, that aligned with my vision and Elias's callous personality. "So, now what? Who set us up?"

"Now we eat. And once we have supped like civilized Humans, we'll talk."

I frowned at the plate in front of me.

"I must say," he continued, "I've enjoyed your Earthen cuisine during my exile. It's a disgraceful abuse of resources to breed and eat meat, but you can't deny that it is delicious." He popped another bite in his mouth. "My men have developed quite a taste for fresh meat as well."

A chorus of snickers went around the table, and the Mundanes cowered against the wall.

Holy gods. I swallowed my disgust and fear. "You're letting them eat people? Are you insane?" I gripped my steak knife.

"Use that knife to eat." His words snapped with command, and the Traiten bands glowed. "And your fork, of course."

My stomach twisted, but I picked up my fork, cut off a small bite, and stuck it in my mouth. I felt like a puppet.

"What do you think of the food?" He waited for my reaction, eyes lit with eagerness.

"I've had better," I said truthfully and set the knife back down.

He sighed and dabbed at the corner of his mouth with his cloth napkin. "Very well. We can address our business directly. I'd like to propose a partnership."

I snorted. "My Sect will never agree to a partnership with the leader of the Brotherhood. You're a murderer and a traitor."

"I'm not interested in a partnership with your Sect. I'm talking about you and I."

I twitched in surprise. "Why would I want anything to do with you?"

Elias rubbed his fingers over his bottom lip. "You've not tried your drink."

"No, thank you." My voice was a growl.

"Drink," he commanded.

I picked up the wineglass and took a sip. I'd never hated him more.

"You really should eat more and enjoy all of that glass of wine. It's quite delicious."

Obediently, I picked up my fork and took another bite of the steak. While I chewed, I examined the space. There were two exits on opposite ends of the room and a wall full of windows on the far south side, but from the second floor of this mansion, I couldn't see more than treetops.

Elias and the table full of monsters eyed me intently as I took another sip of the wine. I'd never make it more than five steps before they pounced. I flexed against the Traiten bonds, but nothing gave. I couldn't access my magic, and I was trapped. I had no idea where I was, but if Agent Lennart kept his end of our deal, Casius should be learning what I'd done right about now. They'd be preparing a rescue. I guessed I had an hour before they found me, two tops.

"I have a proposal," Elias said.

"Not interested," I snapped back.

He laughed again. "I adore your fire."

I scowled at him.

"Are you hungry? Speak the truth."

"Yes," I said. "But I don't want to eat with you."

"I want you to enjoy this meal with me."

"I don't think that's possible. I detest you."

"Perhaps that's a bit too much honesty from you this evening."

"You brought me here. Deal with the consequences." I tightened my grip on the steak knife again.

"You'll do nothing. You will not harm me. Release the knife, Lady Maeve."

My fingers went obediently limp, and the knife clattered back onto the table. I was so helpless. Rage burned through me, hot and strong.

"Please eat until you're not hungry. And drink." He crooked his fingers, and the Mundane man stepped forward obediently to refill my glass. His hands shook as he poured it, and some of the red liquid spilled onto my lap.

The Rakken nearest me grabbed the man by the neck. The man gasped and started sobbing. The Rakken snarled, squeezing the man's neck as he choked.

I have to do something. "Let the man go, and I'll listen to your proposal," I said.

Elias smirked and waved his fingers as the Rakken. "Let him go."

The Rakken loosed his hold, letting the man breathe. He rushed back to the wall, and the two Humans grasped hands silently as they stood there, trembling.

Elias picked up his glass and rolled the liquid around. "Together, you and I could rule both Earth and Aeterna."

"Ruling is overrated," I said. "Comes with a lot of responsibility."

He leaned in, and the humor disappeared from his eyes. "Don't you want it even a little bit? The chance to determine the fate of the world? The power, the respect? Be honest."

"No," I said as the bands glowed, compelling me to complete honesty. "I will never help you rule over Earth. I don't care if you put a hundred compulsion spells on me." I let my loathing show on my face. Elias was despicable. He was the worst kind of power-hungry narcissist who would use anyone and any advantage for himself and never think twice about the price.

"Be still," he said, and I froze. He leaned in until we were uncomfortably close. His breath washed over me, thick with the cloying scent of red wine and meat. The tips of his fingers traveled down the side of my neck. "We could do great things together. With your control over the Earthen Source and my leadership, no one could stand in our way." He kissed my neck.

My stomach squirmed with revulsion. "Don't touch me."

His lips continued down my neck, and fear flashed through me. His command kept me from pulling away. I was completely at his mercy.

The Rakken around us edged nearer, my fear setting off their animal instincts.

"Do you find me attractive?" Elias asked.

"Not anymore," I answered.

He chuckled. "We started something and never finished it. Kiss me, and see if we can reignite the fire."

I leaned in and placed my lips on his obediently. I closed my eyes as Elias's tongue invaded my mouth. My body was under his control, but my mind screamed in protest. His hands cupped the sides of my face, holding me to him. Disgust turned my stomach until finally, he let me go.

"Tell me you didn't enjoy that."

"I didn't enjoy that," I said instantly.

He frowned as he realized the error in his command.

"You can compel my body, you piece of shit, but I will never want you. I would rather die than rule with you."

"I have the power to command you to stab that knife into your own eye, and you still can't control your temper." He threw his cloth napkin on the table. "Frankly, I question your intelligence."

"I'm not the one feeding the Rakken human flesh and then making them sit like trained dogs at your dinner table while you assault me. They are salivating for violence. You feed them your scraps and talk about Brotherhood, but they aren't your loyal dogs, Elias.

You won't even know how stupid you are until they have their claws in your back!"

The tension in the room went up several degrees. The Rakken had followed Titus for a chance at a better future and an opportunity to get out from under the Aeternal Council's classist structure. In Aeterna, they'd had no chance to be anything but laborers and servants. But with Titus dead and Elias as the face of their rebellion—a face that had also been the leader of the Aeternal Council—I wondered if there was any chance to bring the Brotherhood out from under Elias's control.

The Rakken who had choked the Human man said, "She killed our brothers, my lord. Let us feast on her flesh."

Elias clicked his tongue. "Her powers are more valuable to us than her flesh, Brother Brutus."

"Let my men enjoy her body, then. We can leave her alive."

The Rakken around the table leaned in, nostrils flared. They were eager for violence of any kind. I froze, abandoning any hope of shifting their alliances. These were Rakken. They'd been broken and fundamentally changed—forced to spend more time in their animal forms than their human ones. Silas said that the Brotherhood had used magic to further modify their behaviors and thought patterns. They were too far gone and too violent to reason with.

If Elias lost control of his monsters, I would be defenseless without my magic. My fear was feeding the tension in the room, but I couldn't relax. If Elias decided to give me to them, there was absolutely nothing I could do about it.

Elias pushed his chair back and stood in one swift movement, staring down all five Rakken. "She is mine."

Each one dropped his eyes, ceding to Elias's authority, and I almost sagged in relief.

Elias dabbed at the corner of his mouth with his napkin. "You may take these Mundanes to the maze. Enjoy yourselves, whilst I show our guest why she should have more respect for our Brotherhood."

The monsters in human skin jumped to their feet eagerly, grabbing up the Mundanes. The woman screamed and tried to run. Brutus slapped her across the face and tossed her over his shoulder, and the man started sobbing as they dragged him from the room.

"No! Stop!" I grabbed the steak knife.

Two Rakken paused at my outburst, their eyes wide with excitement. The closer one took a step toward me.

"Sit still and be quiet," Elias commanded me. "Keep your cutlery if it makes you feel better, but you'll do no harm with it."

The bands around my wrists glowed again. I clutched the knife in my fist as my anger and fear boiled over, and I couldn't do a damn thing about it.

He waved his hand at the lingering Rakken. "Go. Enjoy your reward."

They dragged the Mundanes out of my sight, and I couldn't say a word.

"Those were the last of our servants." He sighed. "Your mouth is out of control, my lady." Elias walked to the large row of windows on the south side of the room. "Come here."

I rose obediently. Even though I wanted to stab my knife into his back, the command not to harm him prevented me from raising my arm to attempt it. The windows where Elias stood overlooked the mansion grounds, with a clear view over a large property bathed in early-evening sun. In the distance, I noted a large mountain range, but I had no idea where that put me. I could be in another country for all I knew.

Closest to the mansion, eight-foot-tall walls of stacked stones wove around the property in twisted paths that connected at right angles and dead ends. It stretched for miles. *A maze.* Beyond that, a ten-foot wall ringed the grounds, and atop it, wrought-iron spikes kept out any would-be Mundane trespassers. I looked above the pedestrian security to the dome of magic arching over the entire estate. We were in the middle of nowhere, surrounded by miles and miles of maze and under an impenetrable magic shield.

My hope plummeted. There was no way anyone was getting in here. And I wasn't getting out without help.

"Tell me, what do you think of the Rakken?" Elias said.

"They've lost their humanity," I responded. "Elias, let the Mundanes go. You don't need to show me how brutal the Rakken can be."

"I take no pleasure in this. But thanks to your outburst, I will appear weak if I don't punish you. Shifters don't tolerate weakness, because they have no basic humanity. At their core, they respect only power and fear—like animals."

A terrible, excited howling rose from the maze. I covered my mouth as the food I'd been compelled to eat came up in my throat.

"I require them to give the Mundanes a head start." He shrugged. "It seems only fair."

"You're a monster."

"Let go of your Mundane morals, and you'll see the same thing I did. Our society is broken. We let soulless monsters play at being Human and ignore the natural order of things. Under my rule, everyone would know their place, with Humans at the top where we belong."

The woman's loud, desperate scream pierced my ears. A chorus of shrieking howls answered her.

I blinked back tears of rage as I stepped back from the monster next to me.

"Listen to them salivating over flesh." He jabbed his finger at the maze below us. "*They* are the true threat to humanity. The

Rakken were cultivated from the worst attributes of the Shifters. Your Lord Silas saw to that. Under an absolute ruler, creatures like the Rakken wouldn't need to exist."

Surprise slapped me across the face. Silas had told me about the Rakken, how they were trained, and how the Guardians used them to win their battles. But I didn't realize he'd been so involved.

Elias chuckled once at my horrified expression. "Did he not mention it? No, I thought not. Shifters are all capable of becoming as the Rakken are. It doesn't take much. Your Aegis perfected the technique of breaking a man down to his animal in less than eight weeks. It took little effort to strip them of any pretense of humanity and transform them into the most brutal strike force the Council has ever known. Silas excelled at orchestrating the Council's slaughters. And now, I hear they've made him their Lord Councilor."

I refused to believe Elias's version of Silas's history. Even if he had done those things in the past, that wasn't who he was anymore. Silas was not the monster here.

"Tell me what you're thinking," Elias said.

My fingers tightened around the steak knife, but I couldn't make my hand move. "I want to stab you in the eye."

He smirked at the knife in my hand. "It amuses me to see you clutching that blade with impotent rage. It is a good metaphor for your situation."

I ground my teeth and imagined stabbing him. "You blame Silas, but you led the Council that bred and used the Rakken. You're just as bad as any of the monsters down there in that maze."

He frowned. "You don't see it yet. Come, I want to show you something."

I obediently followed him from the room. I fumed, willing myself to break free of his compulsion and crack open his skull as we headed deeper into the mansion. I tried again to access my own magic, but it was still blocked by Elias's command. He had me under his control, and without his permission, I couldn't access my limited powers.

After a lot of twists and turns that led us deep underground and left me lost and aching with the futility of fighting against the Traiten bonds, we came to a dead-end hallway. Elias stopped in front of metal bars welded across the stone passageway, creating a small cave-like cell. I peered into the darkness.

"The Fae are no better than the Shifters," Elias said. "Do you know why they force their children to take truth oaths when they come of age? They'll tell you it's to maintain their connection to their magic. They like to pretend they are keeping themselves pure to allow their magic to flow through them." He chuckled without humor. "Narcissistic Fae-holes. The truth is they're all sociopaths—they lack natural affection. They make those binding truth oaths because their society would crumble without them."

Elias touched his finger to the cell bars, and the whole room flashed with energy. I flinched, and Elias shook out his hand as if he'd received a shock. "It's a clever little trap the Council designed. The cell drains whatever is inside it, fueling the imprisonment."

"Why are you showing me this?"

Elias banged on the bars and called out, "Lady Kianna!"

Another flash of energy flooded the cell, and a pile of rags stirred in the corner. A dirty face and two pale arms emerged from the pile, and suddenly I was staring at the blond woman from my vision. *Lady Kianna.*

Another vision hit me, and I tensed.

A battle spills outside onto the meticulously manicured grounds of the abandoned hospital campus my people call home. Swathed in black combat gear, a troop of government agents storm the field from all sides. They open fire indiscriminately, their bulky guns shooting waves of energy that send dozens dropping to the ground with each burst.

Everything is a bloody mess, and I can't tell who is fighting whom. Bodies fly through the air. Children and families are caught in the cross fire. So much blood soaks the formerly groomed grounds that the green field has turned dark with gore.

I see a horrific sight—Rakken bounding into our midst.

With a gasp, I fell out of the vision. My heart beat furiously in my chest as the newest version of horrors burned through me. The energy fizzled out and dropped the cell back into darkness. The vision of my people dying now included the threat of government agents and the Rakken. I wasn't making things better—I was making them worse. This vision was more terrible than the first time Four had shown it to me.

I must have caused the change when I brought DODSI into this.

"Lady Kianna is the offspring of Lord Nuada and Lady Treva," Elias said smugly.

I held back my reaction. I couldn't let Elias know the promise I'd made Lady Treva to find her daughter or that she was the key to getting the antidote from Nuada. If Elias knew how badly I needed her alive, he'd use it as leverage against me.

And thanks to the latest Fate-inflicted vision, it was clear that Kianna was connected to the vision in which our people would be overrun by an unexplainable and lethal combination of our enemies. If I didn't save Kianna, somehow that would lead to the Fae, the Rakken, and the government converging on our location and a hell of a lot of death.

I peered into the cell. Kianna seemed inches from dying, and I wasn't even sure how to get myself out of this mess, let alone save someone else. I swallowed thickly as my mind raced. Nuada believed the Council had taken Kianna, but it was Elias. If I could get her out of there, I could convince Nuada that the attack was unjustified and get the antidote for the poison spreading through the Citizen Source. A surge of excitement bolted through me.

Forcing my voice to sound uninterested, I said, "Fae can't live without their magic. How is she not dead?"

"I give her enough to sustain her each day but not so much she can break free."

"What are you going to do with her? Why did you take her?"

Elias barked out a harsh laugh. "Her own father gave her to me. Lord Nuada uses her as the justification for his retaliation against the Council. I'm to kill her in one day's time and return the body to the Fae anonymously."

My heart dropped through my stomach. *Nuada gave Kianna to Elias? Her own father wants her dead?* I blinked as my mind spun in circles.

If Elias wasn't lying—and that was a big *if*—Nuada had orchestrated everything just so he could accuse the Council of kidnapping his daughter and retaliate with the deaths of thousands of people. My mind was racing. There was no way Treva knew. She'd released me to find Kianna and made me vow to help. But if Elias was telling the truth, then Nuada wanted to martyr his daughter, and Lady Treva had no idea.

"Do you see now?" Elias said. "They have no natural affection. They're dangerous animals lacking basic humanity."

It was possible that Elias had set this all up to pit the Fae against the Council. He could have kidnapped Kianna and sent the ransom demand to Nuada, pretending the Council had orchestrated everything... my brain was twisting into knots. No. That was too complicated. If Elias was behind all this, he didn't have anything to gain by demanding that the Fae return to Aeterna or by showing me Kianna. As much as I wanted to blame him, Elias hadn't done this.

The probable explanation was the simplest one, as twisted as it was. Nuada had orchestrated everything, just as Elias claimed. Nuada was willing to sacrifice his own daughter to justify killing thousands of innocent Aeternals—all to weaken the Council and make sure the Fae stayed free of their control.

It was crazy, but it also fit what I knew about Nuada. He was an isolationist, and above anything else, he wanted the Fae to be independent. He also intimately knew the Council. The loss of the Fae's Master Healers would be reason enough to want them back, and although the Council was currently reeling after Elias's betrayal, eventually, they would find a way to force the Fae back under their control.

Insane as it all was, Elias had to be telling the truth. Nuada had handed his own daughter over to Elias in order to fake a kidnapping he could blame on the Council. Then he'd used that as justification to poison the Citizen Source and weaken the Council.

I exhaled in sheer frustration. If all of that was true... there was no way in hell he would trade Kianna for the antidote. Our plan wasn't going to work.

Except Lady Treva was desperate to get her daughter back. We'd never intended to rely only on Nuada. We needed the rest of the Fae to know the attack on Aeterna was unjustified in order to force Nuada to give us the antidote. Discovering that Nuada had orchestrated the kidnapping didn't change that plan. It just meant that we needed Lady Treva more than ever.

"Give Kianna to me, and I'll take her back to her people. Nuada's people won't back him when they find out what he did."

Elias snorted derisively. "They won't care. You're missing the big picture, the crux of the problem. The Fae have no natural love, no loyalties. They are nothing more than sociopaths who sacrifice their children for political gain." His eyes burned with the fervor of his belief. "The Shifters are animals. Believe me, I've spent decades among them both, and I know what they are. We are the ones who must rule Earth. *Humans.*"

I looked back at Kianna's cell. I didn't believe what Elias was saying. Lady Treva was truly desperate to get her daughter back. Her anguish hadn't been an act. And Tessa, who was part Fae, was a wonderful and kind person who I trusted with my life. The Fae weren't emotionless sociopaths like Elias claimed.

I had to admit that the Rakken were more animal than human, but Silas had told me the Council conditioned them for exactly that purpose. He hadn't revealed just how involved he'd been in that personally, but Elias was feeding them human flesh and keeping them in their nonhuman forms to fuel their animal instincts. Shifters were not Rakken. They chose their actions just like the rest of us, and just because some Shifters turned into this willingly didn't mean the entire race was bad.

Even Humans had committed so many atrocities against each other that it would take days to list them all. The basest instincts could be brought out in anyone under the right circumstances.

"You're keeping a woman locked in a cage and slowly killing her. You let the Rakken eat people. What's the justification for the kind of monster *you* are?"

"She doesn't have to die," Elias promised. "We want the same things, you and I. With your ability to access Earth's magic directly and my leadership, our reach would be absolute. All the realms would unite under our rule, and all the unnecessary violence and death would cease."

"How can you promise any of that? If what you're saying is true, Nuada is going to get his way, and there's nothing either of us can do about it." *Tell me your evil plans so I can thwart them.*

"The Fae are vulnerable—Nuada knows this, and it's why he attacked Aeterna. The Fae have a haven in this realm, but it's young, and it can't generate enough magic to protect them against the full might of the Council. Help me repair the crack you created in

Earth's binding, and the Fae won't have enough magic to sustain their foothold in Earth."

"But what about the Council?"

"Nuada has already provided the groundwork for destabilizing Aeterna. If we work together, the Fae and the Council will be ripe for picking. Our leadership will be absolute, and peace will follow."

Chapter Twenty-One

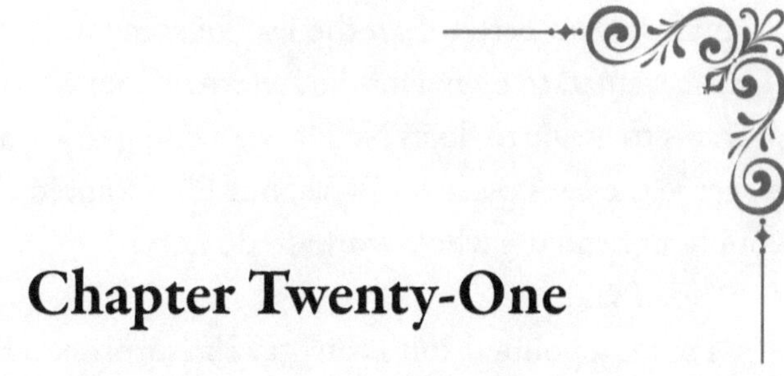

"The Fae haven't done anything to attack us," I said. "I don't see why we can't all be in the same realm. No one has to rule over anyone else."

"The powerful rule the weak, my dear. It's a time-tested truth. You need to think long-term. The Fae will not be content to stay in the small territory they have claimed as their own—generations must expand. In the span of time it takes for your children's children to reach adulthood, the Fae's haven will be mature. They will have enough power to destroy your ancestors' greatest creation, the Earthen Source. Magic will flood this realm, giving them free range across Earth. Do you know what will happen to your precious Mundanes when magic drowns their lives?"

I rubbed Marcel's charm between my fingers as the future Elias painted swam through my mind. "You only want to repair the Earthen Source so you can control it. You don't care about Mundanes. You'd let them all die if it meant more power for you."

He shrugged. "You're getting lost in the minutiae. We have different motivations with the same end goal. I care about keeping the Source intact, just as you do. But if the Fae succeed, and Earth's magic is distributed among all within this realm, there will be no power left to rule. The masses need a leader, or civilization will crumble. More lives will be lost. Together, we will ensure Humanity survives."

Elias was no better than the Fae. In some ways, he was worse. The Fae wanted to be free of the Aeternal Council, and they needed access to magic to do it. Nuada was willing to kill a lot of people to secure the Fae's place on Earth, but Elias wanted to rule, and he would imprison the whole world to do it.

"No," I said.

"I'm disappointed, but I can't say I'm surprised." He ran his finger slowly over his bottom lip. "I'm confident a blood Transference will give me enough of your power to access the Earthen Source, but your ability to channel all that power would have been quite useful. I suppose I must finish what Titus started." He looked me over from head to toe. "A true shame."

A loud boom shook the stone walls around us.

I jumped. "What was that?"

Brutus pounded up the hallway, flanked by two other Rakken I didn't recognize in animal form. "My lord, we're under attack!"

Elation thrilled through me, and a smile spread over my face. I shrugged, feeling the reassuring tug of the tracker glued to my skin. My new government allies had come through, and my people were here for the rescue. "Looks like you're out of time, Elias."

Elias snarled and dragged me through the maze of rooms and hallways. I fought him until he simply commanded me not to. Without preamble, he threw me into a small room with a single window, a desk, and a chair. He pushed me into the chair. "Don't leave that chair. I'll be back for you soon. You have one last chance to reconsider my offer."

He stormed out of the small office, directed Brutus to guard the hallway outside until he returned, and slammed the door behind him.

I had to get out of there before Elias came back. I couldn't wait for a rescue. If I could get back to Kianna's cell, I could work with Lady Treva and get the antidote, even if Nuada had other plans. But that meant getting us both out of there, which was not going to be easy. *No time for a reality check. Do or do not, Maeve.*

I willed myself to stand up, but I couldn't. I was stuck to the chair as strongly as if Elias had tied me there. The compulsion was too strong, and I slumped against an unseen weight holding me down.

I swore vigorously at Elias, letting out my frustration and anger. My foot jittered on the floor. I'd have to think my way out of this, but I couldn't fight the Traiten compulsion.

As soon as I decided that I couldn't fight the command to sit in the chair, a great pressure lifted. I shifted deeper into the seat and stretched out my legs. I counted to sixty in my head before I tried standing up. The pressure returned, and I couldn't do it.

I listened for noise beyond the office door. It had been silent outside for several minutes, and I had no idea if my people had made it through the shielding around Elias's lair. Elias could return at any second and attempt the Transference before my people managed to break through. I didn't have time to sit around.

"Relax," I told myself quietly. "I'm not going anywhere. This chair is great... I could sit here all day."

The pressure let up again. Magic was funny like that. *What did Elias say, exactly, when he told me to stay here? "Don't leave that chair."*

I kept my butt firmly planted in the seat. "I'm not leaving this chair. I have no intention of ever leaving this chair."

With a glance at the door, and hoping the Rakken guarding the other side didn't come to investigate, I planted my heels on the floor and pulled myself forward with my feet, shuffling like a duck to the window. It was getting dark, and my vantage point didn't allow me to see where my rescue was coming from.

Maybe I could lift the chair, swing my butt around, and somehow gather enough momentum to shatter the window. I discarded that impossible idea. There was no way I could do that. And I certainly couldn't drop three stories to the ground and outrun the Rakken through the maze of walls below while holding the chair to my ass.

I shuffled back to the desk and started opening drawers. Empty. Then I remembered the letter opener in my hair and pulled it free. The thin metal blade would be a truly pathetic weapon. Maybe I could ask Elias to hold still for about an hour while I poked him to death. I threw the letter opener on the desk in disgust.

Another explosion thundered so loudly I jumped and landed on my feet. "What the hell?" My left hand gripped the chair's armrest.

I laughed. With one hand firmly gripping the chair, I wasn't *leaving* it—but I apparently didn't have to sit in it to fulfill the compulsion. I slid my hand around to the back of the chair and forced myself to think. Compulsion was a very specific magic. Elias had told me not to leave the chair, but I could stand up as long as I intended to take the chair with me.

I needed my magic. I probably still didn't have enough to skim out of here, but if I had even a minimal amount of magic, I could conjure a weapon. But Elias had told me not to use my magic. What had he said exactly? *You will not access your magic.*

Maybe I could find a loophole in that. I felt for my powers but found nothing. I could sense the magic around me, but I couldn't grab onto anything. Without directly accessing my magic, I couldn't think of a way to get around the compulsion.

Another explosion rocked the house. They were getting closer. I scooted to the windows, anxious for any sign of my rescue. The view from the southern-facing window was only a slice of the entire grounds, and I still couldn't see anything. I listened for other sounds or any indication of what was happening outside. After another minute of silence, I guessed that the shield around the mansion must have been holding—otherwise, the noises would be getting louder.

An idea started to form. I grabbed a heavy metal lamp from the desk and positioned myself next to the door. Eyeing the distance, I took a fighter's stance and launched the lamp at the window five feet away. The glass shattered with a very satisfying—and loud—crash.

The door flew open, and Brutus ran in, surrounded by tainted red magic that bled to black at the edges. I whipped the chair around and slammed it into the back of his legs. The surprise blow buckled his knees, and he plopped into my chair.

From the back of the chair, I wrapped my right arm around his neck, under his chin. I gripped my own left bicep and slid my hand behind Brutus's neck, squeezing hard. The choke hold cut off his air. I'd done this move hundreds of times in practice, and it paid off as he bucked wildly, flailing and choking.

His hands transformed into claws. I yelled as he ripped into my shoulders and neck. But this was life or death, and Brutus was a bastard who ate innocent people. I held on for everything I was worth as he jerked and fought for air. The hold was solid, and his struggles ended quickly. I released him as he slumped unconscious in the chair. I was scratched and bleeding, but I'd live.

Another blast shook the walls. Out the window, the energy of the shield wavered. I rocked from foot to foot as the shield collapsed and shivered out of existence. My people were coming. Casius was going to be pissed, but I knew he'd come to my rescue.

Unfortunately, Elias would have noticed the shield collapse, too, and was probably headed back to start the Transference. I was running out of time.

I dumped Brutus's unconscious form out of my chair, grabbed up the probably useless letter opener, and ran out into the hall. I pushed the chair in front of me, bumping over every seam in the stone floor. The wheels clanked loudly as I sprinted down the hall. The Rakken were going to hear the noise, but I didn't have a choice. I had to find my way back to the cell with Kianna and get out of this damn mansion before Elias found me.

I had no idea if I was headed in the right direction. I paused at the first intersection of four hallways in a miniature foyer. Elias had dragged me through here after visiting Kianna, but I didn't remember which direction we'd come from. I'd gotten too turned around.

I spun in a circle and literally ran into Elias coming from an adjacent hall. The angle of the hallways prevented us from seeing each other until we were almost on top of each other and my chair smacked into his shins. He jumped back and clutched at his leg where the chair had hit him.

I maneuvered the chair between us like a shield. With a curse, he lunged and grabbed the chair. I pulled back, but he yanked it forward with impressive strength. I shifted my weight onto my hands, preparing to deliver a roundhouse kick to his head.

"Stop!" he yelled.

The Traiten bands glowed with magic, and my entire body froze, leaving me awkwardly balanced on the chair arms and a single leg.

He kicked the chair out from between us, ripping it from my hands.

"No!" I dove for the chair.

The compulsion was too strong. I scrambled to get back to the stupid chair, but Elias grabbed my feet and dragged me on my stomach down the hallway. I kicked and screamed and clawed for the chair as it spun away from us.

"Gods dammit, forget about the chair!" Elias commanded.

The compulsion lifted immediately. I flipped over onto my back and kicked Elias in the face. He dropped me and clutched his nose. I scrambled to my hands and knees and reached for the letter opener on the ground.

"Stop!" Elias yelled.

The bands around my wrist glowed, and I froze. The letter opener was just inches from my fingers. I gritted my teeth and tried to make my hand move. I just needed to curl my fingers around the thin blade and use it on Elias, but I couldn't do it.

He booted the pathetic weapon out of my reach and then kicked me hard in the stomach. The blow laid me out on the floor. Pain radiated from my ribs and stomach. It hurt so bad that I had to focus on my breathing as nausea rippled through me. Above me, Elias glowed with power, and blood dripped from his nose as he bared his teeth. He looked feral, the veneer of refined civility gone as he loomed over me, angry as all hell.

"Maeve!" a voice shouted.

Elias and I both turned toward the familiar and totally un-expected male voice. Silas was running down the hallway at full speed, his sword gripped in his hand. With my magic out of reach, I hadn't even felt him through our shared bond. My emotions flipped all over the place—surprise that he was here, utter relief, and finally, guilt. He'd come for me even when I told him it was over between us. I was completely unable to take my eyes off him as my heart stuttered with a dizzying array of emotions.

Behind Silas, three more rescuers followed—Tessa, Jason, and Casius, all glowing with power.

"Stop, or she dies!" Elias yelled.

Silas slid to a stop just inside the small foyer where I was still sprawled on the ground. His stance was aggressive, ready to spring into action. The others stopped behind him, also armed and ready for a fight.

"Maeve, get up," Elias commanded me.

The bands glowed again, and my body moved, sending waves of pain through my abused ribs.

"Hold that blade to your throat," Elias said.

I retrieved the letter opener, and my hand rose to my own neck. With enough force behind it, the edge would be just sharp enough to slice through my skin. Comprehension and then horror flowed over my rescuers as they realized what was happening.

Casius swore.

"If they attack me, slit your own throat," Elias commanded.

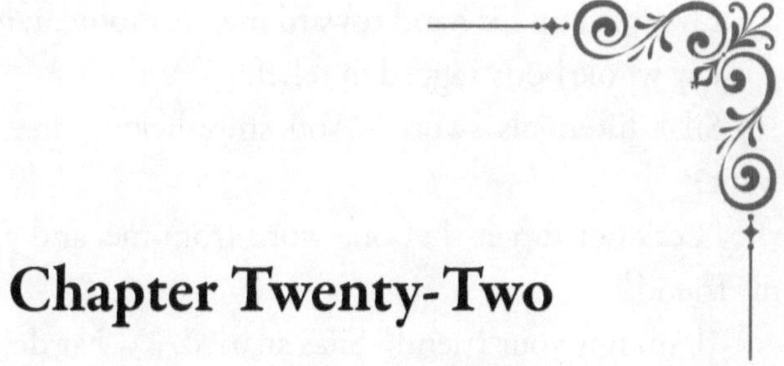

Chapter Twenty-Two

I felt the compulsion slide over me, and I knew I would do it. If any of them attacked Elias, I would slit my own throat. Terror shivered up my spine, wrapping its claws around my neck until I almost couldn't breathe. I didn't want to die.

"Do you want her to live, Lord Silas?"

Silas's jaw clenched, and his whole body tensed. "Take the compulsion off her, and I won't kill you."

Elias barked out a laugh without humor. "You'll kill me the second she's free."

Casius stepped out from behind Silas, and side by side, they faced Elias. "I give you my word. Release Maeve, and you'll go free."

Elias raised his chin at Casius. "Lady Maeve, who is that?"

"His name is Casius," I responded automatically. "He's my mentor and a leader in the Inner Circle."

Elias hummed. "Perfect. Drain his magic."

Pure terror flooded my brain. Elias was going to make me kill Casius. I tried to fight the command, but it was impossible.

I reached for my magic. My flare was still weak from the burnout, but it might be enough for me to hurt my mentor. I didn't want to take the chance.

"Run, Casius!" I yelled.

Casius frowned at my weak aura as my hands rose.

I reached for his magic and—

"Elias, hold!" Silas bellowed.

Elias held up his hand toward me. "A moment, my dear."

My whole body sagged in relief.

Silas lifted his sword. "You shite-licking arse, what do you want?"

"Let's not forget that one word from me, and your Aegis dies, my friend."

"I am not your friend," Silas snarled. "What do you want with Maeve?"

"Let us go, or I'll have her drain all of you." Elias backed down the hall, his eyes glued on Silas. "Come, my lady. We're leaving."

As commanded, I followed Elias, but my gaze snagged on movement in the adjacent hallway. A troop of agents moved stealthily up the narrow corridor, decked out in combat gear. From where I stood in the foyer, I was the only one who could see them. Elias had his back to them, while Silas and my people were farther back in their own hallway, not quite inside the foyer where all four corridors connected.

In the front, Agent Lennart crouched low, leading a team of five soldiers with their guns drawn. If Elias turned around, he'd see them, and he'd kill them with magic in less than a second. They had no idea they were inching closer to their own deaths, and I couldn't warn them without giving them away. And if they attacked Elias, the compulsion would force me to slit my own throat. Lennart wasn't supposed to be here, and he was going to get us all killed.

"If you attempt to harm me, she'll kill herself," Elias said to Silas. "If you attempt to follow us, I will be forced to kill her."

Silas started forward, rage all over his face, the point of his sword lifted toward Elias.

"You're right!" I blurted.

Elias turned toward me, exposing his back fully to the soldiers. His brow wrinkled in confusion. "I'm right about a great many things, my dear. You'll have to be specific."

"We deserve to rule. We're better than the Shifters, the Fae, all of them."

Elias laughed, his face tilted back in a full-throated guffaw. "Are you trying to get out of your imminent death? Speak only the truth."

"Yes." Then I pulled out my best Fae impression and let him hear what he wanted from snippets of truth. "Of course I don't want to die. But the truth is, I would rather die than allow the Fae to rule Earth. And you want to rule, but you need my powers to do it. Our needs align." Every single word was true, and Elias would draw all the wrong conclusions.

He narrowed his eyes.

The agents were nearly at the entrance to the foyer, just a dozen yards from Elias's back. I made eye contact with Lennart and shook my head slightly. He nodded, oblivious to my silent plea to turn back. I held back my frustration and dragged my gaze back to Elias, who was trying to decipher the meaning between my words.

I fed him more nuggets of truth. "If you die, then I die too. We both lose. I'd rather not die." All true. But none of it meant what he wanted it to mean.

Lennart lifted a bulky gun with a squared-off muzzle—it looked like a toy—and fired. A high-pitched whine went off. Elias spun toward the noise, and a wave of energy from Lennart's specialized gun hit him right in the chest. Part of the blast caught me, and I stumbled backward into Silas just as Elias fell unconscious to the ground.

Silas knocked the metal letter opener from my hand and locked me in a grip so tight I could barely breathe. "Let go!" I said, assuring him as best I could around his hold. "I'm totally not suicidal." I felt absolutely no compulsion to kill myself. I examined my wrists. The Traiten bands were gone. The compulsion had been wiped out with the blast from that strange gun.

The blast had hurt like a mother fratcher, but I barely had time to think about it. Silas released me just as four Rakken barreled up the hallway behind the soldiers, screeching and growling. Their predatory howls sent primal fear slithering into my brain.

The agents froze at the sight of the ferocious beasts charging toward them. Their claws dug into the stone floor as they raced toward us. The agents didn't even have time to fire a single round before two Rakken pounced on the soldiers at the rear of their group.

I grabbed for my magic and felt nothing. My entire body was numb. With the Traiten compulsion gone, I should be able to sense *something*. But I couldn't sense any magic around me. It was as if my connection to magic was completely severed. I was completely defenseless—no powers, no weapons. Panicked, I grabbed the letter opener from the floor as the lead Rakken leapt past the Mundane soldiers, easily clearing the entire group of people, and bounded straight for me.

Silas was there before I could jump out of the way. His sword flashed, and he spun his entire body with the blade, his magic twisting with him. The Rakken's head fell from its shoulders before the rest of the body toppled to the ground, still moving from its own momentum.

Three more Rakken tore through the DODSI soldiers, clawing and slicing without slowing as they barreled toward us. Silas ran to intercept them.

"Silas! Weapon!" I yelled.

Bless him—he didn't question why I couldn't conjure my own weapons, and he didn't hesitate. He slid his sword across the floor to me and formed razor-sharp lines of magic around himself as he charged toward the Rakken. I stopped the blade with my foot just as a large hairless monster leapt in front of me.

Silas's blade was too heavy for me, but I managed to heft it and slash across the thick hide of the Rakken's neck. The blow glanced off, barely scratching. I poked the sword toward its eye and almost got my hand bitten off. I was too damn slow with Silas's heavy freaking sword.

I lowered the blade, too tired and bruised to keep it raised properly, and pivoted clear of the Rakken's snapping jaws. The beast followed me, gnashing its teeth and clawing, trying to herd me down an adjacent hallway away from the others. I kept the blade between us as it forced me back, farther and farther. Then Tessa was there, dashing in behind the Rakken to sever its hind-leg tendons in a single swipe of her blade. The beast crashed to the floor, snarling in pain.

With a flash of magic, Silas conjured and threw a dagger to me. *Ripper!* I dropped his sword and caught the seven-inch field knife I'd bought on the streets of Boston. When we first met, Silas had stolen it and branded it as his own until I agreed to answer his questions. It was damn handy that he could summon it now.

The familiar hilt fit perfectly in my palm. Ignoring the pain in my ribs, I dodged in and sliced from left to right on the underside of the wounded Rakken's neck, burying the blade almost to the hilt as I opened a deep gash.

Sharp. Well balanced. I really do like this knife.

I sprang to my feet, ready for another attack from the Rakken.

The agents opened fire.

I dropped to the ground and covered my head. Without magic to shield me, I was no match for bullets. But as the familiar feel of Silas's arms and his magic slid around me in a protective shield, I realized I was safe. The rapid fire, and at least one more whining blast of the strange magic-killing gun, went on for several seconds and took out the rest of the Rakken.

When the firing stopped, I rose and took stock of our situation. Fortunately, my rescuers had also had the good sense to hit the floor—Tessa, Casius, and Jason were all fine. Lennart was unharmed, but two other agents weren't as lucky. One lay dead on the ground, and three more seemed seriously wounded from their encounter with the Rakken.

I swore when I counted up three dead Rakken, now in their human skins, but no Elias. He must have slipped away during the fight. Silas pushed himself to a standing position and stalked in Lennart's direction.

Lennart planted his feet and pointed his magic-killing gun at Silas's chest. "Stand down!"

The tip of Silas's sword rose. "Who are you?"

Lennart's finger tightened on the trigger.

"Wait!" I yelled. "They're not enemies. Agent Lennart helped me get Gia back."

Lennart's gun didn't waiver from Silas's chest. "O'Neill! Tell Highlander here to back down or I'll shoot."

Quick footsteps pounded up the hallway, and more soldiers in tactical gear flooded the foyer behind us. I reached again for my magic. *Nothing.*

Silas's aura flexed with magic, but I put my hand on his arm, shaking my head. We couldn't kill everyone around us without some serious repercussions from the government. And I needed to know what I'd been hit with. If that blast was permanent, then both Elias and I had just lost our connection to magic. I tamped down my panic. I just hoped my state wasn't permanent.

As I instructed Silas to stand down, Casius, Jason, and Tessa were pushed up against the wall, their hands behind their heads, and pistols pointed at their backs by the newest agents, who gaped wide-eyed at the destroyed bodies of the Rakken, now shifting back to their human forms.

Time to try logic. Gods help us.

I showed Lennart my palms. "The man you shot—Lord Elias—he's the one I was telling you about. He's the man who kidnapped me and is orchestrating all of this. You need to let us go so we can stop him."

Lennart took in Silas's leather armor and his sword. "This is the man from the battle." Lennart jerked the barrel of his antimagic gun at Silas. "He's the one in our satellite images with *hundreds* of bodies." Lennart bared his teeth. "You're both coming with us. We have some questions for you, Highlander."

Silas took another step forward, and every gun in the room trained on him. His bloodied sword rose from the ground, and magic flexed around him. "I do not bow to your authority."

Lennart's finger moved onto the trigger. "Freeze. Not another step."

Slowly, with my palms raised, I put myself between Silas and Lennart. Silas growled at my new position, but I ignored him as I spoke to the agent. "Elias is the one responsible for those deaths, not Silas. We need to stop Elias before he gets too far away."

Lennart kept his eyes on Silas. "Elias has been neutralized. He can't get far without his magic."

"Is it permanent?" I tried hard to keep my face neutral. I was pretty sure Lennart didn't know I'd been hit, and I really wanted to keep it that way.

"Temporary," Lennart said grudgingly. "Stunned for a few hours."

I let out a tiny sigh of relief. I'd get my magic back. I'd only gotten a fraction of the blast—and if the full blast took out someone's magic for only a couple of hours, hopefully I'd be well on my way to recovering my own abilities much sooner.

"Then let us find him while he's vulnerable. You *need* us to stop Elias, Agent Lennart. And your people need help." I motioned toward the agents on the floor. Several other agents crouched around them, attempting to stop the bleeding and bandage their wounds.

One man's leg was missing a chunk where a Rakken had torn at it, and the others had wicked claw wounds.

Lennart's lips pursed as a radio squawked in his ear. "The building is clear. Teams one and three, move out." He waved his hand in the air, and his people started gathering up their wounded. "The rest of them can go hunt the big bad guy, but you're coming with us, Miss O'Neill. You promised us information."

Silas stepped forward, his sword raised and magic flaring around him. "You're not taking her with you."

Lennart lifted his gun. "Is this the pissed-off guard who was going to lose his shit after you died?"

Silas's expression went completely flat, and anger flooded through our bond. "You thought you were going to die, and you *still* went forward with your plan?"

The flash of hot anger was the first I'd felt from him since I'd accepted the bond-mating with Ethan, but it was weak. It would probably stay that way until my powers fully returned, but feeling anything from Silas was a relief—as was any sign that my magic was coming back.

"You're not helping, Lennart. We can heal your agents. Let us help them, and we'll part ways as friends."

"None of you are getting anywhere near my people," Lennart said. "You made a deal, and we came through with our end. Now you're coming with us to answer a hell of a lot of questions."

"Look, I promise to give you all the information you need, but I can't go with you right now. I need to help stop Elias."

"Want," he corrected. "All the information we want."

"Fine," I agreed, ignoring the pissed look I got from Casius. "Whatever you want. But I can't come with you right now, not when Elias is still out there. I promise to keep my end of our bargain once this is all over."

Lennart glowered at me and then at Silas, who hadn't backed off even an inch, and finally at the rest of my rescue squad. I got the distinct impression he was deciding if he could take me with him by force.

"Speaking of bargains," I said to disrupt whatever stupid idea was brewing in his head, "you were supposed to give my coordinates to my people."

"And I did. They're here, aren't they?"

"But following me here was not part of our deal. I might even go so far as to say you broke our agreement."

Lennart's face scrunched in distaste. "Fine. You can go, but you still owe us information." He motioned at his people, who released Casius, Jason, and Tessa. "Oh, and I'm supposed to tell you that Ethan is the first turning point."

"Ethan?" My head cocked to the side. "What does that mean? Who told you that?"

"Director Pascal told me to deliver that message word for word. It's not my fault if you don't know what the hell it means." He adjusted his grip on the bulky magic-disrupting gun. "Just hold up your end of the bargain, or you and I will have bigger problems next time we meet."

The agents left as I pondered the message, but I didn't have much time to dwell on it as I faced my disgruntled rescue squad. Every one of them watched me angrily for completely different reasons.

"Oh, stop it, all of you. I'm fine. Gia's safe. I did what I had to do to make that happen because no one else came up with a better plan." I tugged my braid back over my shoulder. "And now we know where Kianna is."

Chapter Twenty-Three

After twenty embarrassing minutes of playing follow the lost leader, I finally found Kianna's cell buried deep within the building.

"Don't touch it!" I said as Jason reached for the metal bars. "It's a magic-absorbing trap."

We stared at the unconscious body on the floor. The jumble of rags and limbs barely stirred.

"That's Lady Kianna?" Casius asked doubtfully as he squinted into the dark cave-like cell.

"Yes," I said.

Tessa whistled between her teeth. "So that's why the scrying wouldn't work. The cell absorbed the conjuring's effect. Shite, she looks like they ran her to the post and back."

"What did they do to her?" Jason asked, his face furrowed in concern.

"She's been cut off from magic." I waved toward the bars in front of us. "That cell sucks energy out of whatever is inside it. Apparently, it's the Council's creation."

One of Silas's eyebrows rose. "I'm impressed that Lady Kianna is still alive. Fae are tied closely to their magic and can't survive in magic-sparse environments."

"Elias said they're allowing her just enough magic to stay alive. I'm guessing they take her out for a few hours each day."

"Are you sure she's still alive?" Casius asked with a dubious twist of his mouth. Kianna hadn't moved, and she was skin and bones. I wondered if they'd been starving her of food as well as magic.

"If she's not, a whole lot of people are about to die with her." I dragged in air to deliver the rest of the bad news. "Nuada orchestrated her kidnapping. He used his own daughter as the excuse to poison the Citizen Source and start a war with the Aeternal Council."

Silas swore loudly and heartily, immediately catching on to the implications.

"Nothing changes," I said. "We still have to convince the Fae that Nuada's actions were unjustified."

Jason, Casius, and Tessa looked confused.

"Lady Treva helped me escape the Elementari so I could find Kianna," I explained. "I don't think she was in on the plan to kill her own daughter. Once we convince the Fae that the Council didn't take Lady Kianna, I think Treva will help us get the antidote, but we have to get Kianna out of there first."

Thanks to Four's cryptic restrictions, I couldn't tell them that I also needed Kianna freed to make sure the latest vision didn't come true. Either way, we had to get her out. I stared at the threads of energy within the cell's conjuring. It was complex. Even at full power, I didn't know where I would start trying to unravel it. Casius examined the convoluted layers with an equally perplexed expression.

With a tug on my braid, I reached for my magic. *Nothing.* I was still running on empty. A small flash of panic hit me, but I pushed it down. It had been less than thirty minutes since I'd been hit with the blast, and I was already drained from my earlier burnout. The magic would come back with time. *It has to.*

But my current situation gave me an idea. "I think I can go in and get Kianna. I'm basically a Mundane right now thanks to the blast from that magic-disrupting gun."

I reached for the cell bars, not waiting long enough for anyone to object. The spell zapped my brain the second I touched the metal. My vision flickered, and the cell flashed with a burst of energy. I fell back, rubbing at my painfully tingling skin.

"That was stupid," Tessa said.

"Thanks. I got that." I shook out my hand. "I think it just zapped me, but it stings like a mother."

Silas reached for the cell door and yanked hard. Power snapped like a rubber band along his flesh, and he swore as he let it go. "And it's locked."

I frowned at the cell. "We need the key."

"Even if we find the key, who's going to go in there and get her?" Tessa asked.

I glanced around the room and found exactly what I was searching for. Elias was overconfident and cruel. He'd hung the key within plain sight of Kianna's cell.

I grabbed it off the hook, and a brilliant idea hit me. "Did anyone see a barn or a stable on their way in? I think it would be on the west side of the building."

Casius looked at me like I'd lost my mind. "You need a horse?"

"They're keeping Mundanes locked up there." I remembered the woman who served me dinner and the hay tangled into her matted hair. "Someplace where there's hay. Like a barn."

"Why would they keep Mundanes—"

"Trust me, you don't want to know," I said. "But any of the Mundanes can go in that cell and carry Kianna out. If there's anyone left."

"I can go back and check," Jason said.

"I'll go with him," Casius said. "We shouldn't go anywhere alone, in case we run into any more Rakken or Elias."

"Agent Lennart said the building was clear," I said.

"Right," Casius said. "But let's still be careful. Don't split up."

They rushed off, leaving Silas, Tessa, and me to guard Lady Kianna, who lay on the ground far back in the shadows, not moving as far as I could tell. I hoped she wasn't dead.

"We need to get her out soon." I chewed on the inside of my cheek, wondering if Kianna knew about her own father arranging her kidnapping. Things could get messy, depending on what she did or didn't know.

Which reminded me about the mess I'd made of my relationship with Silas. Even though I'd accepted a bond-mating agreement right in front of him, he'd still showed up to rescue me. I shifted back on my heels. "So, uh, did you get my voicemail? How did you find me?"

Silas's face played out a range of expressions that could mostly be summarized as frustrated. "Casius brought me with him."

"I thought you left to find Kianna."

"I stayed behind to talk with you when we didn't have an audience. That bond-mating proposal was a ridiculous pile of shite, and then you willingly crawled even deeper into it, and I want to know why. Whatever it is has clearly spun out of your control."

Tessa cleared her throat. "I'm just going to go... over there... and keep watch." She wandered off down the hallway, giving us some much-needed privacy.

Equal parts indignation and love filled me. I'd been afraid my actions had ruined any chance I had to be with Silas, but I should have known better. He wasn't going to give up on us just because I'd agreed to something stupid under duress.

"It's scary how much I love you," I said to Silas.

Surprise flashed across his face and through our bond. His eyes searched mine intently. "Maeve, tell me what's happening—not just with this bond-mating. Something more is going on that you're not telling me. Something big."

I couldn't explain myself without telling him about the visions. And Four had been very clear about what would happen if anyone else knew. I would lose my chance to change the visions, and Silas would die. My people would be slaughtered. I'd already managed to make the visions worse when I involved DODSI. I couldn't risk it.

I shook my head. "I'm sorry, Silas, I really want to but—"

I was saved from further interrogation when footsteps echoed up the hall. Silas drew his sword, and I gripped Ripper tighter. A Mundane man with brown hair rounded the corner. He stopped in midstep, and his gaze froze on Silas's sword.

"I'm supposed to help someone?" he asked hesitantly.

I stepped forward, nudging Silas to the side and hiding Ripper casually at my side. I didn't want to scare the poor man to death—he'd clearly already been through enough.

"Hey," I said slowly. "Are you alone?" I peered down the hallway for Casius and Jason, but they weren't following him. It was strange that Tessa hadn't said anything either when the man passed her in the hallway.

"Yeah. Your friends are looking for the others..." He peered back up the hallway as if he were considering bolting.

"It's okay—everything's going to be fine." I held out the key to him and jerked my chin at Kianna's cell. "We need you to get that woman out of there. The monsters who kidnapped you took her too. Do you think you can help me?"

The man met my eyes, but instead of taking the key from my hand, he winked. "All you had to do was ask, Maeve O'Neill."

Four!

Before I could move, the Fate reached out with his index finger, deliberately tapping me on the palm. My entire body zinged with magic, and everything went white. I screamed. Every cell in my body seemed to reorient itself as magic flooded back through me in a wave of agonizing and euphoric power.

"Maeve! What happened?" Silas called from my side.

My brain was flooded with white light. "I can't see anything!" I cried.

Tessa's voice echoed down the hallway. "Silas? Maeve?"

"Don't move!" Silas's strong grip on my shoulder guided me until our backs were against the wall. We froze, tense, waiting for an attack in the darkness.

After a handful of heartbeats, I whispered into the dark. "Can you see anything?"

"No. Might be a defensive spell," Silas said.

Nothing happened—no enemies lunging from the shadows, no explosion of magic. Slowly, my eyes adjusted, and I gasped when I saw the cell. "The door is open!"

"Where's Lady Kianna?" Silas yelled.

I peered into the dark alcove, blinking away the last of the temporary blindness, and saw her still body lying on the ground. "Kianna's still in there."

"Where did the Mundane go?" Silas demanded.

"Is all well?" Tessa called.

"Stay there," Silas called back. "Wait for Casius and Jason to return."

"I'm pretty sure Casius and Jason didn't send him," I said slowly.

"Come again?" Silas asked.

I sighed, letting my frustration and anger loose. "He's a Fate named Four. That's the second time the bastard's winked at me before doing something shitty."

Silas stood in front of me. "A Fate?" His eyebrows rose in that exasperated expression I was so familiar with. "Maeve, tell me what is going on."

I swallowed hard. "I'm trying to straighten it all out. But I... I can't tell you any more than that."

Silas frowned, and then understanding crossed his face. "What does the Fate want from you?"

I gritted my teeth. "It doesn't matter. If we save Kianna, then everything else will fall into place."

I really, really hoped that Silas would trust me to finish this on my own.

Silas glowered. "Anything a Fate says is designed to twist your head."

"I know. But whatever he did restored my powers." I let magic flood my aura, and Silas scowled. "Look, it's almost over. I just need to finish what I started."

"Is Kianna part of this?" Silas asked.

I clamped my mouth shut. I couldn't tell him anything. *How did I get myself into such a mess?*

"Maeve, tell me what the Fate showed you." Silas's voice was just short of a demanding growl.

"I can't! If I tell anyone, it's going to cause... *stuff*... to happen. I already messed up once, and I can't risk it!"

Silas threw his hands in the air. "Gods dammit! This is utterly ridiculous. You can't trust a Fate, Maeve. They'll fratch up your entire life with no more than a thought. Trust me, I know firsthand."

I swallowed thickly. The Fates had royally screwed up Silas's life with the prophecy that forced him into a bonded mating. I felt terrible that I couldn't tell Silas everything, but I couldn't risk the consequences. "I'm sorry, Silas. We don't have time to fight about this. We need to figure out a way to get Kianna out of there and get the antidote."

Silas glowered, and I stared back until he turned on his heel with an irritated huff and took a deliberate step inside the cell.

"Silas!" I yelled.

He crossed the threshold. Nothing happened. My heart swung from wild alarm to relief, leaving me breathless.

"What the hell?" I exclaimed. "That cell could have drained your magic dry!"

"The Fate disabled the conjuring," he said.

"You didn't know that for sure!" I snapped. "That was idiotic!"

"Much like trusting the word of a Fate!"

He wasn't wrong. I just didn't have any other choice. And I definitely didn't appreciate his methods of pointing it out. "Just get Kianna, and let's get out of here."

Tessa's voice echoed up the hallway. "What's happening back there?"

"We're coming, and we've got Kianna," I yelled back.

Silas scooped Kianna up with ease and carried her out of the cell. She seemed tiny in his arms. She was unconscious and covered in dirt and dried blood, but her chest rose and fell evenly. Kianna was in bad shape, but she was alive, and the lives of everyone in Aeterna depended on keeping her that way.

"Is she going to wake up and skim away?" I asked.

"She won't have any magic for quite some time," Silas said. "Natural regeneration is a slow process. Especially this far from the Fae's haven."

"Let's get her back to her mother before anything else goes wrong."

"Follow me." Silas led the way out, carrying Kianna.

We met up with Tessa partway and then Jason and Casius at the end of the long hallway. They reported that no other Mundanes were locked in the barn, but their faces were white, and Casius looked a little green around the edges. I didn't want to ask about what they'd found, and they didn't volunteer the information.

Silas seemed to know which way to turn at every intersection. Or at least, if he was guessing, he was confident about it. After a few minutes of winding through hallways, we left through the shattered remains of the mansion's front door—a hunk of twisted wood and metal hanging from a single hinge—and into the outer courtyard. A path of destruction led straight through the walls of the maze, leaving no doubt what the loud booms had been. My rescue team had blasted through the shield and plowed a direct path from the outermost wall to the front door, leaving at least a dozen gaping holes in the walls of the maze.

We picked our way through the ruins of the first two-thirds of the maze before our luck ran out and a chorus of shrieks rose up behind us. We all cringed at the brain-piercing noise, the sound triggering a primordial fear that curved around my spine.

Silas shifted Kianna's unconscious weight over his shoulder, and we ran through the destroyed maze as fast as we could. Jason got to the outer wall first. Crouching, he boosted Casius and Tessa up to the top of the ten-foot wall. They helped Jason up, and Silas and I pushed the unconscious Kianna up and over into their arms.

Silas crouched, offering me his cupped hands. "Your turn."

Howls erupted behind us. Ten rows of broken maze away, at least a dozen Rakken raced toward us, twisting through the wreckage. Even though I had my magic back, I couldn't skim Silas and myself out of there. I didn't have a visual on the other side of the wall, and I had no idea where we were. From this side, I would have had to skim us somewhere I was familiar with, leaving the others behind to defend themselves against the Rakken without Silas or me. The only option was to physically climb over the wall and skim out together.

Casius leaned over the wall, his arm outstretched. "Come on!"

The Rakken were too close. There wasn't time to get Silas and me both over the wall, and I wasn't going to leave him to fight on his own. I ignored Casius's outstretched hand and gripped Ripper. I briefly considered absorbing the Rakken's powers, but just thinking about the influx of stolen life magic made me want to vomit. I let my magic rise around me. Missy landed in my other hand, and I braced myself for a fight.

"Stay back," Silas ordered. He unbuckled his scabbard from around his hips, letting it fall to the ground as he dashed forward. Golden power rose around him as he ran head-on toward the Rakken without his sword.

I took a step forward. *What the hell is he doing?*

Energy blazed on all sides of Silas, covering him as he sprinted for a head-on collision with teeth and claws. Silas was twenty yards away from me when he reached the Rakken. Three of them leapt at him. Silas jumped as if to meet them in midair and—disappeared.

I sucked in a breath. *A midleap skim!*

Silas reappeared on the other side of the Rakken, flipping like a gymnast as his magic flashed gold lightning around him. Just as Silas's feet touched the ground, magic punched the air. The power rippled from him in all directions, obliterating everything in a ten-foot radius, including the Rakken.

Fifty feet back, the impact reverberated in my chest as a tidal wave of pure energy hit me. The whole world seemed to pause as Silas's magic pulsed. I exhaled and stumbled forward under the unexpected upsurge of power.

I soaked it in, instinctually absorbing the residual magic through our Aegis bond. When it had finally washed over and through me, I gulped in air. I'd forgotten to breathe. I took in the destruction. Bits and pieces of Rakken were scattered in a perfect circle around Silas. It was horrible and awe-inspiring at the same time. I'd never seen anything like it.

Silas looked dazed as he took a shuddering step forward.

"Silas!" I ran for him.

He was panting when I slid to a stop beside him. "I just need a moment," he said. "That was... difficult so far from my own source."

I'd heard about Silas's legendary battle magic, but it was even more forceful than I'd imagined, like a nuclear blast going off with Silas at the center. And he hadn't even drawn from my family source. *Holy shit.*

It had happened so fast—I couldn't quite wrap my brain around the absolute destruction he'd managed in mere seconds. He'd landed in the middle of an entire pack of Rakken and completely decimated them.

"Why didn't you draw power through our bond, you idiot?"

He pulled me against his chest and kissed the top of my head. "I wasn't sure you could follow orders."

"What are you talking about? Are you delirious?"

He grunted. "I was afraid you were going to follow me, and that particular tactic doesn't discriminate between friend and foe. I can only use it in an open area, where I know my allies are out of range, and I wasn't completely confident you'd stay put if you felt me draw that much power through you."

I snorted as Silas pulled himself together. I decided to let that one go—it felt so good to be in his arms after I'd almost blown up everything between us. Another wave of horrific awe swept over me as we picked our way through the gory destruction and back to the wall. I could imagine how useful Silas's particular skills would be in a battle.

Jason had scrambled back over the wall, and he held out his closed fist. "That was sick, man."

Silas's eyebrows rose as he gave Jason a reluctant fist bump. "Sick?"

"Sick. Awesome. Super cool. How do you store enough power to fuel that kind of offensive maneuver? Actually, first, tell me how you managed to skim while you were in the air like that. The disorientation from your starting point has to be something else."

I rolled my eyes. It wasn't often that Jason acted his age, but apparently, Silas had a new fan. *Just what Silas's ego needs.*

Casius reappeared at the top of the wall. "Stop dillydallying. Kianna's awake."

I reached for his outstretched hand and scrambled over the wall with a boost from Silas. On the other side, Kianna sat propped against the base of a large oak tree, giving Tessa the evil eye. Some of the color had already returned to her skin. That was a good sign. No magic aura yet—also a good sign. We wouldn't want her skimming back to the Fae on her own when we needed to trade her for the antidote.

I crouched at her side. "Lady Kianna?" Her gaze shifted to me, and she seemed a little dazed. I lowered my voice to a soft, reassuring tone. "You're free now. You're going to be okay. Do you think you can stand up?"

"How much time has passed since I was taken?" Kianna looked up at us with wide amethyst eyes, and I corrected my earlier belief that she was pretty despite being covered in grime. She was breathtaking. Even in rags and starved half to death, she was... magnetic.

"At least four days," Tessa said. "That's when your father kidnapped Maeve."

"Who is this halfling?" Kianna asked me.

I looked at Tessa. She was clearly Fae born, with her amethyst eyes and adorably pointed ears. But comparing Kianna and Tessa, the differences between a full-blooded Fae were obvious. They both had Fae features, but Lady Kianna's cheekbones were sharper and her face more angular than what would have passed for human upon close inspection. Kianna was so lean that I'd assumed she'd been starved when I saw her in the cell, but as she rose gracefully to her feet, I realized she was tall and supermodel thin but not weak—another Fae characteristic that made her look slightly *other* and which Tessa didn't share.

"Tessa? Do you and Lady Kianna have a beef we should know about?" I asked.

"Lady Kianna doesn't know me." Tessa rolled her eyes. "She's just an elitist snob, like her parents."

Lady Kianna sniffed delicately.

"You should be grateful we rescued you after your father kidnapped Maeve," Tessa said.

"My father kidnapped you, and you rescued me? I don't understand. Why would you do this?"

"You didn't deserve to die, even if your father is a first-rate Faehole," I said.

Kianna and Tessa both frowned at the slur.

"Sorry." I had to assume that Kianna didn't know that her father had poisoned the Citizen Source or that he'd handed her over to Elias. "I just meant that you're innocent in all this. The fight between your father and the Council doesn't have anything to do with you." I bit my lip and decided to see what she knew already. "I'm curious, though. How did Elias get his hands on you? Weren't you in the Fae haven with your people?"

"I had ventured outside the haven for a short while on some personal business. I never even saw my attackers, and then I awoke in that cell."

There was definitely something shady about her answer—including the question of what she had been doing outside the haven, where magic was almost nonexistent—but I didn't push. She'd confirmed what I needed to know. She had no idea her father had set her up, and I didn't want to complicate our exchange by filling her in on that particular detail. Most importantly, her story didn't contradict what Elias said, and I was more confident than ever that Nuada had his own daughter kidnapped.

Silas walked up to us, and Kianna went stiff. "Do you intend to turn me over to the Council, Lord Silas?"

"Your father has poisoned the Citizen Source," Silas replied. "One of his demands for the antidote is that you are returned safely."

She sank to the ground, kneeling, and her fingertips dug into the dirt. "I am saddened to hear that."

Silas crouched down next to Kianna. "Is there an antidote?"

She seemed to consider her words carefully. "I do not know how my father has poisoned the Citizen Source, nor can I confirm the existence of an antidote."

Silas rocked back on his heels. "So we still have no guarantee that an antidote even exists."

"What will you do with me, then?" Kianna's eyes went wide, and I felt a sudden desire to comfort her. She'd been through so much already, and she needed someone to protect her. She lifted her chin bravely, quivering slightly. "Will you kill me?"

"Your father wrongly attacked Aeterna," Silas said. "We need you to tell your people who really took you. If they agree to give us the antidote, there won't be any reason you can't go home."

She straightened her shoulders. Her face set into a determined glare that reminded me of her mother, Lady Treva. Then it softened. Her hand rose to Silas's chest, the fingers gently splayed over his heart. "You won't hurt me, Silas Valeron."

Silas lowered himself to one knee at her side. "Of course I won't hurt you."

She ran her hand through the hair at the back of his neck. His hand lifted to her beautiful face. Casius and Jason moved closer, smiling down at Kianna.

She really is lovely.

"You love me, don't you?" she asked Silas. "You want to set me free." She kissed Silas softly on the lips. His hands cupped her face.

Something sharp twisted in my heart. The discomfort tore through my stupor, and I shook my head. Something wasn't right. I didn't like what Kianna was doing. I blinked, trying to clear away the buzzing in my brain. It hurt.

The pain brought clarity, and I noticed tendrils of blue magic tangled around Silas. I examined them, following the threads back to Kianna. She had her magic wrapped around Silas, around all of us. The magic was spreading, pulsing with energy that tingled and burned across my awareness.

No. Gritting my teeth, I fought against the thrall that had fogged my brain. I grabbed the threads of her conjuring and broke them with so much force that the magic smacked her on the rebound. Kianna gasped as I held Ripper's blade against her throat.

Silas staggered backward and scooped up the sword he'd laid casually on the ground. "Shite! I didn't even feel the thrall." He looked down at her hands still buried in the dirt. "Fratching hells. She's an Earth elemental."

I pushed the knife a little harder against her neck. "Hands up, Kianna."

She folded her hands into her lap and sagged back against the oak tree. The thrall had clearly drained the little magic she'd regained, and she was exhausted. Casius and Jason were similarly dazed, shaking their heads and reorienting themselves, but Tessa seemed to recover as fast as I had and drew her sword, ready to retaliate.

"Looks like she got her powers back," I said dryly, my knife still at Kianna's throat.

"That was faster than expected," Jason said, rubbing at his temples.

Though lighter than a compulsion, a thrall could still be strong enough to build false feelings toward the conjurer. In the worst cases, over long periods of time, the victim developed total devotion even after the spell ended. Entire religions had been built on strong thralls.

"Try anything like that again"—I got right in her face—"and I'll deliver your dead body back to your parents."

"You cannot kill me." The steel was back in her voice despite my knife at her neck. "Not if you wish to trade me for the antidote."

"You're right." I leaned in closer to her face and dropped my voice. "But I will hurt you. And if you touch Silas again, I'll make it really hurt."

"You've picked an interesting bedmate, Earthen. You have no lack of other options and bond proposals to consider from your own kind. Do you even know what Death's Fury is capable of?"

I bared my teeth at her. "Do you know what *I'm* capable of?"

We stared at each other until Kianna nodded carefully, and I released her.

Silas pulled me aside with Tessa, directing the others to keep an eye on Kianna. "We still have no assurances that Nuada has an antidote. We need a backup plan."

"Clearly, Kianna inherited her parents' elitist Fae-first worldview, but most Fae are normal, reasonable people," Tessa said. "They won't support the murder of innocents. If you can show the Fae that Lord Nuada's attack was unjustified, they'll turn against him. He steered our people down this isolationist path, but we're not all bloodthirsty monsters or Fae-holes." She frowned back at Kianna. "Not most of us, anyway."

"Sorry." I put my hand on Tessa's arm. "I heard the term from Elias, and Kianna got under my skin. I didn't mean anything about you, but I shouldn't have said it."

Tessa grimaced. "Lord Nuada and Lady Treva have driven a wedge between our people and the rest of Aeterna for decades. They believe in Fae superiority. Half Fae, like me, don't even make the cut, but that's not the way all Fae feel—or even most. Our leaders have not done a good job representing us for a long time."

"If we convince the Fae that Nuada was wrong, will they be able to pressure him to give us the antidote even if he doesn't want to?" I asked.

"If you can prove that the attack was unjustified, Nuada will be forced to make amends or lose respect from the people," Tessa confirmed. "They could appeal to our queen for a new representative. It's not unprecedented."

I nodded. "I think that Lady Treva will help us too. We can appeal to her and the rest of the Fae."

"If we can't convince them, we're as good as dead," Silas said. "Nuada isn't going to let us leave their haven alive once we return Kianna."

I tugged on my braid. "It's a risk we have to take. We need that antidote."

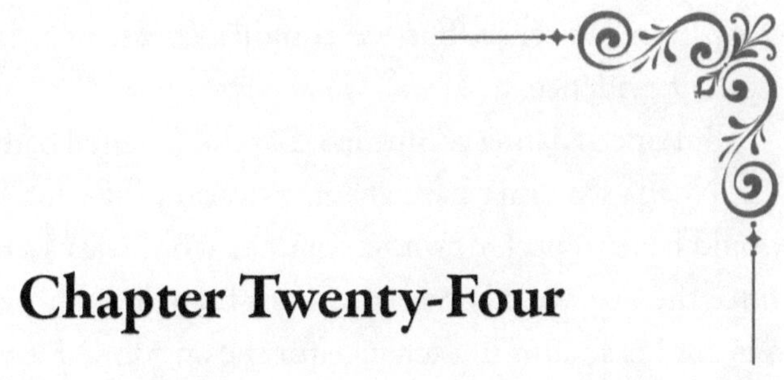

Chapter Twenty-Four

The sun spread the last of its burnt-orange rays across the sky as Casius filled me in on his part of my rescue. When Lennart had called him with my GPS coordinates, Casius had skimmed to the old farm with the others, and they "borrowed" a rusty red pickup truck from the local town and drove from there to Elias's mansion.

We were only about an hour from the barn in Idaho where my mother had died. Elias had built his mansion of terrors in the middle of farm country, drawn there most likely by the knowledge of our old compound sitting on top of a rare rural magic pocket.

Silas marched back to Kianna. "Will you confirm to your parents that the Council had nothing to do with your kidnapping? Innocents are paying the consequences in Aeterna."

Kianna's eyes tightened. "My kidnappers will pay for their actions," she confirmed, her voice hard.

The group gathered around us, waiting to hear the plan. "Silas and I will take Kianna to the Fae haven," I said. "If we aren't back in two hours, send word to the Aeternal Council that Nuada doesn't have an antidote. And prepare our people for a possible attack."

I'd considered telling Kianna that her father was a backstabbing monster who'd orchestrated her kidnapping, but I had no idea how she'd react. If she freaked, we wouldn't be able to pull off a smooth handoff. Not to mention, the only proof I had was Elias's story. It made sense, but we couldn't accuse Nuada of anything without evidence.

But once Kianna confirmed that the Council hadn't kidnapped her, Nuada wouldn't have any justification for what he'd done. He would have to back down. If Kianna's word wasn't enough to convince the Fae, we planned to make a bargain with Nuada—immunity for his actions in exchange for the antidote. He wouldn't want to do it, of course, but I hoped Treva would help us negotiate a deal. The possibility that Nuada would get away with his plans to martyr his own daughter didn't sit well, but I would find a way to warn Lady Treva.

"Lord Valeron will be the only one to accompany me," Kianna said.

"No deal. You're not going without me. Especially not after that stunt you pulled with your thrall."

Kianna's shoulders straightened. "Lord Valeron, I can grant you safe passage and return. By my word, none will harm you, but she would not be welcome among my people. Not when her ancestors restricted access to the magic of this realm, forcing my people to remain in Aeterna, where we are subservient to the Council."

What? That's not what happened. My ancestors had saved the Mundane people of Earth from the Council. The Council wanted to strip all magic from Earth, and we'd stopped them from doing it. Yes, we controlled access to the magic, but... my mind spun. *Do the Fae really view us as the bad guys, perhaps just as guilty as the Council?*

Silas frowned, and I could see the debate playing over his face. Mr. Overprotective was getting a chance to sideline me, and he was tempted to take it.

"Silas, don't you dare. You're not going to keep me out of this one."

He raised his hands in surrender. "Where I go, my Aegis may follow."

Kianna sniffed delicately, and I smothered the urge to strangle her. "That's settled, then," I said. "Silas and I will go in with Kianna. Casius, you should go back to our people and warn them about everything that's happened."

My mentor's fist started tapping on his thigh. He'd had three decades of hiding and putting our people first above anything else, and it was a hard habit to break. I'd taken the opportunity to fill Casius in on Nuada's schemes. I didn't believe everything Elias had said about the Fae, but he wasn't wrong about them outgrowing their haven. It might take a few generations, but they would want more territory, and attacking us might seem like a good option to them.

I put my hand on his shoulder. "You know I'm right, Casius. And we can't sit back and let the people in Aeterna die. Not when we can help."

He shook his head slowly. "We have enough of our own problems, Mae."

"We can't live in isolation. There's too much at stake, and you're on the wrong side of this argument." I remembered what Kianna had said—how we might be part of the problem—and conviction washed over me. "The Mundanes and their government, the Fae, even the Council—all of us have to work together. If we don't, we're going to rip our entire world apart. I won't let that happen. I'm going to do something to fix this, with or without your blessing."

Casius pulled me into a fierce hug. "I don't always agree with you, but I'm proud of you, kiddo. Your mother would be proud too."

Surprise and pride flooded me. His compliments were rare and hard-earned, which made them all the more meaningful. Despite our differences lately, he'd always been a strong and positive influence in my life, and it felt good to have his approval. Especially when I'd feared the exact opposite would happen. Standing up to him, and the entire Inner Circle, had put me on the outside. I'd gone against their wishes when I left with Silas the first time, again when I'd brought him back, and a third time when I'd gone to rescue Gia on my own. I'd begun to wonder if the Circle would still tolerate me as part of their group after all that.

He released me. "Go get the antidote. The Circle will be ready for whatever happens next."

As everyone prepared for their journeys, Silas gave instructions to Tessa to return to Aeterna to update the Council if we didn't make it out of the Fae haven. She didn't like it, but she agreed when Silas pulled rank. Then he and I were momentarily alone.

His voice was low, urgent. "Keep an eye on Lady Kianna. Even when they're seemingly on your side, the Fae are tricky bastards."

I grimaced, thinking of all the ways this could go wrong. *Why can't anything be simple?* "And you watch your back. No more kissing pretty Fae women."

He arched a brow. "Isn't that a little hypocritical?"

I racked my brain for the last time I'd made out with someone.

"You agreed to a bond-mating with Ethan..." His tone was light, but I could feel the emotions coursing off him. A healthy dose of hurt laced his casual reminder of what I'd done. "I gather you have a history there as well."

After Ethan's pep talk about "giving us a chance," it was obvious that my high school flame was definitely harboring some feelings, but I didn't return them. I added Ethan's feelings to the list of things I'd have to deal with later.

"Silas—I'm sorry I hurt you. Alannah would have walked if I didn't. It's important that she stays, but I can't tell you why I know that."

Silas picked up on the reference to my visions. "Why is it so important that she rejoin your Sect?"

My lips tightened as I considered all the things I couldn't say.

"I'm not asking you to talk about the Fate," he said. "Why does your Sect need her to join so badly that they're prepared to sacrifice your personal freedom?"

The vision of Silas dying flashed in front of my eyes, and my voice trembled when I responded with part of the truth. "Money. We need their financial support."

There was a reason my people had hidden on farms and in remote areas where we could create our own self-sustained communities. "Feeding and housing almost a thousand people is expensive. Their assets would be a game changer for all of us. Boston is a great place for us to blend in, the urban pockets of magic are more powerful, but it's a lot more expensive too."

Silas snorted. "So Alannah demanded the bond-mating as a condition of their return. And I'm confident she's already set the condition that the offspring be raised by her House."

My mouth popped open. "How did you know that?"

He raised a brow. "The weaker House needs the heir to increase the powers in their bloodline, and the more powerful one increases their wealth and resources in return. But instead of you getting the benefit of her finances, apparently, that will go to your Sect. You should have gotten a Magister to broker your agreement. They're fratching you left side to right." He glanced sidelong at Casius, making it obvious who he blamed for all of it.

Now was not the time to try to change his opinion about Casius, but I couldn't fully disagree with his assessment of the bogus deal. "Well, I'm not planning on going through with any of it. Alannah just has to believe it's on the table as we negotiate."

"Did you make any binding oaths?"

"No, of course not." The others started heading our way. I lowered my voice. "I'm really sorry I got into this mess. I have to keep up the charade with Ethan until Alannah agrees to rejoin the Sect, but I promise you that I don't have any feelings for Ethan. That's super-old history. When this is over, let's take a vacation somewhere without magic or Magisters or monsters."

Silas's face took on an odd expression—almost pained. "I love you, Maeve O'Neill."

Hearing him say those words sent a thrill through me every time. I ached to throw myself into his arms. "We're going to find a way to make this work. I'm not giving up on us."

Casius sidled up to us with a pointed look at Silas. "I want you to remember all the help you're getting from our Sect, *Lord Councilor*."

"Acting Lord Councilor," Silas and I corrected in unison.

One of Silas's rare boyish grins appeared as magic blazed around him, golden with the hue of his humanity and tapering into bright white around the edges. His white Councilor's robe landed in his hands. He threw the fabric over his shoulder and fastened it around his neck with the gem-studded clasp. Admiring the amazing sight of a flare pulling from two sources at once, I gathered my own pure-white magic around me and felt it settle over me like the softest of cozy blankets. Having my magic back was a huge relief.

Silas bowed formally in my direction and then offered his arm to Lady Kianna. She gazed up at him sweetly and curled her hand over his bicep. I considered smacking her, but I didn't see any thrall magic this time, and Silas didn't seem like he was about to kiss her.

I conjured the thigh holster for Ripper. The weight of the solid seven-inch blade rested reassuringly against my leg. If Kianna kept her hands to herself, hopefully, I wouldn't have to use it before we released her back to her family.

We skimmed without incident and landed just outside the Fells, north of Boston. The early evening had faded to a night draped in darkness. The forest trees twined together, naked of their leaves but so thick they blocked out the meager light from the late-fall moon as we headed deeper off the marked paths. Ten minutes later, we were buried in the forest. I'd have sworn no other living soul had ever visited this area. A sense of ancient magic permeated the entire forest as we went deeper, and the trees and shrubbery were more massive and entwined than their natural age accounted for.

Kianna moved silently and gracefully through the dark woods, leading the way. After a while, I caught only glimpses of her golden hair in the moonlight. Silas took my hand, keeping us together as we followed whatever unmarked trail Kianna could sense leading back to the Fae's haven. We walked some distance farther, carefully traversing the woods until Silas stiffened and pulled us to a stop.

Five Fae waited for us, glowing with blue magic. I recognized only one—Lady Treva. She wore a dark-green robe that draped to the ground, blending against the forest background. The four men beside her wore similar clothing, with the addition of curved daggers tucked into wide leather belts.

We stopped a half dozen feet away, far enough to have time to react if they decided to attack. The back of my neck tingled as if we were being watched from all sides, and I was confident more Fae lurked in the shadows. Now was the moment of truth.

"Daughter?" Lady Treva's face flooded with emotion, and I wondered what Elias would think of this reunion. Surely, even he could sense the sincerity of Treva's love for her daughter.

Kianna and her mother embraced, but my attention was on the two Fae who closed in behind us, blocking our exit. Silas stiffened at my side, his keen eyes taking in every movement in the forest around us.

"We have rescued her from Lord Elias and the Brotherhood," Silas announced loudly enough for anyone in the area to overhear. "As Acting Lord Councilor, I demand an audience with Lord Nuada regarding the safe return of his daughter and restitution for his unprovoked attack against Aeterna."

The four Fae with Lady Treva reacted subtly, shifting on their feet. But I could almost feel a wave of response through the dense forest. We had an audience all right.

"We have much to discuss, Lord Valeron. Come." Treva faded into the forest, moving side by side with Kianna.

"Here goes nothing," I muttered.

"Here goes everything," Silas corrected.

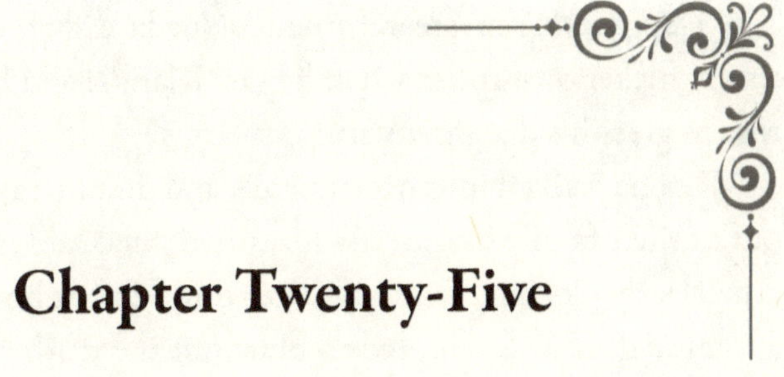

Chapter Twenty-Five

We crossed into the Fae haven, and magic hit us. My breath caught. The hum of it was so thick it vibrated in my chest, making it hard to breathe. The deep, ancient magic I'd sensed in the forest until then was just a trickle compared to the power contained inside the boundaries of their haven. We were surrounded by large, mature trees snaked with vines and foliage. Everything was green and lush, and somewhere in the background, I could hear the gurgle of running water.

From my last visit, I knew the Fae built this haven on a pocket of magic, but what I could feel was more than just a simple surge of power. It had evolved since the last time I'd been there, and it pulsed through every living thing—the trees, the plants, the wildlife, and most especially, the people. Every breath I took felt like drowning myself in Fae magic.

Lady Treva led us down a dirt path to a small clearing with a perfect circle scorched into the ground—the spot where the Elementari had kept me trapped. I shivered at the remembered feeling of being crushed to death under the weight of the fire circle. *Was that only days ago?*

The clearing had acquired two thrones shaped from living trees. Lord Nuada sat in the one on the right. A second throne sat empty by his side, and both were covered in magical symbols and seemed to be growing while I watched. Our escorts stopped us at the edge of the clearing as Treva led her daughter into the center.

"Daughter! You are returned." Nuada didn't show even the tiniest flicker of surprise when he saw Kianna, and he smiled as he rose to greet his daughter with open arms.

Kianna walked into his embrace, and despite my efforts to stay out of their family drama, my lip curled. Silas laid his hand on my arm, clearly picking up on my anger through our bond. Nuada was a total snake. I was tempted to blurt out the truth right there, but I bit my tongue. We had to focus on getting the antidote. Accusing Nuada of kidnapping his own daughter without proof wasn't going to get us anywhere with the Fae. We had to focus on the facts that Kianna could corroborate—the Council *hadn't* kidnapped her. I'd be more than happy to fill in Treva after that and let them sort it out on their own.

Silas raised his voice so the entire clearing could hear. "Lady Kianna will testify that she was held by Lord Elias and his rebels. Your retaliation against the citizens of Aeterna is unjust, Lord Nuada, and I demand the antidote to the poison you spread through the Citizen Source. Thousands are dying because of your actions."

A low whisper spread through the Fae gathered into the clearing, just as we'd hoped.

"Furthermore," Silas continued, "Lady Maeve and I have risked our lives to return Lady Kianna safely to your side, even as your poison spreads through innocents in Aeterna. You owe us a debt. How will you make amends?"

Nuada strode back to his throne and sat, propping his chin on one fist. I couldn't help the little smirk that crept over my face. No doubt, Nuada was trying to figure out how to save face with his people. I was going to enjoy watching him squirm.

"The kidnappers must be punished," Lady Treva finally said. Her face was dark and furious. "There must be justice for our daughter's suffering." A murmur of support rode through the crowd.

Silas stepped forward. "The people of Aeterna are innocent. Take your revenge on those responsible, but your retaliation against Aeternal citizens is unjust, and you must rectify your actions. Give me the antidote."

Nuada rose from his throne and gazed out over the gathered Fae, waiting until they quieted. "Can you prove that the Aeternal Council did not work with Lord Elias to orchestrate the kidnapping?" Silas opened his mouth to deny that, but Nuada continued. "The Council—guilty or not—will use this incident to retaliate against us and imprison us. They have subjugated us for generations, and they will do anything to force us to return to Aeterna under their rule."

The Fae around us started to murmur darkly.

"These *outsiders* claim they were not involved with Lord Elias, yet they were able to find our beloved daughter when we could not," Nuada continued. "They claim the Aeternal Council is innocent when we know them to be anything but. And they know the location of our haven. They cannot be trusted with our secrets."

Gods dammit. Nuada was trying to convince his people to rebel anyway. And his first move would be to get rid of us. Permanently.

"We came here with good intentions and an offer of peace between our people." I turned in a circle, speaking loudly so everyone could hear. Nuada would do everything to block us—we knew that. It was the rest of his people we had to convince. "The Council needs the antidote for the Citizen Source. The Fae want to stay in this realm, free from the Council's reach. And I want to keep my realm safe from an all-out magic war between the two of you. It's in all our best interests to keep the peace. Let's bargain."

The Fae loved a bargain. I'd just dangled catnip, and if the excited whispers were any indication, the cats were very interested. *Just watch out for their claws.*

"Give us the antidote for the Citizen Source, and in return, the Council will not retaliate against your people," I said.

Nuada guffawed. "The Council would never agree!"

I motioned to Silas. "What does the Council want more—the antidote or to force the Fae back to Aeterna?"

Silas said what I already knew to be true. "The antidote."

"If Nuada gives you the antidote, are you willing to make an oath that the Council won't retaliate against the Fae people?"

His mouth curled in distaste. "Yes."

"He doesn't have the authority to make such a promise," Nuada argued.

"He's the new Lord Councilor, so actually, he does."

Silas nodded and, for once, didn't correct me on his title. The other Councilors might not be particularly happy with Silas negotiating without their input, but his word would be binding.

"Nuada, are you willing to give Silas the antidote if he makes that oath?"

Nuada gauged the crowd's reaction as he considered. I was offering him a ridiculously good deal. He couldn't possibly turn it down.

"Your Sect must also make an oath to ally with us should the Council attack now or in the future," Nuada said.

"You ask for more than you give, Lord Nuada," Silas said. "You propose an unfair bargain."

Murmurs rippled through the Fae. It was apparently the right thing to say. Even Treva frowned at Nuada.

"I won't divide our allegiances before our alliance even gets off the ground," I said. "I want us all to live in peace. But I will promise the people of Earth, the Fae included, that my people won't let the Aeternal Council rule in this realm. We'd do everything in our power to stop that, as the Council already knows."

Nuada hesitated, and I worried that he'd refuse to make the deal even though we'd offered him everything he'd promised the Fae people. Maybe we'd underestimated the effect of making this proposal in front of his people.

Treva finally spoke up. "This bargain allows our people to remain within Earth, removes the threat of retaliation, and secures the safe return of our daughter—the cause of our retribution against Aeterna in the first place. We have nothing to lose with this alliance."

Murmurs of agreement spread through the crowd around us. *Thank you, Lady Treva.* This was the moment of truth. We had Nuada backed into a corner. His people were on our side, and we both knew it.

"Do you agree or not?" I said.

Nuada bared his teeth. "We will not accept anything less than—"

Lady Treva laid her hand on Nuada's arm. The Fae around us shifted almost as one toward the forest, and heads bowed. By the time I followed their gazes, I caught a glimpse of long silver hair just as a figure folded back into the woods out of sight—the Fae queen.

I didn't know what Mother Nithia had just done, but Nuada's nostrils flared, and his mouth thinned into an angry line. "I agree to reveal the antidote in exchange for Lord Councilor Silas's word that the Aeternal Council will not take any retaliatory action against me or my people."

I pounced on the agreement before Nuada could change his mind. "Silas?" I asked.

"I agree."

Nuada rose from his throne. "Make your oath, Lord Councilor Valeron."

Relief flooded me as the two men clasped forearms and magic circled around them. I almost couldn't believe this was working.

They made their oaths, acting like they would rather stab each other the whole time, but as the magic wrapped around them, I nearly sighed in relief. If either broke his oath, the cost would be their lives. Magic oaths were serious business.

"Okay, then," I said when they unclasped forearms. We had an alliance with the Fae and the Council. I wasn't sure if I'd just saved Earth or doomed it, but it was done.

From her throne, Treva inclined her head slightly in my direction, and I nodded back in solidarity. I'd fulfilled our deal to return Kianna, and Treva had helped me in exchange.

"Give me the antidote," Silas said.

Nuada returned to his throne, and his face twisted into a smug smirk as he sat. "You already have it."

"Come again?"

"Your Aegis has already enacted it upon your bonded mate."

A sick feeling pooled in my gut. He was talking about how I'd cured Aria—a completely unrepeatable situation on a mass scale.

"You must flood the Citizen Source with magic until the pure outweighs the unpure," Nuada said.

My stomach dropped. There was no way to overpower the entire Citizen Source with clean magic. I had barely been able to do it for one person. Even with the entire Inner Circle, I couldn't channel the amount of power it would take. No one could.

Silas came to the same conclusion. "Son of a shite licker! That is not an antidote! It's impossible."

Nuada's insufferably smug smirk got wider. "I'm sure you'll find some way to achieve the impossible. After all, you're the prime of one of the oldest and most powerful Houses in all of Aeterna. With your source alone, think of the lives you could save."

Silas rocked back on his heels. "You want me to destroy my familial source."

"Not just House Valeron." Nuada leaned forward, and his gaze sharpened. "Only the combined magic of all the Council Houses would be enough to outweigh the poison within the Citizen Source."

"You orchestrated everything so the Upper Houses would collapse?" I couldn't believe what I was hearing. "You're willing to kill thousands, and sacrifice your own daughter, to—what? Gain revenge on the Council members? They'll never agree to destroy their House sources!"

I glanced at Treva. *Was she in on the trick? Did she know there wasn't a real antidote?* But her expression was genuinely surprised.

A fierce smile flashed on Nuada's face. He shrugged one shoulder. "Then they choose the deaths of their people."

Silas's face had darkened into a furious scowl as he faced Nuada. The Council would never give up their power, not even to save the lives of everyone in Lower Aeterna. "You've sentenced thousands of people to die," Silas growled, his entire body tense. "You promised an antidote when none truly existed. You bargained without honor, and you broke your oath."

Nuada's grin dropped. He banged his fist on the arm of his chair and rose to his feet. "The Council has the antidote, which I revealed! It is they who will refuse to act honorably. My oath is not in question."

Silas took a step forward, gripping his sword hilt. Magic ignited through his aura. Fae all around us tensed, and blue magic flexed throughout the clearing, ready to attack.

Nuada motioned toward Silas's sword. "Kill me, and you've broken *your* oath not to retaliate. Your death would follow mine."

Silas lowered his sword. "You will pay for what you have done, Lord Nuada. The blood of thousands is on your hands."

"Nothing important comes without sacrifice."

Lady Kianna left her mother's side to stand behind Nuada. She closed the distance to her father with quick steps and reached up as if to hug him from behind. Instead of an embrace, her hand slid across his neck from left to right.

Nuada arched, and his mouth gaped open as the flesh of his neck parted. He grabbed his throat, but blood gushed through his fingers, soaking the front of his robe in crimson.

"Is that what I was, Father? A sacrifice?" Kianna growled.

Nuada dropped to the ground, and I saw the bone-handled knife clutched in Kianna's fist. I recognized the carved handle. It was the same knife Treva had used on Silas as he freed me from the Elementari.

"No!" Lady Treva cried, rushing forward. "Kianna! No!"

Kianna grabbed her mother and pulled her against her chest. Kianna's arm jerked, and Lady Treva shuddered—once, twice. She pulled back from her daughter, an expression of shocked disbelief on her face. Kianna released her, and Lady Treva slid to the ground with the bone-handled knife sticking from her bloodied chest. I watched in horror as Lady Treva fell beside her husband, their daughter standing over their dead bodies in furious triumph.

A wave of power pulsed from Kianna, and her magic burned like a rising blue sun. There was nothing innocent or beguiling about Kianna's expression now. She stood over the dead bodies of her parents, and her lips curled into a triumphant sneer. Magic soaked her aura, and her head rose as she surveyed the Fae in the clearing. No one said anything, and no one moved to stop her.

Kianna's voice was loud and fierce. "My parents worked with our enemies to kidnap me, their own daughter! They planned to have me murdered to fuel their schemes of revenge. They dishonored our people with their lies. They have paid the price for their deceit!"

She looked out into the wooded glen surrounding us. I followed her gaze and realized that she was waiting for the Fae queen to reappear. When she did not, Kianna beamed with triumph. Hundreds of Fae had drifted closer, moving silently through the forest like moths drawn to the flame of Kianna's fury, until we were completely surrounded.

"I will honor our ancestors! And I will honor our future as I lead us to our freedom!"

A low murmur grew into a chant. The cries gained a rhythm and pulsed with magic as the Fae surrounding us chanted. "Freedom, freedom, freedom!"

Gooseflesh rose along my arms. Silas's magic rose, and I gripped Ripper. There was no way we'd be able to fight our way out of there. We might not even have time to skim if they decided to attack.

Kianna bared her teeth at us. "Although it is not what you wished, you have your answers, Lord Valeron. My father's oath is fulfilled."

Silas spoke in a careful tone. "As you say, Lady Kianna."

Kianna glowered at me. "You speak of alliances. But we will not trade one master for another."

Murmurs of agreement surrounded us.

The weight of this moment filled me with a sense of fate. Kianna had killed her parents in cold blood—even her mother, who wasn't involved with Nuada's plotting. Treva had done nothing but love her daughter. The woman standing in front of me did not understand that kind of love. Maybe Elias had been right, and she wasn't capable of feeling it.

"No one wants to control you or your people," I said carefully. "We can be equal partners together in this realm."

Magic flowed around Kianna like a violent blue storm of energy. "I promised you safe passage, and unlike my parents before me, I will honor my word. But know this, Lady Maeve. The Fae will not submit to another ruler—another council. We declare our claim on this realm and our freedom!"

The magic of her people pulsed in time with their chants. "We are not allies. Prepare yourself."

Silas gripped my arm, and his magic pulled us out of the Fae haven.

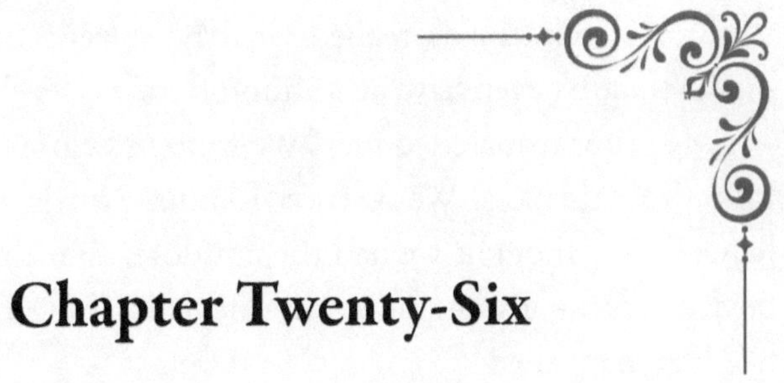

Chapter Twenty-Six

We landed just outside the perimeter shield surrounding the campus in Boston.

"What the hell just happened?" I asked.

Silas dropped his blade into its scabbard with an angry snap. "The Fae have a new leader."

Crisp spring air filled my lungs as we passed the multistory brick buildings lining the central quad area. Half a dozen families were on the grass outside, enjoying the warm sun of an early-spring day. A few glanced up as we walked past. It struck me that no one was afraid. Our people had finally found a home where they felt safe, and I really, really hoped I hadn't just screwed that up.

"Kianna just killed her own parents." My brain was having a hard time catching up. Yes, Nuada had orchestrated the kidnapping, but I hadn't in a million years thought Kianna was going to murder him and become the Fae's new leader. "Did she just *claim* our entire realm for the Fae? Is that a declaration of war against my Sect?"

Silas grimaced. "I think we'd best prepare for the worst."

"Shit, Silas. She killed her own mother..." Treva had done everything she could to save her daughter, and Kianna had killed her without any remorse.

"Her death was unfortunate. Kianna must have believed her mother was involved. Perhaps she was. We may never know the truth of it, but Nuada reaped what he sowed. That shite-licking mongrel didn't even have an antidote!"

My grimace matched his. "We were *this* close to a peaceful solution to this mess. We rescued Kianna. Nuada agreed to an alliance, and I thought we had the antidote... but then it just crumbled. Everything went sideways, and I don't even know how the hell it all happened."

Silas scowled. "Unbelievably, I think we were better off with Lord Nuada. Lady Kianna is unpredictable."

Tamara walked out of the administration building and spotted us. She nearly skipped over to us, her beautiful curly hair bouncing with every excited step. "Maeve! You're back!" She pulled me into an unexpected hug. "Casius told us about Nuada and the kidnapping. I can't believe you're not dead."

"Thanks?" I hugged her back.

"Did you get the antidote?" she asked, glancing between Silas and me.

"No," Silas and I snapped in unison.

I held up my palms, stalling the upcoming barrage of questions. "It will be faster if we can get everyone gathered together so I don't have to go over this twice."

"Everyone's already in the circle room. I just left." She glanced at Silas. "No offense, but we made some additional security modifications to the shielding the Lord Councilor built."

"Acting Lord Councilor," Silas corrected mildly.

She gave him a skeptical look. "Right. No big deal. You're just a regular guy like the rest of us."

Her sarcasm earned her an amused smirk from Silas.

"Everyone?" I asked. "Did Alannah sign?"

"Not yet, but she insisted on being involved, which means Levi and Gia are there too. Wouldn't want anyone to be left out." Tamara rolled her eyes.

Alanna's power-grabbing habits were going to be a problem, but I felt a little surge of hope. She hadn't signed the agreement yet. Maybe there was some wiggle room for my own ill-considered promises. "Good. I need to get everyone up to speed anyway."

"I need to return to Aeterna." Silas frowned. "I have ill news to deliver."

"Tamara, can you take him to the portal? I have to deliver my own bad news, and I need to update the Inner Circle about Kianna as soon as possible."

I really wanted to pull Silas into a kiss. But I'd agreed to a bond-mating with Ethan in front of my entire Sect, and I still couldn't risk Alannah walking away from the summit. As Silas and I stared at each other, all the tension and desire built silently between us.

Tamara cleared her throat, embarrassed. "Should I, uh, give you some privacy?"

I took a deliberate step back. "Don't forget to come back, Silas. I heard a rumor you were planning to spend a lot of time here."

"I'll return as soon as I'm able. Try not to make any binding oaths while I'm gone."

"Deal. See you soon."

"Soon," he repeated. The word was loaded with promise, and I had a hard time turning away, not knowing when we'd see each other again.

While Tamara took Silas to the Aeternal portal at the center of the campus, I made my way over to the circle room in the eastern wing. My brain sped through everything I needed to share with the Circle about the Fae's new leader and her threats against our realm. But I froze in midstep as I remembered our spy.

Someone inside our Sect had helped the Mundanes get on our campus. I'd assumed they were working with Elias, but if Elias hadn't orchestrated the kidnapping... then our spy was working with someone else. And it just occurred to me that Elias had no idea who Casius was when they'd met in person. If Elias had a spy on our campus, surely he'd know who our leaders were.

When we rescued Kianna, she'd mentioned my various dating options, including a bond proposal from one of my own people. And she knew who I was, even though I'd never met her. I felt like such an idiot for not realizing earlier. The spy was working for Kianna.

I swore. Kianna had tried to blow us up with the first Mundane victim, and when that didn't work, she'd tried to get Elias and me to kill each other by kidnapping Gia. It all made sense if Kianna had been planning to overthrow her father from the beginning—before Nuada had her kidnapped. Maybe Nuada figured out what she was up to and had taken her out of the picture. Kianna clearly had different views about what the Fae should be doing to secure their freedom. Proactively taking out threats and claiming our entire realm for the Fae might be just the beginning.

My head was spinning. Kianna had put her sights on us from the beginning. She'd said it herself—they needed the Earthen Source to escape the Aeternal Council's rule. And she blamed our ancestors for binding Earth's magic, giving the Fae no other options but to stay in Aeterna, under the rule of the Council. The Fae would be coming after us—after the Earthen Source—to secure their freedom.

But how could I tell all of that to the Inner Circle without giving away what we knew to Kianna's spy? First, I had to find out who the spy was. I couldn't imagine anyone in our Sect betraying us to someone who wanted us all dead. But it had to be someone in the Inner Circle. The bond-mating proposal hadn't been announced to our Sect yet. Only the Circle and the delegates knew about it, which meant that our spy was someone we trusted. My initial instinct was the delegates, but they hadn't even been on the campus when the first incident occurred.

Except Alannah. She and Ethan had showed up seconds after the first Mundane killed himself. *Could she have been trying to sabotage the summit before it started?* Alannah would be a perfect candidate—power hungry, interested in herself before all others. She'd discredited me and blown up the talks with impossible demands. She'd threatened to walk away multiple times. But I didn't have any proof. I'd have to find some connection between her and Kianna—proving that Alannah was the spy.

When I made it to the circle room, everyone was seated at the stone table, arguing. Ethan was the only onlooker, leaning casually against the wall behind his mother's chair. There seemed to be some sort of disagreement going on between Alannah and Levi. *Another attempt to tear apart our Sect?* All eyes were on the two of them as I slipped into the back of the room unnoticed.

I spotted Gia standing at the table, cradling her stomach. A huge well of relief sprang up inside of me. I didn't like the woman—she'd been nothing short of nasty to me—but I was relieved to find her standing there, alive and safe. Seeing her was a reminder that I'd managed to avoid all the deaths from the visions, and that meant the terrible attack on the campus quad wouldn't happen. Silas was safe. We all were.

The idea of losing Silas made me choke up. I pushed the sudden surge of fear down. Everything had been fixed. There was no reason to keep stressing about the visions. It was over.

Gia noticed me staring. She rose from the table, stretched casually, and made her way over to me. The argument between Levi and Alannah had pulled in Jason and Rhonda, and no one paid much attention to Gia as she slipped away from the central stage.

She stopped in front of me and put her hands on her hips. "I signed the agreement to rejoin the Sect."

I blinked in surprise. "That's great."

"And I owe you an apology." She grimaced. "I begged Marcel not to go after you. I told him it was too dangerous, but he thought you could fix everything that had gone bad after your mom died. He believed you were the key to reuniting the Sect." Her hand moved protectively over her stomach. "He died because he went to find you, and I blamed you for it."

A familiar wave of anguish washed over me. She was right. Marcel lost his life searching for me, and that guilt had twisted in my gut ever since I got my real memories back. But no more. I couldn't accept responsibility for the choices of others. I missed my brother so much—it was like a physical ache in my chest—but I hadn't asked him to risk his life trying to bring me back.

I tugged on my braid. "I never wanted any of this to happen, Gia."

A watery, bittersweet half smile crossed Gia's face as she cradled her stomach. "Marcel was his own man. Stubborn, just like you. It wasn't your fault. Just... make it worth his sacrifice. Be the leader your brother thought you would be."

"I will," I said sincerely. I glanced at her belly again, and a lump caught in my throat. "I'm so sorry. I didn't know the baby was his."

"It's a girl." A mischievous look spread across her face. "I'm going to name her Marcille O'Neill."

I made a face. "That rhymes."

"I know." She chuckled. "It's Marcel's punishment for dying on me and leaving me alone to raise our baby. I hope he's listening now and cringing."

I held back a laugh. I liked her spunk. What she was going through was enough to crush a person. I really hoped her fiery spirit would get her through having this baby and raising it on her own.

I might have been pushing the boundary of our newfound truce, but I couldn't resist saying, "I want to be there for you and... Marcille. We're family. You don't have to do it all alone."

She put her hand on my forearm. "I think I'd like that. Just don't run away on us again. When things get tough, you have to stand up and fight."

That stung, but I nodded. "I learned that lesson the hard way."

Ethan swept over, and Gia went back to the main floor, giving us unnecessary privacy as he pulled me into a huge hug. I let him do it, but when I tried to pull back, he held me tighter. "I was so worried," he said, stroking my back. "I can't believe you handed yourself over to Elias. And when I heard you'd gone to bargain with the Fae, I was so worried. You can't trust Lady Kianna, Maeve. There's something off with her."

Surprise punched me in the gut, and I pulled away from him. "Wait. You know Kianna?"

Ethan went pale. "I..." His gaze slid to his mother, who was still involved in the heated debate with the others. "She, uh..."

"Ethan. Tell me right the hell now. How do you know Kianna?"

Ethan's cheeks puffed as he exhaled. "Kianna came to us and offered an alliance." His voice was a frantic whisper. "It's not what you think."

"What happened, Ethan? I need to know everything."

"We just wanted to hear her proposal, but her terms were ridiculous. We told her no, and she left. That's all, Maeve, I swear."

"Is your mother working with the Fae?" I would kill Alannah with my bare hands. I would choke the life out of her right on top of the stone table.

"No!" His voice dropped even quieter. "No, I swear it. We didn't want anyone to know because we knew how it looked after the Fae attacked you. I didn't think... I didn't realize Kianna was involved until they said you'd found her at Elias's compound. I'm so sorry. If we'd known she was part of this, of course we would have said something. I swear we would have."

Proof! I had the proof connecting Alannah to Kianna. But Ethan... *Could Ethan be in on it too?* They could have snuck in the pendant when he arrived and coordinated the timing of the second attack. *But what about the first attack?* He and Alannah had shown up early. Maybe they'd been watching us...

No. It had been years and years since we'd known each other, but I just couldn't believe Ethan would do something like that. He wasn't the type of person who could kill innocent people and work with our enemies for his own personal gain. And he'd just spilled the beans about meeting with Kianna, which he never would have done if he was working with her. Alannah was another story, though. She was absolutely capable of scheming and betrayal on that level.

Ethan gathered both of my hands in his. "I'm so sorry. You have to believe me."

"Maeve! Oh, my dear, we were so worried," Alannah called.

I frowned at her. Ethan and I had drawn the attention of everyone in the room with our urgent whispers. Alannah's eyes dropped to our hands, and her smile widened.

I gently extracted my hands from Ethan's grasp. A pang of guilt hit me. Ethan had no idea that his mom was the traitor, and he seemed to have genuine feelings left for me. Agreeing to the bond-mating had given him false hope. I had to straighten that out sooner rather than later, but it was going to hurt him, not to mention exposing his mom's betrayal.

I was so, so tempted to accuse Alannah right then and there, but I'd learned from my past rash actions. Alannah had no idea I was on to her, and I would figure out a way to use it to our advantage. Maybe we could feed false information to Kianna through Alannah and thwart whatever Kianna was planning.

With a wary eye on Alannah, I moved to the center of the room and took my place at the stone table. "Lord Nuada and Lady Treva are dead. Lady Kianna murdered them." I made the announcement as blunt and direct as possible, scrutinizing Alannah for any out-of-place reaction, but she acted just as surprised as the rest of the Circle. "Kianna has declared the Fae the rightful rulers of Earth. They're going to attack us for control of the Source. I don't know when, but it's coming."

Tamara scowled, and Casius went rigid. Ethan stared with an open mouth, guilt written all over his face. *No, he definitely can't be the spy.* He was an open book, and he clearly felt bad about the secret meeting with Kianna. All around the room, people reacted with surprise and fear.

Alannah was the first to speak, her face reddened in outrage. "What did you do?"

There were so many reasons I was not responsible for the mess with the Fae, and anger burned on the tip of my tongue, but I wasn't going to let her bait me anymore. Especially since I could see now how she'd sabotaged us left and right. I inhaled slowly through my nose and spoke to the group, ignoring her outburst.

"Nuada arranged for Elias to kidnap Kianna," I said. "He framed the Council so he could use his daughter as an excuse to murder half of Aeterna and weaken the Aeternal Council. Kianna found out and killed both of her parents. And now she's declared the Fae the rightful rulers of this realm, which means they've declared war on us."

"So much for rescuing her ungrateful ass," Casius said. "What did we ever do to the Fae?"

"The Fae haven isn't going to be enough to sustain them forever," I explained. "They need a magic-rich environment, and we control the biggest source of magic in all the realms."

People all around us shifted uneasily.

I had more bad news to deliver. "The panic in Aeterna has totally incapacitated the Council, just as Nuada planned, and now they can't come to our aid when the Fae attack. We're a huge target with no allies."

More muttering spread as people realized that what I'd been saying all along had happened—we'd weakened our allies in Aeterna by not working together. We were on our own against the Fae. With an eye on Alannah, I carefully skipped over what I knew about Kianna's spy, but I needed to talk to Casius as soon as possible.

"No good deed goes unpunished," Casius griped.

"My people aren't signing up for a mass slaughter!" Alannah said.

"After all the arm twisting you did to get me to agree to the bond-mating, you're just going to walk away?"

More sabotage to cause friction and chaos. How could I have not seen it before?

"This isn't our fight," Alannah said.

Levi started bobbing his head vigorously, and I gritted my teeth. I wouldn't let Alannah tear the others away.

I switched tactics. "Fine. Run. But what if the Fae attack you first? You're smaller and weaker than us. Or what about the Brotherhood? Can you withstand an attack from the Rakken? Can your Mundanes? Don't pretend this threat is only against us, Alannah."

She frowned, but I wasn't done with everything I needed to say. "You demanded a seat at this table, but you have yet to sign on the dotted line. *We* have strength in numbers. *We* have a direct connection to the Earthen Source. *We* have a shield to protect you. We are your future, not the other way around. Out there, as the second-biggest group of magic users, you're also a target. So you choose…" I inhaled deeply. It was time to stand up for what I knew was right. "And I'm not a part of the deal. I won't accept the bond-mating as a condition of your return."

Alannah rocked back on her heels. "If you won't keep your word, then my people will not join your Sect!"

"I'm not going back on my word. You can formally propose a bond-mating agreement, but it won't be a condition of rejoining the Sect. And I will have a Magister broker the deal between our houses. I want fair terms with payment going to House O'Neill, not this Sect. I'm not selling myself off as part of your return package."

"You can't be serious," Alannah said.

The look of outrage on her face was incredibly satisfying. I was so done with Alannah's posturing. She needed us, not the other way around. She'd twisted everything into a power grab, sabotaging us at every turn, and we'd let her do it—playing right into her schemes to break apart our summit. I wasn't going to play her games anymore.

I expected Ethan to be angry, or shocked at least. But he had the expression he wore when he was tinkering with his creations—a little perplexed and trying to puzzle through it. I hoped he didn't take this personally. He was a good guy, but enough was enough.

The seconds ticked by slowly. The tension was so thick I could hear my heartbeat in my ears. I didn't think Alannah would walk away. If she did, she would lose her access to the Inner Circle and valuable information she could feed to the Fae. But it was risky. Her entire goal might be tearing apart the summit, and if she left, the future of our Sect was uncertain. Gia's group had already signed, but Levi would likely walk, and we'd be weaker without their support during the fight against the Fae. And as Casius had so often pointed out, we'd be weaker in the long term without Alannah's numbers and their financial connections. Not to mention, my people would blame me for all of it.

If Alannah walked, I'd be forced to reveal her as the traitor sooner than I wanted. But I stood tall. Sometime over the course of this whole mess, I'd grown a backbone. I needed to do what I knew was right, let go of my guilt, and become the leader I was meant to be. I couldn't meet everyone's expectations of what they thought a good leader was, but I would never be Alannah's puppet. I refused to back down, and I refused to glance around for approval from the Inner Circle.

"Mother. Enough," Ethan said. "I'm not going to force a bond on Maeve. *I* refuse the deal."

"Ethan!" Alannah's head whipped toward him so fast I half expected it to keep spinning all the way around like the demon she really was.

"No, really. Enough is enough. Her uterus isn't for sale to the highest bidder. I don't want any part of a forced bond." His jaw was set as he stared down his mother.

I almost cheered as a glowing affection for Ethan returned to my heart. Finally, he was standing up to her. It had taken him twenty-five years, but he'd done it when it really counted.

"This is a bonded mating," she argued. "An agreement, which she already made."

An idea hit me. Even though Ethan was officially backing out of the mating, too, I needed a way to save face with the Circle. They already believed I was unreliable and uncommitted, and if I blew the entire Summit apart, they might never trust me again. Alannah wanted leverage within the Sect, and I could offer an olive branch to keep her and Levi at the summit.

"Alannah, I won't agree to breed an heir for you." Her face darkened, but I plowed forward. "But I will agree to a bond with Ethan." Both their faces scrunched in confusion. "An Anchor bond. As my bonded Anchor, Ethan will have equal access to Earth's source. I won't be his bonded mate, but I will share the magic with him. Over time, his capacity to handle magic will increase, just as mine has. Or you can walk out of here and give it a go on your own."

All eyes were on Alannah. I was offering a good deal that would benefit all of us, and even Levi was scowling at her as she held out for a surprising amount of time. Alannah's mouth pursed, and she seemed far from happy, but she wasn't stupid. She didn't have a solid reason to leave any more.

She lifted her chin. "I accept your offer."

The little nod of approval from Casius was everything.

"Does that work for you, Ethan?" I asked, just to be sure.

In response, he reached out for my hand. I let him. His voice was soft, meant just for my ears. "I'll take whatever you're willing to give, Mae."

I spoke just as quietly. "This is it, Ethan. My heart already belongs to someone else."

He didn't act surprised. "Does that someone scowl a lot and have an ego the size of the planet?"

I chuckled. "Yeah, that's him. Friends?"

"Friends," he agreed. "As long as we're in this together."

I'd done it. I'd brought the splinter tribes home and figured out a way to build lasting alliances for our Sect without selling myself in the process. Once I revealed Alannah as the traitor, their people would have Ethan to keep them on the right course, and Ethan would have a reason to stick around because of our Anchor bond.

Proud of the deal I'd made on my own terms, I suddenly had an idea about bringing in even more powerful allies. "What if we channel the Earthen Source to cure the poison in the Citizen Source? We can cycle it through in phases, just like a blood transfusion, and clear out the poison. I already did it on a smaller scale for Aria—the Lord Magister's daughter. It could work, and once the Council isn't dealing with their own problems, the Guardians could help us against the Fae."

"No," Casius said firmly. "That's just exchanging one problem for another. If we let the Aeternal Council set up a foothold into this realm, they will not leave willingly. Ever."

"I agree," Levi said. "The Aeternal Council cannot be trusted."

"What about the government agents?" Ethan asked. "If the Fae attack us here, DODSI will definitely notice a magical battle in the middle of Boston."

I'd almost forgotten about DODSI. The vision of their agents shooting innocent families on our campus flashed in front of my eyes, and I wrapped my arms around my middle. That vision was never coming true—none of it was going to happen. Not since I'd stopped all of Four's visions.

"We have an understanding with DODSI," I said. "Director Pascal helped me with the kidnapping situation. If the Fae attack, they're willing to help us, and they have powerful technology that disrupts magic."

Saying they would help us was a massive stretch of the truth. I hoped DODSI would help, but I had no guarantee. But I wanted Alannah to tell Kianna we had powerful allies. Maybe it would give the Fae second thoughts about attacking us.

"A short-wave disruption blast?" Ethan asked, his eyes wide with excitement. "I've been working on a design for that... how long does it last?"

Considering the horror I'd felt when I first learned about the gun, Ethan's response was surprising. I gaped at him until I remembered his passion for tinkering with magic and mundane objects. "Agent Lennart said a full hit at short range lasts about an hour." I glanced at Alannah. "Long enough to disable our enemies during an attack."

"How do you know the Mundanes won't use those weapons on us?" Alannah demanded.

Levi shifted forward on his toes. "This is a serious threat that must be dealt with. Mundanes have repeatedly tried to annihilate us throughout history. They fear what they can't control—"

"DODSI isn't trying to kill us," I interrupted before Alannah could rally everyone into full freak-out mode. "We need an alliance with anyone who is willing to live peacefully together—including the Council and the Mundane government. Everyone gets a seat at the table, or we'll just be setting ourselves up as another version of the Aeternal Council."

Casius folded his arms. "We don't get involved in other people's problems."

"These are our problems," I said, cutting off the old argument. "The whole world is our problem, and it's been that way since our ancestors bound all of Earth's magic into a single source."

I remembered what Kianna had said when she blamed my people for the Fae's situation in Aeterna. This was the third time that someone had tried to kill us for control of the Earthen Source, and it wouldn't be the last. We needed allies, or it was only a matter of time before someone took that control from us.

"We need to help the Aeternals so they can back us against the Fae," I said. "Right now, Silas is telling the Council they have to flood the Citizen Source with massive amounts of untainted magic to remove the poison. The only way they can do that is if the Upper Houses destroy their familial sources."

Casius snorted. "They'll never agree to that. It would destroy their personal bases of power."

"Exactly," I said. "Which is why we're in the perfect position to help, and we can set the terms of a new alliance. Together, we can stand against the Fae."

Jason, Casius, Levi, and Alannah all started talking at once. They were all over the place, talking about our allies and our enemies, what our terms would be, and who we could and couldn't trust. Everyone joined in, talking over each other.

Without any warning, something ripped inside my chest, followed by a stab of pain straight through my brain. I clutched my head and screamed.

"Maeve!" Multiple voices rose in alarm.

My knees buckled, and I hit the ground hard. Screams ripped from my throat as pure energy burned through my brain. I couldn't think. I couldn't breathe.

"Someone help her!"

Magic tore through me, too strong and unfiltered. I screamed again. Power flooded every one of my senses, transforming the world into shades of burning white until I couldn't feel my body. Wave after wave flashed through me on the heels of the previous ones, and my entire body spasmed. The magic burned out of every pore—my mouth, my eyes. I was vomiting power.

"Form a conjuring circle!" Casius yelled. "It's an attack!"

After an eternity of agony, the power ripping through me lessened until it was almost bearable. I gulped breaths as the excruciating weight of the magic was drawn from me. Tears leaked from my eyes. I dragged in air and forced my body to unclench. Every muscle had gone rigid, and every nerve felt burned.

As my brain started to function again, I lifted my head and found Casius crouched over me. "Maeve! What happened?"

My body was drenched in sweat, my muscles sore. The drum of my own heartbeat pulsed against the inside of my skull. "It's not..." I licked my lips and tried to focus.

The power had hit me but no one else. I'd felt *something* besides the pain, like the magic was familiar. With the conjuring circle channeling away the brunt of it, I finally realized what I was feeling. The magic that had consumed me under its crushing weight was a backlash directly from a familiar source. And it wasn't mine.

Fear as strong as the debilitating pain washed over me. "It's Silas."

Chapter Twenty-Seven

My legs were jelly as I sprinted across the open quad toward the administration building and the portal. My lungs burned, but I pushed myself forward with blind panic, only dimly aware that the rest of the Inner Circle raced after me, calling out for answers.

The guards outside the atrium moved to stop me. I didn't have time. I hit the first with a blast of magic that sent him flying. I hit the second one in the throat with the heel of my hand before he could react.

I raced across the hard marble floor to the center, where the gateway to Aeterna stood. The portal was inactive—the three long rectangles of carved stone, stacked like an ancient doorway, lay dormant. The magic symbols were dark without energy, and a new shield surrounded the entire structure.

I ran at full speed into the shield, expecting my Sect's sigil to allow me to pass through. But I rebounded and felt flat on my back. In a blind panic, I slammed my magic against the barrier, trying to rip it apart. Pain exploded in my skull as the shield held. *I need to get through!*

"Mae!" Casius grabbed my shoulders and shook me. "Tell me what's happening!"

The bond with Silas had been severed. I couldn't feel his magic at all. Sheer terror had taken over my brain, but I managed to bark out a response. "I have to get the portal open! Silas needs help!"

I'd led the entire Circle into the atrium after me, and I searched their confused faces. *Why isn't anyone helping me? I need to get the damn portal open!* But they didn't understand. I had to make them understand. "I can't feel Silas through our bond! The backlash was from his source, and now I can't sense him anymore. He's going to die! Help me! I have to stop it—the Fate said I could stop it."

"Wait a minute, Mae." Tamara placed her palms on either side of my face and forced me to look into her earnest brown eyes. "Help us understand. What Fate? What's going on?"

"Please, someone's got to help—"

The portal flared with magic. We all dropped on instinct, but the shielding around the gateway caught the pulse of magic and contained it.

A mob flooded out, dozens of people in tunics and caftans and headscarves—women, men, children. Every color of magic surrounded them. They ran through the portal, panicked, as they spread out in every direction. The mass of people hit the shield and started screaming and pounding at the magic barrier. Dozens more flowed through, with more behind them.

"Back up, back up!" Casius yelled.

Terrified people kept pouring through the portal, more and more, until they became a gushing stream, all pushing and yelling. Within moments, a hundred people filled the shielded area around the portal. The front rows clawed and raked at the barrier with bloody hands. The noise was overwhelming—cries, screams, pleas for help in an incoherent stampede.

I was rooted to my spot in utter shock and confusion.

"There's more coming through!" Tamara yelled.

Casius grabbed me and dragged me to Jason. I couldn't hear what he said over the overwhelming noise of the crowd, but power rose around Casius and then Jason. Casius held up three fingers, and I figured out what he was doing. As a security measure, the new shield required three people to disable it. I'd forgotten that in my panic earlier. I joined their circle, and we each grabbed a section of the shielding spell and flexed our magic in unison. The shield shivered to the ground, disabled.

The front line of people crashed forward, some knocked to the ground under the surging crowd, with more still coming through the portal. I stumbled backward away from the rampage, all the way to the edge of the atrium. They rushed through the gateway, filling the large space.

"What's happening?" Casius yelled. "Maeve!"

I couldn't form words, and I didn't know what was going on.

A wave of magic blasted outward from the portal, and the concussion hit me in the chest. Everyone stumbled from the force, many falling to their knees. Terrified screams followed, until the entire atrium was like a war zone, with people shoving and fighting each other to get away from the portal. But they had nowhere to go.

"Open the doors!" I screamed.

Somehow, my voice carried over the mass of people in the atrium. The main double doors on the east side of the floor banged open. Light flooded the space, and people ran toward it to the quad outside.

I grabbed Tamara and threw a shield around the both of us. The mass of fleeing people flowed around it like running bulls on their way to safety.

"What's happening?" Tamara yelled.

The press of people was too great. At least a thousand people had poured through the gate, pushing and fleeing Aeterna. The flow wasn't slowing down either. I scanned their faces, trying to understand. All I saw was terror.

Another wave of magic blasted out of the portal, and the people around us were knocked off their feet. My shield protected

Tamara and me. I gaped in horror as the gateway reversed, flexing backward like a tide sucked outward.

Everyone turned toward the portal, the same primal survival instinct drawing all our attention to the unnatural sensation. The sound in the room was drawn out with it, creating a perfect bubble of silence that seemed to steal our collective breath.

The portal slammed shut. The pressure in the air popped, and a silent boom reverberated in my chest, shaking the floor at my feet. The symbols on the portal drained of magic and became dark stone once again as the pressure in the room returned to normal. People slumped to the ground, covered in grime and blood. Some wept, covering their faces, while others stared blankly at the portal.

I released the shield and grabbed the arm of a man wearing a Guardian uniform. "What happened?"

He looked at me, blinking slowly. "It's gone."

"What? What's gone?"

"Aeterna."

It was my turn to stare in shock. "What do you mean? The entire realm is gone? That's impossible."

He shook his head, his eyes unfocused.

"What happened?" I demanded, shaking him. "Where is Silas? Lord Valeron! Where is he?"

Something seemed to click into place in his brain, and he focused on me. "The Citizen Source collapsed, and everything just crumbled. Lord Silas was holding the gateway. They're... it's all gone. Fates curse us!" He started sobbing and dropped to his knees.

Shock floored me. *No.* There was no way that Aeterna was just... gone. There were almost seven thousand people living there.

Casius's magically enhanced voice carried over the crowd, calm and authoritative, as he instructed people to move outside. Slowly, in a postpanic haze, people followed the commands and began to make their way toward the exit. Parents were clutching their children, sobbing and dazed. They were bleeding, limping, and carrying nothing more than the clothes on their backs. People began calling out for their missing loved ones. The floor was covered in injured people, moaning and sobbing. Some weren't moving.

"Dear gods," Tamara gasped at my side.

Silas. He was on the other side of that portal. *No. He can't be gone.* I'd felt the backlash from his source, and I didn't know if anyone could have survived that. But I couldn't believe that he was dead. A new wave of determination welled inside me. There were thousands of people trapped on the other side of that portal with Silas. Their escape had been cut off, and they needed help.

"Casius!" I twisted and pushed through the crowd of dazed refugees making their way outside until I found him in the quad, directing people. "Casius! There are still people trapped in Aeterna!"

He was directing a reasonably alert-looking woman in a Guardian uniform to send the wounded to the medical building, pointing in the right direction. "How do you know they're still alive? From what I'm hearing, Aeterna imploded with the destabilization of the Citizen Source. We'd be opening a portal to a magical-disaster area."

"People were still coming through when the portal closed. Someone said Silas was holding it. We have to try!"

"If we open that portal, the shockwaves of magic could rip into this realm. It would kill us all."

My mind raced. "We'll put the shield back up." I grabbed his arms. "We have to try! There are thousands of people still trapped in Aeterna." Tears burned my eyes. "Please, Casius, I'm begging you. Silas is back there, holding the other end of that portal. We have to open it up again so they can get through."

Casius squeezed my shoulders. "They're dead, Mae. I'm so sorry, but there's nothing we can do."

"No! I refuse to accept that. We don't know unless we check. Help me, Casius. Help me, or I'll figure out a way to do it myself!"

Casius searched my face for a long moment before he nodded. I ignored the pity I saw there, and Casius and I rushed back toward the portal. On the way, we flagged down the rest of the Inner Circle, plus Ethan and Gia. Levi and Alannah were nowhere to be seen, but everything was in chaos, and we didn't have time to find them.

The atrium floor was almost empty except for debris and more than a few bodies that littered the ground. After stepping carefully through the wreckage, we positioned ourselves around the gateway.

"Everything appears intact," Tamara said, examining the portal stones.

"Put the shield up. I'll activate the portal from inside."

Casius frowned. "Maeve—"

"Someone has to activate the portal on our end, and it can't be done outside the shield. Stop wasting time. I'm the strongest one here, and I'll put up my own shield.

"I was going to tell you to use Ethan as your Anchor. You'll need him."

I didn't even have time to feel embarrassed. "Ethan?"

Ethan's magic rose around him. He was ready to help without argument. I felt a surge of gratitude as I grabbed his arm and reached for his aura. We didn't have an Anchor bond in place yet, but his magic wasn't totally unfamiliar to me, and I connected with him quickly. His power was like a warm cup of coffee on a cold morning, solid and comforting. The second I felt his magic wrap around the core of my own, I built a protective shield around both of us.

Casius, Jason, and Tamara pulled the portal shield up once more, and I faced the dark stones. If Casius was right, and everything was gone on the other side, we were about to get hit with a shit ton of magic backlash as soon as the portal opened to Aeterna. If it opened at all. I channeled another burst of magic into the shield protecting Ethan and me and placed my palm on the stone gateway. *Failure isn't an option. Silas is on the other side of that gateway.*

I let my magic flow. The runes flexed with energy, but the portal stayed closed. *Dammit. It has to open.* I shoved more power into the sigils.

Ethan's connection wrapped around me, bearing the weight of the magic with me. I pushed harder, directing the power at the dark stones of the portal. Something was wrong. Opening the gateway between our realms shouldn't require so much energy.

The portal continued to resist until the sigils carved into the face hummed with magic, vibrating the marble floor under my feet. But the familiar pulse of energy creating the portal between realms didn't come.

Dammit. Come on! I reached deeper, past the outer edges of my magic and into the very core of my powers.

Everything went white.

Everything is so blindingly bright. I can't see. Blinking, I shield my eyes with my hands. The light is emanating from everywhere. My vision adjusts slowly, and I realize I am standing in the Fate's temple in Alaska.

The spacious room is carved from white stone, with columns stretching to soaring fifty-foot ceilings. Magic symbols cover every surface, radiating power. The only furnishing in the room is a high-backed white chair. It, too, is carved with sigils.

Without being told, I can sense that time has stopped moving forward. I'm in a bubble outside of mortal cares, and nothing outside of this moment matters.

I was worried about something, but I can't quite remember what. The frantic feelings are distant, and they don't concern me anymore.

It's all too easy to ignore the pesky edge of panic like a fly buzzing around my head.

A man appears in the chair. I look down at him, completely unsurprised. His face is average and forgettable, but I know he is the same man who visited me in the Elementari and the one who released Kianna from her magic-draining cell. The knowledge starts to trigger something urgent in my brain, but I can't put my finger on the emergency.

He winks.

Four, *my memory supplies. He calls himself Four.*

"Are you going to stop me?" I ask, but I can't quite remember what it is that he's stopping me from doing.

Unlike the oracle child who occupied this temple previously, this Fate's face is full of expression. He barks out a laugh as he slings one leg across the arm of the chair and leans back. "Why would I do that, Maeve O'Neill?"

My own name slaps me back into awareness, and panic hits me. "Did I stop the visions? Is Silas going to die?"

"You all die." He chuckles, like mortality is a joke only he can understand.

I lean in, searching his face for some hint of the truth.

"Your Moments are filled with death, Maeve O'Neill. It cannot be helped. Unless..."

"Unless what?" I demand. I'm desperately licking up the crumbs of hope he's offering, but I don't care. I have to save Silas.

He leans forward in his seat, serious now. The power behind his stare makes me feel like I'm being choked by magic. "You are uniquely situated to help me with a problem. If you scratch my back, I will scratch yours—as the mortal saying goes."

"What do you want from me?"

What can I do that a Fate can't do for himself?

His eyes flare with magic and bore into my soul. "That depends on you."

He chuckles again, and I start to remember that I don't trust him. He's threatening me—twisting my brain—and I shouldn't be here. I need to escape before he makes everything worse.

"You told me Silas didn't have to die. You said I could stop it."

"Mortals die. It is not a threat but a statement of fact. I'm giving you the opportunity to save them all for a while longer. But there is a price you have to pay."

I stare at him blankly. For the first time, he's being direct with me, and I can't even form a coherent response. "What? What's the price?"

"Some would consider it a gift, really. What I'm offering you is so much bigger than you can even imagine." He circles his hand in the air. "There has to be three. And the Fates are overdue for change, Maeve O'Neill."

"What do I have to pay?" I sputter.

"A life for a life. Where one path ends, the other begins. The choice is yours."

The vision ended. I blinked, and suddenly, I was standing back in the middle of the grand atrium. The portal to Aeterna flared to life.

A mass of people rushed through, shoving into our realm and safety. They ran in every direction, and their screams were as thick as the black smoke pouring through the portal. Everything was utter chaos.

"Maeve! Snap out of it! Mae!" Ethan pulled me to the edge of the atrium as hundreds and hundreds more Aeternals scrambled through the portal.

I climbed onto the old reception desk and scanned their faces, desperate to see any sign of Silas. I nearly choked on my tongue when I finally saw a familiar face. "Stephan!" I scrambled down, pushing my way to him. His arm was draped around Aria, and they both looked terrified. "Aria!"

Stephan's eyes were rimmed in red. I'd seen that exact look in his eyes before—in the first vision. He opened his mouth, but my hand flew out in front of me, demanding that he stop.

Something pulses through me, as strong as the Fate's magic, creating a moment where I try to fight this reality.

No. *I refuse to accept what Stephan is about to tell me. I'm trapped in a bubble of time—a split second before he speaks and makes his words my reality. But fate pulls me forward.*

A thousand people pressed around me, just the same as my vision.

I push my way through the crowd. People are sobbing and crying.
They cheered in celebration.

They weep with loss. A final knot of people slips through before the portal closes. A figure rests across their shoulders. Dark hair. Strong, wide shoulders.

A white cloak.

A body is draped across their shoulders, a scabbard hanging from his hip.

"It's Silas," Stephan Valeron said, and the reality I couldn't avoid burst in on me. I'd done everything I could to stop this Moment, and it had happened anyway.

"No!" I screamed, elbowing through the crush of bodies. They lowered Silas to the ground, tangled in his long white Councilor's robe. I dropped to my knees at his side.

Tessa grabbed me, gripping my forearm in the way of the Guardians. She opened her mouth and shattered my fragile reality into a million jagged shards. "He's dead."

Chapter Twenty-Eight

I reached for Silas through our bond. *Nothing.* Where our Aegis bond should be was... absolutely nothing. No tiny spark to hang on to, no flare of cool, strong magic. He was gone.

His handsome face was serene, relaxed. Those strong, stubborn features completely at rest.

I had done everything—*everything*—the Fate had showed me. I'd stopped all the deaths in the visions and jumped through all of Four's hoops.

A wail escaped me. "This wasn't supposed to happen!"

Distantly, I heard Stephan's voice. "The Citizen Source collapsed on itself... he channeled our House's source..."

Clarity hit me like a sucker punch in the face. I'd been set up from the start. I'd let Four lead me around like an idiot, triggering catastrophes all around. My brain replayed the chain of events like a reel of bad memories. Every single vision had led to the next, altering the path just enough to trigger an even bigger problem.

"Expended too much magic..."

Every one of my visions had been the key to an even more terrible disaster. The Fae had claimed Earth. Thousands of people had died in Aeterna. And none of it had saved Silas.

"The portal started to collapse..."

A life for a life.

Your Moments are filled with death.

Four had set me up. The bastard said I could stop it. He said I could choose, but it was a lie. It was all lies, and Silas was dead.

Rage filled me as I stared at Silas's lifeless body. My magic rose up, and everything became shades of white. "I did not choose this!" I sank power into my words and screamed at the skies—at Fate. "Do you hear me?"

Kneeling, I gripped Silas to my chest and pulled on the magic. I dove past the outer binding of the Earthen Source and slammed straight into the heart of our magic without a conjuring circle. I didn't care if it ripped me apart. I felt so angry, so betrayed.

"Maeve! No!" Ethan's voice was distant even though he stood next to me. I felt his power try to wrap around me, anchoring me, but I ripped past it. The pain wrapped around me like a blanket as I buried myself in the ancient powerful core of Earth's magic.

Time ceases.

Three figures form from the whiteness of pure magic. They circle around Silas and me, watching. I recognize two of them—the Fate I first saw as a child oracle in the mountains of Alaska, and Four, who did his best to ruin my life. The third Fate is a tall man hooded in a black robe that covers an unnaturally thin frame. It pools at his feet and hides his face. With a sickle, he'd be the Grim Reaper.

Magic fills every particle around us, burning with energy but leaving us untouched. I'm surrounded by so much power it's sizzling across my skin, but I don't care about that or the fact that the Fates can wipe me out with a single thought. All I care about is the pain in my heart.

"You lied to me!" I scream at Four.

The Fates respond as one, and the words swell with the magic connecting us. "His fate is decided."

"You bastard!" Magic twines around me, heavy and dense, as I take it into me, absorbing the energy and begging the weight of that power to equal my pain.

I want Four to hurt. He should feel the pain clawing through my chest until he drowns in the sheer agony. I want the magic to rip us all apart and make my pain felt by the whole world.

"A life for a life," Four says.

As I cradle Silas's lifeless body, I know what I have to do. If Silas is going to live, I have to pay the price.

"He is not going to die!" I drop to my knees and slam my palm down on Silas's chest, punching all the magic I have into him. I will every bit of the power I can channel, everything that's inside of me, everything I can call from this space connecting magic between realms. I won't stop until I make this right—until I keep this terrible reality from happening.

Reaper Fate shoots forward and grabs me by the arm. "Stop!"

I scream in fury. I don't have words or meaning, just raw pain pouring from me. He can't stop me. I won't let him.

I take everything from the Fate. Soul-searing magic rips through me as I drain the power the Reaper Fate contains, pulling and pulling at the seemingly endless well of his magic. He tries to escape, but he can't rip free of my grip. My pain is too strong.

I hear Four's voice inside my brain: "Your Moments are filled with death, Maeve O'Neill." And suddenly, I'm surrounded by Four's powers, expanding my own. I'm a vast reservoir—a well of power without beginning or end—and my will is his fate.

"Silas will not die," I declare, and strong, ancient magic reverberates through my words.

Panic slaps across Reaper Fate's features, but I don't care. I can't stop. It's a lifetime and only a moment until... I've taken all of his magic, and he disappears from existence.

I can't pause to consider my actions. The pain of the magic I'm holding inside of me and the pain of my loss are too great for rational thought. I slam all of that magic into Silas.

The shock wave of power pounds me back into my own reality.

A thousand veins of magic lit beneath Silas's skin like forked bolts of white lightning etched in his flesh. He gasped, arching his back as if he were being electrocuted, and his eyes flew open. They were pure white.

Silas slumped back onto the ground, unconscious, but my entire world righted itself as his chest rose and fell with deep, steady breaths. Alarmed voices swelled around us, and my awareness returned to my physical body and the people around us at the campus in Boston. The power I'd infused into Silas was seared into my retinas as an echo of the powers I had absorbed from the Fate. Magic was everywhere, floating uncontained across the atrium, caused by the explosion of power centered on us.

All of that barely registered as I held the man I loved in my arms. "Silas?" I wiped away my tears and snot and sweat.

Silas jerked upright like the dead rising. He moved so fast that I didn't have time to get out of the way, and he headbutted me as he sat up.

"Ow!" Pain slashed across my forehead, and I pulled away, clutching my face. "Shit! Ow. Silas!"

"Maeve!" Silas pulled me against him, his hands running over my face. "Are you all right?"

I wiggled my nose and checked my hand for blood. *Not broken, not bleeding.* But it still felt like I'd run face-first into a wall.

I opened my mouth, and hysterical laughter bubbled from me. I gripped his shirt in my fists and inhaled the warm, spiced scent of him. "You're alive!"

Silas took in his surroundings with wide eyes. "Did I just... die?"

I FLOPPED BACKWARD onto my bed and buried my face in the crook of my elbow. I was exhausted mentally, physically, and magically. The former recovery room I'd been assigned for my bedroom was designed for two patients, but it held only a single bed, a dresser, and a small desk. It was spacious but sparse. I never spent any time in my room unless I was sleeping—it didn't feel like home. I missed my basement apartment in Boston, and I missed my family. I missed when life was simple.

Silas and I had worked all night fortifying the campus, posting guards and patrols, and checking the perimeter shield. When we were satisfied with that, we helped the Aeternals find places to sleep. Every inch of extra space in the campus buildings had been assigned to the refugees. People bunked in patient rooms, on the gymnasium and cafeteria floors, and finally, on the grassy quad outside, with all the blankets and temporary shelters we could find. Thank goodness the early-spring temperature was above freezing. Winter camping in Boston would be quite a shock for Aeternals used to moderate year-round temperatures.

We estimated that three thousand Aeternals had escaped the collapse of their realm. All of them were now refugees without Earthen identities. Thousands more hadn't made it out. Families had been separated, and the weakest hadn't been able to skim to safety, but of course, the members of the Aeternal Council had survived, and they were already making demands. I let Casius and Jason deal with them. I just couldn't.

We'd attempted to open the portal back up a second time, but it was hopeless without the insane boost of power I'd received from the Fates. The gateway between our realms was damaged beyond repair, and all of Aeterna might be destroyed. The collapse of the Citizen Source had destabilized everything that had been built with magic—which, in Aeterna, was pretty much everything.

Early that morning, Silas crawled into my bed, and we both passed out for a few glorious hours until Tessa delivered breakfast and informed us that the Inner Circle was meeting at noon. My efforts to save Silas had widened that tiny crack in the Earthen Source into a gushing waterfall of magic, and Casius wasn't happy. Everyone in Boston had felt the impact of that power—even the Mundane news outlets reported effects of some kind of shock wave or earthquake felt throughout the city, though they didn't know what had caused it. I was honestly surprised we hadn't heard from our friends at DODSI. Knowing my luck, it was probably only a matter of time before they came knocking. Plus, I owed them answers to all their questions.

I sighed. I'd made such a mess of things. The entirety of our knowledge and power wasn't going to be enough to fix what I'd broken reopening the portal and saving Silas. So despite only a few hours of sleep, I dragged myself out of bed and spent fifteen minutes under a hot stream of water in the women's locker room, trying to come up with a solution that would satisfy the Inner Circle. I didn't have any brilliant ideas, but my musings were cut short when I realized Tessa was guarding the door and scaring away everyone else who wanted to use the bathroom.

There was a light knock on my bedroom door before it clicked open.

"Are you awake?" Silas had showered and changed into a clean set of Guardian fatigues that came from gods knew where.

His eyes had returned to their normal steel gray, not the blazing white of the Fates. We'd both gotten a boost from what I'd done, but the details of it were hazy—it didn't seem real. Facing the consequences was going to suck, because I remembered one thing clearly—the price still had to be paid. *A life for a life.*

"Maeve? Is all right with you?" Silas slipped into the room and closed the door quietly behind him.

I realized I was staring and hadn't answered him. So much had changed so fast, and I didn't want to talk about it until I'd had a chance to process everything. The fact that we were all alive was a miracle.

From Silas and Tessa, I'd managed to piece together everything that had happened in Aeterna. Nuada's poison had infected the users of the Citizen Source, but no one realized it was eating up the power within the source as it spread. When it burned through all of the magic available, it went supernova and imploded. Silas drained his own House's magic into the Citizen Source, burning through the entire Valeron Source in an attempt to stabilize the power.

When that wasn't enough, everything started to collapse. All hell broke loose, and only the people in Upper Aeterna, with easier access to the main portal to Earth, were able to escape quickly. By the time the citizens from Lower Aeterna were able to make it through, there wasn't any power left to hold open the portal. Silas pulled the last of his family's magic in an attempt to hold the portal open for as long as possible. Lady Cecilia had joined him and helped hold the portal open. They'd saved thousands of lives. Both of them had burned through all of their magical resources and kept on pushing until they had nothing left to give. Lady Cecilia had died, burning through her core magic in the process. I swallowed back a lump of emotion—she'd been a fierce advocate for her people and a good person.

Silas would have died, too, without the power I stole from the Fate. I shuddered. The vision, and the reality, of Silas's body being carried on the shoulders of the crowd of panicked people was too much for me. I'd killed a Fate to bring him back, and there were going to be repercussions. Silas needed to know what I'd done, but it was kind of a blur, and I really didn't want to think about it yet.

Where one path ends, the other begins. A life for a life. I'd made a choice, and I definitely didn't want to think too hard about the consequences.

The bed dipped as Silas shifted closer. He lifted my arm off my face to peer down at me with an expression that was hard to decipher. "We need to talk."

Is he freaking out? I was freaking out.

"Aria and Stephan? The baby?" I asked, delaying the hard questions that would surely follow.

"All fine. They're settled into a room in Building Four."

"Did you find Commander Corin?"

Silas's mouth went tight. "He didn't make it out. His last known location was in the Lower City..." He ran his hands through his hair and released a huff of air. "Most of the Guardians were down there, enforcing the quarantine. Less than a hundred made it through before the portal collapsed."

"I'm so sorry, Silas." I placed my hand on his forearm. This whole situation was terrible. Thousands were dead, and their entire civilization was gone. And all of it was needless.

Silas held my gaze, and that strange expression returned. "How were you able to bring me back from death? You didn't even have an Anchor."

I finally realized what the expression on his face was: awe.

Well, shit. I don't deserve that. I scowled. "I caused catastrophe after catastrophe until I cracked Earth's source wide open. I've lost count of all my stupid mistakes." I tugged on my still-damp braid. "You should be yelling at me right now."

Silas raised his eyebrows. "I started the collapse of an entire realm when my actions allowed Nuada to return to Aeterna, destroyed my House source... and apparently, I died. Let's not start... what do Earthens say? Pointer fingers."

There wasn't an ounce of guilt on his face. *How does he do that?* I'd been buried in guilt for months ever since I led the Brotherhood back to my Sect's compound in Pennsylvania. I had all those deaths on my hands, and now I'd broken our source and killed a Fate.

I forced myself out of the old destructive thought patterns. If anyone should be blamed for what I'd been forced to do, it was Four. He'd set me up.

Silas intertwined his fingers in mine. "What you did was incredible, and truth be told, I don't understand how it was possible."

"I killed a Fate to bring you back," I blurted.

My announcement brought him up short, and his eyebrows rose. "Come again?"

I swallowed hard, remembering the details of what I had done. It felt like a dream. My actions hadn't mattered while the pain of losing Silas burned through me, but he needed to know what had happened. So I told him about the visions and how I'd done everything I could to stop them from coming true—each death I'd averted to save him.

"And then you died anyway," I concluded. The echoes of that pain burned behind my eyes as I blinked back tears. "Four promised me you would live, but he tricked me into causing your death. I was so angry, and I was willing to do anything to save you. I channeled all the power I could..." I took a breath. "I didn't even really know what I was doing, but I think I went directly to the Earthen Source, Silas. One of the Fates tried to stop me, and I—I drained him. I used his magic to bring you back."

"Holy shite, Maeve! You could have died." He stood up and started pacing, running his hands through his hair.

Finally, Silas was freaking out. But true to character, it was about all the wrong things. He wasn't even worried about the cost of killing the Fate, just that I could have died doing it. Pissing him off felt amazingly normal, and I pulled him back onto the bed and curled onto his lap. His arms wrapped around me, and I leaned against his strong, broad chest.

Warm breath ruffled my hair. *Alive.* He was alive and breathing. And so was I.

"You're so damn reckless with your own life," he said. "If you'd brought me back and died in the process, how could I live with that?"

"That didn't actually happen," I pointed out.

"Never again, Maeve." He pulled back to stare me down, the strong lines of his jaw tight. "I would *never* choose my life over yours. Promise me you'll never make that decision again. It was stupid and reckless and... reckless."

"You said reckless twice."

"You were *really* reckless."

A tight knot uncurled in my chest. He was angry, but he was alive. "I didn't do it out of guilt. I did it because I love you, and I couldn't let you die, Silas. I had to do everything in my power to keep you with me, because I refuse to be separated from you again." I put my hands on his face, staring into his eyes. "I won't apologize, because I'm not sorry. You would never choose your life over mine, but I feel the exact same way about you. I couldn't let you die."

His eyes roamed over my face, lingering on my lips and sending tingly heat through my chest. My exhaustion fled as desire kindled low and fluttery inside of me.

"Well, that does answer one of my questions." His magic blazed. The golden color at the center of his aura—normally a reflection of his human heritage—shone pure white. His flare looked like mine as I directly accessed the Earthen Source.

I let my own magic fill me until my aura was pure white. That was normal in my case, but I could feel extra power coursing through me. The fact that we were hopped up on Fate powers was probably the only reason either of us was still conscious. The last time I'd pushed that much magic through me—saving Aria's life—I'd passed out and needed a boost from Silas's source.

"Don't get a big head," I said. "Speaking from experience, it'll fade with time."

He hummed. "Does the Inner Circle know what you did?"

"I was hoping I wouldn't have to get into all the details." I bit my lower lip. "They get a little freaked over this kind of stuff."

"I think the cats are out of their boxes. My flare has been freaking people all night."

"Please don't say that to anyone else." I snorted and then lost all my humor as I thought about the upcoming meeting with the Circle. "We're going to have some explaining to do."

"A small price to pay for being alive."

I smiled sweetly up at him. "By my count, that's the second time I saved your life. When are you going to learn to say thank you?"

My heart picked up as he shifted to his knees and moved me backward onto the bed with his body. Slowly, deliberately, he pinned me to the mattress with the weight of his hips.

"Then allow me to rectify that and express my deepest gratitude," he said, his voice low.

A delicious tingle ran through my abdomen as his fingers slid under my clothing, trailing over my flesh. I tangled my fingers into his dark, tousled hair. He kissed the sensitive skin behind my ear, and I let my hands roam over his shoulders and the strong muscles of his back, traveling lower to tug at his shirt.

It felt so right to have him in my arms, and I was more than happy to forget the rest of the world as he fisted the fabric behind his shoulders and pulled it over his head with one hand. As our mouths connected and his hands moved over my skin, pleasure cascaded through me.

The fabric between us disappeared in a flurry until we were both naked and breathing heavily. Hovering over me, he was hard angles and muscle, his gray eyes dilated with desire. His dark hair was tousled from my hands, his lips pink and swollen from my mouth. He was mine, and I wasn't ever going to let him go. Fate be damned.

My heart skipped a beat. "I can't believe you tried to die on me."

"Fratch, Maeve. I owe tribute to every god known to every race in this whole blighted world that you're alive after what you did."

I reached out to him through our Aegis bond, and the flood of power and shared emotion between us filled me just as joyfully as magic. His clever fingers moved lower, stroking and building my entire world into a frenzied tornado.

"Silas," I pleaded. "I need you..."

It was too much. The feeling was too big, and I needed more. I hooked my leg around his strong, muscular thigh and pulled him closer. He murmured my name, kissing and stroking me as our mouths and bodies moved together. The pressure built between us until I couldn't take any more. Pleasure overwhelmed me, and I rode the wave until he joined me.

Watching him come undone on top of me was exactly what my soul needed. It was that exact moment that I knew we were alive. Together. Nothing was going to tear us apart again. Not our responsibilities, our mistakes, or even death. What we had together was too big. Too right.

We collapsed onto the bed, our arms and legs still tangled, our bodies sweaty and completely spent.

"Remind me to express my gratitude more often." Silas planted a gentle kiss in my hair as he curled his large frame around me.

We fell asleep in each other's arms, and I let the sound of his heart beating soothe away the last of my pain and fear.

Chapter Twenty-Nine

"It's too risky." Casius leaned against the mahogany desk in the old chief of staff's office, tapping his fingers on his thigh.

"I agree," Silas said.

Great. Now they're best friends? I'd brought Silas with me to convince Casius about our spy before the Inner Circle meeting, but my plan was backfiring.

"But—we could feed Kianna misinformation and make her think we're more powerful than we are. It could hold off her attack."

Silas had paced from one side of the office to the other as I brought them up to speed on everything I knew about Alannah's connection to the Fae. He stopped between Casius and me, planting his hands on his hips. "I agree with your conclusions. Alannah's behaviors as well as her connection to Kianna are highly suspicious. But whatever information you feed her isn't going to offset the risk. You can't restrict her movements unless you want her to realize you suspect her of being a spy. Which means she'll have the opportunity to sabotage further negotiations and feed sensitive information to the Fae."

"But—"

"There's just no way we can risk the kind of damage she could inflict," Casius said. "We have to do something to prevent the danger to all of our people. It's not a spy movie."

"I realize that," I said, letting anger snap in my tone. "I just think we should consider all of the options and not act rashly. I already planted the seed about DODSI being our powerful allies. If she tells Kianna that, maybe we can keep the Fae off-balance long enough to recover from this situation."

"No amount of misinformation will cover up the precariousness of our current situation," Silas said. "We now have almost four thousand people on this campus—all of the Fae's declared enemies in one location. If Alannah were to do something to compromise the shield..."

"The Guardians can follow her," I said.

Silas crossed his arms. "That is far from a fool-proof plan."

A knock sounded at the door, and all of us jumped up as Silas released the privacy spell so Casius could answer it.

"Ethan, Alannah—" Casius's voice was strained as he opened the door and saw who was on the other side. "Now is not a great time."

"We need to talk, Master Casius." Ethan pushed his way into the room, and Alannah followed, her high heels clicking on the wood floor. For once, she didn't seem smug. Her hands were clasped in front of her, and as she chewed on her lower lip, I noticed she'd foregone her usual brightly colored lipstick. Her fingers started fidgeting.

Ethan's jaw was set in a firm line as he faced the three of us. "I know what you think, but you're wrong. My mother didn't betray us to the Fae."

My mouth dropped open. *Dammit*. Ethan wasn't stupid—he'd realized my suspicions after he spilled the beans about Kianna's visit, and of course he believed his mother was innocent. I hadn't even thought about how he would react. I was such an idiot.

"Tell them, Mother," Ethan said.

Alannah cleared her throat. "I should have told you about Kianna's visit and her proposal for an alliance between my people and the Fae."

"Damn straight," Casius said. "You look awfully guilty, Alannah. I never would have expected this from you, of all people."

Alannah twined her fingers together, and I noticed that the bright-red paint had chipped on one nail. "I know, Casius. And I'm sorry for that. When we learned about what Nuada did—I didn't want to cast any suspicion on us. We sent Kianna away. That was the end of it, I swear."

"Why should we believe you?" I asked. "You did everything you could to sabotage our summit—and you tried to pull everyone else out with you! You did exactly what the Fae wanted. Keeping us apart makes us weaker."

Alannah straightened her shoulders, and some of her usual heat returned to her tone as she said, "Questioning poor leadership is not the same as sabotage. I came here to negotiate rejoining the Sect, but you didn't make it easy! You have questionable allegiances"—she motioned at Silas—"and then you run off, risking access to our source when you almost get yourself captured by the Brotherhood's leader. If I were a spy, I'd be cheering you on and watching you self-destruct!"

I flinched.

"Mother," Ethan warned. "You're not helping."

Alannah picked at her chipped nail. "I came to prove my innocence. I'm offering to take a truth oath to clear my name."

Silas, Casius, and I looked at each other. Truth oaths were tricky business. The oath acted strangely on someone under duress—the caster's perceptions of truth or the intent of the question almost always influenced the response. False confessions and half-truths were the most common outcome of a truth oath that had been forced on someone else.

But if Alannah took a truth oath voluntarily, the magic reacted much more reliably. She wouldn't be able to lie outright—but much like the Fae, she could twist the truth if she wanted.

I shrugged. "It can't hurt."

Casius closed the office door and motioned for Alannah to sit in one of the chairs. "Be as direct and straightforward as you can, Alannah. We're not in the mood for games."

Alannah's magic rose around her, a shade of golden-red that didn't quite edge into orange. Somewhere in their family tree, they'd had Shifter blood, but I knew that neither she nor Ethan had enough of it to change shape. I could only imagine what Alannah would be in animal form—something sneaky and aggressive for sure. *Maybe a feral rat. Or a rabid skunk.*

Alannah formed the truth oath conjuring, and once it settled over her, I said, "Do you swear to tell the truth, the whole truth, and nothing but the truth?"

She raised a judgy eyebrow at my choice of oath. "I swear."

So help us gods.

"Start with a question she won't want to answer truthfully," Silas suggested.

"Is blond your natural hair color?" I asked immediately.

Alannah rolled her eyes. "No. I'm covering up my grays."

"You have to ask her something harder than that," Silas said. "Something she really doesn't want to answer."

I racked my brain for something Alannah wouldn't want us to know.

Ethan stepped forward. "Who's my father?"

Alannah froze. "You don't want me to answer that, Ethan."

"Actually, he's wanted you to answer that question his whole life," I said. "Who is it?"

Alannah's gaze slid to Casius, and I knew the answer a second before she said, "Casius is your father."

Casius's fingers paused midtap, and he grimaced. But he didn't look surprised—and as Ethan and I stared in utter shock, I realized that Casius had definitely already known.

"Holy shit," I said. "I did not see that coming." But then I remembered the secret glances and hours of talking during social events. They definitely had a history. I just hadn't realized that it included making babies.

"Why didn't you tell me?" Ethan asked them.

"I'm sorry, Ethan," Casius said. "It's... complicated."

"As interesting as this family drama is," Silas said dryly, "I'd like to get back to the questions at hand. I believe we've established that Alannah is telling truths. Do you agree?"

With a sympathetic glance at Ethan, who looked shell-shocked, I nodded. "Yup, that was a big ole truth bomb right there."

"Did you meet with Kianna to discuss a potential alliance?" Silas asked Alannah.

"Yes. But I'm not her spy."

"Did you make an alliance of any kind with her?" I asked.

"No," Alannah replied.

"Say it," I said.

"I did not make an alliance of any kind with Kianna or any member of the Fae."

Silas lifted his chin toward Ethan. "Did anyone else make an alliance with Kianna?"

Alannah's face was earnest. "To my knowledge, none of my people made an alliance with Kianna or any of the Fae, including Ethan."

I twirled Marcel's charm through my fingers. "Why didn't you tell us about Kianna's visit?"

"I didn't want to look guilty by association," she replied.

"Any other reason?" Casius asked.

Alannah pursed her lips. "I briefly considered the option of an alliance in the future if things didn't work out to rejoin the Sect. But that was before Nuada's attack on Aeterna. I haven't considered an alliance with any of the Fae since that happened, Casius. I swear."

Silas lifted his chin, satisfied. "That seems thorough to me. Any other questions?"

"What about a thrall?" I asked.

"A thrall?" Alannah's eyes widened in horror. "I'm not under a Fae thrall."

"You wouldn't know if you were," I replied.

Ethan swore. "Is Kianna capable of a thrall strong enough that we wouldn't be able to detect it?"

I raised my eyebrows at Silas. With just a fraction of her powers, Kianna had managed a thrall that captured four people. At full power, she'd be capable of a lot more, including much more subtle manipulations. In the long term, it would be a very strong method of control that maybe wouldn't be detectable even by experienced magic users.

Silas's magic glowed, and so did the sigil that allowed him to see the patterns within conjurings as he walked slowly around Alannah and Ethan.

"What are you doing?" Ethan demanded.

Silas ignored Ethan while he circled them, searching. He paused behind Alannah, and his lips pursed slightly. I couldn't sense anything, but the master-level conjuring Silas had earned during his Guardian training might be able to detect more subtle magic.

"Do you see anything?" I asked.

Behind her back, Silas tipped his head slightly toward Alannah before he took a casual step backward, putting himself subtly between our guests and the door.

Shit.

I let my magic rise around me. "Alannah... I need you to *not* freak out."

Alannah's eyes were wide with panic. "I'm not under a thrall! Casius? You have to trust me! You know I wouldn't betray our people. I didn't do anything!"

"You wouldn't even know if you were," Casius said gently. "You may not even remember if Kianna doesn't want you to."

"There are trace amounts of Fae magic on Alannah," Silas said. "Have you had more recent contact with any Fae?"

Alannah shook her head, but her face had gone paler.

"It could be a very subtle thrall or perhaps the remnants of one that has worn off without sustained contact." Silas looked pointedly at Ethan. "Anyone who came into contact with Lady Kianna while she had full access to her magic should be suspect also."

Ethan flinched back. "Me? I didn't—I'm not under a thrall. I'm not a spy."

"Oh my gods," Alannah said.

"How do we break a thrall we can't even see?" I asked.

"You can't break something you can't detect," Casius said. "I'm sorry, but we need to detain both of you, or Kianna could use you to cause further damage."

Alannah gritted her teeth. "Then all of this was pointless."

"No, wait!" Ethan said. "What if we disrupt our field of magic—the thrall would be broken."

"You mean like, hit yourself with a disruptor blast?" I asked.

"Exactly. I've been working on a prototype."

"Are you sure, Ethan?"

"What other option do we have?" Ethan asked. "We need to make sure we aren't under her influence."

"Fine," Casius said. "Let's do it and settle this."

"I volunteer to shoot them," Silas said.

"Silas!" I said.

Silas smiled. "I hear it hurts."

Chapter Thirty

I frowned at the huge crack running down one side of the table through half of the twelve magically binding sigils. At my side, Silas squeezed my hand. Casius had delayed the Inner Circle meeting until Alannah and Ethan had recovered and we were certain they weren't under a thrall. The next morning, we all gathered around the broken meeting table, and everyone was there to witness my colossal screwup. The Inner Circle was there—Casius, Jason, Tamara, Seth, Rhonda, and I. Alannah, Gia, Levi, and even Ethan stood witness to the disaster too. If you also counted the surviving Aeternal Council Members—Silas, Alaric, Octavia, and Nero—it was a nice full tribunal.

Casius's brow crinkled with confusion. "You put the powers of a Fate into him how exactly?"

"I'm not sure..." I didn't have the words to explain how I'd brought Silas back to life. I'd pulled as much as I could through the Earthen Source and then absorbed the powers of a Fate. I had no idea if that magic had mixed and backlashed or if I'd somehow torn through the binding around the Source on my own by drawing too much power.

I'd already tried to explain it twice, and no one knew exactly what had happened. Not even me. We'd been at this for hours, everyone was agitated, and no one had answers.

"All that matters is that she broke the Source." Alannah's accusation echoed off the empty rounded walls of the circle room.

Alannah's attitude about me hadn't improved after my accusations about her being a traitor had forced her to reveal her deep, dark family secret to clear her name. I glanced at Ethan, who had been keeping a cool distance from both his mom and Casius. They had some things to work through, and I felt bad for him, but we had more pressing problems to deal with first.

For the second time, we hadn't opened up the meeting to the entire Sect. What we had to discuss was too sensitive, and with three thousand extra people on the campus, we couldn't have managed to meet in one place anyway.

Tamara threw me an apologetic glance. "Technically, Maeve broke the *binding* around the Source. And I think it's just... cracked *more*. Not completely unbound. Otherwise, magic would have entirely flooded this realm."

Anyone with a lick of magic ability could sense the power leaking from the stone altar in front of us. But that didn't mean we knew how to fix the problem. Repairing the conjuring that bound the Source to our Sect was of a level of complexity and skill we just didn't have anymore.

Casius tapped his fingers on his thigh. "How are we supposed to fix this?"

"It isn't possible." Tamara sighed. "If I had a fraction of our ancestors' knowledge and the raw power of their conjuring circle... maybe."

"Maeve can absorb the loose power and put the binding back together," Levi said.

I grimaced. "I don't know how to do that."

Levi slapped his palms on the stone altar, leaning in. "Maybe if you hadn't spent half your life hiding, you'd be of more use now when we need you!"

"Do *you* know how?" My voice came out sharp, and I felt immediately guilty. This really was my fault, and I shouldn't snap at

Levi when I deserved every bit of censure in his voice. "No one knows how to do it."

Levi threw his arms up in the air. "We have to try something!"

Silas cleared his throat. "The Aeternal Council has the knowledge you need to rebuild the binding."

Every single one of us stared at him in surprise. The Council had first ordered the binding around the Earthen Source for their own purposes, but I'd assumed they'd lost the knowledge, like we had, over the centuries.

"You're offering to help us?" Casius asked slowly. "In exchange for what?"

"They're not in a position to bargain," Alannah said shrewdly. "They have several thousand helpless people in need of sheltering. They have to help us in order to protect their own asses from the Fae—who hate them more than they hate us."

Lord Alaric inclined his head. "As the lady has so crudely put it, if you agree to shelter and protect our people, the Aeternal Council will help you repair the binding around the Earthen Source to the best of our ability. But I must say up front that we cannot guarantee the outcome."

"And boost our perimeter shield," Alannah added. "You have to help us rebuild the binding around the Source and strengthen the perimeter shield around the campus again—and I know for a fact that he"—she pointed at Silas—"knows how to do that."

Silas bared his teeth in a poor impression of a smile, and I was glad he wasn't currently wearing any weapons. "We agree to your terms."

The other Councilors' heads bobbed, and I realized they'd already agreed on their plan.

"No time like the present," Levi said. "The binding is unstable. We have to repair it before things get worse."

"Let's start with the shield," I disagreed.

"Maeve's right," Casius said. "Defenses first. We have to secure the campus, then we'll worry about repairing the binding."

Levi shook his head emphatically. "We can't repair the perimeter shield yet. Can you even conjure a shield of that magnitude without the power of the Source?"

That's a good question, actually.

"Maeve, can you get enough energy without directly accessing the Source?" Casius waved his hand, indicating the concentrated, unformed magic around us.

It would be a lot harder to gather in all that power, especially if I had to be careful not to harvest the magic from the people around me. I pursed my lips as I considered the possibilities.

Alaric cleared his throat and motioned toward Levi. "He's right. You cannot build a master-level conjuring without direct access to a source. Both the shield and binding can be accomplished in a day, but you need the power first."

I shrugged. It would certainly be a lot easier with the full power of the Earthen Source behind our conjuring circle.

"Fine—we'll fix the binding first." Casius nodded to Silas and Alaric. "Will your people add their powers to ours?"

The Councilors shared a look before Silas said, "We will join your conjuring circle as a show of partnership."

"Tamara, do you want to take the lead?" Casius asked.

She stepped forward, lifting her chin with determination. "Absolutely."

"We need a connector between the two conjuring circles, and they can't draw on your source until it's repaired," Silas said. "I'm assuming Maeve is still your most powerful *navitas.*"

"A what?" I asked.

Silas seemed to search for a way to explain. "Can anyone else draw more pure power than you without a source?"

Even when I didn't have a direct connection to the Earthen Source, the practice I had drawing and holding massive amounts of raw power had given me a higher capacity than anyone else in the Sect.

"Yes, Maeve is the best choice for that," Casius said.

"But without a direct link to a source, her focus will be split between gathering enough energy and providing it to the lead," Alaric said. "I suggest we use a second *circutio*, with a *sublatis ancorus* for her."

"A what?" I repeated, feeling utterly useless.

"You need an Anchor," Silas clarified. "I can do it, since we share a bond already."

I braced myself. "Actually, Ethan has agreed to be my Anchor."

Silas's eyebrows rose.

"He, uh, called off the bond-mating, and I asked him to be my Anchor instead."

Silas seemed to think that over, but his expression didn't get any happier. "Ethan," he snapped.

Ethan stepped forward cautiously. The two men stared at each other. I braced myself for violence.

"You need to establish the Anchor bond with Maeve," Silas said. "Do you know the ritual?"

"No," Ethan said, swallowing. He looked ready to bolt if Silas so much as twitched in his direction, and I didn't blame him at all.

"Very well. Maeve, may I have your knife?"

I debated the intelligence of giving Silas a knife when he had that particular expression on his face. But I was fairly confident Silas wouldn't actually use it to stab Ethan, so I handed Ripper over. I sent him reassuring vibes through our bond, but I wasn't sure I was getting through.

Silas directed Ethan and me to face each other and clasp forearms. Then he carefully slid the knife flat between our arms. Alannah scooted closer.

"Loosen your grip," Silas said gently and then he set the edge of the knife against each of our forearms, balanced between the tension of our grip.

Silas clasped his hands around our delicately balanced arrangement, his aura flared, and the threads of magic wove around us. The energy circled around our bared arms, each one tenuous until it joined with others and became the strong, complex tapestry of a bonding spell. Silas pushed gently, and the knife broke the flesh on both our arms.

Our magic mixed through our blood, binding us in a powerful blood bond, which would allow Ethan to act as my Anchor and vice versa. Unlike the Aegis bond between Silas and me, this bond didn't include an emotional connection. But it did tie us together in an intimate, magical way. Taking responsibility for anchoring someone was putting your own life on the line, and the trust went both ways—if he bailed during a conjuring, the backlash could kill me. Despite the complicated way we'd gotten to this arrangement, I was grateful my Anchor was someone I could trust.

The ritual complete, Silas released us, wiped Ripper clean, and handed it back to me. With a tiny tug of magic, the shallow cut on my arm healed.

"Thanks, Ethan," I said. "I'm glad we found a way forward that works for all of us."

"I've always got your back, Mae," he said with a wary eye on Silas.

To Alannah, I said, "We're in this all the way. Are you?"

Alannah produced a stack of papers with a small burst of her magic. "We're signing on the dotted line."

Jason snatched up the bundle and turned to Levi. "What about your people? Will you rejoin the Inner Circle?"

Levi pulled his own much smaller contract out of his satchel. "I'm looking forward to it."

Casius's nod of approval radiated through me like a small sun. *We did it.*

"Let's get this party started, then," I said. "We'll need to key Alannah, Levi, and Gia to the Source."

Casius motioned to each of the delegates and positioned them at the stone altar that represented the binding around the Earthen Source, producing a ceremonial knife for each.

When I first saw the table back in Pennsylvania, I'd assumed it was a fancy round conference table, but now I knew it was the physical representation of the binding my ancestors had performed on all of Earth's magic. Each symbol carved into the surface represented a complex master-level conjuring required to bind all of Earth's magic into a single source. We used it for all of our Inner Circle meetings for the symbolism, but it was also the access point to the binding conjuring.

We added the former Aeternal Councilors to the arrangement, with me positioned as the Anchor link between the inner and outer conjuring circles. We'd pulled in twelve additional people and arranged my own secondary conjuring circle focused on absorbing the loose magic leaking around us and feeding it to me. Finally, Ethan stood beside me as my personal Anchor.

"Ready?" Tamara asked me.

"Let's do it," I said.

With a determined furrow of her brow, Tamara kick-started the twelve-person Inner Circle by building a small orb of magic in her palm. Although she couldn't access Earth's source directly until we repaired the binding, there was plenty of loose magic for her to gather. Each of the Aeternal Councilors produced an orb of magic, which a member of my Sect incorporated into the circle. Working in tandem with their counterpoints, they built the strength of the magic, passing energy around the circle until the magic peaked in a burst of white power.

The same thing happened with the outer circle, binding the second group of twelve together, and I reached for both circles at once, connecting them together through me. Although its strength was nowhere near what I'd absorbed by accessing magic directly from Earth's source, the magic of the double circle was impressive. Linked to both, I had the capacity of a much bigger conjuring circle. Even connecting to two circles at once didn't feel like a strain. It was almost easy. My capacity was nowhere near its limits as I pushed the power from the outer circle through to the inner one.

"We're ready, Casius," I said.

Gia grimaced and Levi twitched with nerves as Casius drew a blade lightly down each of their palms, instructing them to place their hands over a sigil on the altar. Alannah took the cut without flinching, regally placing her palm on the table. When they were all in position, the Inner Circle members wove our magic around them, joining them by blood to the binding around the Earthen Source. Each of them flared with a brilliant white aura before stepping back from the altar.

"Connect with the blood sigils," Silas instructed the group.

I moved closer to the stone altar as the other members of the Inner Circle cut their palms deep enough to draw blood and placed it over their sigils. Then the members of the outer circle built their connection, until the combined power of our double circle pressed into the altar, and a white ball of magic formed in the center of our stone table. Its brilliance was too strong to look at directly, and the strength of it pounded in my chest, making every beat of my heart and every lungful of air burn with its power.

The energy built between us, and everything blurred outside of the conjuring circle and our growing magic. I was so focused on our work that I only distantly noticed an extra tug of Levi's magic. I realized what was happening just as he picked up the ceremonial knife on the table... and stabbed Casius in the back.

Casius cried out and arched backward. Levi stabbed Casius again before any of us could react, and my mentor fell forward onto the stone table.

"Casius!" I screamed.

A wave of foreign magic hit us. With a shiver of power that had everyone raising their heads at the same time, the perimeter shield around the campus collapsed. My stomach knotted with sickening familiarity as dozens of strangers skimmed into our midst, and blue magic filled the room. *Fae.*

Our connection fell apart as all hell broke loose. The massive amount of magic I'd been pushing into the circle whipped backward and punched me in the gut. I doubled over.

Tamara reached out for Casius, and a Fae sword pierced her through the chest. We both cried out as her blood splashed across the stone table. Without warning, Ethan dropped beside me, the contents of his gut spilled across the floor by another attacker.

I pooled my magic into a sphere of energy—and pain ripped through my middle. Silas hopped onto the table, an expression of horror contorting his face as he scrambled toward me. I blinked, following his gaze to see a sword sticking through my abdomen.

I grunted and fell to my knees. I wrapped my hands around the blade's tip, but I couldn't feel anything as my brain absorbed the reality of what was happening very slowly.

Silas cleared the table and raced toward me with his sword drawn. I couldn't do more than gasp as Levi appeared between us, glowing with magic. Levi whipped magic at Silas, slamming him back into the wall opposite. He fell, and three Fae jumped on him. Silas's aura flared—

The sword in my stomach jerked free, and the shock of it ripped through me like fiery, desperate claws. I folded in on myself, collapsing to the floor, as Kianna stepped into my field of vision. The golden helmet atop her head resembled a crown, and her long blond hair swung loose down her back as she raised her sword into the air—slick with my blood—and bellowed in triumph.

Hot blood soaked through my clothes and slipped through my hands, pooling on the ground. My vision darkened as Levi and Kianna started a conjuring circle at the stone altar. The Fae were building the layers of a massive spell. Everyone in the Inner Circle was dead or dying, and I wasn't able to do anything more than bleed out on the floor as Kianna began to bind the Earthen Source under the control of the Fae.

Too late, it all clicked into place in my brain. Levi was the spy feeding Kianna information. And we'd just given him—and through him, Kianna—access to the Earthen Source. I shuddered as my blood spread across the floor, leaving me cold and horrified. It had taken Kianna seconds to destroy everything I loved.

My mistakes had cost us everything. I should have punched Four in the face the second he showed up outside that Elementari. I should have left Kianna in that cell. I wished with all my heart I could go back and do it over. Every misstep and every mistake I'd made along this path to hell was crystal clear to me in this final, horrible moment.

A burst of pure-white magic surged from across the room, and I gasped through my own blood as Silas surfaced and Fae went flying. The power of a Fate flooded through his eyes, turning them white just as Kianna gained control of the Source.

It's too late. Kianna had gained access to all of Earth's magic, and we were out of time.

Kianna screamed. Her aura blazed white, and an explosion of magic cascaded outward in a shock wave of visible energy. She had connected with the Source directly, but she couldn't control it. The power pouring through her was too much. The impact hit everyone around her. Levi cried out as his body disintegrated, ripped apart by magic. Gia, Alannah, Alaric, Nero—everyone still standing was caught in its wake.

Directly in front of me, Silas braced himself and threw his hands out, forming a shield conjured from powerful Fate-level magic. Like the surf hitting a lone rock standing tall in the ocean, Kianna's uncontrolled power hit Silas and broke around either side of us.

Kianna cried out again, and the outpouring of power slowed, folding in on itself like a curling tide. She was gaining control. If she couldn't rein in the massive power coursing through her, everyone in the room—everyone on the campus—was going to die. And if she managed to control it, she would gain access to the Source, and the whole world would become enslaved to the Fae. Either way, I had to stop her.

A sob stole my last breath as I realized what kind of leader I was meant to be. I had one life to give, and I wasn't going to waste it.

I forced myself to my knees and opened my arms wide as I took everything riding on Kianna's uncontrolled wave. At the same time, I drew on my own connection to the Earthen Source and pulled on the Aegis connection with Silas to access the Fate powers still coursing through us. I took all that power into myself, and then I let it go. I held absolutely nothing in reserve, not even the core of magic that sustained my life.

My power exploded outward.

The Source pulses, and time skips.

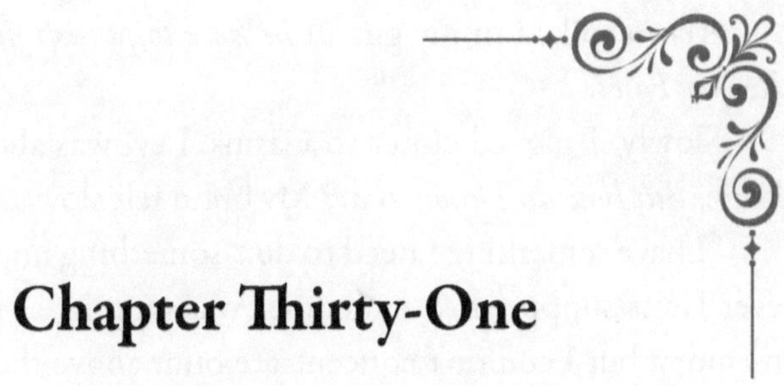

Chapter Thirty-One

The source pulses again, sending a heavy thrum of magic through me.

My hand stretched toward the sigil engraved on the stone table in front of me. Casius stood on my left with Levi on his other side, one hand frozen in the act of reaching for his knife.

Everyone was frozen. There wasn't a single twitch or heartbeat among the two dozen people in the room. The conjuring building in the center of the stone altar was the only thing moving—magic flowed gently as though ruffled by an unfelt breeze around the stone table. My brain fixated on the patterns looping and turning inside to out like a wind spinner on an endless loop.

Four appeared across the table from me. "What an interesting Moment we find ourselves in."

Stepping back from the table felt like moving through a swimming pool of thick honey. This was the same trick the child Fate had used in the Alaska temple to freeze Titus and his men.

"What did you do?" I asked, looking around in confusion. Something was about to happen—or it had happened. I could feel the pain still ripping through me. But I couldn't quite remember why.

He laughed. "Oh no, it's not my Moments that are filled with death, Maeve O'Neill."

"What's happening?" I demanded. "Why are you here?"

"There are consequences that follow actions."

Alarm spiked in my gut. *Is he here to punish me for killing the Reaper Fate?*

Slowly, I moved closer to Casius. Levi was about to pull that knife. *But how do I know that?* My brain felt slow and confused.

"I have something I need to do... something important." Whatever I was supposed to remember was tapping at the back of my memory, but I couldn't concentrate on it above the buzzing in my brain. "Can't the consequences wait? You're immortal—let's pick up this conversation in a few centuries."

I searched for Silas, suddenly afraid. I needed to stop something. *The visions?*

"I didn't stop this Moment," Four said. "You did."

I pushed down my rising panic. "What do you mean, I stopped this Moment? How could I...?" A terrible thought occurred to me. "Only Fates can stop time."

He tapped his forefinger against his temple. "You're catching up. Very good. The first time can be disorienting. You *changed* your fate, Maeve O'Neill, and I've come to warn you."

"Warn me about what?" *I need to stop something bad from happening.*

He looked pointedly around the room, and I took in the frozen people stuck in their own timeline. I remembered blood splashed across the stone table. *Casius dead. Silas standing alone in a sea of magic. A traitor.*

"Wielding a Fate's powers is dangerous," Four said.

I pressed both palms against my stomach, trying to stop an unexplained sharp pain. "How can I stop this?"

"What you do with this Moment is yours to decide. But know that each time you wield this power, you change your fate."

Kianna's sword sticking out of my stomach. The Fae surrounding the stone altar.

But it hadn't happened—yet. *Or again?* Levi was about to pick up that knife and stab Casius in the back. *Levi is the traitor!*

Levi would betray us to the Fae. I had seconds to... *do what exactly?* I could kill Levi, but that wouldn't stop the Fae from skimming in and taking everyone by surprise. I could yell out a warning, but we needed more than a few seconds to change the things that Four had put into motion.

Kianna was going to take control of Earth's magic, and everyone I cared about was going to die. There were thousands of people on this campus, and beyond our walls, the regular Mundanes didn't stand a chance.

"You're thinking too linear," Four stated as if he could read my thoughts.

"How do I stop this?" I begged.

"This Moment is the end of a series of events. Triggers you already pulled. Think bigger—a pattern emerges."

"The visions," I whispered. "I thought I was stopping the visions, but I wasn't, was I?"

He winked. "A web of choices."

"You did this." I remembered now, and my anger rose. "Why did you set me up?"

"You were too tempting," he admitted with a sigh. "Your Sect's control of Earth's magic, the Transference of power from the Brotherhood, and then your connection to the Valeron Source. The sheer capacity for magic you hold—we haven't seen the like before. It takes centuries to guide the perfect genetics among mortals, but there you were"—he snapped his fingers—"a perfect candidate that none of us saw coming."

"A candidate for what?"

"Three had grown too attached to the mortals. He delayed what needed to be done. We all saw it, but I was the one who made it change. If I waited for the natural order of things, my mortal friend, you'd be dead many times over. You just needed a nudge in the right direction. But I did not see *this* change coming, and I find myself surprised." His expression morphed, and for the first time, the mask of jovial unconcern slipped from his face. "I'm not certain I like this feeling."

"I can't stop this," I realized out loud. People I loved were in danger. Silas, Casius, Ethan, Tamara, even Alannah and Alaric—none of them deserved to be the casualties of Four's scheming. "They're all going to die."

"Individual concerns are too small and linear for you. You are bigger now, Maeve O'Neill. It's time to accept your fate."

"Bigger," I repeated. I had to think bigger, without linear time stopping me.

Four had tricked me into this situation, and nothing was ever going to be the same. My brain finally accepted what I'd known since the Moment I killed Three. I'd stolen the Reaper Fate's powers. And if I had the power of a Fate, there was a lot I could do about this Moment.

I locked gazes with the Fate who had caused everything in my life to fall apart. "I really, truly hate you."

The bastard winked, and I knew what I had to do. I'd spent my entire life learning how to control complex magic. I had to *change* everything. Every true turning point had to be redone. And Agent Lennart had already told me what I needed to know right after they rescued me from Elias's compound. *Ethan is the first turning point.*

With my new Fate powers, I examined the web of events leading to this Moment and knew what I had to do. I'd already pulled the trigger, and Four was only distracting me. He was scared of the change I was about to enact—which meant it could work.

I drew once more on the Fate powers inside of me. Stretching everything until I nearly broke, I took more magic than my brain could have conceived of before Four came into my life, and then I reached into the past.

Change hurt. It hurt a lot. The Source pulsed, and I found myself in the rec room.

I gripped the boxing glove in my teeth and ripped the Velcro strap open. "I'm probably the one who should be apologizing."

Ethan's head tilted, and a grin tugged at the corners of his mouth. "For calling my mother a bitch?"

I rolled my eyes. "No. I have no regrets about that."

He chuckled, and I remembered why I'd liked him in high school. He was nothing like his uptight mother. This was the slightly awkward kid who'd gone behind his mother's back to imbue a paper airplane with enough magic to carry a single daisy to my second-story bedroom window in the middle of the night.

I freed my other hand and tossed the gloves back onto the rack.

This was... different. Like déjà-vu and lucid dreaming, I knew I had been here before, but my head was spinning as my future merged with the past. Some instinct I didn't quite understand had drawn me to this Moment—a private conversation with Ethan before Nuada's trap or Gia's kidnapping and my resulting visit to DODSI. This was the Moment when Ethan told me about his tinkering and the magic disruption field he'd been working on.

I grabbed Ethan's arm, startling him. "Ethan, your mother is going to force me into this bond-mating. She'll back us all into a corner, and I'll accept under duress. But you're still a decent person—I know you. And you're going to stand up to her and tell her that you won't accept the bond if I'm being forced into it."

"Maeve, is it such a bad thing? I mean—"

I waved my hand, cutting off his speech about rekindling old flames. "Ethan! This is where our future changes. You want to be part of this Sect? Then help me save it! You're going to think I'm crazy, but that magic disruptor thingy you've been working on—"

"How did you know about that? I haven't told anyone about that." He flinched, confusion and surprise painted across his face.

"I've seen it, Ethan. I've seen the future—" I almost choked on the words. I was so furious with Four and terrified for my people. I sounded like a crazy person, but I had to alter what had happened. I could still hear the cries of the people I loved as they were murdered.

"I absorbed the powers of a Fate, Ethan, and we have one shot at saving everyone. You've got to finish that weapon and give it to the DODSI agents, or we're all going to die."

His eyes went wide, and I could see the wheels start turning. The beautiful thing about people who lived every day with magic was the ease with which they accepted the impossible.

Ethan had caught on very quickly, but keeping myself in the past felt like bench-pressing the world. I couldn't sustain it forever. I needed to move forward, and I didn't have time to go slowly with Ethan.

"The government has a special gun that can short out magic with a single pulse of energy. If you could figure out how it works..."

"It would have to be only a temporary effect," he mused. "Other than a long-term binding, I'm not sure how you could short out someone's magic, and I've never heard of anything like it."

"Right! Yes. It only lasts for a few hours. Thomas's supplies are in a storage closet in Building Two. The code is 02144. Try not to make it too superpowered, okay? Give it a recharge delay and a limited burst of power." I thought of Agent Lennart. "Maybe make them blow up on occasion."

"Maeve, are you going to be okay? You're freaking me out."

"I don't know, Ethan. I really don't know." I handed Agent Lennart's business card to Ethan. "You need to get the disruptor to this man as soon as they take Gia. Tell him you're holding up my end of the bargain when you call."

Ethan's eyes went wide. "Who's taking Gia?"

"I can't tell you everything. Give DODSI the disruptor, or we're all dead. Actually, make two—keep one for us. I'm counting on you, Ethan. And don't talk about this again—even with me. We can't risk changing anything else about the past." I realized I was doing to him what Four had done to me, and the knowledge he now had would be an incredible burden. I grimaced. "Sorry."

Fervently hoping I was doing the right thing, I gathered the Fate's magic coursing through me, let it fill me until it burned, and focused my powers on the next turning point.

I OPENED MY EYES INSIDE DODSI's headquarters. The power faded as I burned through it, and I almost stumbled into the wall. The magic of the Fates was addictive, and I wanted more. The second jump had taken a lot out of me, and I could feel the Fate's power decreasing each time I used it. I didn't know how much longer I could hold this.

I didn't let my brain dwell on the space-time continuum, or whatever I was breaking into little bits. This twisting of time was enough to make my brain explode, but the abilities I'd absorbed from the Fate endowed me with an innate sense of the timeline. Without that, I was sure I'd never have seen the connections between what had already happened and when they'd been put into motion. I was hopping through my own past, finding the places where the webs of time and decision overlapped, and adjusting them to my will.

At least it looked like I'd gotten my timing right. I'd arrived to DODSI's secret base about ten minutes earlier than I had the first time, but instead of walking into the front reception area, where Lennart was waiting for me, I had chosen the break room. Lennart would bring me in here to explain the truth about magic to him, which meant I only had a few minutes to put my alternate plans into place.

With a smirk, I snatched a chocolate-glazed doughnut out of the pink bakery box on the counter, opened the door to the break room, and headed up the hall. After a few close calls requiring me to duck down adjacent hallways so I wouldn't get spotted, I found Director Pascal's office. Conveniently, his name was on the door. I knocked.

"Come in," his deep, resonant voice called.

I opened the door and closed it quickly behind me. He glanced up and scowled. "Who are you?"

One of his hands crept below his desk. I help up my palms. "I'm Maeve O'Neill. You've been surveilling my people, the Earthen Sect of Harvesters." His brow furrowed. "You know, the ones with unexplainable magic abilities."

Recognition and then alarm spread across his face. "How did you get in here?"

"I skimmed in, using magic. You were right about us—we have the powers you suspect, we're using magic, and everyone you know is going to die if you don't listen to what I have to say right now."

His hand stayed under the desk, but his voice was calm. "Is that a threat?"

He was extremely calm under pressure, and I doubled down on my impression that he would make the smart call. I really hoped I was right about that, because a whole lot of lives were riding on the deal we were about to make.

"It's not a threat. Believe it or not, we're the good guys, and we're all that's standing between you and some really nasty people who want to take control over Earth. If you help me, I'll tell you everything you want to know about magic and our people. And I'll give you a weapon you can use to disrupt magic."

By the time I finished laying out the full details of my offer, his eyes were wide. "Why should I believe anything you're saying?"

"They say trust is a two-way street, and I'm willing to be the first one to start walking on it," I said, but my brain almost seized as I quoted him and then realized he'd been quoting me. "Didn't Agent Lennart tell you I was coming in to meet with him?"

Pascal frowned. "Why are you here, Miss O'Neill?"

"I need help with a prisoner-exchange situation. In about thirty minutes, you're going to walk into the break room, pretend to meet me for the first time, and make me believe you know a whole lot more than you actually do about who I am and my people when you call me the Aegis of House Valeron. You'll tell me I'm walking in blind with a weak exit strategy. Eventually, you'll hook me up with an LWT, and after I leave, you're going to mobilize teams one and three to follow me to the exchange site."

His eyes went wide, and I knew I'd struck the right chord of mystery and knowledge of their operations. "If you help me, my associate will give you a weapon that can disrupt magic before Lennart leaves to track me."

For the first time, I wondered if I was making everything into an even worse situation. I was handing over a weapon they could use against us and potentially tipping the balance of power in their favor.

"Go on," he said.

It was too late now. This was our only option if I wanted to save the lives of everyone on our campus and prevent the Fae from ruling over the Mundane world. Plus, it had already happened. The DODSI agents had already used that gun on us. In a brain-twisting revelation, I realized I was the person who'd made that happen.

If I didn't give them Ethan's weapon, they wouldn't be able to use it on Elias and release me from his Traiten compulsion. Everything after that point would be different—and I'd likely be dead. *But all that came before I did any of this.*

My brain was really starting to hurt, and staying in the past was depleting the rest of my powers. Every second felt harder and more draining than the last. I didn't have time to second-guess myself. I'd just have to trust my new Fate instincts over my limited brain capacity to understand all the turning points. I grabbed a sticky note and a pen off Director Pascal's desk and scribbled the location of Elias's compound on it.

"Three hours after you drop me off, Lennart can take the disruptor and show up at this location. You'll get a chance to capture the former leader of the Aeternal Council, Elias Marius. He is one of the most powerful magic-using Humans in this realm. He's also a real asshole, with a pack of... demonic dogs ready to defend him, so tell your guys to be careful.

"I will be with three other people—don't hurt them. One of them is going to be a pissed-off guy with a sword, and Lennart needs to make sure he doesn't start a fight with him. They're on the good-guy team."

It came out of my mouth before I recalled those were the exact words Lennart had used. They'd seemed a bit strange at the time, but now I realized he had been quoting me. My head hurt, and I needed a drink. Badly.

"Also, have Agent Lennart tell me that Ethan is the first turning point. Word for word, 'Ethan is the first turning point.'"

Lennart's hint had helped me put all this together at the right time in the past. *Future. Future-past. Screw it.*

Pascal's dark-brown eyes were assessing as he pursed his lips in thought. "This is a lot to agree to before you give me anything."

"You'll get the magic-disrupting gun, Director Pascal. My colleague will be in touch soon."

"I want more than one weapon."

My answering smile was too sharp as I let the powers of the Fate build again and shine out of my eyes. Pascal flinched as I leaned forward and planted both hands on his desk. "I'm counting on that, Director Pascal, because I haven't gotten to what you're going to owe *me* yet."

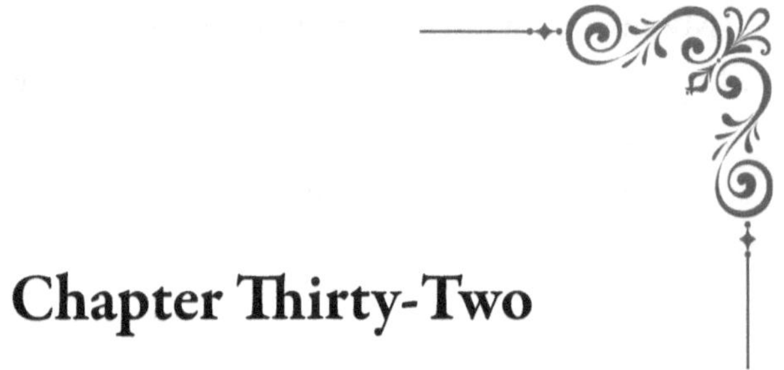

Chapter Thirty-Two

The power of the Earthen Source pulsed like a drumbeat in my chest. My palms started to sweat as my brain oriented back to the current Moment. I'd used up an enormous amount of magic to pull myself through the connected web of past events, and I could barely feel the Fate's powers anymore.

I'd intended to come back earlier and redo the entire last day, but I'd returned only minutes before Kianna's attack. My fading Fate powers had let me down. If the natural timeline played out, in less than five minutes, I'd be bleeding out on the floor, everyone would be dead, and Kianna would be on her way to binding the source under her control. I started to shake, almost too tired to keep myself vertical. I was done. I couldn't go back any farther, and I wouldn't be able to manage that again.

"Access your sigils," Silas instructed the group gathered in the circle room.

I touched Ripper in the holster on my thigh. Everything seemed a little unreal. I locked eyes with Levi a quarter of the way across the table. His expression was completely neutral. No guilt, no remorse. He was about to stab Casius and betray everyone in this room, but there wasn't even a trickle of sweat on his brow. We were all going to die, and Earth was going to fall because of him, and he didn't even seem nervous. *The bastard.*

I gripped Ripper's hilt, and Levi's eyes narrowed as he caught me staring. I couldn't resist asking him the question that had been nagging at me. "Why?"

Why would he betray us all? What does he have to gain from it?

Levi grabbed his knife and lunged toward Casius's back. With a surge of adrenaline, I pulled Casius out of the way, and Levi's blade sliced into my mentor's shoulder instead. Casius cried out as he fell back against the table—shocked but alive.

Levi threw a shield around himself. It was a feeble defense against someone who could manipulate magic, and I tore through it with a swipe of my hand. I knocked his knife away as he stumbled back and gave a swift kick to the outside of his kneecap. He doubled over in pain. I slammed my elbow below the base of his skull, and he dropped to the ground. It should have kept him down, but he rolled onto his back, and his aura flexed with white power from the Source.

Before Levi could do anything with that magic, I stabbed Ripper into the side of his neck, burying it between his vertebrae. I ripped the blade sideways through the spinal column, and he went slack like a puppet cut from its strings.

Seconds later, it was over. Levi lay flat on the floor, dead. It had all happened so fast that no one else had reacted. I'd barely had time to think. He'd lunged at Casius, and I'd reacted on instinct and training.

The room was completely silent for the space of a heartbeat as everyone stared in shock. I had no idea how to explain what had just happened. Then Levi's entire body shimmered, and a glamour spell dropped away, revealing a young, delicately featured face and slightly pointed ears. *Fae.*

Shocked gasps surrounded me as the details slid into place in my brain. This wasn't Levi Porter. The Fae had obviously used a glamour to send someone who looked like Levi. He was young, likely not yet considered an adult—too young to have taken the binding truth oath all Fae took upon adulthood. They'd probably killed the real Levi to take his place, and we'd fallen for every bit of the deceit, welcoming a traitor onto our campus and giving him access to the Earthen Source, just as Kianna planned.

"Maeve!" Silas ran to my side. He and Tessa both flared with magic.

"What in the flaming hells is going on?" Casius demanded as he gripped his bloody shoulder. "Who is this Fae?"

I'd stopped the spy from killing Casius, but we had *minutes* until Kianna attacked. We had to prepare ourselves, and everything was going to hell as people freaked out.

"Stop!" I yelled. The infusion of power I put into my voice worked, and everyone froze. "This Fae was sent to betray us, gain access to the Source, and give control of it to Kianna."

"How is that possible?" Jason demanded. "Our wards block outside magic. We can *see* a magic conjuring, for crying out loud! His flare would be blue!"

I couldn't remember if Levi had used his magic before he attacked Silas—he must have. But other things fell into place, like his discomfort with Tessa and the way he reacted when I casually thanked him. He'd even come up with alternative explanations to our concerns about a spy.

I swore. "The Fae wouldn't have needed to put Alannah or Ethan under a thrall—they had him, and we didn't suspect a thing."

Alannah's face was pale. "What about the traces of Fae magic you found on me?"

"That could have been from contact with Levi, or maybe it was just a decoy so we would suspect you," I said.

Silas dug into the satchel that the fake Levi always carried, emptying the contents onto the ground next to him. Seven vials of blood spilled out. He swore. "He's been using a long-term glamour."

"What do you mean 'long-term'? That's not possible," Casius said.

Silas collected the vials into one fist. "It's exactly what it sounds like, and it explains why his flare wasn't blue. A long-term glamour requires ingesting the blood of the victim every couple of hours, and the victim doesn't usually survive that much bloodletting. It's outlawed for a reason." Silas's magic rose. The vials incinerated in his hand, and Alaric nodded in approval.

"As soon as he got access to the Source, Kianna planned to use his connection as a way in. It was going to work too," I said.

There was a chorus of swearing.

As bad as that was, there was worse coming. "The Fae are about to attack," I said. "They will try to take over the Source. Help is on the way, but we have to keep the Fae from controlling Earth's magic at all costs. They're going to surprise us, and we're all going to die if we're not prepared this time."

Casius clutched as his bleeding shoulder, scowling. "How do you know all this? What—"

"I know because I've *seen* it." *Well, damn. Aren't I being all mysterious and Fate-like.*

We didn't have time to convince everyone with logic, so I let the power of the Fates fill me again. Even though I'd burned through most of what I'd taken from the Reaper Fate, my whole body reveled in the feeling of their expansive magic filling me once again.

The shocked gasps around me confirmed what I knew would happen—the aura around me had become blinding, just like the child Fate I'd first encountered in the Alaska temple, and my eyes glowed with pure power. People shielded their eyes.

Silas was the first to recover, bless him. He pulled the sword at his hip with a reassuring ring of metal. "Tessa, rally the Commanders. Get the Guardians to the weapons lockers. Work with Maeve's people, and find enough space outside for a defensive position."

"Alaric, you and the other Councilors need to warn the Aeternals," I added. "Anyone who can fight needs to get to our weapons cache—send them to Commander Tessa. Then take the others and run. Get as far away from Boston as you can."

"How dare you presume to order us—"

I cut him off with a slash of my hand. We did not have time for his blustering. "Get those who can't fight out of harm's way, or you will be responsible for the deaths of the rest of your people. You choose."

He took a step back, and I made a conscious effort to tamp down the magic leaking off me. "Aria is outside this building. If Kianna gets past us, they will kill everyone on this campus and use their magic to take over Earth. Put your ego aside for a hot minute, and do something helpful."

Alaric's white cloak flowed behind him as he turned and ran outside, and Nero and Octavia followed him with zero objections. The doors of the auditorium banged closed behind them, and I hoped that they would be able to get the Aeternal refugees out of harm's way. I hadn't given them much time, but it was already better than the first time.

Casius's power rose around him, projecting his voice across the campus and out over the quad. "Everyone—Protocol Red. This is not a drill." To us he added, "Form a circle. Everyone not in the Inner Circle, get to your breach posts."

Thank the gods for the paranoid old bastard and his breach drills. Everyone knew where to go and exactly what to do. They ran for their assigned posts, and that left the Inner Circle, Silas, and our guests—Alannah, Ethan, and Gia—inside the room with me.

I met each of their shocked gazes, using the last precious seconds we had left in the hopes they would understand exactly what was at stake. "I know you don't understand everything that is happening right now. But we are the only chance for thousands of defenseless people on this campus. And if the Fae get control of the Source, Earth will fall under their control too. We can't let Kianna outside of this room, and we can't let the Fae take the Source. We are making a stand right here and right now for every life on Earth. Make it count."

Every head in the room nodded in grim determination.

"Tamara, can you put up a shield around that stone altar? Kianna knows it's the access point to the binding." She nodded, and I turned to Ethan. "I need your prototype disruptor again."

His face was pale. "Are you sure this is going to work?"

It occurred to me that Ethan had never been in a fight for his life. He'd gone through the same basic training I had before they split from the Sect, but it had been a decade since he'd last held a weapon with any intention of using it. He didn't know our current drills, and he barely used his magic other than to tinker in secret. He'd just become my Anchor, and the power coursing through me had to be scary as hell. In fact, I was still glowing with it. The weight of it flowed through me like an invisible current, and I knew he could feel that through our Anchor bond just as I could sense his magic.

"I need you to trust me." I tried to appear reassuring, but my glowing eyes probably killed the effect I was going for.

Ethan collected himself, and his magic flared a tranquil yellow, like sunshine and daffodils. The bulky gun landed in his hand, and a small spark of hope lit within me. It looked just like the one Agent Lennart had used on Elias. My crazy plan might just work.

"Thanks," I said as he handed it to me. "You did the right thing. Now, take your mom, and find somewhere safe to hide."

"But—I'm your Anchor."

"If things go bad here, your people will be the only group that can stand against the Fae. You too, Gia. You need to take care of your people—and my niece."

Gia hesitated before she nodded. I sighed in relief. I didn't need any of them dying with us today.

Alannah tugged on Ethan's arm, her face tight with alarm. "Come on, Ethan. We need to go."

The three of them left, but before the doors slammed closed, Tessa ran inside with five of her Guardians. She spotted me still glowing with Fate power and slid to a stop, glancing from me to Silas, who had accessed his own magic and also glowed with pure-white eyes. "The two of you might want to consider some matching sunglasses."

"I'm not planning on keeping the look," I said, tamping back my magic. I didn't need to burn through what was left of the Fate's powers too fast. "Did Alaric get the Aeternals off the quad?"

"They're working on it." She grinned. "I saw the Councilors running out of the building like their hair was full of snakes and fig-ured the action was happening here. Am I right?"

"For honor in battle," Silas said, gripping Tessa's forearm in the way of the Guardians.

"For glory in death!" Tessa replied, and the Guardians closed their fists over their hearts, saluting.

Maybe three minutes had passed since I'd killed Levi. In the original timeline, I probably had another three or four minutes. But I didn't know whether Kianna was waiting for some kind of signal from him or if they had a prearranged time to attack. I peered up at the balconies above us. The last time around, Kianna had attacked only from the first floor, quickly overwhelming us. But I had no guarantees this time, since I'd started changing things.

"Jason, seal all the doors. Don't forget the upper levels," I ordered. "No one is getting past us."

Everyone conjured their weapons, and we gathered with our backs to the stone table, twelve people to defend against Kianna's dozens. The Guardians, Tessa, Silas, Casius, and I were seasoned fighters. Tamara, Jason, Rhonda, and Seth would need to rely on their magic as best they could in this tight space. We didn't have time to rally more people to help. Within seconds, the conjuring circle was up, and I felt the magic of the Earthen Source amplified within me as well. We were as prepared as we could be.

Except... everything was different now. I'd messed with the past, and I needed a backup plan. I closed my eyes and focused on finding Elias. I wouldn't have even considered what I was about to do without the power of a Fate coursing through me, but as I located the familiar energy of the Brotherhood's leader, I didn't hesitate. I built the layers of a skimming spell, and then I folded it on itself, creating a pocket of space. I mentally reached through it, and with a magical tug, I skimmed Elias into the circle room.

The former Lord Councilor landed in front of us, stumbling to his knees. He still wore the same outfit he'd had at his McMansion, and he hadn't shaved for at least a few days.

I smirked at the Mundane handcuffs around his wrists. "Looks like DODSI caught up with you."

I shot Elias in the chest with the disruptor, and it was damn satisfying to watch him crumple to the ground. The weapon had a kick. I wasn't expecting that, and it almost slipped out of my grip. A high-pitched whine indicated what I assumed was a recharge cycle that lasted about three seconds before it clicked and quieted in my palm. I made a mental note of the delay—three seconds was an eternity in a fight. It wasn't hot, so I tucked the bulky gun into the back of my jeans, summoned Missy into my right hand, and patted Ripper in my thigh holster.

Silas drew his broadsword, and his aura flared white. He lifted his chin at Elias. "What are you going to do with him?"

"Remember the visions I told you about? Elias is our leverage against the Rakken that are probably about to show up. Make sure he's visible, and only kill him if you have to." I shrugged. "But feel free to kill Kianna any way you can. Especially if you get the urge to start kissing her."

A short-bladed katana landed in Silas's left hand. He flashed an appreciative look at me that I could feel tingling through our Aegis bond. "Gods damn, you're scarier than all five hells." He pulled me into a quick, fierce kiss before he hoisted Elias onto the center of the stone table.

I surveyed the group. Everyone looked a little freaked, but Rhonda had gone completely pale, and I patted her on the shoulder. "It's going to be okay. We're already changing the future."

The Guardians, along with Casius, Seth, Rhonda, and Jason, were positioned in front of the stone altar, glowing with magic and ready to fight. I stood in front of it all with Silas and Tessa next to me, swords in hand.

"Ready for all hell to break loose?" I asked.

"Sounds like fun," Silas said.

"We really need to work on your use of Earthen phrases."

"Oh, he means it," Tessa said with a grim smile plastered on her face.

Everyone in our group pulsed with the potential of undetermined fate. I could feel it like a tangible presence between us. A long moment hung in the air as we waited for the Fae to attack. Then a wave of magic hit us.

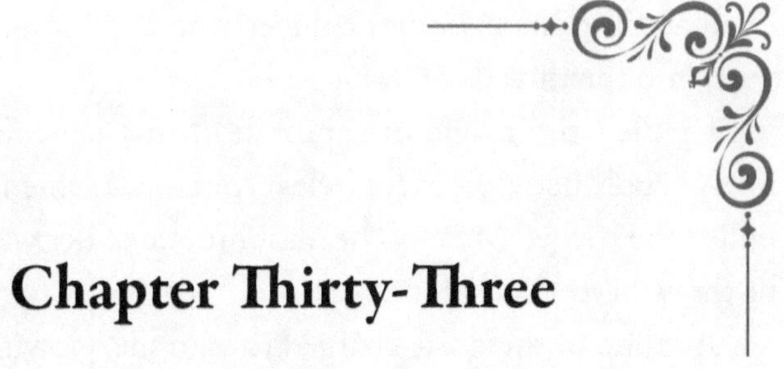

Chapter Thirty-Three

At least two dozen flares of energy burst around us, filling the small auditorium with Fae warriors. Kianna appeared with a golden helm atop her head and sword in hand, glowing with brilliant-blue magic. Her gaze swept across the room before her face creased in confusion. She'd clearly been expecting a surprise attack and a massacre. When she spotted me, she jerked in surprise.

Surrounded by the Fate's burning magic, I relished her wide-eyed shock. A feral smile spread across my face as I pointed to not-Levi lying on the ground. "Your spy is dead!" I raised my sword toward Kianna. "Your attack has already failed."

The Fae stilled as my words hung in the air, but righteous anger burned in Kianna's eyes.

"Leave now, and we can live in peace." I let the full power of my magic loose around me, pulling on the remainder of it until my eyes glowed white again. "Yield, or face your fate!"

There was a tangible weight around Kianna, as real as magic. It held a sense of unbalanced fate that shivered across my skin. She could decide which way fate tipped for her and everyone in this room. Maybe even everyone on Earth. The power of possibility was as heavy as magic. I inhaled it and let it fuel me.

Kianna lifted her sword into the air and screamed. The Fae burst into action, but this time, my people were prepared. Magic and metal clashed. Yells of bloodlust and determination filled the small auditorium as bodies collided and the Moment spilled forward into the threads of fate.

I pulled the magic disruptor from my belt. There were too many people between us for a clear shot, but I aimed at Kianna and pulled the trigger. Most of the blast hit one of her warriors as Kianna threw herself out of the way.

A group of three Fae charged toward me, glowing with bright-blue energy as the disruptor cycled through a recharge, whining loudly. I threw a wave of magic at them. With the crazy magic mojo I was packing, I created a blast that was bigger than I'd intended. All three Fae flew backward off their feet and slid at least five feet along the floor before they hit the curved wall behind them. The wave of magic almost took out Casius and Tamara, who'd been a half dozen feet away from my targets.

Shit! Just like Silas's battle magic, I couldn't use my powers effectively in tight spaces. With less than thirty feet from wall to wall in the circular room, we were packed in too tightly.

It was incredibly hard to let go of the supercharged Fate power coursing through me—it actually hurt when the world faded back into dull colors and linear knowledge. But I managed to let it go as the Fae spread quickly across the room, attacking with weapons and magic at the same time. They engaged my people in small groups, two or three to one. I parried briefly with one of the Fae until he took a sword in the back from Casius.

The disruptor clicked in my hand, and I sent another blast toward Kianna. Two Fae and a Rakken fell, and Kianna scampered back behind her people.

I couldn't get a clear shot. We were outnumbered, and we wouldn't be able to hold off their attack forever. I had to get closer and cut off the head of the snake, but Kianna was using her warriors as shields.

Silas was fighting with his long sword and the shorter katana like a fiend—blocking the Fae attempting to reach the stone altar. Like me, Silas couldn't use his magic offensively, so he held them at bay with steel, alongside Tessa and the other Guardians, while my people provided cover with magic. My momentary distraction watching Silas almost got me stabbed with a long, thin blade by an overzealous Fae. At the last second, I dashed out of the way, earning a deep gash on my upper arm. I grabbed at her magic and pulled. The energy floated between us, ready to be snatched away from her and oh so tempting.

I'd made a vow never to kill for magic again. It was a slippery slope full of small choices that chipped away at my soul. So I gritted my teeth and let go of the power. It snapped back into the woman, whose eyes flew open wide as she tumbled backward.

The disruptor clicked and stopped whining. I shot the Fae woman in the chest and slapped a healing spell on my upper arm. The gun whined as it recharged, and more Fae sprinted toward me from across the room.

Three. Two. One. The gun clicked, and I caught the first two warriors with a blast from the disruptor, but the last one made it through. The gun whined again, and I didn't have time to wait. I dropped it on the floor, and cursing my super-juiced-up magic, I raised Missy the Messer with both hands.

With a slightly curved blade and a grip similar to Ripper, the sword was a lighter, shorter version of the efficient German blade, and I was very good with it in tight quarters, thanks to my daily training. But the Fae male charging me was huge, and he wielded a two-handed claymore with a sharp edge on each side of the blade. It must have weighed at least five pounds. With one good hit of that massive blade, I'd be a goner.

With a flick of his hand, he sent a blast of elemental Fae magic flying at me. Trying to use only a scrap of my magic, I formed a shield between us. It was sloppy, and I slid a few steps backward from the impact, but it saved my life as his magic slammed against it.

The male didn't give me time to recover, jumping after me with his massive sword already swinging. I spun out of the way, deflecting a jarring blow with a clang of metal that vibrated up to my elbow. He kept trying to hack me in half as I dodged out of the way. I couldn't get close enough for a decent hit with my shorter blade, and I was running out of room. Every attack and dodge brought my back closer to the wall. He was faster, stronger, and wielding a bigger sword. But I'd been fighting above my weight my whole life—I had learned to be smarter.

With my back almost to the wall and nowhere for me to go, he raised his sword above his shoulder in a high-guard position, ready to heave it downward like an axe. If he knew what he was doing, he'd smack my sword down and then use the rebound momentum to thrust up and through my chest. *Killing blow.*

I lifted Missy to parry, and he brought his massive blade down hard. The instant our swords touched, I let mine drop out of my hand and hopped sideways. My blade clattered to the ground, and without any resistance to stop him, his sword smashed full-force into the floor. He grunted from the impact.

I summoned Ripper into my right hand, stepped inside his guard on his left side, and stabbed the blade between his ribs, right into his heart. He yelled and threw out his fist, but I was already dropping to the ground. I squatted and spun on the balls of my feet as I snatched my sword off the floor. Gripping it with both hands, I completed the turn and slashed the blade across the backs of his unguarded legs.

He screamed as I sliced through both of his hamstring tendons, and then he dropped. I ended his pain with a quick thrust through his throat and scanned the room. I'd ended up behind the stone altar. In front of me, Silas and Casius were the only ones keeping the Fae away from the table, and the shield was gone.

Tessa was a quarter of the way around the circular room with two of the Guardians, holding back the Fae trying to get out through the first-floor exit. I didn't see Tamara or Seth anywhere, but Rhonda's lifeless body lay on the table with a hole in her chest.

Oh, Rhonda!

Because life was stupidly unfair, Elias lay next to her, still unconscious from the disruptor blast and perfectly alive. Electric bursts of magic brought more of Kianna's reinforcements each second, piling into the tight space. They desperately outnumbered us at least three to one.

With a yell and another thrust of her sword into the air, Kianna sent her people toward the stone altar. I raised the disruptor, but there were too many people between us. I couldn't get a clear shot at her, and now that the recharge was taking up to a minute, I couldn't afford to waste any of my shots.

"Silas!" I ran up behind him, and he glanced over his shoulder at me. "There's too many!"

Silas stepped back from a wild swing aimed at his collarbone. A swift countercut took his attacker off guard, and Silas kicked her in the gut, sending her sprawling backward. "We need to retreat!"

"We can't let them take control of the source!" I yelled back.

"We need reinforcements!" Casius shouted as he flung wild waves of energy into the surging Fae.

"Reinforcements are outside that door!" Silas called back.

Dammit. He was right. It was too tight in the room for either of us to use magic without hitting our own people. Casius and the others couldn't keep their magic going much longer without help. We were outnumbered, and Kianna's people kept coming. We needed a chance to regroup. I put my back to the stone table. When not-Levi had caught us unaware, he'd been the one to give the Fae access to our binding sigils. Kianna didn't have him now, and it would be much harder for her to break through the binding.

I glanced down and found Tamara bleeding and barely conscious under the stone table. Her eyes were wide and terrified and her skin pale from blood loss. Next to her, a Guardian had died with his blade still clutched in his hand.

"Outside!" I yelled. "Retreat to the quad!"

I pulled Tamara to her feet, looping her arm around my shoulder. Silas and Casius cleared a path toward the doors, holding the Fae back with magic and steel. As we neared the exit, I deconstructed the conjuring sealing us all inside the circle room, and the magic shivered out of existence.

In the hallway, Tessa took Tamara off my shoulders. "We're clear. Seal the doors!"

My stomach twisted with anger as I pivoted back toward the circle room. We'd lost Seth and Rhonda, and two of the Guardians hadn't made it out with us.

At the door, Casius panted with the effort of holding the Fae back with wave after wave of magic.

"Go!" I let my aura fill with power. *No need to be reserved now.* I let my magic loose and blasted energy inside the circle room.

Fae blue magic surged inside as I kept up the barrage, buying time for a retreat. Their personal shields blocked most of the damage, but I lifted the disruptor and took a wild shot, hoping maybe my luck would improve and it would hit Kianna in her conniving, lying face.

Silas slammed the double doors shut, and I slapped a single-layered seal against the outside. It wouldn't last long, but I didn't have time for anything more complex. Silas and I ran outside to the quad. The general alarm was blaring, and people ran in every direction, panicked and yelling.

I stared in confusion at a shimmering wall of magic arching overhead. It wasn't the perimeter shield around our campus. It wasn't our magic at all. I swore when I realized what it was. The Fae had built a barrier around the campus, and no one was getting out. Screams filled the air as thousands of evacuating people realized the same thing. *We're trapped.*

I saw Casius on the rooftop of the administration building. The call for breach posts had sent everyone in my Sect except caregivers and children to the tops of the buildings around the campus, and the people up there were already glowing with magic and ready to fight. The rest knew to head for the tunnels, but the Aeternal refugees were in a frenzy on the quad, trying to flee on the ground level.

About eighty Guardians had assembled on the grass in front of the central building, each one armed with various weapons and flaring with magic. Tessa had already started issuing instructions, and the Shifters had changed into their animal forms.

Silas pulled me over to the Guardians and gave them a shorthand tactical update. "We have a half troupe of hostile Fae—levels four to five. Reinforcements inbound. Primary target is Lady Kianna at six plus. Maeve has a magic-disrupting weapon, a single burst with a two-minute recharge cycle." He glanced at me appraisingly. "She's mage plus, but broad. Nonoffensive. I want her behind the line."

Tessa nodded. "Are we going back in?"

"How long will your seal hold?" Silas asked me.

"A few minutes," I guessed.

The frantic screams of trapped people running in all directions had me examining the Fae shield again. "I have to get the families out of here."

"Agreed. Get to higher ground, and work on getting that barrier down. We'll hold Kianna inside the building and give you the time you need."

"We need to get Kianna away from the stone altar," I disagreed. "She's trying to gain control of the Earthen Source."

"How long do we have?" Tessa asked.

"I'm not sure. She doesn't have anyone on the inside this time, so it will take her longer to break into our binding spell." I tried to guess how long it would take me to tear through someone else's conjuring. "Twenty or thirty minutes maybe?"

"She'll consolidate her forces inside until she's gained control of your source," Silas said. "We should have time to rally and set up a strong defense. We'll split and conquer. You get that barrier down, and I'll get us back into the building."

A loud magic-infused explosion blew the doors of the administration building apart, and dozens of Fae burst out like a violent wave of a storm-tossed sea, crashing onto the quad.

I swore. Kianna wasn't fortifying inside—she'd used our retreat to bring in more Fae to slaughter us while we were trapped inside our own campus.

"Get that shield down and your people out!" Silas yelled at me. "Tessa, stay with Maeve."

"No—Silas. I don't need backup. Tessa is one of your best fighters. You need her."

Silas and I locked gazes. "High-powered magic mojo," he said.

"It's what I do." I lifted my chin at the charging Fae. "Have fun."

"For glory in battle!" Silas shouted.

"For honor in death!" the Guardians yelled in unison.

They rushed toward the building and our enemies, forming the front line of our defense. *Our only line of defense.*

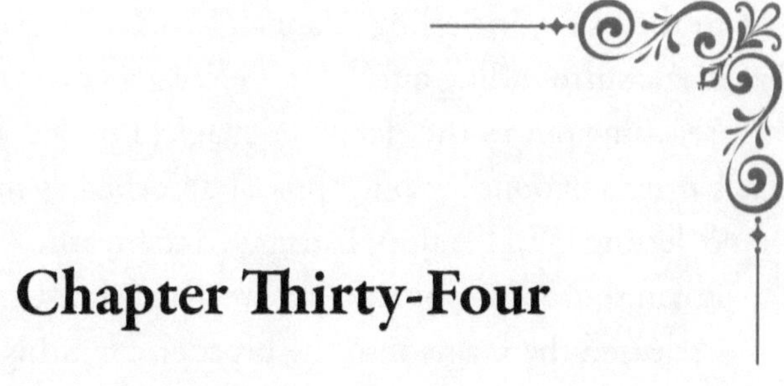

Chapter Thirty-Four

My heart skipped a beat as Silas, Tessa, and the Guardians charged toward the Fae warriors. They crashed together with the force of a tidal wave. The clash of metal combined with the screams of Humans and animals assaulted my senses and filled me with fear for their lives.

My heart pounded as I ran to the rooftop where Casius and the Inner Circle had gathered. The faster I got the Fae barrier down, the sooner I could help against the Fae. By the time I found the stairs, pounded up them, and forced open the access door to the roof, my people were working together to conjure and hurl spheres of energy onto the heads of the Fae below. They used the technique I'd developed, one person pulling in the magic and the second redirecting it into projectiles.

"We have to get that barrier down!" I yelled.

"Form a conjuring circle," Casius directed.

"Ethan!" I was relieved to find him still there but honestly surprised to see Alannah with us, helping. "I thought you left."

"I already told you—I've always got your back. What's going on down there?" Ethan asked. "You didn't stop Kianna?"

"No, and we don't have much time. I need an Anchor. Are you up for it?"

I extended my hand toward Ethan. He took it, establishing the Anchor bond faster through physical contact. Then I opened myself to the circle, including Alannah and Gia. I glanced up at the Fae magic surrounding our home. "Here goes everything."

Reaching out to the elemental magic, I pulled power from the Fae barrier surrounding our home. I absorbed as much magic as I could, letting it fill me until I struggled to breathe.

Ethan squeezed my hand. "We're here, Mae. Use the circle."

I released the magic into the broader conjuring circle, and the pressure eased. I focused everything on the barrier trapping my people and pulled more. The conjuring above started to waver, losing a tiny bit of its stability.

The Fae's barrier was destabilizing, but the process was slow going. The power growing inside our circle pulsed with energy. I had an idea. Instead of absorbing more power out of the Fae's conjuring, I could smash through it with the magic we'd already stored.

"I'm going to try something," I warned Ethan.

With his magic securely anchoring me, I reached for the sphere of pulsing energy in the middle of the conjuring circle. I took all of that magic and used it to form a dense orb of power between my hands. Manipulating all that magic left me sweating, and the urge to keep it for myself made my hands shake, but with one final push, I hurled all the magic at the shield.

The energy slammed against the Fae's shield. The sky lit with a brilliant pulse of power as crackling magic cascaded across the barrier. The conjuring fell apart, and our people cheered.

Jason clapped me on the back. "Nice work."

I smiled back at Jason and the rest of the circle. Down on the quad, families scattered out of harm's way, escaping the campus. The Guardians had already taken down more than half the Fae, and the rest were retreating back inside the building. Silas and Tessa had split the Guardians into two forces, each leading a group toward the building's main doors. They'd be inside in no time.

A screeching howl tore through the air. My head whipped around to the southern side of campus just in time to see several dozen Rakken tear onto the quad. Even though Four's vision had shown me this exact scene, my stomach dropped as I watched them invade our home.

"Holy shit! What are those?" Ethan yelled.

"Rakken!" I yelled. "Form offensive pairs, and hit them from above!"

Casius had drilled us for just this type of attack, and my people reacted quickly. Spheres of magic rained down from the rooftops as fast as the magic was gathered, but the Rakken were already on top of the Guardians.

Silas's group was hit from behind. The Guardians at the rear were forced to turn, leaving less than half their force to fight the Fae while they dealt with the ravenous demon dogs. The Rakken bounded straight into their ranks, taking down Guardians with each massive swipe of their claws. Silas was at the front with the Fae, and I could see him directing fighters to the back, but the Guardians couldn't face both enemies at once—they didn't have enough people. They were getting smashed between the Rakken and the Fae.

Tessa's group doubled back, attempting to get behind the Rakken ranks, but that created an exit for the Fae they'd just pinned against the building. The Fae rallied and pressed into the Guardian front line, forcing Silas's people to break ranks.

All I could do was watch from above as the whole battle went to hell. *Dear gods.* This was unfolding exactly like my vision—panic on the main quad, and a force of Fae and Rakken attacking my people.

Below me, Silas danced through the battlefield with deadly precision, fighting sword to claw. Surrounded by seasoned fighters and enemies with animal reflexes, Silas pivoted, whirled, and parried in a blur of motion that I would have sworn was only possible with magic. There wasn't a single movement wasted or a single slip of his sword, but it wasn't enough.

The Rakken were tearing through the Guardians while the Fae regrouped and started barraging the field with magic. My people couldn't risk hitting our allies, and as the fight mixed all sides together, our magic strikes from the rooftops slowed to a stop.

"I'm going down there!" I skimmed to the quad and landed beside Silas, the disruptor already raised.

"What are you doing?" Silas yelled as he slashed at one Rakken and kicked a second in the face.

"Saving your ass!" I shot the Rakken he'd just kicked. It dropped immediately, shimmering with magic as it transformed back into human form. "You can thank me later!"

Another Rakken leapt from over seven feet away. Its powerful frame stretched across the distance, claws first. *They always pounce.*

I dropped the whining disruptor and conjured Missy into my hands as I ran to meet it. I slid underneath like I was stealing home base and thrust my blade up into its soft belly. It twisted in midair, reaching for me with those razor-sharp claws. My blade sliced along the length of its stomach, but the tough hide protected the demon beast from a mortal wound. *Not deep enough.*

The beast landed behind me and spun. I was already on my feet, running like my life depended on it. It bounded after me. It pounced again, and I dove out of its reach and stretched to swipe the blade across the side of its thick neck.

With my arms extended over my head, I didn't have any way to cushion my landing, and I fell hard on my side. My momentum rolled me across the grass. The Rakken followed, teeth snapping inches from my head. I sprang to my feet, just barely avoiding razor-sharp teeth.

The Rakken had several deep bleeding wounds, but it barely slowed down. The giant, hairless creature stalked forward, and I scrambled backward, acutely aware of a pulsing pain in my ribs from the hard landing on my side.

"Maeve!" Silas kicked the disruptor toward me. It slid on the grass, right between the Rakken's legs. I scooped it up and pulled the trigger.

Nothing happened. The stupid thing was still recharging. I swore, tossed the useless hunk of whining plastic at the Rakken's face, and raised the long Messer blade again.

The Rakken ran forward at full speed, teeth bared. I braced myself for another round of dodge and slash, but I'd lost the element of surprise, and it was much, much faster than me. Its claws were going to slice me to shreds before I could get out of the way.

Silas barreled into the Rakken from the side and grabbed it around the neck. The weight of Silas's entire body hit the beast in the side, forcing it off its feet. They flipped over each other. I saw metal flash and heard a scream of pain that sounded human.

"Silas!" I rushed after them, slashing my blade to either side as I cleared a path through the battlefield. I couldn't tell who had been hurt.

They rolled twice more before the Rakken slammed into the ground on its side. Silas landed on top, and his momentum carried him through another rotation and up onto his feet. Silas's sword was buried in the soft juncture between the Rakken's neck and sticking out through the base of its skull. The Rakken didn't get up.

"Fun!" he declared, a wide boyish grin on his face.

I huffed. "I'm still not sure you know what that word means."

Silas pulled his sword free, scooped up the disruptor, and tossed it to me. "We have to get to Kianna."

The gun clicked in my hand, ready to fire. I glared down at it. *Stupid hunk of plastic.*

Movement snagged my attention to the eastern side of the quad, where a knot of black-clothed agents swarmed into view with tactical helmets and visors covering their faces. Each held a clunky, almost fake-looking gun with a square muzzle. *Disruptors.* A matching group swarmed onto the quad from our other side, and I almost cheered.

True to his word, Director Pascal had sent reinforcements. The government was here, and they'd brought lots of guns. The tide of this battle was about to turn in our favor.

The agents spread out, and waves of disrupting energy fanned across the quad. The Rakken went down—but so did the Guardians. I swore and dropped to the ground. The Mundane soldiers didn't know—or maybe didn't care—about the difference between our groups.

Within seconds, the crossfire between the Mundane soldiers took out at least ten Guardians. The Fae started hurtling magic at the DODSI agents. A Rakken leapt out of the main fight and bounded into the middle of the Mundanes, tearing through them with brutal efficiency. Someone finally got off a shot from a disruptor, but at least half the group had fallen before the Rakken went down.

Wild shots of magic-disrupting energy flew everywhere, and even the families trying to escape were pinned in again by the DODSI agents firing indiscriminately. Children, women—the DODSI agents didn't seem to care. It was chaos. *Just like my vision.*

"Aren't they supposed to be on our side?" Tessa yelled, ducking under a blast of disruptor energy.

"Fall back!" Silas yelled. "To the buildings!"

As we ran, I spotted several all-black vehicles with black-tinted windows at the edge of campus. One of the large vans had various conspicuous antennae and a communication satellite mounted on its roof.

"I need to find Pascal! He can call off the Mundanes!"

"Go!" Silas agreed.

I pulled magic around myself and formed it into a skimming spell. Unfortunately, I didn't stop to think about the panic I'd cause when I appeared in the middle of their operations and ran straight for the communications van, where I hoped Pascal would be.

The agents started shooting, but their bullets hit my shield and dropped.

"Stop!" I ordered. "I need to talk to Pascal!"

They didn't stop.

"Pascal!" I infused magic into my yell.

Director Pascal emerged from the van, wearing a bulletproof vest and a headset. "Cease fire!"

"What the hell is wrong with you?" Agent Lennart emerged behind Pascal decked out in assault gear and a matching headset. He raised a fully automatic assault rifle and aimed it at my chest.

Four more agents with rifles surrounded me. I ignored all of them and turned back to Pascal. "Your people are attacking everyone with magic! They're shooting down women and children!"

Pascal started barking orders into his radio, listening in his earpiece. "They can't tell who the enemy combatants are."

I needed a way to fix this problem, and fast. I formed my magic into a skimming spell and pushed extra power into it—enough to carry two people.

I turned to Lennart. "You're coming with me." I didn't give him time to object as my magic wrapped around him.

Lennart fell on his ass as we landed on the rooftop. He scrambled backward, fumbling to raise his gun. I held my hand out to help him up, but he pointed his assault rifle at me again.

"What did you just do?" he demanded.

"Don't be a baby."

"Maeve? What are you doing?" Casius demanded. Lennart whipped the barrel of his gun toward Casius, who flashed his empty palms and backed up. "Did you just kidnap Agent Lennart?" Casius asked calmly.

"What? No. He's going to tell his people who the enemy combatants are from here."

Lennart and Casius shared a look.

"Did I forget to explain that first?" I asked sweetly. "Get up, Lennart. You look ridiculous."

He popped to his feet with an angry huff and managed to lower his gun.

"Tell your people to shoot anyone who has a blue aura!" I said, pointing at the Fae on the quad.

"Their—what the hell do you mean by 'blue aura'?"

"He can't see magic," Ethan reminded me.

"What the hell is he thinking?" Casius demanded, his attention focused on the field below us.

Silas had somehow gotten himself surrounded by Rakken, completely isolated from the other Guardians, who had retreated to the edges of the buildings. He was fighting the closest ones off with his sword, but there were too many of them. He was completely outnumbered and surrounded on all sides.

Silas's magic rose suddenly, and I could see the pure white of his eyes even from the rooftop as he channeled the Fate's powers. The Rakken closing in on him backed up, but it was too late. His magic snapped outward like unfurling wings, and he *moved*. As if the magic gave him actual wings, he twisted and flowed through the battlefield almost faster than I could follow, mowing down everything around him.

I watched in awful fascination as Silas unleashed his legendary battle magic. I'd seen some of the technique when he'd rescued me from Elias's stronghold, but this was... more. Instead of a single blast, his magic moved with him like a physical weapon, obliterating everything in its wake as it cascaded from him and over his enemies. It flowed with him as he danced across the battlefield, both a weapon and a shield. Silas's battle magic was beautiful and devastating, and I didn't feel a single tug of magic through our shared bond.

He poured more power and speed into each movement, destroying everything in a thirty-yard radius. The Rakken dropped, obliterated by magic. Nothing survived.

Death's Fury. The Angel of Death. I'd known all these names for Silas, but now I understood. When Silas stopped moving, he stood alone and surrounded by death—at least two dozen dead Rakken lay around him in a circle of destruction.

"Holy shit—is that your Highlander?" Lennart asked.

I shook myself free of shock and awe. "Tell your people he's on our side! Take out any of the Rakken—err, giant dogs—that escaped!"

Lennart started barking orders into his radio, and the government agents swarmed the remaining few Rakken, mowing them down with bullets and blasts of magic-disrupting energy.

The Guardians rallied to Silas, who seemed completely fine even after the massive use of power, and Lennart directed the agents not to shoot them. A wave of relief washed over me. Silas was fine, and the Rakken were no longer a threat. Asking Director Pascal to show up—just as he had in our vision, but this time on our side—had paid off. The vision hadn't come true like Four had shown it to me. We'd managed to change our fate.

As the field below cleared, Silas looked up at the rooftop where we stood, as if drawn to me through our bond. His eyes still glowed completely white. I gasped. *That is freaky as all the hells. Did I look like that?*

Jason whistled between his teeth. Lennart swore. "That's something you don't see every day."

Silas and Tessa's groups merged in front of the administration building. Lennart instructed the DODSI agents to take up a perimeter position at their backs. While Silas handled the Rakken, the Fae had retreated inside, where Kianna was attempting to take over the Source. She'd had almost an hour to break through our binding. She had to be getting close.

"We have to stop Kianna from getting control of the Source. We don't have much time," I told our group.

"What's the plan?" Casius asked.

"First, we need Lennart's people to make sure the rest of our families get out safely," I said.

"No way. Uh-uh." Lennart backed up. "You are not going to transporter me again."

"You can take the stairs." I pointed at the door leading to the stairwell and barely refrained from laughing in his face.

"Freaks," he growled before he jogged across the roof and out of sight.

With the DODSI agents now sufficiently informed and on our side and the families off the campus, I was ready to focus on stopping Kianna. "We need to reinforce the binding spell and block Kianna until Silas and the Guardians can get into the building. Once they're in, we can go in and help finish this for good."

The Earthen Source was a collection of magic energy. Unlike a smaller source, like House Valeron's waterfall, it wasn't a physical thing. It was a collection of all the energy and potential of every living thing. My ancestors took all of Earth's untapped magic and controlled access to it by creating a protective layer that only we could access. If Kianna broke through that, she'd control all of the magic in Earth. We had to reinforce the protective binding and stop that from happening.

I fingered Marcel's charm around my neck and took a moment to center myself. There was a good chance that stopping Kianna would take more power than I had. *Am I willing to make that ultimate sacrifice?* I wanted to be the kind of leader my mom had been—one who was willing to put the needs of our people above her own life. But I also needed to be the type of leader who would make the smart call and not throw away my life uselessly to appease my own guilt. Silas had taught me that.

Even though the magic I'd gotten from the Fate was fading, I had the power to stop Kianna. But every time I used their magic, it was harder and harder to come back to myself. I didn't know what would happen if I completely released myself to it, and that might be exactly what was needed to stop Kianna.

"Do you know how to reinforce the binding?" Tamara asked me.

Our ancestors had been too busy running and hiding to teach us how to do anything with the protective binding they'd created around Earth's magic. No one alive could replicate what they'd done, not even the Council. But I could see magic, and I could manipulate it. I had Fate power at my fingertips and the right abilities. I had to try.

"We're going to find out," I said.

"We're too far away," Tamara said. "Even with a double circle, our efforts would be more effective if we had line of sight on the access point."

I tugged on Marcel's charm and looked down at my feet. Kianna and her people were almost directly below us in the circle room. "I can skim us to the top level of the circle room balconies."

Alannah's eyes went wide. "*All* of us? That's twenty-six people!"

"She can do it," Casius said with confidence.

"Form two conjuring circles," I said. "The second Silas's Guardians are inside, I'll skim us around the upper balcony."

"We can form a protective shield between us and the lower floors," Alannah said, and I nodded.

While Casius directed everyone into two circles, I pulled Ethan aside. "Look, I know this is probably more than you signed up for. Are you still okay to be my Anchor?"

He grabbed my hand. "I'll do whatever it takes to keep you safe, Mae. We're in this together. You know that." Despite his brave words, his expression was pinched. His lips twisted.

"But...?" I prompted.

"But I'm not sure I can Anchor as much power as you're capable of channeling. You're going to burn me out way before you reach your limits."

I bit my lip. He was right, and we both knew it was a risk. With the Fate's powers, I had access to more power than everyone in the Inner Circle combined. And it wasn't unheard-of for an Anchor to burn out if their partner pulled in more power than they could handle. Even if it were possible to work with more than one Anchor, I didn't think it would help.

"You're right. It's too risky. I'll do this without an Anchor."

Ethan squeezed my hand. "That's not what I meant. I just need you to say you'll be careful. I trust you."

I chewed my lip. Without an Anchor, I could lose myself to the overwhelming power of the Source, but worrying about Ethan would limit my ability to do whatever was needed to stop Kianna. Really, what I needed was Ethan to help bring me back if I lost control.

"I don't need you to channel everything with me," I told him. "I can handle the power on my own. I just need you to keep a hold on the normal, human magic that makes me who I am. We're bonded by blood and by friendship. You know me. I trust you to bring me back if I go too deep. Do whatever it takes, Ethan. I don't want to lose myself."

He nodded solemnly and pulled me into a hug. "I promise."

Below us, the Guardians broke through the door and rushed into the building. On the field, Lennart's agents were almost finished getting people safely off the campus, but if Kianna broke through the binding, she was going to lose control of the magic and kill everyone around her. I didn't know exactly how far that blast of power would reach, but we could all be at risk—maybe even the entire city.

We didn't have time for second-guessing. Silas's group was already on their way in, and we needed to be in place when they got to the circle room. I was doing this, and I was planning on making it out alive.

"We're going in!" I grabbed the center of both circles and slid into place as the connecting point between them. Just a few short months before, I would have found this role challenging. Now it was nothing.

The connection to Earth's magic came easily—a good sign that Kianna hadn't broken through our binding yet—and I pushed power into the threads of a new conjuring. It rose above us, creating a glowing sphere of white light the size of a beach ball.

A terrible ripping sensation in my chest made me cry out. The sound was echoed on the field and from the rooftops as every single member of my Sect felt what I had. The others in the conjuring circles called out in confusion. I'd felt this before when Silas's source was being torn to shreds. But it wasn't Silas this time—it was the Earthen Source.

Time just ran out.

Chapter Thirty-Five

"Kianna's going to lose control of the power!" I yelled. "We have to go in now!"

Ethan grabbed my hands, and I let him wrap his magic around a core part of me, holding back a small reserve of power between us through our Anchor bond.

I opened myself to the power of the Fates once more. It was like stepping into the sun, but I couldn't dwell on the ecstasy coursing through me or the way the world became brighter and clearer. I couldn't lose myself.

I wrapped myself in the magic and twisted all of that energy into an enormous skimming spell. With everyone holding hands, I skimmed the entire group onto the upper viewing balcony of the circle room. All twenty-six of us landed in a circle, ringing the room. I bent over, gasping for breath. That was it—I was done. I'd burned through everything I had left from the Fate. I was down to my normal levels of magic.

Our shield shimmered into place. The Fae immediately started lobbing waves of offensive magic at us. The protection held, and their magic couldn't hurt us.

On the central lecture stage on the first floor, Kianna had both palms flat on the stone altar. Magic poured through her, lighting her from the inside out as she took control of the Earthen Source. A second ring of Fae and a third surrounded the altar, all of them glowing with elemental magic.

At Kianna's side, Elias was conscious again, and he had joined the conjuring circle along with the rest of Kianna's people. I swore—of course those two treacherous, self-centered narcissists would figure out a way to work together. Apparently, it was too much to ask for them to just kill each other and end all our misery.

Kianna had probably helped him alert the Rakken. The irony was, if I hadn't brought Elias here in the first place, the Brotherhood wouldn't have been involved in this fight at all. I'd actually caused them to show up, like some kind of self-fulfilling prophecy. I really hated this Fate stuff.

Right on time, the first-floor door to the circle room flew off its hinges, along with a huge chunk of the wall. Plaster and wood exploded into the auditorium, and Guardians poured through, led by Silas and Tessa.

With a quick check on Ethan's connection to me, I dove into the power of the Source. I didn't pace myself or ease into it. I took as much power as I could and then pushed it back into the Circle. The magic pulsed with each beat of my heart, sending shock waves through me as I dove deeper. It felt like drowning. I couldn't breathe, and I could barely think—all I knew was that I had to keep going. I had to stop Kianna before she took control of Earth's magic.

Something slipped out of place. I was pulling so much power that it was straining the limits of our double circle. Jason had passed out on the ground, slumping against the ornate balcony railing, but everyone else kept their eyes locked on me, their expressions determined.

I was going to lose my people to the strain. Gritting my teeth, I held more of the magic within me, hoping to lessen the impact on my circle, and then I let my awareness slip fully into the Source.

I float without my physical body in front of an incomprehensible sphere of magic. It's a molten ball of energy, heavy with the power of Earth's life—a thick bundle of threads, each holding millions of individual strands of energy. Each thread is a life made of complex decisions and yet-to-be-realized potential. They twist and weave and build together into a complex tapestry of intertwined lives full of choices. The connections tangle among themselves, pulling, pushing, and creating the web of all life on Earth.

The deep complexity of it all intrigues me, and with the expanded awareness in this place, I can feel the power of the Fates tingling along my flesh. So much potential and so many options. Life, death, change—all of it is contained here inside the core of Earth's magic.

A stab of physical strain registered briefly as another loss in my conjuring circle. Someone else had fallen out. The weight of the additional magic bore down on me, but I shoved the physical pain away, focused on the magic and what I needed to do.

Something is wrong with the energy contained here. I can sense it. I move away from the fascinating tapestry of Earth's magic until I see the binding my ancestors used to contain it.

Compared to the core of pure magic, the binding around it is rudimentary in its structure and design. It's meant to restrict access to all but my people. It's like an ugly patchwork blanket thrown over a glowing orb of beautiful magic light.

The binding is threadbare. Pure energy seeps from jagged cracks in the pattern, and there's a large rip down the center. The impression of wrongness bothers me. It's not balanced, not symmetrical. It's blocking the beauty underneath.

I can see where the layers of the binding have weakened. It would be so easy to fix them, to pull and fuse the magic back together.

I hesitate. The idea feels wrong to me. I don't want to fix the binding—I want to set all this beautiful energy free. There's so much potential, and I know that trying to contain it is wrong.

But there was a reason I needed to do this. It's important, somehow, that I keep the magic trapped behind the ugly binding. As I try to remember that reason, I become aware of another presence in this ma-trix of power. With the awareness comes the physical representation of her. I know her, but I can't place her name. She is Fae, with long blond hair and a warrior's crown atop her head.

She is focused on the core of magic, completely unaware that I am watching. She changes the binding, building different layers, and the beautiful glow of white energy begins to fade behind her new binding. I don't like what she is doing, and I want her to stop.

Stop, I command her.

An expression of recognition slaps across her delicate features, con-torting them into an angry snarl.

I remember her name. Kianna.

Her mouth moves, but I can't hear her words. She isn't solid enough in this space between.

STOP. I put more power behind the command.

Kianna's face twists as if I've struck her, and I remember other faces contorted in pain. Faces but not names—the details feel just be-yond my reach in this place. There is so much pain in life, and with death comes release.

Kianna wants to control Earth's bound magic, but I can't let her do that.

She is a collection of energy. The threads of magic that form pat-terns of interwoven magic make up the fabric of who she is. Her life is no more complex than a woven piece of cloth, a tapestry that is no longer needed. I can unravel those threads and end Kianna right now.

And with that thought, I unmake her. The threads of Kianna start to unravel. She fights and wails in silence, but I am her Fate. She cannot stop me.

At Kianna's core is a strong thread of magic. I reach for it and hold it between my fingers. Her life is hanging on by a single thread.

Anchored, I realize. Someone is anchoring Kianna's magic.

A bone-white ring appears in my hand. It's carved into a delicate rose. A thread of magic stretches across the void from the ring to Kianna, shimmering and pure.

"Your mother didn't betray you," I say to Kianna. "She loved you."

"Liar!" Kianna screams in rage, and it vibrates along the tenuous thread between her and the bone ring, turning it black and brittle.

"She didn't deserve to die," I tell her, holding the thread from Treva's ring to her daughter. Kianna's mother has woven her tight into the tapestry and anchored her with love.

"She wouldn't have stood in my way if she truly loved me! She deserved to die!"

I close my fist around the final thread anchoring Kianna to her mortal existence. It shatters like ice in my palm, erasing Kianna from existence.

I should feel... something. But I don't. I hold no guilt. Life and death and change will always come to pass. Kianna made her choices, and ultimately, a single life is meaningless within the tapestry. It's so beautiful here inside magic's chaotic order.

Something tugged at my physical awareness, demanding my attention. It felt heavy and mortal, and I didn't want to pay attention to it.

From nowhere, a thread winds tightly around my waist, shimmering with urgency. An Anchor. It pulses almost painfully, reminding me of why I came. The original binding around Earth's magic is ripped in places and overly thick where Kianna attempted to patch and control it. The wrongness strikes me again as I focus on it.

I remember something my father told me. Our ancestors tried to protect Earth's magic by binding it, but they stunted the development of Earth. I think about the people I love who have died trying to protect the Earthen Source from those who want to control the world. The Council hunted us for access to that magic, then the Brotherhood, and now the Fae.

The magic within Earth belongs to everyone and no one. It is too powerful, too important for one group to control. It is time to honor the true desire of my ancestors and protect those who cannot protect themselves—from us. I will protect Earth by unmaking our greatest mistake.

I need to set the magic free.

The decision feels right. I reach for the binding and begin to tear it away. It breaks like the silken threads of a spider's web underneath my fingers as I rip and rend it. My determination grows as I destroy layer after layer, and magic swells around me.

I have to set it free. I reach for the final threads of magic—

A slash of intense pain burned through my physical body, and I stopped and pulled back into myself. I drew in a heavy gulp of air laced with agony.

"Maeve! Stop! You're tearing apart the Source!" someone yelled.

I couldn't quite think of his name.

The physical presence pushed deeper into my awareness, and I became aware of the two circles surrounding me. My feet weren't touching the ground as power pulsed from me in time with the beat of my heart, thrumming against the magic that flowed through us all.

Anchored. They've anchored me to my physical body, and it feels too heavy. Too mortal.

My head felt too heavy as I took in my surroundings. Around the open-air balcony, three members of my circle had fallen, and the others had fear stamped over their features. The sandy-haired man nearest me was frantic with worry, yelling my name.

"Ethan?" My voice sounded strange to my own ears.

His warm, familiar power surged through me. "Mae!"

My physical body lowered until my feet touched the ground. No one moved as they stared in shock and horror, frozen in their own time. But this time, it was I who had moved away from the linear equation.

And I wasn't alone. Two Fates stood in front of me on the balcony, glowing with incredible power.

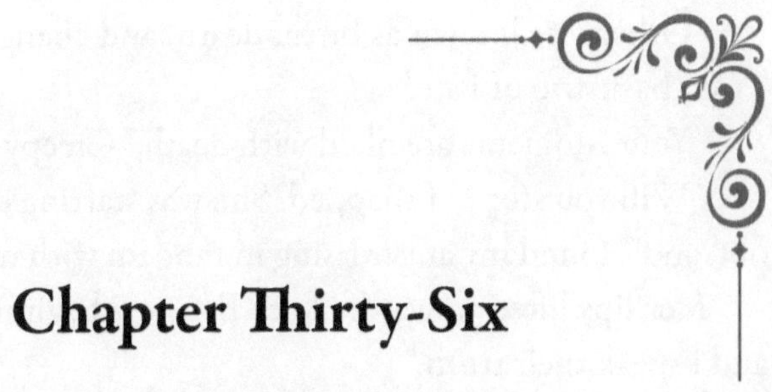

Chapter Thirty-Six

Four stood with the creepy child Fate I'd encountered in Alaska. They both glowed with magic so pure it couldn't be comprehended by mortal eyes. Seeing the Fates made my body even heavier with a feeling that pressed on my chest and made it hard to breathe.

The weightiness in my body had a name: Rage. As soon as I named the emotion, it burned through me, hot and demanding.

"Four!" I yelled at the Fate. "I should have known you'd be here, pulling the strings. I refuse to be your puppet anymore."

Four's mouth was a thin line. "It's time to accept the consequences of your choices."

"You tricked me into everything that happened. How was that a choice?"

"Your Moments are filled with death," the child Fate said in her saccharine voice.

I glared at Creepy Fate. *She could have been a little more helpful last time around.* "I'm a little busy right now. I don't have time for your doublespeak."

"What will be has already come to pass," she insisted.

I rounded on Four. "You're going to have to find someone else to be your puppet. I'm done with your lies and tricks."

"There is balance in fate," Creepy Fate said. "Beginnings, endings, possibility."

"Otherwise known as birth, death, and change." Four winked. "Your basic trio of Fate."

"Your Moments are filled with death," Creepy Fate repeated.

"Will you stop?" I snapped. She was starting to really freak me out, and I found my anger rising in tandem with my fear.

Her lips lifted upward. "I see the new beginnings before you, and I speak their truth."

"Two was an oracle in a past life," Four said with a shrug that felt stilted. His reactions felt like a mockery of humanity. Like he didn't quite feel the emotions but had studied the movements. "She oversees new beginnings—birth and rebirth on a large scale. And you probably figured out that I oversee change. You already met Three when you erased him from existence. Ironic, since he oversaw endings." I cringed, and Four seemed to study my expression again. "Don't worry. He lost his interest in existing a long time ago. Which is why we're here—it's time to move forward, and we need a third."

I felt the space around me start to fold, just like it had when I'd used my Fate powers to pull myself through time. "Wait! We can work this out—I didn't mean to kill Three! You can take his powers back!"

"You're using our magic to tear apart the Earthen Source. It seems you've taken it upon yourself to impact fate on a massive scale. There has to be a balance to what you've done."

That made me pause. Everything I'd experienced had felt like a dream, but it was real. I'd been fully within the Source, and I was moments away from destroying it.

Holy shit, I just killed Kianna with my thoughts. The realization of what I'd done hit me, and I started to panic. I'd lost touch with my own humanity. Nothing had mattered inside that space of pure magic. I'd come so close to losing myself. If Ethan hadn't brought me back... I shuddered and looked at the people around me. Everyone was frozen, including the Guardians and Silas still fighting the Fae on the first floor.

Kianna was gone, but the damage wasn't undone. The Fae were still fighting, and I could feel the dangerous instability of the Source. Kianna had started something, and I had to finish it.

I couldn't condone what had been done to all of Earth's people. My ancestors bound Earth's magic and kept it for themselves. They'd done it to protect Earth from Aeterna, but the end result was the same.

"Kianna won't be the last one to try to control the source. I have to end this."

"Your Moment is to choose," Creepy Fate said.

"Choices have consequences," Four warned. "We cannot interfere in the free will of mortal lives."

I snorted. "You sure as hell interfered in my life."

"You always had your free will, Maeve O'Neill."

The weight of their stares was like all the magic of the Earthen Source flooding me at once. I swallowed around a sudden lump in my throat. I was literally messing with Fate. Any deal I made was going to be permanent.

I'd made a choice to kill a Fate in order to save Silas's life. And I was about to make a choice for all of Earth, to set things right for all of us. I couldn't expect anything less than to pay for my own actions. If my life was the cost for that, it was a sacrifice worth making. A sacrifice any good leader would make.

"I've made my choice."

"We have an agreement," Four said, and they both disappeared.

Power pulses through my awareness, and I am pulled back inside the Earthen Source. I take in the infinitely complex weaving of all of Earth's magic. Just a few remnants of the binding remain, and my conviction returns. It's time. I have to set the magic free.

The power soaks into my being, and I let it fill me until I am ready to burst. I don't dare let myself sink into the immense power and potential of the magic, because I know I would lose myself, and I have a responsibility to see this through. I reach for the last threads of the binding, prepared to undo the greatest mistake in the history of humanity. With a final yank, I pull away the last of the binding around the Source and set Earth's magic free.

The magic pulses, crashing over me with unrestrained power.

I rode the waves of magic back to consciousness, returning to my body lying on the balcony. With a groan, I pushed to my elbows and found everyone who had joined in the conjuring circles sprawled across the floor. The backlash of magic had knocked us all out, and the entire roof of the circle room had blown away. Magic was *everywhere*. It floated around us, thick like fog.

In a daze, I leaned over the balcony. The people on the first floor were all unconscious except Silas. He stood in the middle, looking up at me with pure-white eyes.

It reminded me of the first time I'd used my powers and lost control. I'd drained more than half a dozen Rakken of all their magic, killing them. Silas had stood just outside my circle of destruction, staring in horror. "What have you done?" he'd asked.

My heart stuttered, and everything inside of me ached to *feel* his strong arms around me. I needed him to tell me that I'd made the right choice and the price would be worth it.

I blinked, and Silas stood in front of me on the balcony.

"I set it free," I whispered. "I set magic free."

What have I done?

I knew what I had done. I'd done the unthinkable. I'd set magic free, and right or wrong, there was going to be a Fate to pay.

The pure white of Silas's eyes faded away, leaving the steel-gray gaze of the man who loved me sometimes better than I knew how to love myself. He pulled me into his arms, and the strength of his embrace grounded me.

"I just meant to stop Kianna," I told him. "But there will always be another Kianna, another Brotherhood, another *someone* who wants to control all that power and use it to hurt people." The words kept spilling out. "I—I ripped apart my ancestors' greatest creation. Four warned me that there would be consequences to my actions—saving you, changing the past. But I kept going back for more. Nothing else mattered."

"The Fate's powers are addictive," Silas said. "Everything is skewed when you're in that space. It's as if nothing else matters."

"I think I might have lost a piece of my humanity. I killed Kianna in there, and... I didn't feel anything," I confessed.

"If you truly lost yourself, you wouldn't feel remorse now. Once you stop caring about the blood on your hands, that's when you have to worry about the state of your soul."

"You told me that when we first met," I said. "After I lost control of my magic, I remember thinking you were probably one of the only people who could understand what I was going through."

He held me tight against his chest.

"How do I know I made the right choice?" I asked.

"Because you did what you always do."

"Screw everything up?"

"You followed your heart. No one can ask anything more of you." He twined our fingers together. "Right choices, wrong choices—you can't control what other people think. It's the intent of your heart that matters."

"I should have listened to you when you warned me about the Fates."

"You definitely should have listened," Silas said, some of his earlier anger slipping into his tone. "But whatever happens, we'll deal with it together."

"Thank you, Silas. You always know the right thing to say."

His mouth lifted at one corner. "Save your gratitude for later, when we're alone."

I laughed. "Deal."

Ethan moaned and sat up, pulling us out of our short reprieve from reality. "What happened?" He took in the loose magic floating through the air and up at the sky visible through the hole in the roof. "Holy hell!"

"Are you okay?" I asked. "I felt you keeping me anchored. I didn't mean to go so deep into the Source, but you brought me back just in time."

Ethan's magic rose around him, and he went pale as he saw it. It was no longer a burning white. Without a direct connection to a source, the power that had radiated through his aura was gone. Now only a pale golden-yellow magic emanated from him.

"Oh, Ethan!" I gasped. "I'm so sorry. I burned you out—"

"It's not just Ethan." Silas motioned toward the others, who were beginning to awaken. Everyone had lost their white auras. Various shades of magic—all of them weaker than before—glowed around them. I let my own powers surface, and just like them, my aura was no longer white. My magic was a spring green—reflecting a surprising mix of Human and Fae heritage that I'd previously had no idea about. *Holy shit.*

Casius stumbled toward us with a large bleeding gash on his forehead. "What happened?"

Ethan's voice was a shocked whisper. "The Source is gone."

"I don't understand," Casius said. "The Source is gone? That's not—it's not possible. What the hell happened?"

Others gathered around us, confused and on the edge of panic as they realized their magic was all but gone. "I unbound Earth's magic," I said. "I destroyed the last of the binding so no one could control it ever again—not even us. I set the magic free."

Casius opened and closed his mouth several times. People stared blankly as they slowly absorbed the enormity of our situation. Silas stood by my side, but I could feel his confusion through our bond.

"I don't know what all this means yet," I admitted. "But we'll figure it out together."

Casius, my mentor since I was old enough to hold a knife, looked at me like he didn't know who I was. I'd chosen to make a sweeping change for our people, and it wasn't going to be a popular decision. I'd just put the needs of the whole world above the needs of my people. Without meaning to, I'd separated myself from them, and it was possible I'd never be a trusted member of the Inner Circle again. As our eyes met, I saw all those things reflected in Casius's gaze.

"I'm sorry," I said, choking on my words. "We're responsible for every life in every realm on this planet. I had to make the right choice for all of us."

The Fae on the first floor started stirring, and I looked over the railing to see several of them gaining consciousness. For the most part, their auras were the same as before—strong and blue with their own Fae heritage. But some of them now had mixed hues revealing broader access to Earth's magic. They'd been changed, just like our people. And that wasn't going to be the last change from unbinding magic. Not by far.

BY THE TIME EVERYONE was conscious again, Silas and I had all our enemies sorted into three groups under protective boundaries—two for the Fae and Elias under his own special dome.

Tessa and the knot of Guardians with her were all glowing with their own shades of magic. By the looks of it, the Aeternals had roughly the same amount of power as my people. Silas was the only one with extraordinary access to magic at the moment—but the Fate's magic would fade like mine had.

Just as we finished, the doors to the quad banged open, and DODSI soldiers stormed into the circle room, filling the small auditorium with the whine of charging magic disruptors all aimed in our direction. Lennart's angry scowl zeroed in on me as he pointed the barrel of his bulky plastic gun at my chest.

I raised my hands. I shouldn't have been surprised, given that I'd just destroyed the Source with the intention of creating equal access to magic, but the weak aura of power around Lennart made me pause. A few other DODSI agents glowed with traces of magic energy—most tinted in the golden shades of humanity.

Director Pascal entered the room last, and he didn't have an aura of magic around him at all. He stopped dead in his tracks when he saw Elias. His voice was loud and clipped as he demanded, "Do you mind explaining what the hell just happened, Miss O'Neill?"

Silas stepped forward with his sword in hand, putting himself between me and the head of DODSI. Lennart shifted to track Silas, moving his finger directly over the disruptor's trigger. At least a half dozen agents did the same thing, and everyone tensed.

"Director Pascal," I said, "please ask your men to stand down before someone gets nervous. We're all friends here."

Director Pascal looked pointedly at Silas and his sword. Little did Pascal know that Silas could do a lot more damage with his magic if he wanted.

"Silas," I said calmly, "this is Director Pascal. He's the leader of the Earthen government agency I told you about. We're all going to need to work together, so it would be really nice if we don't start our partnership off with bloodshed."

Silas and Pascal took a moment to size each other up. Then Silas shifted back a few steps and sheathed his sword. Director Pascal signaled for his men to relax, and the tension in the room ratcheted down several levels.

"Director Pascal, this is Silas Valeron, acting leader of the Aeternal Council, and this is Casius Palmer, leader of the Earthen Sect of Harvesters." I pointed at Elias, trapped and silent under the magic barrier. "You already know Elias, *former* leader of the Aeternal Council and dumbass traitor to everyone. Sorry, I had to borrow him for a bit."

Pascal scowled again, but I plowed forward. "For those who didn't already figure it out—magic is available to everyone." I motioned toward the DODSI agents. "That means we all have equal access, and no one person can control Earth's magic. Not even me. So I suggest we all work together and figure out a way to get along."

Director Pascal's eyes had gone wide, but it was Agent Lennart who spoke first. "Are you saying that regular people now have magic powers?"

He had no idea about his magic yet. This was going to be interesting. "I'm not sure about all Mundanes, but a few of you already have it."

Lennart narrowed his eyes.

Director Pascal said, "You can't just release magic to everyone on Earth. It's going to change everything we know about civilization."

He was right, of course. Everything about Mundane life was about to change. "It's going to be a little messy, but the alternative was subjugation to those who had control of the power. Personally, I'd go with a few changes to society over slavery."

"Changes?" Director Pascal sputtered. "Try mayhem. Years of chaos and the crumbling of society as we know it."

I rolled my eyes. "You're being a bit overdramatic, don't you think? I—"

Casius laid his hand on my shoulder. "He's right, Maeve. The consequences of magic flooding Earth are going to be wide ranging. We need to get ahead of this before the entire realm plunges into total anarchy."

"Exactly." Pascal pointed at me. "You have to fix this."

"Me?" I said, astonished. "What can I possibly do?"

"Take it back."

My mouth gaped, but the words didn't happen for a few seconds. "There's no take-backsies," I said. "This already happened. I can't undo it."

"Magic is spreading in this realm," Silas said. "We need a coalition between all our people—your government, the Circle, and the Council—if we're going to peacefully transition everyone together."

"And the Fae." I glanced at Tessa and then at the twenty or so Fae warriors trapped under the protective dome of magic.

"They just tried to kill us," Alannah objected. "You're suggesting we offer them an alliance? They should be punished for their crimes against us. Our people died today!"

Lord Nero spoke up for the first time in his rumbling bass. "I agree. Fae caused the collapse of our entire realm. We have a chance to bring them to heel whilst they are weak."

I swallowed hard as I remembered Rhonda's lifeless stare and the two Mundanes Kianna had compelled to kill themselves. But I also knew that the Fae were people just like us. Tessa had reminded me about just how easily prejudice led to suffering.

"Their leaders have misled them," I said. "There are hundreds of Fae who did nothing wrong. They deserve a chance to live peacefully with the rest of the magic community. We can't just decide anyone else's place in society—you've seen how that turned out in Lower Aeterna. We can't make those same mistakes again." I frowned at Elias. "People will follow monsters if you make them desperate enough."

With a wave of my hand, I pulled apart the barriers around the Fae.

The Fae warriors stood tense and wary as I addressed them. "Your leaders died because they couldn't see a future where we lived in peace. Lady Kianna wanted to control the Source and everyone in this realm. I'm showing you a different way. If you're willing to take an oath of peace, we can work together, and you'll have equal rights in this realm."

One of the Fae males stepped forward. He was tall with distinctive green eyes that set him apart from other Fae with the more common amethyst coloring. "And if we do not accept your alliance?"

I considered him for a long moment. I could practically feel the weight of this moment tipping fate for all our people. "Then you're free to go."

Casius and Silas hissed behind me almost in unison.

I ignored them. "You can go in peace. But your children and their children will look back on this day with regret. You could have secured the freedom you've been desperately seeking without bloodshed and without bloodthirsty rulers throwing away your lives in their quest for domination."

More than one Fae seemed to consider my words, and their defensive, fearful expressions transformed into relief as they realized I was letting them go.

"I hope you'll return when you're ready. As a group or as individuals. Tell your people that everyone is welcome."

The group stood silently as if not quite believing my words before they started to skim away one by one.

Jason's lips narrowed into a thin line. "I'm not sure that was wise, Maeve."

"I'm doing what I believe is right." I glanced at Tessa and Silas. "It's the only thing any of us can do."

Casius had remained silent during the entire exchange, eyeing me with a wariness that I wasn't sure I'd be able to repair. Part of me couldn't believe what I was doing—speaking for our Sect and making decisions for the whole world. But I was neck deep in the mess I'd started, and I had to see this through to the other side. That started with making sure our new alliance would be successful.

"Director Pascal," I said, "are you willing to make an alliance with us to live peacefully together? Think of all we could accomplish for the betterment of the entire world. Magic can heal, end world hunger, and spread a new era of cooperation across the globe. Are you willing to be on the right side of history?"

His complexion had gone a little pale. "I'm not sure I have the authority to do that."

Silas's magic flared around him, blindingly bright, and the Fate powers shone through his eyes. Pascal took a stutter step backward.

"Then get the authority, or bring us someone who has it," Silas said. "If your government doesn't want to be the first to make an alliance, I'm sure there are others who would jump at the chance."

"Is that a threat?"

"It's an offer of alliance," I said immediately, "just like the one I just extended to the Fae. Talk to your leaders, and come back when you have an answer. You know where to find us."

Pascal was taken aback at my dismissal but recovered quickly and motioned for his people to leave.

"Wait!" I called. "You forgot someone." I motioned toward Elias glowering from under the dome of magic. "We made a deal, and I promised you a full download of everything you wanted to know about magic. Elias is full of all kinds of useful knowledge. You can have him back. Consider it a gesture of goodwill."

I released the magic trapping Elias, drew the disruptor from the waistband of my jeans, and shot him in the chest. He crumpled before he could so much as sneer at me. The disruptor clicked in my hand—*Now it works?*—and I shot Elias again. Director Pascal flinched. Silas raised an eyebrow.

"Feels great every damn time." I tucked the disruptor back in my jeans and tried to look a little less crazy. "Just keep shooting him to keep his magic under wraps."

Silas laid his hand on my shoulder. "These Mundane guards will not be able to hold him forever. They don't know the extent of his abilities."

"Agreed," Casius said. "He's too dangerous to just hand over to DODSI."

The agents tied up Elias, preparing to cart him away to some underground prison cell for the rest of his life.

I sighed. "I'll remove his magic so you don't have to shoot him every hour for the rest of his life. As much as he deserves it." I glanced as Casius. "Does that work for you?"

Casius frowned. "It takes the power of a direct source to bind someone's magic permanently. Without that, you can't—"

"Maeve and I can do it," Silas said.

With a nod, I connected to Silas's powers, relishing the way the Fate magic still inside him made the world burn brighter. My power from the Fate faded every time I used it. Soon it would disappear. I felt a hollow ache in my chest as I thought about never feeling that power coursing through me again. But it was for the best. The power was too addictive and too cold. Every time I accessed it, I could feel my emotions—my connection to humanity—take a back seat.

Silas's aura flared along with mine, and we placed our hands on Elias's unconscious head. I closed my eyes. Focusing on the magic within me, I visualized the threads of a binding spell, and we wove them together two at a time. With the power from both of us, the complex weaving of the magic was easy, and working with Silas was like a dance as he wove threads of his own. We were in sync, moving together without needing to talk through each step.

Someone swore quietly behind us, but I ignored it. I didn't want to think about how creepy these abilities were. When the binding spell was complete, I mentally pulled all the threads tighter and pushed it over Elias's unconscious form. Silas tied it off, and I was satisfied that nothing short of a direct connection to a very powerful source would break it. And since I'd just destroyed the Earthen Source, and magic in Aeterna had imploded, there was no way Elias was getting his magic back.

The agents left with their prize, and I watched him go with deep satisfaction. Everything bad that had happened to me in the past several years was tied to Elias in one way or another. Stripping him of his magic and throwing him in a deep, dark hole was poetic on several levels. I hoped he never saw the sun again. I let the remainder of the Fate powers slip away as I turned my attention to the future. It was time for a new alliance. With everyone on equal footing, we would usher in an era of peaceful coexistence.

I looked at the magical leaders of our community. "Are you ready to change the world?"

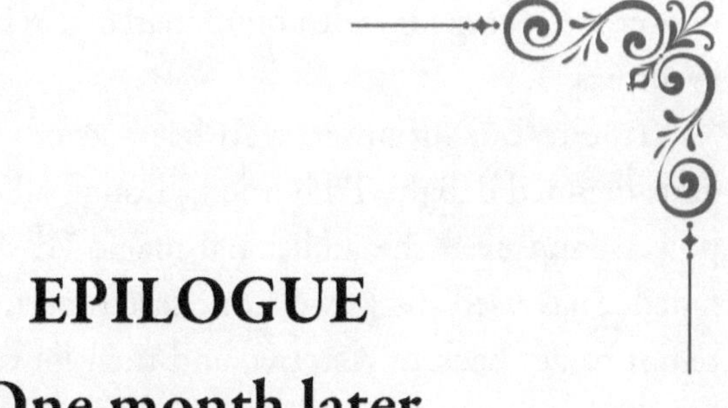

EPILOGUE
One month later

THE SENSATION OF HOT sand giving way to the cool, wet sand beneath my feet was perfection. I wiggled my toes deeper as I relaxed on the sun-drenched beach of our private island and let loose a heartfelt sigh of contentment.

Silas emerged from the ocean, naked as the day he was born. His olive skin had darkened during the past three days, turning a golden-brown that looked sinfully good. I took a moment to appreciate the view as he walked toward me, totally unabashed at his own nudity. My own pale hide had gotten some sun, mostly in the form of freckles, despite the daily slathering of sunscreen and the beach umbrella Silas planted in the sand for me each day.

I handed him my latest creation.

"What is this one called?" Silas asked.

"It's a piña colada."

He tasted it and made a face. "Why are all your favorite drinks so sweet?"

I took my drink back and took a sip of the deliciousness. "That's why I only made one. You clearly don't have good taste."

I gave him a towel, which he used to dry his face and hair then slung around his shoulders, leaving the rest of him to air dry. He caught me eyeing him with more than casual interest and raised his eyebrows.

True to our promises, we'd been strictly magic free. It was a gods-damned delight. I'd burned through all of my borrowed Fate powers, and even the additional magic I'd shared with Silas had faded. Silas used his powers one last time in an unsuccessful attempt to get back to Aeterna, and then he went cold turkey. The temptation to use our godlike abilities came with too high a price. Both Silas and I felt that we were losing touch with our humanity every time we accessed the Fate's powers.

When Silas suggested camping out on an island for a week, I'd patiently explained to him that I wasn't rich, and private islands weren't cheap. Then he clued me in to the fact that despite the collapse of his entire realm, he wasn't without resources. Apparently, the Upper Houses of Aeterna had invested significant money in the Earthen realm, and the members of the Aeternal Council hadn't been left destitute by any stretch of the imagination.

I didn't begrudge them continued funds, because the Council had been surprisingly helpful. It didn't hurt that they had to live in the same dorm rooms and eat the same food as everyone else. They contributed millions to quickly renovate the rest of the hospital into living quarters for the nearly four thousand people packed into our campus. We also added several recreational buildings, speeding the process along with magic.

Unfortunately, none of the Fae had returned yet, but we would have room for them when they did. And I was already planning a visit to talk to Mother Nithia. I needed them to know that I was serious about an equal partnership.

With no way back to their own realm, the former Council also provided magic expertise to supplement our defenses, energy consumption, and other technology, putting us well on the path to becoming a self-sustained community.

When Silas and I left for our island, they were transforming every available green space into gardens and organizing work shifts for cleaning, food prep, and other necessary functions to support such a huge group of people. In the past month, we'd grieved together over those we lost and had found a new place and role for everyone regardless of their heritage or former magic ability. We were all the same now, with the same access to open magic.

All of that was hidden from prying Mundane eyes by a shield Silas and I helped erect over the entire campus. Even to satellites, we'd appear like a mostly abandoned hospital campus—which was a good thing, since we weren't making much progress with DOD-SI.

As magic spread from our access point in Boston, all the stars and stripes of the US military had descended on our campus. We tried to forge an alliance, but they didn't want to join us on equal footing. They wanted to be in control, and they wanted to suppress all knowledge of magic. After we got past the threats and plans for mutually assured destruction if we ended up as enemies, we hacked together a compromise of sorts. Our people had erected magical barriers just outside the city borders, keeping the slowly spreading magic in a localized area around Boston. We couldn't "take it back," but we kept it contained. For the moment. Our goal was to show them that a peaceful transition from Mundane to magic was possible, and Boston was the proving ground.

"We could go into town tonight," I offered. "Get you a whiskey neat or a really great scotch. I think you'd like it."

"Tonight," he replied huskily, "I have other plans."

I bit my lip. "Oh? What did you have in mind?"

A sly grin slid onto his face, and he reached around to unknot the beach wrap tied behind my neck. "Would you like a preview?"

My stomach lurched violently. I held up the remnants of my drink, wondering if I'd gulped it down too fast. The funny feeling in my stomach tied itself into a familiar knot of anxiety as an un-welcome guest crashed our private island party. "Four!"

Silas jumped to his feet, dagger in hand and ready for an attack. I blinked at him. *Where'd he get a knife?*

The Fate was wearing his average-Joe persona, clothed in a ter-rible imitation of vacation wear—a loud red-and-white Hawaiian shirt and khaki shorts with flip-flops. He even sported a wide straw hat atop his head.

Four looked Silas up and down. "Did I interrupt something im-portant?"

Scowling, Silas wrapped his towel around his waist. "You're not welcome here, Four."

"I came to collect on our deal."

For the past month, Silas and I had tried to figure out a way to handle the situation with Four. We'd obsessed over every inter-action with the Fates and every vision—at least what I could re-member—trying to figure out a plan for handling this moment. We knew Four would be back to collect, but we hadn't expected him so soon. I'd hoped it would be years before an immortal Fate would bother to think about me again, not weeks.

"You tricked me into doing your dirty work," I said. "The way I figure it, you wanted that Reaper Fate—Three—killed. I did you a favor, and borrowing a little magic in return makes us even."

Four waggled his finger at me. "Oh, no, no. You're forgetting the part where you used those powers to change the trajectory of your fate a second time. You skipped right through your own time-line, altering it as you saw fit. And you used our powers a third time to free magic in this realm. I warned you of the consequences, and you made your choice. You made a deal, and you can't keep what you didn't pay for."

"She doesn't have the powers anymore," Silas said. "That's not a fair deal."

"The deal was made of her own free will. She got exactly what she wanted, and now she must pay the cost. I need a replacement for the Fate of Death."

My brain was racing. I wasn't ready to pay the price. Not yet. Not when I'd had so little time with Silas.

"Every choice has a consequence." Magic rose around Four, and the blinding-white power emanating from him outshone the sun. He reached toward me—

"No!" Silas yelled.

Four's power pulsed, and I slipped into one of his visions.

Brilliant white magic rises around Silas. He lunges between Four and me, his knife swinging. His first swipe misses as Four steps backward supernaturally fast. Silas drops into a leg sweep, and Four casually lifts his index finger and steps outside the linear timeline.

But I learned that trick also. I draw on Four's powers, stealing magic directly from him with such aggressive force that he stumbles backward. In two bounds, I reach the Fate and kick him in the chest.

He grunts but doesn't go down. I reach for his magic again, already anticipating the rush it will give me, but he raises his hand, and I'm stuck. Every movement is like swimming through molasses, and I can't get through it.

Four steps casually behind Silas. His eyes are locked on me as he places his hands on the back of Silas's neck and twists violently, snapping his neck with unbelievable ease.

"Stop!" I grabbed Silas by the arm, yanking him back. "Stop, or you're going to die!"

Four smiled at me, and I wanted to punch him.

"I'm so sorry, Silas," I said. "I did all of this to keep you alive, and if we fight him, you're going to die. I can't let that happen. I made a choice, and I'm willing to pay the price."

Silas's expression was angry and confused. He tensed, holding back on my word only. If Four so much as winked, I knew Silas would react, and it would be the end of everything I'd fought for.

I reached up and held Silas's face in my hands. It was so unfair that I had to give him up to keep him alive. We'd finally managed to be together, and it killed me to say goodbye to him after so little time together. "I'm willing to pay the price for saving your life—everyone's lives."

"What were the exact terms of the deal?" Silas gripped my wrist, tethering me to him as he demanded answers from Four.

"Maeve O'Neill used the powers of a Fate to save your life, and she agreed to pay the price. 'With great power comes great responsibility.'" Four winked. It was all fun and games and movie quotes to him. But this was my life he was messing with.

Silas's teeth ground together, the muscles of his jaw flexing. "What was the price that she agreed to?"

"A life for a life," Four said. "She must take the place of the Fate she killed."

"There's got to be another way," Silas said, his eyes flicking between me and Four. "I won't let her pay for my life with hers. That is not a trade I am willing to make. What about my free will in the matter?"

Four painted an expression of deep pondering on his face. He started tapping his chin as if in thought, and I was absolutely positive he'd had this moment planned from the start. "Magic was set to spread across earth, creating change on scale that was forbidden to me. And then you stopped it." There was real anger behind his eyes. "You barricaded the magic inside the borders of the Mundane city. Why? Why would you stop the spread of magic after everything we did to set it free?"

I glared at him. He'd set me up to take out the Reaper Fate for some kind of internal Fate politics and so he could incite change on a global scale. Four played me, and like an idiot, I hadn't realized until it was too late. But his anger was real, and Four was capable of erasing me from existence with nothing more than a thought. I had to tread carefully.

"The Mundane government threatened us," I said. "They have weapons that can hurt us and ways to imprison us. We had to stop the spread of magic until we can prove that it's safe."

Four's face twisted into a snarl of fury, morphing from average Joe into something ancient and dangerous that made me plant my heels in the sand to keep myself from stepping back.

"You said *we*. 'Everything *we* did to set magic free,'" Silas said. "Why do you care if magic spreads across Earth?"

Four's mask of studied human emotion slid back into place. "I'm the Fate of Change. It's what I do. Which is why I'm willing to make you a new deal. First, you must finish what you started—set magic free."

"Is that it? That's the price I have to pay?" That was too easy. I already planned to make exactly that happen.

"Oh, no. Your chaos will amuse me, but it far from satisfies your debt. We need a Fate to replace the one you killed. We require balance in our trio."

"I already told you that I don't have the powers anymore—they faded. It's all gone, so I can't become your Fate of Death or whatever."

"Oh, I don't want you," Four said. "I want Death's Fury."

My stomach dropped.

"It has a certain symmetry, don't you think?" Four said. "The path was circuitous, but what could be more ideal than Death's Fury taking up the mantle of the Fate of Death?"

Four raised an eyebrow in a near-exact impersonation of Silas. "Don't tell me you didn't notice the power that still courses through you."

"His powers are fading. They're almost gone, just like mine," I said.

"You put all of Three's magic into *him*. What you had, Maeve O'Neill, was a fraction of the power he still has. Residue of the transfer—that faded, but the powers inside Silas Valeron will never fade."

Silas had gone very still. "What exactly are the duties of the Fate of Death?"

"You'll shepherd fated Moments of death when required." He waved his hand casually. "And I'll need your help on some special tasks here and there."

"For how long?" Silas asked. "My entire natural life span? Longer?"

"No," I said. "Silas, no!" I let my magic rise around me. It wasn't as impressive as when I'd had the powers of a Fate, and it wasn't even close to what Four could wield, but I wasn't going to let him take Silas without a fight.

"A decade is all we need," Four said. "You'll shepherd fated Moments of death for ten years, and then I'll consider the bargain upheld."

"And I can stay with Maeve?" Silas asked.

"When you're not doing the work of a Fate, you can stay wherever you want. But you cannot use the powers of a Fate outside of your duties. I can't have you going around mucking with mortals' lives," he said with absolutely no irony in his tone. "If you do, I will collect on our deal by reclaiming both your lives."

"Silas, don't do anything rash," I begged. "We have time to figure this out."

"It's a fraction of his lifespan." Four spread his hands open between us. "I'm doing you a favor."

I'd never wanted to murder him more. It was a deal with the devil, a bargain that was sure to end badly, because Four was a tricky bastard whose deals always screwed the other person over. I opened my mouth, about to tell Four where he could stick his offer.

"This is a one-time offer," Four said to Silas. "A handful of years from you or a life from her. I don't care which."

I shook my head at Silas. "Don't. We can figure this out some other way—"

"Choose now," Four said.

"Deal," Silas said. "I accept your terms."

Acknowledgements

First and always, my gratitude and love to my husband and kids, who make space for me to pursue this crazy author thing. Thank you to my "guysies." You know who you are. You are my fan club and my therapists all in one, and sharing the journey with you makes it twice as fun. Thank you to the amazing team at Red Adept Publishing and especially my content editor, Alyssa Hall, who made this story shine. And finally, thank you to my readers. This wouldn't be possible without each and every one of you. I am still amazed and grateful that you have trusted me with your time and your imagination. If you enjoyed this book, please consider leaving a review online so we can continue the journey.

Book Three of the Bound Magic Series is coming! For updates, links to exclusive content, and the latest information on author things, please visit my website www.bpdonigan.com[1] and follow me at www.facebook.com/BPDonigan.

---

1.   http://www.bpdonigan.com

Also by B.P. Donigan

Bound Magic
Fate Forged
Fate Broken

Watch for more at https://bpdonigan.com/.

About the Author

B.P. Donigan was born and raised in Alaska. She left to attend college in rural Idaho, graduated from not-so-rural Utah, and finally moved to very-not-rural Boston, where she lived and worked for ten years.

After paying her dues to extreme winters, she resides now in sunny California, with her two kids, two dogs, and one amazing husband. Like any good superhero, she spends her days building her cover story behind a desk and her nights saving the world (on paper, at least).

Read more at https://bpdonigan.com/.

About the Publisher

Dear Reader,

We hope you enjoyed this book. Please consider leaving a review on your favorite book site.

Visit https://RedAdeptPublishing.com to see our entire catalogue.

Don't forget to subscribe to our monthly newsletter to be notified of future releases and special sales.